The Copper Pipe of Time

The Copper Pipe of Time

W. Lawrence Nash

I thank Mr. Robert Westover for both his moral support
and his intelligent and thoughtful comments on the progress
of my drafts.
Other Titles by W. Lawrence Nash

Frank McCord and the Foghorn Blues.

Frank McCord and the China Blues, or, Here a China, There a
China, Everywhere a China China.

The Perfect Monster.

On the way:

Frank McCord and the Time Crystal Blues

Contents

Chapter 1: Don't Blame Me

With his shoulders back, Charles F oster faced the gleaming array of test subjects mounted on his laboratory wall. His astounding research was proven and done and it was perfect. A circular blue ink stain highlighted the pocket of his white shirt as he looked up at the four huge Fresnel lenses installed as skylights above him. They were magnifying and hot and they jumped with energy from the brilliant day forming outside. They patterned the laboratory floor with their refractions and made him into a living pointillist experiment as their concentric rings traded patterns under the passing clouds. He lifted his head and with no regrets he reached to the rack on the wall and picked out what he needed. He took one slow deep breath, looked to the heavens and did what he had intended to do and Charles Abernathy Foster was gone.

To begin the day, Charles had carried his steaming coffee into the living room to wait for the dawn. The aroma of his custom Peruvian blend trailed behind him and filled the house. It was the best coffee in the world and his special order had just arrived. Charles inhaled deeply over the scalding brew and luxuriated in its bouquet. He peered out the east window to check the light. In the valley below, windows appeared from nowhere as the city awoke. Foster was anxious to see how the sky was developing. He needed the dawn to break right and the day to be brilliant and sunny. His plans relied upon the sun and today was the culmination of thirty years of work. His final project was finished. He tapped the antique barometer hanging near the door to the garage a couple of times to make sure it wasn't stuck. It had never been stuck and he had never heard of a barometer that was stuck but he had seen his father tap the same barometer in the same way and he liked the memory. The barometric pressure showed 80.69 kilopascals. That was 28.33 inches of mercury. It was up from yesterday and as he did every day, he set the gold colored constant indicator to correspond. He walked over to his writing desk and sat down feeling fidgety. For a few seconds he waggled his monogrammed fountain pen between two fingers, then pulled it open to record the barometer readings. His specially made ink had a low viscosity and the old pen leaked and made his fingers blue. He opened his leather-bound day book and neatly he entered the figures. He was content with the realization that after thirty years of making such an entry every morning, this would be his last one. He circled the date. He smiled a smile of anticipation at the relief this day was going to bring to him and with as ostentatious a flourish of finality as he could muster, he signed off for the last time. He double dotted the end of his signature and slipped his big leaking pen into his white shirt pocket. His tuxedo pockets were sewn closed to protect the shape of the tailoring.

Charles Foster had never owned a tuxedo. He had been undecided on how to approach this day as it was to be a special day of firsts and lasts for him. This day, he wanted to experience special things. The tuxedo he chose was a nice one. It was bespoke tailored for him from the Gucci stable of formal wear and it fit him elegantly. He had had it fitted three months ago in New York. It was a light English wool Tom Ford design with a grey stripe, with Jacquard stitching. At $4,600.00 it was a bargain for looking good at his big send off. He dressed slowly while he listened to his favorite nocturne, the Chopin Nocturne Op 27 # 2 in D Flat Major. Its tempo and dynamic envelope stated perfectly his initial angst over his decision for that day and exactly like him it resolved itself to a perfect conclusion. When he finished dressing, he strutted in front of his bedroom mirror and he really looked fine. Somehow the cut of the jacket made him want to stand up straighter. *Too bad only a couple of people will see me. I should have done this Ford thing earlier.*

Today was the most climactic day in Foster's life and for the first and last time he had decided to take his prized show car to the Foster Industries head offices. Religiously he kept the car under a spider-proof cover in his garage. It had never held a passenger nor spent a night outside. Today he was taking it to his office. What he did today, would be his last statement and he regretted he would not be around to witness the reactions. This sort of statement could not be written on paper.

He went to the garage and ran the door up from the inside and stood in the dark looking out at the quiet street while he waited for the light. In the distance a coyote howled a mother's disappointment at a fruitless night of hunting. Unlike every other day in the last thirty years, Charles felt no urgency to be at his office and he sipped his coffee slowly. He had calculated the dew point would be around 60 degrees that day and he was content to wait before he exposed his car. He slipped off the cloth protective cover and as usual he caught it on the hood ornament of the flying speed goddess. She leaned her chrome body forward with languid trailing arms carrying sleek and seductive wings above an arched back. Her posture demonstrated her speed but she led with a defiant chin and it always snagged the fabric of the cover. His 1931 Auburn was a cream color convertible with deep brown enamel on the exposed radiator and also on the contour lines running back to the boat tail. The license plate he had inherited was the measurements of his beautiful flying speed goddess. 1.2.12. One inch by two inches by twelve inches. The automobile had wide whitewall tires on chrome spoked wheels and he loved it. It was his only toy. It was a 1931 8-98 Boat Tail Speedster with a straight eight Lycoming engine and it was built to run with ease at 100 miles per hour. He had never done that, but today he planned to hammer it.

Charles lived at the highest point of 70 rolling acres of mixed farmland and hardwood bush. He had planted various species of maple forty years ago, along with sourwood for their white blossoms and their attraction of bees to his fruit trees near the house. Their autumn colors were astounding. Yesterday he had taken his lunch and picnicked in a clearing giving him a line of site to the estuary of the Borstal river and the sea. He would soon be far beyond those. He intended this to be his last day occupying the world as he knew it and as the time approached, he had become more contemplative of the event and more determined to proceed. He wondered what they would say about him afterward. He wondered who might miss him if anyone. He wondered, wherever he landed, whether there was someone he could miss in return. It was fascinating. He had no family to speak of except for his employees and he would miss them without a doubt. For more than thirty years he had taken the time to sign their thousands of Christmas dividend cheques personally. His main plant employed 2300 workers and he had treated them well and he had been able to make them efficient too. They were his only family. He hoped they might miss him some. The Foster conglomerate of twelve companies was thriving and it should continue on productively without him.

Then there was his Vice President of Operations. He and Charles Foster had been together for twenty-five years and he was a minority shareholder in Foster's closely held company. Their relationship was not a collegial one. Foster's

3

departure would provide reciprocal relief to each of them for not needing to deal with the other. There would be no missing. The VP's given name was Melvin but the world knew him as Bully. Bully Gregious. Bully's sidekick of twenty years and Vice President of Strategic Planning was Ms. Malveena Drago. With a ruthless efficiency, she did ninety percent of Bully's work as well as her own and she was incapable of the sentimentality required for missing or being missed. In her mind those inanities were not in aid of anything.

Charles Abernathy Foster removed the canvas top from his 8-98 Speedster and got in and turned on the ignition. He stepped on the starting switch button and pulled the dash throttle control all the way out. The motor fired immediately and he pushed the throttle half way back in and left it idling in neutral. The driver's door hinged at the rear and he left it swinging fully open and walked back into the house. The engine burbled nicely behind him. Slowly he looked around the house to gather a last memory of it and walked to be sure whatever should be off was off and whatever should be on was on. From habit he set his entry alarm and as he exited his house he had a sudden twinge to take his barometer with him. He laughed at himself and hopped into his little beauty. The engine sounded good and he eased the throttle into a closed position and listened. *Fine. It is hot and ready.*

A pocked Macadam road ran past his front gate and wound down to the left for a mile then ran on the flat for six miles. From there it wrapped around the mountain in a continuous descent down to the river road and the Foster offices. He settled his Speedster onto the flat stretch and checked the Auburn's speedometer. The needle on the round-faced dial pointed to 65 miles per hour. He pressed down the accelerator and the engine hummed a higher note and entered the 80 octave. It was colder than he expected with the top down and it felt good. He hammered the pedal and the speedometer crept to 93 when he heard a clattering noise. *Hm. Valve spring whip. I will have to replace the spring or maybe just put a washer at the.. Charles.* He shook his head. This was the last trip for the Auburn. He pressed the accelerator hard to the floor and at 102 the clattering left, the hum was steady and happy and he felt like a free man but he was running out of road. He allowed the gear resistance to slow him and he entered the downslope at 40 miles per hour. He was a little disappointed he hadn't gotten a speeding ticket. He would not be around to pay it. The security

4

guard at Foster's River Road executive offices did not recognize the car but when he saw the boss, he waved him in. Foster parked in the hatched no parking zone at the main entrance and entered the foyer humming the old Jimmy McHugh song 'Don't Blame Me'. He liked the Nat Cole version best and he had the 1958 disc in his collection.

Darryl Turnbull was the front foyer security guard and he did a double take at Foster in his tuxedo. He usually came in wearing jeans and a sweatshirt.

"Whoee Mr. Foster. You shore is purty." They laughed at his hick caricature and Foster strode happily into the elevator and sang as loudly as he could up to the executive offices and laboratory. *Don't blame meeee.* He had always wanted to do that. Bully Gregious heard him coming and he fished out a couple of cheques from the top drawer for Foster to sign.

Foster poked his head into Bully's office and swept on in. The door was open as usual so the rare passerby could see how hard Bully worked at sitting there.

"Charles. You have on a monkey suit!" Charles wanted to strangle Bully as a parting gesture to him but he refrained.

"Yes Bully, I do. Monkey suit by Gucci. Do you like it?"

"I do Charlie, but I have never seen you so duded up." Foster began to reconsider his decision to refrain from strangling Bully.

"Well, I am pleased you like it." He smiled, not wanting to use any of his remaining time on this kind of badinage.

"Going someplace special, eh?"

"Yes Melvin, I am going someplace, special. Yes. I am going."

Bully knew he was in for trouble when he heard the 'Melvin'. He had never come out of a 'Melvin' conversation in good shape.

Charles reversed out of Bully's doorway and strode past Ms. Drago's office next door and continued singing on toward his lab on the other side of the corridor. *If I can't conceal the thrillll that I'm feeling, don't blame meee.*

Charles stopped channeling Nat Cole and turned to the Zone 8 surveillance camera mounted high on the wall directly opposite the door to his laboratory. He stood still and looked into the glistening bluish lens and smiled his best smile and said good morning to the distorted fun house reflection. He held the pose for a full ten seconds. He wanted no questions as to whether it was him going into his laboratory. He felt perky in his new tuxedo so he saluted the camera. He positioned himself to block the view of the keypad and punched in his four-digit security code. He alone knew the combination. Even the custom manufacturer had no record of it. Foster had built an override mechanism which was a Morse code. Only he was aware of that function. He had designed and patented it. Old man Davis the installer had tested it and he was deceased. Foster's keypad was primarily mechanical with no electronics except for a counter limiting the number of attempts at entering a code. It also had the capacity to accept a user code which extinguished after one use. He had given one such to Bully Gregious for emergency entry, but for Bully, one time in the lab was likely one time too many. Bully was not remotely interested in anything developmental, patentable, scientific, technical or new. He wasn't really interested in anything; not innovation, not any of Foster's fourteen patents pending nor the 56 which were active. With effort he tracked the ones expiring and dealt with them. He was satisfied with the status quo. Thankfully he had been clever enough to hire Malveena Drago to carry the load of the mundane day to day exigencies in operations.

The keypad accepted Foster's pass-code. Four heavy steel bolts retracted from the top and bottom of the door. With finger pressure, he pushed open the perfectly counterbalanced blast door and stepped inside his laboratory and swung the door closed behind him with a thunk. The bolts re-engaged. He looked around for a place to hang his jacket and chuckled to himself. There were no hangers. He threw his Tom Ford jacket on a lab stool. He would not need a tuxedo wherever he was going.

Chapter 2: Bully Meets Madcow

Two unsigned dividend cheques stared up from Bully Gregious' desk and berated him for not having made Foster sign them when he was in Bully's office. The cheques were right there on his desk waiting for Foster's signature and he had let himself be distracted. First came the singing in the elevator. What was that all about. It was abnormal. It had never happened before and it made Bully nervous. It was unnatural for a man of Foster's age to be so excited. Bully resented it. Bully had not been excited about anything for decades. Then the unexpected flash of the Gucci monkey suit walking through his door all buoyant and striding with something going on nobody had told Bully anything about. And then came the dreaded "Melvin". It should be called the Melvin of Damocles. Usually Foster just finished Bully off right on the spot following the first 'Melvin' but no. Not today. He left him with a hanging Melvin and went singing down the hall into his bloody lab.

The previous morning Charles Foster had entered his executive parking spot at dawn. The mist was heavy off the Borstal River and it continued to crawl up over the banks to shroud the flats and claim the land. The dimness had kept the halogen lights on. The gulls had not tried to get above it but hunkered smaller and quiet on the pavement, still using the stored heat from the sun. Charles checked in through security and entered Gregious' office directly. He sat at the desk and pulled over a small stack of cheques. Bully's desk used to be his desk. He had left it without a single marring coffee cup ring and now the stickiness made it difficult to move the paper around. He was there to sign the last few of 2300 Christmas bonus cheques. He had first signed the bonus cheques personally when he had one employee. Now it was a ritual he demanded of himself to sign each and every bonus cheque by hand using his same old fountain pen and his thin pale blue ink. It was his last signing for Foster Industries. He had timed it to finish up by 1:00 pm. He was going home to take his last walk through his grassland and to smell the sun in his woods.

Bully had wondered what the rush was to sign the bonus cheques. It was months until Christmas. In fact, it was barely the end of the third quarter. As minority shareholders, that was when Bully and Malveena received their dividends. Now, the cheques sat on his desk, unsigned, and Foster was locked in the lab. At any moment the Malveena monster would be coming through his office door, demanding hers. Not only that, there was still the 'Melvin' thing. Not that he didn't deserve whatever was coming to him for something he did or didn't do or forgot or put off or neglected. He was sure any or all of those categories applied but the Melvin stress was just too much.

His digital clock blinked a change in the hour. His hand trailed a perspiration track on the leather desk top as he picked up the clock to see it better. He had caught the movement but he couldn't read the digit. His wife had given him the blasted thing.

"Why Bully, you can see this from one hundred feet. It is beautiful. And red numbers too."

"Thank you, Lucretia."

He had asked her for a clock and he got one. All he had wanted was a simple analog battery clock with a white face and a quiet sweep second hand to hang on his wall across from him. At ten feet he could read that. But now he had this flashing red monstrosity sitting on his desk, and yes indeed, he could read it from one hundred feet but not from three feet and he had left his reading glasses at home. He slid his chair back until the clock came into focus. 2:00 pm. He estimated Foster had been in his lab about two hours. That was enough time for him to get his thingamajigs set up and bubbling or whatever.

Bully Gregious punched the phone line to the lab and let it ring ten times. Foster did not answer but that meant nothing. He often became so engrossed with an idea, he heard nothing, lost track of time and forgot to eat. Charles Foster often worked 24 hours straight. Bully set the alarm on the digital clock for 3:00 pm to remind himself to call the lab. With that done he fell asleep in the sun. He jerked awake at 2:45 and slid back from his desk to see the time. *I bet he left while I was asleep.* He dialed the extension for the security room.

" Frank? Bully Gregious. Run back the tape on the Zone 8 camera and see what time Mr. Foster entered the laboratory and when he left it if he did." Bully waited on the line. Frank was back within the minute.

" Mr. Gregious, he went in at 11:40 and he has not come out. He is still in the lab for sure. His blast door is the only game in town. One door in, one door out. Do you want me to try him?"

" Yes Frank, go ahead."

Bully heard the line ringing and there was no answer. " Thanks Frank. I will try him again myself later."

The office was hot from the Fresnel lenses in the 12-foot ceiling and Bully dozed off and on. The noise was picking up in the parking lot behind him as the coming and going shifts slammed their car doors. Bully was oblivious to it. The clack of Malveena's Jimmy Choos woke him into high anxiety as she sambaed into his office.

" Cheque Bully, cheque Bully, cheque, Bully." She snapped her fingers and held out her hand. " Cheque Bully, cheque for Malveena."

Bully stared at the blinding red digital clock. He couldn't see it but it was better than looking Malveena in the eye.

"Go away Malveena."

"Oh yes Bully, when I get my, when I get my, when I get my cheque."

He looked down at the dividend cheques and back to Malveena.

" Bully! They are unsigned! Why did you not have Foster sign them?"

" I didn't see him."

" Bully. I heard him bellowing in the elevator. I heard him walk down the hall. He stopped. Where did he stop, Bully? He stopped and came in here. And you Bully, you idiot, did not get him to sign the cheques. The big guy can sing 'don't blame me' all he wants Bully, but not you. I do blame you. You are to blame! "

Bully withered under Malveena's onslaught. He decided the best defense was an offence. " You can't talk to me like that Malveena. I am the Vice President of Operations. I'm your boss and don't you forget it."

Malveena tried something on her face which copied a smile.

" Oh. I see. Yes. How could I forget you are my boss."

She reached onto his desk and spun his day book around so she could read it. The day page was empty except for one entry which was circled. `Pizza King`.

" Making an acquisition all by ourselves are we Bully? Busy in the franchise business are we Mr. Vice President? Don't know the corporate by-laws, hmm? Don't tell me. You have never read them. Well let me tell you. Acquisitions and divestitures may be done by Charles Abernathy Foster Esquire and no one else. But I believe I may have misjudged you. You are not really acquiring a chain of pizza parlours, you have simply acquired and demolished by yourself, a large Pizza King pizza, slathered with cheese, bacon, pepperoni, mushrooms and pineapple."

She paused for effect. "That's my boss."

Bully lifted his head with a defiant look and said nothing. What really irked him was Malveena had been exactly correct about the toppings.

Malveena looked Bully over and targeted the evidence of pizza smeared on his shirt. He followed her eyes down to the smear. He shot his hand to cover it and caught the button and popped it off so his hand slid inside onto his belly. He put his other hand outside the shirt to cover the hand inside.

Malveena shook her head. " Lovely, Bully."

Her voice became silky and that was bad news. " Bully, you are absolutely correct. You are my boss. Fine. Boss me. Do it."

She pulled up the heavy oak chair from the corner and sat directly opposite Bully. She pulled her skirt down over her knees a little, put her Jimmy Choos together and tipped her legs a perfect 5° to the right and clasped her hands demurely, just as she had been taught by Miss Manners' book of etiquette. She had assumed the perfect seated protocol for a young lady. She sat motionless and dutifully and fixed her eyes on Bully's eyes, waiting to be bossed. Bully was helpless. Malveena always did this to him. She was a beautiful, relentless killer. Bully said nothing and he broke eye contact and he lost.

" I thought not." She stood up and slid the chair hard back to the corner and it made a track in the wax. She checked her Dolce Gabbana. It was 5:00 pm.

" That's it Bully. I want my cheque." She leaned over Bully's desk and punched the line to the security cameras.

" Frank, run the tape back in Zone 8 and see if Mr. Foster is still in his lab." He was.

" Bully, get over there and hammer on the door and get him. You will only need him for a moment. He won't mind." Bully was in no hurry to get his Melvin treatment.

" Malveena, that is a blast door. It is soundproof and two feet thick solid steel. I don't happen to have a hammer in my pocket to knock on the door. Do you?"

" No, I don't, but I know who does."

In two minutes, Wilf Norgren from maintenance showed up with his hammer. It was a sledgehammer. She had not specified. She had just said 'hammer' and he had had it for two years and this was the first chance he had to use it.

" Hello Ms. Drago. What do you want me to do?"

" Nothing. Give me that." With two hands she dragged it behind her down the hall to the laboratory with Wilf and Bully following. She attempted to swing it. It was heavier than she anticipated and she took a huge chip out of the tile and bounced the hammer against the door. Steel on steel reverberated through the building. Nothing happened. No Foster.

" Wilf, call him on your walkie talkie."

Wilf did as he was told and there was no answer. Bully was enjoying himself. He stood with his hands on his hips and his white unbuttoned belly hung over his belt. Malveena hit the door harder and it rang like Big Ben and continued ringing on a high pitched sustain.

" Bully. Make it stop."

" What do you mean make it stop. You hit it."

Gradually the piercing harmonic diminished and after sixty seconds or so it dissipated altogether. There was no activity from inside.

Wilfred had been trained in emergency response and he had never used it. Now was the time. Any conscious person in that laboratory would have heard Big Ben. If Mr. Foster was not in there that was fine. If he was in there and didn't react to the sledge hammer, he needed help. Wilf called 911 and asked for everything they could send. Within a minute they could hear the sirens.

The fire department emergency response team was there and inside and on the second floor in under five minutes, with three men carrying resuscitation equipment. The paramedics arrived three minutes later. No one had any idea of how to deal with the door.

No, there is not another entrance.

That is against the fire code.

No, this is an exempted high containment facility and there is not another entrance.

The police arrived a few minutes later and in short order there were nine emergency personnel in addition to the triumvirate with the sledgehammer

11

milling around the door to the laboratory in a seven-foot-wide corridor.

Downstairs Frank had a clear view of the action from Zone 8 on his monitor. The fire department called the station about a ladder truck to get to the skylights. They were on their way.

The police called up their cutting torch man and apprised their SWAT team leader of the situation and how they might break in. They were on their way.

They called the architect and requested the blueprints of the building. The drawings were on the way.

Brown and Son locksmith was on the way. Yes, he knew about the door but he had told them not to expect much. This was a tough nut to crack.

Frank patched into the intercom and turned up the volume. "Doesn't anyone have the combination to the door?"

Everyone looked at everyone and Bully blinked crimson and attempted to cover his belly. All the responders looked at the company people for help. Malveena looked at Bully. Bully bent over and began backing away from the throng like a supplicant leaving the king. "I do... did... might.. wait here. Don't go away. Nobody leave." He turned and fled down the corridor and into his office. Dimly he recalled sometime probably fifteen years ago Foster had given him something about the laboratory door and he thought it was probably a combination. He had probably written it down. It was somewhere. He fell into his chair and put his head in his hands. Why was it always him. Malveena came steaming in after him.

"Bully. These combinations were all changed eighteen years ago. It was shortly after I arrived. You were not operating with a computer then. Where would you have written it. Think Bully."

Rivulets of perspiration were drenching him as he struggled to recall. He pulled a tooth marked yellow pencil from his pencil mug and began crunching it between his teeth. Depressing the soft wood with his bite helped him calm down. The panic left and Bully smiled as it all flooded back to him. He pulled open the right-hand drawer in his desk and fished to the back. He could feel it. He held the short pencil up triumphantly. Foster had given it to him and told him to put it away.

"Here."

It had been sharpened to a nub and four digits of its product catalogue number remained. That was the code. His combination was 3675. The last remaining product numbers. He ran back down the hall.

" Here it is. I have it. The combination is 3675."

Small delays in reaching a victim were important and the resuscitation teams were frustrated. One of the young policeman snuffed, " Figures."

Bully looked at him, perplexed. " What do you mean, `figures`?"

" 3675 on a keypad is d o r k. It spells DORK."

The relief at getting the combination released laughter they did not know they had. It was uproarious. Bully punched in the numbers and the bolts slid back and the first responders poured through the opening to rescue Foster. The temperature inside was one hundred and thirty. Foster had not turned on the evacuation fans and the heat generated by the lenses overhead streamed out and along the corridor. Malveena stopped dead and retreated toward the cool of her office.

" Bully I'm not going in there. That heat would be the end. I know you want to get to Foster but I can't do it."

Bully didn't care whether he went into the laboratory or where he went away from the snickering. He had been made to feel a fool most days in his life and if he was honest with himself, probably every day in his life, but never quite like this. His mentor and colleague and owner of the company he worked for had given him DORK for his password. He hoped Foster was in the lab and he was nice and crispy by now.

The emergency response teams moved with urgency into the heated laboratory. The first fireman saw the switch panel and started the high velocity evacuation fans. Each man wanted to be the one who found the body. They charged in eight directions and came up empty. They heard the ladder squad scrabbling on the roof. Shadows of moving heads cast onto the floor from the skylights and the lead fireman waved them off. Charles Foster was not visible. Two burly swat team members trundled in carrying a two-man steel battering ram and looked with disappointment at the open door. The cutting torch specialist was flicking his finger on the torch nozzle. The door was beautiful. Never been cut. His team leader warned him off with his head. The excited architect burst through the door waving his drawings, followed closely by Brown junior, the lock specialist. The swat team secured the washroom with expectations of disaster but that too was empty. A policeman pulled on the handle of a two-doored storage cabinet just inside the blast door. It would not open. He smashed the handle off with the butt of his rifle as Wilf stepped around him and opened the other unlocked door. The cabinet was empty. One by one they opened every closet, every storage bin and every cupboard. There was no mistake. Charles Foster was not there.

The balance of the day was occupied with reviewing video tape. The continuity of the videotape was examined by the police experts and it proved continuous and uninterrupted and pristine. Tape experts ran the tapes backward and forward ad nauseum and the result was always the same. It was conclusive. Charles Foster went in, Charles Foster had not come out and the laboratory was empty.

Wilf retrieved his sledgehammer and went back to his custodial work. He had wanted just one swing, just one. But it was always the same. The big shot got to do it. He knew he would get blamed for chipping the tile floor.

Bully had had enough of the drama. All this craziness around him was making him crazy inside. *Let the police do what they do. Dust for fingerprints, fine. Fill the place with dust for all I care. Witness interviews, fine. Video tape analysis from our security cameras. Wonderful. Pah! I bet the guy who draws the chalk outlines is disappointed. So, Foster is gone. Too bad. Here today, gone tomorrow. No. Gone today here tomorrow more likely. He'll be back.* He wandered down to Malveena's office.

"Well Malveena, that disappearing stunt was a neat trick wasn't it. Old Charles is full of them isn't he. Trouble is, who's going to sign our dividend cheques."

Malveena did not seem to be perturbed at all.

"In the end, it doesn't really matter, Bully. The Foster Industries by-laws provide for this. In the event the signatory is incapacitated or unable to fulfill his prerogative, we may collateralize our shares against the value of our dividends. In other words, we get our money right now and temporarily the company takes control of some shares until things are sorted out."

Malveena saw Bully was blank. "You have no idea what I'm talking about do you."

"No Malveena, I don't. You tell me I'm getting my dividend money. Good.

Foster can spin."

" Bully, you are the consummate Philistine."

"Thank you."

Melvin Gregious trudged back to his office and fell into his chair. There was no question whether Foster would be back. He and Foster still hadn't had their 'Melvin' conversation. Maybe Foster would be kind enough to give him some more passwords.

The policeman of broken cabinet fame poked his head through the door opening and rapped his clipboard on the door jamb. " Excuse me Mr. Gregious. We can't find an inventory of the laboratory contents. Do you have a copy?"

Of course he did not have a copy. What was this man thinking.

" I do not have a copy of anything to do with that miserable lab. It had nothing to do with me. Ask Malveena about the inventory. She is the sabre toothed one next door. Ask her."

"I've already done so Mr. Gregious. She has nothing. She said to ask you. An inventory is required for an assessment of the crime scene. Here. Use this clipboard. I'll be here for several hours yet. Give me a copy when you're done and keep one for your own records. I will sign your copy and date it for you. You may need it later."

Bully didn't like the sound of that. It was more or less a threat. And crime scene? What in the devil was he saying.

" What do you mean crime scene? Why is there a crime? Some mean-minded reprobate decides to make like smoke up the chimney and suddenly there's a crime?"

Bully snatched the clipboard from the young officer's hand and headed for the lab. The officer hurried along behind him. They had not looked up the chimney.

Bully entered Foster's laboratory, clipboard in hand. There was not much of an inventory and of what there was, few things had names known to Bully. The bench tops were clear with the exception of some Erlenmeyer flasks. Bully didn't know what they were called. He counted them and called them small, medium and large beakers. He opened the closest cupboard and put them away. The officer heard the clinking.

" Mr. Gregious. You moved the glassware. Don't do it again. Don't move anything. Don't touch anything. Just do an inventory to the best of your ability and then give us a copy. We will ask you about the individual items at a later date. Please."

The policeman looked fifteen years old and Bully was getting a mini-Melvin lecture from him. Bully pouted his way around the laboratory. He counted the glassware under the counter tops. He counted the burners and the retort stands. One Gucci tuxedo jacket. Looming above the main workbench was Foster's rack thing whatever that thing was. Xylophone? He dated the worksheet, signed his name and left the laboratory. Bully had no intention of waiting for the forensic team to complete their work. He spoke back over his shoulder.

"Close the blast door when you leave. The bolts drop five minutes after closing so don't leave anything behind." The police worked through until 2:00 am. They made a quick final sweep of the space and pulled the mammoth shining door closed behind them and five minutes later the bolts dropped and locked it down. Bully's one-time entry code extinguished.

Bully was wrong about Foster coming back. Foster did not come back. Six weeks passed without communication from Foster or any information suggesting he still existed. His abandoned Auburn convertible was taken to the outdoor police pound and given up to the sun and to the rain and to the auction.

In the third month following the disappearance of C.A. Foster, at the request of the two senior vice presidents of Foster Industries, the police designated Charles Abernathy Foster as a missing person.

Important people are always imagined to have been seen in many places soon after their picture is circulated and that was the case with Charles Foster. He was seen everywhere. He was seen in old newsreels. He was seen all over the world but none of the leads led to anything. Malveena started her internal countdown to declaring him dead. She wasn't sure quite how that timeline worked but she was going to see if somehow, she could expedite it. Then she would reorganize the company to her liking.

Foster's Houdini act was big news. Foster Industries was the largest employer in the region and his disappearance was taken very seriously by the court. The corporate status of his conglomerate was one of a closely held corporation and

Foster had constructed meticulous and exhaustive by-laws for all contingencies including this one. The company governance was set out within a framework even Bully could understand if he had read it. Malveena had it memorized and that was good enough for Bully. The court reviewed the documents related to Foster's disappearance along with the police report and they found no indication of suspicious activity other than remarking upon the impossibility of Foster's one way in, one way out evaporation and why would someone abandon a $4,000.00 jacket. The judge would not have done it.

The court ruled. Until such time as he was declared legally dead seven years hence, or in the interval someone approached the court with proof he was not dead, or failing a duly executed power of attorney, the court ruled his assets, private laboratory and capacity for acquisitions or divestments by Foster Industries were frozen. Melvin Gregious and Malveena Drago were to remain in place and they were authorized to continue day to day operations. No additional shares could be issued or moved in or out of the treasury and no dilution or share splits were allowed. Bonuses and dividends carried on as before. Bully was named signatory for the annual dividend.

The months dragged on for Bully and his usual sloth deepened. His attention to the status of Foster's patent portfolio was careless and competition began to erode some of the income stream. Malveena gave the layoff notices as the production became glutted but everything had a bright side. There were fewer Christmas bonus cheques to sign. He was tired of the decisions and tired of chairing two meetings a year and he was ground down by Malveena's pathological furies.

Front reception buzzed Bully out of his doze. He fumbled at the phone and put it on speaker. The speaker spit and crackled and distorted the receptionist's voice.

"Mr. Gregious?"

" What. What is it."

" Mr. Gregious, there are five gentlemen here to see you."

" What?"

" Mr. Gregious, there are five gentlemen here, and you gentlemen are from where?"

Bully could not hear what they said with the distortion from the speaker phone.

" Mr. Gregious, they say they are from Macau."

" Madcow?"

" Yes sir. Macau."

Bully knew about Madcow. His son Lenny had been telling him all about it. Lenny read it in the library and the real name was something spongy. Spongeformitis he thought it was. Mad cow disease. Makes you crazy and then you die. And Bully had a leather couch. He did not know the disease had been named after a place but he wanted nothing to do with it.

" Tell them to get out and go away. I am busy. Tell them that too."

" Sir, the gentlemen are wearing Armani suits and if I am not mistaken, I notice their wristwatches are Rolex and Patek Philippe. They seem to be serious people, sir." She put the fifty-dollar bill in her shirt pocket.

The Patek Philippe got Bully's interest.

"Mm. Well, send them up in five minutes. No make them wait. Send them up in seven minutes."

Billy had no papers to clean up on his desk. He had been doing nothing. He didn't know whether he should put papers there to demonstrate his busyness or leave the desk empty to show his efficiency. He decided to leave it empty. It was less work. He walked to the window and centered himself there, with his hands behind his back looking contemplatively out over the Borstal River. His pose would demonstrate his corporate élan when they came to his open door.

The elevator door opened with a ding to announce the second floor. Bully heard the feet coming and he put on his most thoughtful face. There was a knock on the door frame and the lead man from Madcow walked energetically to Bully and held out his hand. Bully took it and at that moment thought of the disease and dropped it like a red-hot brick. He proceeded to scrub his hand on his pant leg.

The main man hardly seemed to notice. Bully walked and sat behind his desk, still rubbing it off. The other four men from Madcow went to the window and stood looking at the view. On the left they could see just the edge of the library building and, on their right, they admired the sweep of the Borstal River as it spread open to form its estuary.

The main Madcow proffered his card to Bully. It read, 'Roger Tam.

Director of Acquisitions. Macau International Gaming.'

Bully took the card and spoke his thoughts out loud.

" So that is it. Not Madcow, Macau." Bully did not know where Macau was but wherever it was, it was superior to Madcow.

Roger Tam laughed. " That is very good. Madcow indeed! Ha! Mr. Gregious, your reputation for humor precedes you. They told me about you. Be prepared for that Melvin Gregious, they said. May I call you Melvin?"

" Yes. Melvin is good."

" Thank you, Melvin. By the way. I see my colleagues are captives of the view from your window. I hope you don't mind them not joining us. At any rate, I was warned about you, about Melvin Gregious, what a wit. Oh, what a wit! Madcow. I have never heard that before. Allow me. I'm going to write it down." He laughed again and waggled his head in admiration as he made a little note on the edge of his binder. Bully liked him.

" Melvin, I have something for you."

He unzipped his black satchel. "You are the first person to see this. It is because of your reputation for innovation and foresight you are seeing it today."

He pulled a neatly folded architectural rendering from a folio. He looked over his left shoulder to be sure his colleagues standing at the window were not listening. This was between just him and Melvin. He proceeded to open the drawing on Bully's desk while he asked, " May I open this on your desk?"

Melvin nodded affirmatively to the already opened drawing. Bully stood with his fisted hands on the edge of his desk to get the rendering in focus. The man opposite him mirrored his position exactly. The architectural rendering showed an elevation of a beautiful new building sitting on the edge of the Borstal River, surrounded by more beautiful out buildings. Melvin and Roger lifted their heads from the drawing in a perfectly matched tempo and looked into each other's face. The two moguls smiled at the possibilities.

He looked at Bully's arm and at the leather strapped Sears $29.00 watch Bully wore. Roger Tam began to shake his arm as if something was bothering him.

"Er, Melvin I hesitate, to, but, well, we are friends I think?" Bully nodded.

" May I try your watch? I was gifted the one I am wearing and I can't get it comfortable and it just doesn't feel right for me. I asked my wife for a watch and she got me this one. Who would pick this."

Bully understood perfectly. *Exactly. Like my clock.*

Mr. Tam continued. "Now your watch, it settles well on your arm, it looks comfortable."

Tam slowly and elaborately removed his Patek Philippe and placed it center square on Bully's desk. Bully knew precisely what it was. He had begged Lucretia to let him get one. Not one so good as that one, but one of its poorer cousins. On his desk was one of the finest timepieces in the world. He had seen the exact watch advertised for sixty-seven thousand Euros. It was a platinum model.

Mr. Tam rubbed his arm in relief. "Melvin, may I try on your watch?"

Bully unbuckled his watch and the strap stuck to his perspiration. Roger took it and held it flat in both hands to admire it. He strapped it on eagerly and beamed like a man who had been to Lourdes. They made the trade.

At Roger Tam's insistence Bully retained the architect's renderings for his consideration and they agreed to meet again in Bully's office in three weeks. *Time to show Malveena how Bully does business.*

Chapter 3: Be Careful What You Wish For.

Janet Pilcher arrived home later than she had anticipated and she was in a foul mood. The engine overheat light had flickered red all the way up the hill and it was two weeks past warranty. Her brows were furrowed and she was discouraged by her pointless day. Janet dropped her purse onto the front hall bench and rubbed her temples in a slow soothing circle and exhaled slowly and completely. She crossed her arms and massaged across both eyebrows the way she had seen a guy do it on the internet and she caught the clasp of her watch on her necklace. With gritted teeth she extricated herself by bending open a loop in the gold chain and now that needed fixing. Maybe Harry could do it.

She jerked open the louvred hall closet door and hung up her white jacket. It was wrinkled and it needed washing and she put it out of sight and slammed the louvred door but it wasn't built to slam and a piece of white plastic flew out of the upper track and spun dead on the tile floor. Janet sat on the front hall bench and removed her shoes and rubbed her feet. Her low pumps had never been too tight but now they were. Surely, she hadn't gotten fat on her feet too.

She heard her son rustling upstairs and trudged up carrying her shoes. Two stairs squeaked to remind Janet of the weight she had gained as she moved toward his bedroom and listened to his quiet one-sided conversation. She stood at the open door and sighed to show her frustration as her fists directed themselves to rest on her hips.

"David Pilcher! Good grief Davy! You are 13 years old, not five. Are you kidding me? Talking to your imaginary friend! Talking to little Dopo! What is wrong with you?" She wanted to take it back but it was too late.

"Ah Mum. Don't worry. I like to say things that's all. See how it sounds, you know? Just run it by myself and see how it sits. Dopo doesn't say much anyway, just listens, and I get stuff off my chest. If you hear a thing said, an idea, sometimes it lands on you better than just running it around loose inside. I can look at it better, you know?"

Janet was quiet. She did know. She had just arrived home from a $240 per hour session with a 29-year-old psychologist from Berkeley who didn't say much, listened to Janet verbalize her thoughts while interspersing an "I see" or a "hmm" and watched the clock. Janet wondered where Dopo's office was. Janet grabbed Davy, bear hugged him and immobilized him and kissed him on the sweet spot on the back of his neck. "I love you Davy."

Davy squirmed away and as he left the room to go downstairs he stopped and turned and said, "I love you too Mum."

He started down the stairs and spoke quietly. "That was nice wasn't it Dopo." Dopo was in his office and he seemed to agree. Davy shouted back to his mother.

"The tide is out Mum. I'm going down and walk on the flats for a while."

Janet didn't answer. She could kick herself. She was so worried with her husband losing his job and the plant closing in a few months and she was taking it out on Davy. Foster Industries employed half the town and it was closing.

School was out for Davy at last and this was the first day of holidays, with two beautiful months of sun and sea and sky and free time streaming ahead of him. Already Davy was searching for something to do. He knew if he asked his mother on the first day, "What is there to do" that was the end of him. From the hat rack in the front entrance, Davy grabbed his kangaroo skin hat his father had ordered for him from Australia, tied it up under his chin and headed out the door. Working his arms into his jacket, no one told him do it up and he made for the seashore a mile down the hill and over the bluff. Sunshine filled the sky and Davy wondered what did the sunlight move out of the way to do it. The sunlight had to take up space. It couldn't just be and come and go without moving something else out of the way to get where it wanted to be. And did what was pushed out of the way just fill back in again behind the light or could something else get in there and go with the light if the timing was right? *I bet it goes to fill in where the light just came from. Or maybe it goes to fill in where the light is going.* He thought on it. He should read about it. He would turn his mind to it.

The wind had swung offshore and the day was a little cold for late June. The breeze was abating after three days of storm but Davy still tied down the hat to hide his fresh out of school haircut. Above him the clouds moved fast and tufting as they furled and unfurled their sails in an endless armada racing out to sea. Davy walked down the hill quickly as if what was there would be gone if he didn't get there in time. The boardwalk was mostly empty of strolling families and only a couple of people were out on the pier. The bay was flat and shimmering and with the tide going out like today, there was a wet desert of shallow furrows stretching for 500 yards, with small fingers of water being sucked slowly away. The three o'clock sun was still warm and its angle flattened the retreating water even more, and gave it that distant blend which erased the horizon line. More easterly, there was a channel which had been dug for the marina and for the pleasure craft to shelter there, and the boats were moored and bobbing inside the enormous piled stone breakwater. The storm driven spume of the previous week had coated the boats with a viscous salt crust and a few owners were out and scrubbing their beauties with long handled brushes. The gale had thrown hundreds of polished and peeled silver logs the size of telephone poles around the arc of the bay and pickup-sticked them against the rocks protecting the shore. They were strewn along for miles in both directions, piled one on top of the other in impossible balance. They were perfect for sitting against as a windbreak from the offshore wind. Davy found a good log, with dry sand which was dropped and piled into a dead spot out of the wind. It was the perfect height for his back and he sat down on the sand in front of it and burrowed in to get comfortable.

"This is a good spot, Dopo."

Davy heard no disagreement. Davy took off his shoes and wiggled his toes down into the warm sand until his feet were covered. He put his hands behind his head and leaned back looking up at the clouds and thinking how they controlled the sun. The sun was supposed to be all powerful yet the clouds foiled it at the whim of the wind to keep it from doing its job of warming the ground. The distant caws of the gulls fighting their way in against the running offshore breeze and the squarking and clamor of the fights over the feast along the strand played in Davy's ears. It was wonderful and he smiled. He knew Dopo liked it too. There was no symphony as beautiful as the skree of the wailing sea birds.

The clams were making their telltale blowholes everywhere in the wet sand and the seagulls were doing their aerial bombardment onto the pier. Davy watched as a very large and beautiful three-year-old white gull snatched a clam from its lair and soared with it in triumph, high above the pier. It suspended itself against the wind which was switching onshore from the south, tipped and

23

rolled its wing over to sideslip some lift and dived like a strafing airplane at the pier below. It dropped the clam onto the thick wooden plank surface and smashed the clam open, making a noise like a pistol shot with the impact. Davy's beautiful bird got away with the easy meal before he lost it to a rival. He watched the gulls by the hundreds moving along the shore, riding the strong updraft streaming up the face of the bluff, wheeling and side slipping and diving in their endless squadrons along the boardwalk. The barrage of clams continued onto the pier and life was good for the gulls.

The gull he was watching swooped past with a one-winged wave and landed about ten meters away and looked directly at Davy. He could see now that it was a four-year gull, as it had almost all its white feathering. That took four years. This gull was the biggest gull he had ever seen. Big ones had a wingspan of 48 inches or so but this one was bigger. This was Gullzilla. *Good one* thought Davy. He would use that in his first essay when he got back to school. He smiled to the gull. Dopo smiled too and the mocked gull took off with a poop.

The elevation of the sun pointed at supper time. The gulls were landing on the wide beach too as the thermals keeping them up were weakening and flying was harder work. He got up and brushed his feet off and put his socks and shoes on. He was wearing his favorite socks with red stripes with stars in alternating rows. They seemed wizardly to him. With a sigh he turned to go home with the wind. His father would be home soon and Davy wanted to be there. He liked seeing his dad come home. He kicked at a large clam shell and noticed the bore hole in it. *Moon snail* thought Davy. They could bore in and clean out a clam as clean as a whistle. The people flying kites on the beach were leaving too as the winds were dropping and it was not so easy now to keep a kite up. He heard the cries above and it seemed the birds shared his haste to get over the bluff and up the hill to home. Davy loved the sound of the gulls and how they announced the end of the day as if they had never seen the setting sun before. They would come inland and sit like queens on their thrones atop the exhaust vents on the rooftops. They searched for radiant heat and wherever they could find it they battled for their turf and snuggled in for the night.

The climb back up over the bluff and up the hill was thoughtless for Davy and he passed a few older folks struggling at it. His shadow striding beside him was longer than he wanted. His dad must be home by now. He turned the

corner to his house and there was a plumber's truck in the driveway. *Huh.
That's funny. Dad usually does this stuff himself.* The sign on the van
announced 'Rickman's Plumbing'. He knew the plumber's son, Brian Rickman,
from school.

The back gate of the plumber's panel truck was open and Davy walked
quickly to the front steps. He grabbed one of the first drooping beans from his
mother's scarlet runner beans tied up with fishing line at the edge of the porch.
They were getting big and they were sweet and delicious off the vine. Later they
would be stringy and tasteless but Davy would snitch one every day until the
vines were taken down in October.

He could hear voices coming from the kitchen as he squeezed through the
partially open front door. He walked into the kitchen to join the discussion and
he leaned his weight onto his hands flat behind him on the face of the counter
and held onto the remains of the bean pod. He then realized his hands were
probably dirty from fiddling down at the pier and were making smudges on the
paint but he did nothing because he didn't want to interrupt.

The plumber was saying to his dad, "Harry, the old iron pipe has to go. It is
the original plumbing from when the house was built 55 years ago and it won't
stand up to the water pressure and in some spots, it has rusted through. It is
not a joint that came loose, the pipe itself has had it."

"I understand that Frank. I simply cannot afford it. I just want to replace
what has split and put a couple of good junctions on each end and leave it at
that. I may have to sell the house and I'm not going to put the money into a
new copper plumbing system. I'm not doing it."

This was the first Davy had heard anything about selling the house. He
knew Mum had been worried about money lately and he had heard rumors
about bad things going on at Dad's plant. *That must be why Mum has been so
edgy lately.*

Mr. Rickman went down to the basement to cut the pipe and Davy followed
him to watch the work. The new pipe was 3/4-inch copper pipe and it was great
looking stuff to Davy. It gleamed in the light and bounced a special reflection
around the basement like nothing he had seen. The concrete floor was wet and
slippery from the burst pipe but most of the water had gone to the sump and
there was no flood. Rickman wore rubber boots anyway.

25

Mr. Rickman checked for defects and soft spots by tapping with his ball-peen hammer along the same water line and there were two other areas needing replacing. He got to work right away so Janet had to finish the dinner with no water from the tap. She had already prepared sauce for the pasta before the pipe burst so she panned out some water from the back of the toilet tank and boiled that.

Davy did not really want to eat. He wanted to watch Mr. Rickman cut and size and solder the pipe. Rickman measured and quickly cut two pieces of about seven feet each. He had two small pieces left over that he allowed to fall on the floor as he cut them. The second one landed on the first piece and made an amazing sound. One was about 8 inches long and the other one was about 6 inches long. Davy wanted to have those pieces of pipe but he wouldn't ask for them yet. He watched the skilled hands of the plumber fit the copper pipe and sand then wipe the ends with flux. The small propane torch heated up the junction and Rickman held the end of the coil of silver solder against the joint to seal it up. The wood joist behind it began to smoke and a small flame started where the sharp blue end of the propane flame wrapped around the joint and contacted it. Suddenly, the solder flowed like lightning around the joint and made a beautiful silver collar where the two pieces touched and they were now soldered securely together. Mr. Rickman sure knew what he was doing. The little flame went out as soon as the torch stopped feeding it.

"Um Mr. Rickman, er... Can I have those, those extra pieces of pipe you cut?"

"Well, okay Davy, sure you can have them. What are you going to do with them anyway? They are not good for very much."

"I'm not sure what I will do with them. They just look neat and I guess I just like them."

"Ok kid. Take them away. It saves me cleaning them up." Rickman wiped his hands on the cloth he had stuck in his belt. His hands weren't dirty but it was an ingrained habit to wipe off his hands as a gesture of completion of the job he had been working on. Davy grabbed up the two pieces of pipe and hefted them, one in each hand.

"Thanks Mr. Rickman. These are really something. Thanks again."

He rushed up the cellar steps and through the kitchen to his room on the second floor and he forgot he had not eaten anything. He couldn't believe the treasure he had in his hands. He put the two pieces of pipe side by side on his bed running parallel to the long dimension and put his face very close over them and looked at them. He picked up the longer of the two pieces. He put it back down and picked up the shorter of the two pieces and put it down.

"Davy. Come down for supper."

He picked up the two pieces and turned them to run across the short way of his bed, with ends open toward the window. He got onto his knees and rested his arms looking at the pipe.

"David!"

"Just a minute Mum. Coming."

The westering sun shafted through the corner of his window, finding the gaps forced by the wind through the maple tree outside his room. The slats of light hit the ends of the pipes and bounced in through the openings and shone out the other end toward Davy. The longer pipe was beautiful, but the shorter pipe. The shorter pipe. The light hummed. It sung. It danced through the pipe and pirouetted with freedom out the near end and burst onto the wall behind him. Davy could not leave it. It seemed to speak to him. *Wow Dopo. This is something else.* Dopo nodded, quiet in the viewing.

Davy heard the stomps coming up the stairs and quickly he grabbed the smaller piece of pipe and stuffed it under his pillow. He did not know why. His mother stood at his open door with her hands on her hips. She did not usually get to this point so fast and Davy knew this was the time to look repentant. He moved as fast as he could while rolling up his sleeves to imply he was intending to wash his hands before dinner, but it didn't get him off the hook.

"And wash your hands."

They sat eating their dinner quietly and they were not talking which was unusual. Davy looked back and forth at the faces of Janet and Harry Pilcher and they were each strained in their own thoughts. The plumber had the water back on and Harry got up and took his plate to the sink and washed it off. A bit of grit showed up and he pursed his lips. He had forgotten to run the water for a few minutes to clear the pipes after the plumber did his cutting and soldering. He put the plate down and ran the water until it cleared fully and then he walked noiselessly into his small study and sat at his desk surrounded by his shelves of books. Davy got up to join him.

"Finish your supper Davy."

Davy sat back down and chewed as fast as he could and got up to join his father. He looked back.

"Thanks Mum."

Harry was sitting there in his small office looking vacantly at the empty expanse of his leather desk top. Harry Pilcher was an intense man but when he sat in his study surrounded by his books, the rigidity dissolved and the real Harry Pilcher emerged. This was the Harry that Davy wanted now. He had to ask.

"Dad, are we, are you and Mum really selling the house?"

Harry looked up at his concerned son and smiled. "Well, it could be, but houses come and houses go and wherever that is, we all will be there together. Besides, plans change and maybe the powers that be won't actually close the plant. So, don't be thinking about it. I know what to do."

That was the end of it then. If his father knew what to do, then that was enough for Davy. Davy sat on the floor and looked at the books surrounding the two of them as he often did. The titles were familiar to him and they were a treasure of fantastic imagined worlds for Davy. Some books were newer and about economics and accounting and they did not appeal to him. Others were older and some were from his Dad's boyhood. Davy began to read the titles aloud to his father. White Fang. Nelson and the Slaying of the Monster, The Tale of Two Cities, Woodstock and the 10 million. The Dancing Wu Li Masters, The Sea Wolf. Sun Tzu and the Art of War, Treasure Island. Shogun. Man and Superman. *What a world* thought Davy.

"Some of those I have had since I was your age, Davy." His father saw the look on Davy's face and smiled at the memory of his same fascination for those old books. Davy was transporting himself when his father broke in.

"See any particular one you like?" 'Monster' had caught Davy's attention as it always did.

"That one. The Monster and Nelson."

Harry pried the book from its slot and watched the other books lean into the gap at the release of pressure along the shelf. "This Nelson book might surprise you with what it is. It is a true story and I don't think you will be disappointed.

The Monster's name was 'Bonaparte'."

Harry opened the well fingered book randomly fifty or sixty pages in and began reading.

"The French fired on the up-roll as they were trained to do, to take down the masts and demolish the rigging but this cannon shot came early and well below the height of the roll, touched off too early by a panicked French gunnery crew. The cannonball from the French ship *Redoutable* hammered the *Victory* close to the waterline, at the upper edge of the gun port on the third gun deck. It blasted through the three feet of oak planking, tore a hole in the port side bulwark and blew a thousand stiletto-like shards of wood fifty feet across the main gun deck and cut down a swath of men with a vicious blizzard of jagged oak pieces. The four-ton smoking gun heaved back on its carriage, tearing out its ring bolts, the breeching cables now severed by the impact of the cannonball and tore away its side tackle restraints. The eight-thousand-pound monster swung crazily at an angle and jammed in the gun port and screeched a larger rent in the wall. Blood slicked the sand covered planking and a dying monkey lay thrown against the midships barrels. A sponger with his left arm torn open by a flying piece of oak, gently moved the small body out of the carnage and with his good hand he placed it resting midships and shook his head in understanding and sympathy. He too had been a monkey."

Harry stopped there and looked at Davy who had his mouth open. Davy was mesmerized. *Blood on the planks and a dying monkey?*

"Dad, can I, er, may I read that book? I will be very careful with it. I will."

"I know you will. In fact, any book here is yours to read. One at a time and you may not take them to school. Agreed? Understand?" Davy was more worried about losing a book of his father's than Harry was at having it lost.

"Yes. I do understand. I will be careful. I promise."

Harry handed his son the Nelson book and Davy took it as if it were an eggshell. He forgot to say thank you and he took it to his room and stood it on his dresser and looked at it. That night he read to the spot about the dying monkey and he was in love with the amazing ship and the amazing men and the amazing sea. He reached for his pipe and scanned the horizon along the line of ceiling meeting the wall. Nothing on the horizon. He devoured Nelson and The Tale of Two Cities and Woodstock and the 10 Million and he intended to mow down all the books. He was learning things happened if you intended more.

The summer passed apace, filled with sand and sun and Dickens and London and Kerouac. Davy's mind was expanding right along with his vocabulary. His thoughts were turning to the upcoming year at school and he looked forward to it. It had been a split grade and he knew most of the kids. He heard he was getting Mr. Hill as his home room teacher, or "Tilt" as the older kids called him. Davy carried the six-inch pipe around with him incessantly for a couple of weeks and he wore a hole in his right pants pocket in his favorite jeans. He switched it to the left but that didn't work. He needed it on his right for quick grabbing. He badgered his mother to make a little holster to attach to his belt to hold the pipe and she did so. She thought it was much better than having to mend the holes in his pockets and soon enough the pipe would go the way of all flitting interests of her bright little boy.

Davy's pipe was on his belt in the special leather sheath at all times. His mother had cut the sides from an old purse and put a snapper flip-top to close it and Davy felt somewhat like a gunslinger. He and his pipe swaggered the mile down to the sea every day and he sat on the silvered driftwood logs with his bare feet on the sand and curled his toes up and down as he scanned the horizon with his make-believe telescope and looked out for trouble. Looking though his pipe, the world was different. It had parts. Not just a big picture, but important smaller parts. He thought sometimes the pipe was even guiding him where to look, but that was ridiculous. *That is stupid, isn't it Dopo?* Dopo did not comment.

The labor day long holiday weekend was the last before school resumed. The weather had turned unusually hot and it was busy at the seaside with the tourists and families gathering up the last few days of summer into their memories. The tide was beginning to ebb. There was no undertow in the gentle retreat and the toddlers sat down in the warm water and splashed and the parents looked around for approval of the wonder of their unique child. The gulls were everywhere. They had become so accustomed to the people by the end of the summer they sat on the railings along the pier within arms reach hoping for something good to happen. They would do this for 15 years or so until the next generation took over. They were beautiful up close and made the world happier looking at them and marvelling at their flight and the squabbles and the mess, and if you wanted to, they satisfied your need to complain.

Davy could not wait to get back to school. He had his new spy pipe. He had the gunslinger's holster and his favorite old jeans which his mother had attempted to disappear because he had grown three inches over the summer holiday and they were too short. He had rescued them twice from the rag bag.

He knew the classroom would smell of potted geraniums which he hated and a new layer of dust collecting, linseed oil laden dust bane, which gritted under your feet and stuck there which he hated; and newly varnished everything which never got done until the last week and still reeked, but he wanted it. Then there was Mr. Tilt. That would be something new. Davy was an only child and he had no older sibling to get the scoop from about Tilt, but he had heard enough about him to make the year interesting. He had seen Tilt from a distance poking long bony holes in the air with his long bony fingers to make his point. Mr. Tilt was 6'5" and was always postured at a non-vertical angle depending upon what he was emphasizing in his speech. Hence, Mr. Tilt. Davy knew he would be asked about his holster and he knew he would not show anyone but he hoped and anticipated being asked. He was practising how to be mysteriously non-committal.

The opening day of school at Charles A. Foster Elementary School was hotter than any day in the last two months. Even Charles Abernathy Foster looked as if he were complaining. He hung in portrait in the main foyer on the wall above the office counter. He had donated the land and had gotten the zoning changed for a school and they thanked him with a portrait, which now had been in place for about 30 years. It was Foster Industries where Davy's father worked and which was closing in six months or so. The closing date was April first. Foster had disappeared under mysterious circumstances about four years ago. He often locked himself in his lab to work undisturbed and one day he just never came out. There was no note, no mess and no suspicious occurrences. He just never came out of a lab with no windows and one combination secured steel blast door. And now Bully Gregious, his partner of thirty years, was closing the largest plant in the Foster conglomerate of companies. Davy often stopped and examined the interesting old face in the oil painting. He had taken to saying hello to it. Foster had a kindly, benevolent look to him but his steel blue eyes seemed to examine Davy when he passed by the

31

office. Foster would be your best friend and your worst enemy thought Davy.

The sea breeze which usually moderated the climate and freshened the air had deserted the coast so the occasional sea smell came through the east window of the classroom, now opened by Tilt to a generous one-half inch as his concession for that day. The galvanized pail filled with dust bane was in the corner with its scoop, the floor was strewn with it and the geraniums stank. Davy was thankful for the smell of the recently done varnish which somewhat overcame the geraniums. He sat in the row next to the window on the side chosen for the higher class in the split grade. Other children were filtering in and he knew them all except for one girl who came and sat directly beside him on his right side. She did not look at him but just adjusted herself and placed a pad with two perfectly aligned pencils on the desk in front of her as if to say, 'Let's get this learning thing going.'

Davy shifted a little to show off his holster but apparently, he was invisible. The children were given peel back badges with their first names on them for the first two weeks of school, for the benefit of both the teaching staff and the pupils. He peeled off the sticky back and stuck his name on his left shirt side with just a slight wrinkle. It said David. The girl had already done hers. It was perfectly smooth and perfectly horizontal and hers said Mildred. *Mildred. What a name.* He had an aunt Mildred. *Who would give a child a name like Mildred.* He looked out the window while the class hummed with excitement and he wondered whether he was missing any pirates on the horizon past the breakwater. He wanted to spy right now and his hand moved on its own to the flap over the pipe and flipped it open.

Tilt came clicking martially into the classroom with his highly polished officer's boots as if he were still with his army regiment and he slammed the door. There was no good morning from him and not one cursory pleasantry to welcome the nervous lot to their new school year. One long arm waggled a bony finger for emphasis.

"Where you are is where you will sit. I will not move you. You have chosen your own place and that is where you will stay and that is where I will write you on the roster. If you can't see, I can't help it. You chose it. If you hate your neighbor, deal with it. If the sun hurts your eyes, close them. If you can't see the board, move your head so you can see it."

He was tilting forward now and aiming his long first fingers on both hands to the highest farthest corners of the room, apparently pointing out the spatial location of the statement he was making. Still standing at a tilt, he glared down his aquiline proboscis as if it were a pointing device and he scanned across the faces of the children and made quick little tilts to the ones he thought looked suspicious. Davy and Mildred each got a tilt. Having finished with the warm welcome, he spun around toward the green board and picked up the chalk and began scratching numbers onto the surface. He could make the chalk squeak and squeal whenever he wanted and today he wanted. The children gritted their teeth and covered their ears and old Tilt smiled and hummed as he set out the sums. Tilt was of the old school. The school board had issued iPads to this grade level, but Tilt would have none of it. He demanded paper notes and cursive writing. If the little darlings wanted to transfer their work to their devices, that was their own business but he would not participate. In his class it was chalk and paper and pencils. He understood well cursive writing and organizing the written sentence structure helped with focus and mathematics and the spatial concepts of physics. He would not give that up. Tilt did not give much homework, but when he did it had to come back to him written. Until they forced him to do so, he would not see an open electronic device in his class. Cell phones were labelled by the owner by name, left outside the door in a box and if one of them rang or hummed or buzzed or beeped through the closed door, he ignored the sound, knowing every student feared and hoped it was theirs and they were missing a call or a marvellous text or some wonderful collaborative derision of one of their enemy friends. If a student brought one in to his class and it went off, he sent them out and would then give a test to the rest of the class. If the class got tested, they knew whose fault it was. Not his. He liked that.

He had been at the board less than fifteen minutes and somehow, he was already covered in chalk. He slapped his hands together, enjoying raising the dust and he hawked and then spat on the floor.

"Do these problems. Let's see if you remember anything from last year."

He walked to the pail of dust bane in the corner. The dust bane was made with linseed oil and sawdust and a green gritty granular mystery material which somehow stayed behind when the floor was swept. He picked up a scoop full and tossed some of it on the spittle to make a little pile. It was a bit high so he squashed it with his foot and returned the scoop to the pail. By the end of the day he made a small mountain range of these, s*ort of like the Apennines* he thought; and the linseed oil smell almost defeated the geraniums.

Davy looked at the sums and equations which the class would work on for an hour. He had done them as quickly as Tilt had written them and now he had nothing to do and there he would sit. He had been at school for less than an hour and he was already bored and dissatisfied, longing for the places in his head. He looked absentmindedly over to what Mildred was doing and she too was finished all the lines of figures. She did not seem to mind it. She was thinking. She sat with a peaceful semi-smile and a posture which said she had it, whatever it was, all under control. Mildred was really different and she really irritated Davy.

The sun was climbing in the east and running hot into the classroom. Tilt liked the windows closed and the place was heating up. Davy wandered to an island. He came back and flew with the gulls out over the bay, looking down at the boardwalk. He could not hear the clams hit from such a height. He soared back down and he put a harness on White Fang and saw him bristle. He pulled out his pipe which he had sworn to himself he would never do in the classroom. Something made him do it. The telescope went up and he began to scan the horizon. He looked west to the far reaches of green slate clouds, he scanned north through the bane of the small Apennines mountain range, he scanned east and brought the pipe into perfect communion with the sun and it took him.

A blinding flash grabbed Davey and caressed him into oblivion. He had his eyes closed against the light of a million stars but the light also came from within and it was not something to be blocked by his eyelids. He floated as if in a stream of the purest gold and before the thought of it could express, he landed with his feet spread and chest up, standing on a hard wooden floor under a brilliant blue sky. The floor seemed unstable to him but he had no concern for balance. He was suspended as if in a world of gelatin imbued with a memory of gold. He saw as if through a thickened air. He saw but did not know or think of what he saw despite the fact he was seeing it. He saw all from a distance as if a bystander with no capacity to understand or a need to remember or act yet he

34

was a part of it all. He saw a wave of clarity approaching with the speed of a shock wave and with a thunderclap it tore away the miasma of his unthinking suspension. He stood in the burning heat of the brilliant sun and suddenly out of balance, he fell hard on his back on the tilting wooden floor. Dizzy, he slipped his pipe back into his holster and lying on his back with his arms spread limply and gone of strength, he stared up in dread at a terrible blue sky.

Chapter 4: Volley and Thunder

Davy closed his eyes to stop the spinning in his head. He could not make sense of the sea smells and sounds around him as he stretched his arms wide in an attempt to stabilize himself on his back. He felt the grit of sand under his hands and the burn of the sun on his face. A sharp kick to the ribs from a horny calloused foot spun him around and pointed him at two bare brown feet splayed below cut off white trousers.

"You there! Monkey! Get bleedin' up and get bleedin' below!"

Davy's eyes were watering as he attempted to get up. He flashed his right hand to his leather sheath and it was closed and secure. The deckhand thought the lad was making a reach for a knife and he reacted. He delivered a vicious open-handed slap to Davy's ear and knocked him back down. A single weathered hand picked him up by the belt at the back of his pants and skidded him hard along the sand strewn deck and over the brink and down through an open hatch. He bounced down the ten steps splitting his forehead on the ladder and landed with his shoulder hard on the edge of a black, stiff leather bucket. It wrenched his neck to one side and he landed on his belly face forward to the bucket. The bucket was blazoned with a gold "GR" surmounted by a crown. A thunderous shout tore into Davy's brain as he struggled to his feet.

"That boy! You! Bring that water! There! Be quick about it! Move it."

A small red-haired boy covered with black dust scuttled toward Davy carrying and dragging a slopping bucket of water too heavy for him between his legs with both hands. Davy backed out of his path attempting to clear his head and staggered again and fell on his injured shoulder against a monstrous gleaming black 12 pounder cannon weighing two tons. He put his hand to his throbbing forehead. It came back with blood on it and he wiped it on his pant leg and leather pouch. This was definitely not what he had imagined in Tilt's classroom while waiting for dull sums to be solved. He had imagined Admiral Nelson on the *HMS Victory* with its billowing sails and blazing cannons and valour, not a split forehead, kicks to the ribs and a throbbing ear. Despite that, here he was.

I visualized being here and here I am. Somehow, I have used the light and the pipe to do this. GR written in gold on the bucket. George Royal. He was indeed on Nelson's flagship the *HMS Victory*. He blanched.

Good grief Dopo! This could be bad. Dopo was non-committal.

The gun captain spun at sensing someone out of position in the gun crew. "You!"

The stentorian voice bounced around the deck. Every man quick-looked to be certain the 'you' did not mean him. The gunner looked Davy up and down. He did not know him. There were thirty powder monkeys on board and he dismissed the fact of not recognizing this particular youngster. He saw Davy was cut and bleeding from a gash and contusion on his forehead and marked how he stood there speechless and immobile with a pale and vacant look.

"Get below lad. Go to the cockpit." Davy stood motionless, not understanding.

"Get to the orlop deck, boy."

Davy did not move, not knowing what or where the cockpit and orlop deck were. The gunnery captain thought Davy was concussed and uncomprehending from the blow to his head.

"Spider!" he shouted.

The red-haired boy of the heavy bucket appeared in three seconds.

"Sorr."

"Get this lad to the cockpit in the orlop and come directly back. Bring back two full charges."

The charges for the cannon were heavy but as far as Spider was concerned, he was going to prove he was the man to do it. This was a 12 pounder and the lightest gun on the ship and the Gunnery Captain had his eye on Spider. His duty was to supply his gun with powder filled cartridges from the below decks armory. When action commenced, Spider the powder monkey must deliver the charges for his cannon without cease or the battle was lost. And today a pasty bleeding boy was interfering with him showing how fast he could do it.

"Boy. Come with."

Spider grabbed Davy by his shirt shoulder and tugged him into tow behind him. Davy had been tossed through the hatch from the quarterdeck onto this, the first gun deck of the HMS *Victory*. There were 30 black and gleaming 12 pounders on this deck identical to the one Davy hit his shoulder on. Each of

37

them weighed two tons and at that they were the smallest guns on the ship. The young powder monkey inspected Davy and found him wanting. He was standing too tall. He looked too directly at rank and he lacked submissiveness. *A dance with the cat will change that soon enough I reckon.*

For self preservation, at 11 years old, Spider had learned well the furtive and wary look of cowering to authority. He was red haired and small for his age but he was already toughened and sinewy and he was very strong from heavy work. His usual role was one of invisible servitude but now he became voluble. Spider was thrilled to outrank someone and he was curious. He could not resist this rare chance to speak on duty.

" Yer big ter jus' be startin' ain't ye? Pa wanted yer gone?"

Spider cackled like an old man at his riposte and Davy was surprised by the incongruity of the little boy with the old man's cackle. Davy said nothing.

Spider turned to Davy and attempted a demeanour befitting his current control over Davy.

"So, I be takin` ye t'orlop. Likely is they be puttin' some pitch on t'yer gash. But I stays out of it, away from seein' it. Savvy? T'orlop gore ain't a want for Spider. Maybe cuts ye they do, he does, sorgeon Beatty. Come out missin` a thing or two if y'ain`t keerful. In quick times the sorgeon gets a might hasty wiff his 'tensils if ye get the drift. Lops as 'e gets more pressed like eh? Does more then, more it is. Now stay with, lad, stay with."

Davy got the drift and he did not like it. Together they hurried down the first ladder to the second gun deck where there were 24-pounders. They passed down the next ladder through to the main gun deck where the 32-pounders were. There were 30 of them weighing four tons each with 15 on each side waiting to deal death at the waterline. One more deck down was the orlop where the ship's surgeon worked and Davy and Spider moved along the lantern lit passageway toward the stern and the orlop and its cockpit. Spider's agitation grew with every step as he imagined some grisly happening he might stumble upon. Davy sensed the fear and spoke to him.

"Spider, what is your real name? Surely it is not Spider."

The red-haired boy hesitated. His old name was an ephemeral thing.

"No, 't'ain't Spider. I think it be Gareth. It be Gareth. And you? What's yer naim? Yer true."

"Davy. No, David. My friends call me Davy."

Spider said nothing. Friends were not common in Spider's world and he reserved his right of first refusal.

"Yer on yer own now boy. Now ye be on yer own. I be stoppin' here. Go through that door, there."

He pointed to the ship's surgery and scurried back the other way to the ladder leading down to the hold and ran to the armoury to get his powder charges as ordered. He was sure he was being timed.

Davy was feeling dizzy again and he half fell and staggered into the cockpit. The ship's surgeon Dr. Beatty, took one look and grabbed Davy and laid him on a futon style bed. He looked at the cut which was now clotting and bleeding less freely. He covered Davy with a heavy grey blanket.

"You stay there for just a bit lad. You will be fine."

The surgeon looked Davy over and ran his gaze slowly and poignantly over his strange dress. That he had shoes was odd enough, but the cut of his breeches and the high-quality leather belt and sheath worried the doctor. This may be the son of a baronet or earl or such, on board for his first taste of it. *Well, let him taste that the cockpit is mine.*

"We may be in action at any moment. Listen here. Nod if you understand me." Davy nodded.

"If we beat to quarters you are out. Understood? Out you go. Find anywhere to lie down boy, but not here. I will need this space soon enough."

He turned back to his work where he and two women assistants resumed laying out saws and compresses and bone rongeurs in ordered rows along side the tourniquet straps lined up for limb amputations.

Davy stayed put under the warm cover for half an hour in a restless daze. He sat abruptly to see the cockpit empty and he wobbled out and into the gangway back along the way he had come. He could smell food and he realized he was very hungry. He could only guess what time it was but the lamps had not been lit except in interior passageways. He had heard the bells but he had no idea what time their ringing of two times then once again connoted. *Dopo, I have no idea of what time it is. Do you?* Dopo did not answer. Apparently, he had no idea either.

It was three bells, one and one-half hours into the afternoon watch when

Davy pulled himself unsteadily up the ladder onto the main gun deck. The planks were immaculately polished pegged oak. The deck-head was low and painted white to give some illusion of space and as Davy shuffled forward his hair brushed the painted surface. He stopped beside a 32- pounder cannon. It weighed four tons and blasted 32-pound cannonball two miles. The black gleaming monster was even more wonderful than he had visualized from his father's book about Nelson.

Gunnery captain Watson leaned against his gun, waiting to give the word. His 14-man crew were all big men and hard, made strong and fit by training. They were lounging close by their quarter and taking some ease while they could. Soon enough the blast and carnage would engulf them. They ignored the boy. At the call to action, they were virtuosos at the side of their belching four-ton monster. They lived for this and they were trained to it better than anyone on earth. They were resolute men who carried and slung thirty-two-pound iron balls and rammed cartridge and ball down the throat of their gun and sponged the bore to clean the sparks and manhandled four tons of cannon out the gun port and blasted the hell out of the enemy and dodged the sixteen-ton recoil and did it again and again and again with mindless sublimity until they were dead or victorious through what might be twelve hours of bloody, smoke filled deafening terror.

Davy moved shakily forward with his feet spread wide trying to keep his balance. White fleece sponges hung down from the end of stiff ropes at the ready for a replacement at each gun. Davy did not see the ramrod stored on the deck-head above him and he ducked into it and reopened the cut on his forehead.

All guns were fully back against the breaching ropes as if they had recoiled there and were secured by ring bolts on the ship's side. The muzzles were inside the gun ports which were closed and secured by a port bar and lanyard.

Davy's head throbbed but it was clearing. If he was on the *Victory* at the day he had intended, the great man Horatio Nelson would be on board at this very moment, likely in conference with his captain. Davy thought it was Captain Hardy. I*s that right Dopo?* Dopo did not disagree. What neither Davy nor Dopo knew was Nelson was at that moment laying out his battle plan for all the Captains of his 27-ship fleet.

Davy spotted Spider's red hair down the way. Spider was seated at a two-plank bench with four other boys and a man. They were jammed between two 32-pounders and Davy made for the table. He was ten feet from it when the hail came.

"We shall beat to quarters!"

The snare drum began hard and sharp and the shout went out, loud and proud and the men had what they were waiting for. The rhythm of Heart of Oak, the official march of the Royal Navy, beat them to quarters. The opening paradiddle on the drum told every man-jack this was an exercise and not the opening salvo against old Bony. The tumult and activity astounded Davy. The benches and tables disappeared. Every loose piece not needed for fighting was taken below decks. Wordless efficiency sped the task and every man knew what to do, when and how to do it and where to put what he handled. All wood items like mess tables, benches and furniture were sent below the main and gun decks. *Victory*'s six boats were let down and towed behind to limit cannon hits creating flying splinters. The decks were cleared for action in 10 minutes and the 800 men crammed into the 227 ' HMS *Victory* were at their stations and ready for the word.

Davy did not know where to go within the mêlée. Spider saw him and grabbed him by the shirt and hurled Davy out of the way against the side of the ship into the alcove on the bulwark where the mess table had been. Striking his injured shoulder hard, Davy tumbled onto Bert, a weathered older man who was huddled there to make himself small. Bert was a runner. He was short and of a height to pass along the rail below the line of sight of the snipers in the rigging of the enemy ships. He ran messages when the din was too much. Little Spider gripped two crushing hands on Davy's shoulders and looked hard in his eyes.

"Don' ye move hif ye vallies yer skin. This be a full battle drill. You stays put and ye doesn't move an inch. Sit and don' move."

"Time! Time! Time!" shouted Watson to the gun deck.

The fourteen men who had been lazed and idle near the gun sprang to their positions at the cannon like panthers released from a cage. Gunner Watson jumped in behind his gun breach and checked the second hand on his watch as he buckled on his belt. The belt held a pistol, cartridges and percussion caps, fifty primers and a priming wire to run through the vent to puncture the cartridge bag in the gun. He stood directly behind the four ton 32- pounder, looking at the gun port, awaiting orders from the deck officer. His 13 men stood motionless in perfect equidistant lines on each side of the cannon waiting for the word. Their eyes did not leave his face as they primed every muscle for action. Spider stood a little to the left and in rear of the gun, having received and now returned with his passing box under his left arm. He stood erect and on edge, with the pressure he exerted down on the box cover with his right hand blanching his fingers. In the passing box he held his gunpowder cartridges.

Bert looked in admiration at the perfect configuration of the fourteen-man gun crew. "Beu`iful ain't it. Now that there gunner." Bert pointed at Watson. "He be a sen'r war'nt officer an' a good'n. He be the boss o' the gun and powder. That there gun and carriage, she weigh mor'n four ton. We don' want 'er gettin' frisky like on t'deck."

Watson bellowed the word. "Silence!"

The men froze to the demand and riveted their gaze on their gun captain, awaiting orders. Davy and Bert were sequestered at the midpoint of the row of 32 - pounders against the bulwark on the starboard side of the *HMS Victory*. The glistening black cannonry stretched away in both directions. Bert's eyes gleamed as he pointed to the officer stepping toward them to the beat of the drum. The blue coated lieutenant strode onto his stage which was the gun deck and on his word the symphony of mayhem began.

He ordered. "Man the starboard guns! Cast loose and Provide!"
Fifteen gun crews attacked the downbeat in perfect unison. Their tune was a martial piece which when played well concluded with a crescendo in under two minutes. They did not rush the tempo nor did they extemporize. The music they played was written for them alone. They knew the score by heart and anticipated every direction from their conductor. Gunnery captain Watson was there to keep them on time.

The first Loader quickly cleared the gun port while the first sponger pulled the bore protector out of the muzzle of the gun.

"Ten seconds," shouted Watson.

The gun captains centered the four-inch rope restraining the sixteen-ton force of the recoil of the 32-pounder and kept it straight. Eight side tackle men sprang to the pulleys and hooked the train tackles to the side training bolts and the eye bolt in the rear of the gun.

"Sixteen seconds." The pace accelerated.

The outer blocks of side tackle were hooked to the side training bolt on both sides of the gun.

"Thirty-four seconds."

Sponges and rammers were placed together on the right side of the gun in overhead brackets.

"Forty-one seconds! 'Op it you lubbers!"

Two men worked at the hatchway receiving shot and wads from below.

"Fifty-two seconds," read Watson's watch.

There was so much happening at once and so fast Davy did not know where to look. Davy marvelled at the physiques of the men. Their forearms were bigger than Davy's thighs. He pitied any foe having to fight hand to hand on a rolling deck with any one of them, let alone with a battle axe. The biggest were the handspike men who levered three tons up off the carriage to aim the gun.

"Sponge your guns", came the cry.

In a blur the first sponger angled out the port and his arms rippled as he inserted and rammed the sponge down the barrel to the breech, wetting it to the depth of the bore. Sparks extinguished in the vacuum of the withdrawn sponge.

"Sixty-three seconds!" screamed Watson, urging them on.

"Load cartridge and ram!"

Spider moved like lightning and passed the powder charge from his passing box to the first loader, who leaned to the port and drove the charge home to the breech with one enormous thrust of the rod.

"Load Round!"

The first shot man passed ball and wad to the first loader. He spread his feet and pivoted in a perfect arc and propelled the wad and 32 pound shot down the open muzzle of the cannon as if it weighed nothing.

"Ram round!"

The ramrod drove the round and wad deep against the charge. Watson loaded the gunlock as if it were a pistol and pulled back the hammer and cocked it.

"Run Out!"

43

The back muscles of eight side tackle men screamed as they fought the rolling sea and held the carriage of the four ton gun hard up against the ship's bulwark with the muzzle protruding out of the gun port. The Gun Captain sighted his target and the two handspike men levered up the breech.

"Six degrees," called the gunner.

In slid the quoin to read six degrees on the gauge and the handspike men released the pressure on their levers and seated the cannon.

"Clear the Gun!"

The gun crew flew back out of the recoil path of the big gun and hoped the four ton cannon would not jump the breeching. Hot guns jumped at firing and a torn breech killed many a crewman in the recoil.

"Fire on the down roll."

Watson pulled the lanyard and the explosion of the powder shattered Davy into a full body tremor. The force of the detonation blasted out the thirty-two pound cannonball faster than the speed of sound. The gun carriage flew back against the breaching cables with a force of 16 tons while its projectile flew on to obliterate anything within 2 miles of the ship. The 50 gun starboard connonade continued gun by gun from bow to stern along the length of the ship. All decks had loosed their broadsides and together they had delivered one tonne of hot iron. Spider was animated in his arachnid disjointed way. He jumped two little hops and stood at the ready to pass on his next cartridge. Along the line came the order from every gun captain.

"Silence."

"Silence."

"Silence."

At Davy's gun, gun captain Watson shouted to the world.

"Ninety-seven seconds!"

The gun deck erupted in cheers. They had made fine time in high seas. No navy in the world could match it. The music was finished.

Lord Nelson made sure every gunner in the navy had a watch with a second hand. The entire sequence for his gun had taken 97 seconds. The gun crews were ferocious to have times better than their adjacent guns. Many a coin changed hands on the best gun wager. The *Victory* ran three more drills in quick succession and the all clear was drummed. Good gun crews could load and fire three full broad sides of 50 guns in five minutes. *HMS Victory* did it in four minutes in rolling seas and sometimes less in soft swells. Every man knew drills such as this made the difference between life and death and between victory and defeat. This was the advantage the Royal Navy had over every fleet in the world and they knew it. The *Victory* has been training like this for 22 months. The French had not. The guillotine had stripped them of their officer class and their crews had no stomach for the cut and thrust of war.

Bert was proud of the men around him. He had been in a 12-pound gun crew and had seen action on *HMS Bellerophon* at the battle of the Nile, eight years previous. He leaned to Davy and croaked through his toothless grin.

"It bain't be lookin' so nowadays lad, but I be a rippin' good tackleman on the 12 pounders in me day."

Davy nodded. His hearing had not yet recovered from the two hundred explosions of the gun drill.

This gunnery practice had been live. It was the last opportunity for live rounds as Nelson was closing in stealthily on the united French and Spanish fleet and cannon fire could be heard for many miles. Benefactors of Nelson saw to it Captain Hardy was supplied with extra powder and perfect shot for the purpose of training. It was not so throughout most of the fleet of 27 ships. For this drill the *Victory* was beating up an East Northeast 10 knot wind and the sound of its firing had been carried to the lee, back away from the location of the enemy who was somewhere to the east. Nelson had six frigates and schooners tailing and pinpointing the location of the French and Spanish fleet for the last mad dash into combat.

Six bells rang. Davy reckoned that was 3.00 pm. He was still shaking visibly from the noise and powder inhalation but no-one remarked upon it. They had all been there at one time and for some of them it had been years before they did not react the same way to the fury, vibration and drama of a cannonade. The smell of food was everywhere and Spider and the boys had dropped the table top from its hooks and were bringing up the benches from below decks. The mess tables and bowls and the square plates and benches were back in place in short order. Davy guessed the saying to "have a square meal" came from this very thing.

Each mess got its own food from the galley and today they were having the usual staples. Davy's mess was filled so eight were at table including a young fellow named Roatley. The salt pork, peas and oatmeal, with butter and cheese seemed wonderful to Davy. He had never had beer but he was going to have it today. Each sailor had a daily ration of 6 1/2 pints of beer and a full tankard was sat in front of every man. Davy sat with Spider on his left and Bert on his right. Bert began to look amusedly at Davy. Davy had been very thirsty. He had thrown back half the tankard of beer and he was feeling interesting. He had that look on his face that every one of them had had at his age and they knew how it was.

Davy turned to Bert.

"Bert, you said you were a 12-pounder tackleman. That is wonderful Bert. And Bert, that barrage, that cannonade thing, was amazing. I never saw anything so good as that."

Bert had a wistful look. "Yes bucko, I was one of them oncet, years ago. Good I were too. On a good team I was."

Spider smiled and he was pleased Davy had been thrilled with what he and the men had done. He was also a touch jealous because Spider himself had never seen a full cannonade from beginning to end. He had always been on the move and running here and there and staying sharp and being quick.

The men at mess ate well. They had 5000 calories a day and needed them all. Davy drained the rest of his beer. He felt good. He rubbed his hand up and down the pipe and sheath as he heard eight bells. The ship was pounding more now and the wind was up. The creaking timbers spoke of the stresses 26 miles of rigging placed on the *Victory*. Davy liked the increasing roughness and wondered if this was the day he thought it was. He turned to Spider.

"What day is this? What is the date?"

Spider and Bert were nonplused. Never had the day or the date mattered to them and they didn't know how to answer. Davy did not persist, but he knew very well what he had intended and wished for with his pipe. This was certainly the day before the battle. He knew the increasing seas and the squall wind coming up would lead to the heavy rain of the night before the conflict. Bert got up smartly from the bench. He was going on watch and the wind was cold and he was getting his one wool cardigan.

Davy said to him, "Bert, best to get a slicker. It's going to begin to rain in a couple hours and it won't let up until two bells or so on the night watch."

Bert looked amused. *The young lubber ain't been on the seas but oncet and now he's a bleedin' hexpert on the wevver.*

The men began hanging their hammocks above the mess. Each man slept at his station in his quarter and could be battle ready in seconds if circumstances demanded it. The strength of the squall was increasing and every joint in the ship complained about the torque, but the *Victory* was weatherly, stiff and fast. She, like about half of the fleet had a copper bottom making her faster than her sails would suggest. This weather would not bother the *Victory*.

Davy climbed into his hammock and breathed out in relief to be lying down. His forehead had swollen and around his eyes some fluid puffed his face. He was exhausted and excited and sleepy from the beer, all at the same time. He did not know what to do. He knew from his books tomorrow there would be a sharpshooter in the rigging of the French ship *Redoubtable*, looking to shoot Admiral Nelson. Should he tell the deck officer? Should he tell Spider and Bert? If he did something, it could change all the history he knew, that everybody knew. If he did nothing, perhaps his being here was intended not by himself but by the light. Perhaps the light carried all intention and Davy just joined in and he was intended to be here to change things. So, he might change the intended history by doing nothing, also. He could be wrong both ways. It was difficult. The swaying of the hammock gentled Davy into a fitful unpleasant sleep. Around him and throughout the gun decks, 450 men slept cheek by jowl like so many bees in a hive and dreamed of Devon and Tahiti and swaying hips and big brown eyes. Above decks in a driving black horizontal rain, 300 men worked across slick timber and plumbed the night with their eyes, looking for the enemy.

Chapter 5: Spider Is a Brave Man

Davy awoke to the sound of eight bells and the rain had stopped and it seemed the wind was down. The slowness of the roll told of heavy swells. It was a new watch and he felt no need to sleep. Men aloft were coming down and the next watch was climbing like a band of acrobats up into the shrouds. Vigilance was never at rest. The galley hands began gathering eggs from the crates and indignant hens gave voice to a fine day beginning afresh. Most men were awake but not stirring. They understood the clash with the combined French and Spanish fleets was imminent and hundreds of their mates would not survive it. They thought of home and greenery and knew this might be their last dawn and they wanted to see it. While the men ate and rested, Nelson on the poop deck ordered his fleet into two columns and the men on the main gun deck felt the shudder of the force on the sails as they strained into the new heading. Davy did not know what happened but he felt the change and heard the timbers creak in response to the new stresses. Overnight Nelson had spent one solitary hour resting on his futon. He was a restless sleeper at best and as usual was fighting sea-sickness so he stayed on his feet.

At four bells Davy sat down with his mess at his gun. Roatley was on watch at the quarterdeck and not there at the table. The crew were digging into a congealed pile of something foreign to Davy and he raised both eyebrows involuntarily when he looked at it. It stuck to the ladle as it was passed. Bert saw the look.

"Burgoo it be called. Good for ye."

It smelled good and it tasted alright. It was porridge doused with molasses. Davy saw Spider and Bert were not so much looking at Davy as examining him. His clothing was cut strangely, he carried himself with a self-assurance which belied his age, yet he seemed not to know how to do anything. It was as if he had been plucked from the ether and dropped onto the ship.

Bert began. "Bucko, ye has a strange way of it, don't ye. A speakin` and a hair and a toff belt that's a mite strange. And a dirk in a scabbard. Hoity. Yer different sez I. Ye differs if you get my drift." He ran his tongue around and around the large gap between his two remaining upper eye teeth and smacked a little sloshing sound. He had an old man's cackle but he was not old. He was hard and sinewed and a good friend to have in a fight thought Davy. He carried a dirk open in his rope belt like most of the old hands and it was sharp and he looked at home with its blade.

"Then if I thinks on it, I be differing too."

Bert had scars all across his neck and it looked like the edge of a healed burn at his collar. His ear was torn. Davy changed the subject away from himself.

"What happened to your ear?"

"Oh, my ear. Yes." He smiled as if whatever had happened was worth it. "Yes. That was a good'un. It were in Marseilles. As pretty a port as was ever done but full of Frenchies it was." He looked at the cut of Davy's clothes and his eyes narrowed in suspicion. "Ye don' be Frenchy do ye" Davy shook his head sombrely as if in an oath and Bert continued.

"Well. The lass was just my taste and perky if ye sees it." Davy did not see it. He wondered if Mildred would be called perky. "She was quick like and straight after me earring and...."

"We shall beat to quarters!"

The Royal Marine drummer rolled hard to the rhythm of Heart of Oak. The juices surged in every man, for the enemy had been sighted. Nelson's eyes on the sea were five frigates spying the waters to pin down the exact location of the French fleet and now they had done it. The war was on.

Davy could hear the pounding of the feet of the Royal Marines and the cries to order as they formed up. He was frozen and his heart raced and he knew he was beet red. This was the real thing. *Well Mildr.. Dopo, this is a fine mess isn't it.* He was sure Dopo nodded. Davy wondered what happened if he got killed out of his time.

"Clear the Decks". The French and Spanish gun decks were already cleared for action. Villeneuve had ordered his fleet to prepare for battle as soon as it was at sea.

The British crews sprang to action. They distributed fuses to those manning the guns. They stuffed hammocks into netting above the bulwarks and stowed mess tables and stools. They tore down the partitions separating the officers' quarters in the stern. Furniture was thrown overboard, the armory issued small arms, galley fires were extinguished and the decks covered with sand. Bert swept the wooden breakfast bowls and the square plates off the table and into the canvas table bag and thrust it into Davy's gut.

"Stow it below!"

Davy saw the drill yesterday and he tore down the ladder watching where others were taking the same. He dropped his bag into the bin and stepped two at a time up the ladder to the main deck and rushed to the alcove in the bulwark where Bert huddled, ready for action. No sailor knew the battle plan. It was immaterial to him. He was honed to his tasks and wanting the test and he knew it would be a hard one. The Royal Navy relied on its training and the iron will conditioned into its career sailors to prevail against any foe. Superior gunnery and tactics always won the day. Eye to eye broadsides of one ton of steel that blasted at the enemy every 90 seconds proved devastating and the man to man, controlled frenzy of a boarding party with axes, bayonets and grenades finished the job. Despite that, every man in the fleet understood the enemy was prepared for this. The allied fleet of France and Spain outnumbered the British and their ships were the largest fighting machines on the seas. They had at least four ships of 100 guns or more in their combined armada and the gigantic Spanish man of war Nuestra Senora de la Santisima Trinidad had 1100 men on board with 136 guns on a massive four decks. Nothing could withstand it.

On the morning of 21 October, the wind had fallen almost to a calm. Despite the speed of the sleek copper bottomed English ships, the approach to the combined French and Spanish fleet had taken six hours. The overnight squalls had vanished and the day had cleared to the beginning of a blue sky, with swells still running high. The sailors in both fleets knew this promised a heavy gale within a day. The wind had switched around to west northwest. Davy could hear the subtle change of the creaking coming from new stresses on the ship as different timbers were being asked to take the load. The deckhands crowed they now had the weather gage advantage in the clash with the French. They could sail with the wind and the French fleet would beat upwind. It suited Nelson and his captains.

Over the last several weeks Nelson had set out his audacious plan, a plan which departed from what any opposing fleet could expect and one which no British Royal Navy had attempted. Nelson would not lay his ships along their line and trade salvoes, he would go straight at them. He and Vice-Admiral Cuthbert Collingwood, his second in command on the *Royal Sovereign,* would cut though the enemy line and divide it in three and confound the French and Spanish alignment. Nelson sent out the signal to all ships, "England expects that every man will do his duty".

At last, Collingwood's Royal *Sovereign* which was leading the lee column, was able to open fire. The *Royal Sovereign* waited until it was well inside the usual 600-yard point blank range before it unleashed its 32-pound guns. The French and Spanish Grand Fleet were sailing in line about two hundred yards apart and stretched for six miles. At right angles to the enemy line, *Royal Sovereign* forced its way though a gap between the Spanish all black ship *Santa Ana* and the French *Forgueux,* who's bowsprit was almost touching *Santa Ana.* Collingwood released a triple shotted broadside which penetrated the *Santa Ana*'s stern and traveled the full length of the enormous Spanish ship from stern to bow and wiped clean the entire main gun deck. Men from the *Santa Ana* could be seen clinging outside the lee of the ship hoping to escape the onslaught. Collingwood's gunners continued with a running four deck cannonade of one ton of hot steel each 90 seconds until the trailing British line came to their aid.

Captain Hardy on the flagship *Victory* turned to Nelson. "Where do you want me to break through sir?"

"I don't care where you break through. Head for the closest ship."

Victory broke the line between *Bucentaure* and *Redoutable* and the order came from the deck lieutenant.

"Treble shot. Treble shot!" and the order passed down the batteries.

Spider passed the cartridges and the running fire of four-gun decks from a range of a few yards through the stern of Bucentaure swept clean the gun decks of Admiral Villeneuve's flagship. It tore the ship apart and dismounted 20 guns. Despite that, *Victory* had been taking terrible damage in the run to cut the line and she was trembling with the impact of the French hammering to her rigging and hull. The majority of *Victory*'s fore mast was taken away and part of the main mast was damaged. The French fired on the up-roll as they were trained to do, to take down the masts and demolish the rigging but this cannon shot came early and well below the height of the roll, touched off too early by a panicked

51

French gunnery crew. The ball from the *Redoutable* hammered *The Victory* close to the waterline, at the upper edge of the gun port on the third gun deck. It blasted through the three feet of oak planking, tore a hole in the port side bulwark and blew a thousand stiletto-like shards of wood fifty feet across the main gun deck and cut down a swath of men with a vicious blizzard of jagged oak pieces. Blood slicked the sand covered planking and Spider lay motionless and odd angled, bleeding profusely. A sponger with his left arm torn open by a flying piece of oak, gently moved the body out of the carnage and placed it resting midships with his good hand and shook his head in understanding. He too had been a monkey. The four-ton smoking gun heaved back on its carriage, tearing out its ring bolts, with its breaching cables now severed by the impact of the cannonball and tore away its side tackle restraints. The eight-thousand-pound monster swung crazily at an angle and jammed in the gun port and screeched a larger rent in the wall. The gun captain was stunned and staggering, looking right and left for what was left of the battery of four guns. He did not see he was about to be crushed between the careening cannon and the bulwark.

"Move!" shouted Davy and with one quick stride he body-checked Watson to the deck as the flipping 2000-pound gun carriage missed the gunner's skull by one inch and split against the deck head. "Thankee Boy" was all he said.

Number two sponger saw the action with the gun captain and also saw Spider down and he grabbed Davy by his damaged shoulder. "You! Get to the armoury. Cartridges. Now."

Davy jumped to action, not knowing whether little Spider was dead or unconscious lying at midships. His face flushed with excitement then paled with the understanding of the impact of the battle and now he was forced to play a part. He ripped Spider's passing box off the boy's limp arm and slung it over his left shoulder which shrieked with pain. He ignored it and spun to the hatch leading down to the armoury. Powder cartridges were stored in the armoury on the level below the orlop but where exactly the cartridges were and how to deliver them was another thing. He wanted to do his part but did he really have a part. What would he change or could he change in the flow of history if he helped. He was not here in the real battle in 1805. A cuff from Bert moved him to action and down the ladder he went. The powder boys were on the run at every deck and he followed them down to the armoury. Davy Pilcher was a powder monkey.

The flying lines of determined boys led him. He looked like a landsman but he moved like a sailor. The cascade of cannons above sent shock waves of pressurized acrid smoke throughout the ship. Davy forced himself to breathe. He had pondered and worried over the decision all night and he now decided he must warn Nelson. He was at the farthest point from the poop deck and the ship was in torment from bombardment. He did not know the fastest way to Nelson but he started up the first ladder to the second gun deck and passed blackened and bloody reserves streaming down to fill in Watson's crew.

Captain Thomas Masterman Hardy stood on *Victory*'s poop deck with Horatio Nelson, Baron of the Nile and Burnham Thorpe. He wore no officers coat but instead an old frock coat blazoned with four stars. He had lost an eye and an arm in service to the king.

"Hardy." Nelson Pointed. "That signal, there, in the French line. From Admiral Villeneuve on the *Bucentaure*. Look, there, Hardy. Is that not a signal to change course for his fleet?"

"By God, I think it is. They are running away."

"Damn his cowardly eyes, we will not let him. We will not let them!"

High above the *Victory*, a single wisp of smoke came from the rigging of the *Redoutable* and the wind carried it off and hid the spot from where the sharpshooter fired his musket ball. No-one heard the report of the rifle amid the din of cannonade nor did they watch the discreet black enlarging hole blossoming on the breast of Horatio Nelson. His back showed red with a spreading plume and he fell at Hardy's feet, still conscious.

"I hope you're not wounded, my Lord?" Hardy cried.

"They have done for me at last, Hardy," Nelson gasped.

"I hope not!"

"Yes," Nelson said. "My backbone is shot through."

Davy burst out of the hatch onto the poop deck with his knee cut open from the protruding splinters on the damaged first gun deck ladder. He saw a prone form on the deck and a dark stain emerging around it. He was too late. Captain Hardy was bent over Nelson and he ripped open the frock coat and buttons flew along the deck. Davy stopped the one spinning near him and dropped it into his sheath for safekeeping for Admiral Nelson.

Hardy turned in a panic to Davy. "Lad, get Dr. Beatty here, Fast. Run." Hardy put his coat under Nelson's head and a handkerchief over his face.

Davy returned in two minutes and leapt up the last two steps onto the planks of the poop deck. Struggling up behind him was Dr. Beatty, smeared with blood and soaked in perspiration from the heat of his surgery in the cockpit. He appraised Nelson quickly and looked up at the weeping Captain Hardy.

"Not here Hardy. I can't do anything here. You men, there, leave that keg. Bring the admiral to the cockpit at orlop deck and keep your mouth shut about this. Extra tots." He raced ahead to prepare his implements.

Davy pushed up behind the frantic parade and willed it forward to the surgery. The cockpit on the orlop deck stank of sand and rum and blood saturated sawdust. It was jammed with injured men waiting patiently to be seen by *Victory*'s Surgeon, William Beatty. Beatty charged through the injured men with orders. Close behind him came the prostrate form of Horatio Nelson followed by Davy. To a man they called out for help for Nelson as a sergeant major and two seamen from the quarterdeck carried him through. They knew the famous frock coat and loved the man as he passed.

Beatty removed the handkerchief and looked at Nelson's eyes. Nelson spoke clearly to Beatty.

"Ah, Mr. Beatty! You can do nothing for me. I have but a short time to live. Look to the men."

The battle raged on and one by one, the French and Spanish ships struck their colors. The cacophony of the battle slowly faded away and at 4.30 in the afternoon, the battle was over and Sir Horatio Nelson was dead. The Royal Navy had not lost a ship.

The British fleet made way to Gibraltar with the remnants of the enemy fleet in tow as prizes. The songs rang to the halyards and extra rum fueled the voices in joy and exultation of life.

'Once more we sail with the Northerly gales, towards our island home, our mainmast sprung, our sailing done, and we ain't got far to roam;
Our stuns'l's bones is carried away, what care we for that sound,
A living gale is after us, thank God we're homeward bound.'

Davy sat cross legged on the main deck. His heart was both torn at the loss of

Nelson and warmed that both Spider and Bert had come through. Spider lost no limbs but he was splinted on three arms and legs and wrapped like a mummy. Bert had not a bruise. Davy's forehead contusion was a beautiful blue. His 20-year-old mess mate Lewis Roatley, sat writing a note to his mother. *A man should witness a battle in a three-decker from the middle deck, for it beggars all description: it bewilders the senses of sight and hearing.*

"I agree", said Davy, looking over Roatley's shoulder. Roatley looked up at Davy and marvelled this bruised and powder covered little boy in the odd shirt and pants could read.

The sea began to increase and the sky told of rough weather. The wind was blowing curls off the swell tops and twisting the wave troughs into corkscrews. The gale continued to grow and began to derange the control and headings of the already damaged British fleet. The towed ships torqued and gyrated in what was a furious storm with gale-force winds which would last six days. Admiral Collingwood who had taken over for Nelson, signalled the fleet to destroy or disable the ships under tow. The pride of the French and Spanish navies foundered and ran aground and sunk on the treacherous shoals of Trafalgar.

Despite the rampaging of the monster Napoleon Bonaparte on the continent, Gibraltar was a land at leisure. It was a safe haven for the fleet, but no man had leave. Some of the lads were swimming and the sea was cooling down under high cloudless blue skies. The wind was blustery out of the east as *Victory* bobbed and swung at anchor. The crew was healing its wounds and thinking of green places and quiet. The sand blown from the beaches two miles away gritted in Davy's teeth and he thought of home with every squark of a gull. It was 2.00 in the afternoon. The sun would be just right in a few minutes for an attempt at going home. Davy flipped open the top of his sheath and fingered his pipe. It had been calling him somehow. *Dopo, this thing seems to have a mind of its own. I hope it knows what its doing!* Dopo thought it might.

Davy walked over to Bert and shook Bert's hand. Bert let Davy do it and looked at him with acceptance. Somehow, he knew Davy was leaving. He went back to Spider. Spider laid at 45 degrees on a plank in the sun and enjoyed being treated like an invalid. His nose was alone in getting sunburned as most of the rest of him was bandaged.

"Gareth, you are a brave man."

Spider welled up and a large tear rolled down his cheek and he made no attempt to quell it. Davy loved the powder stained little boy and he leaned over and gave him a kiss on the forehead as he had seen Captain Hardy do for Lord Nelson in his dying. It was a fine thing.

In full view of the crew he turned and lifted his pipe to his eye and scanned into the blazing sun. They watched the lad play at having his own spyglass and they smiled. They all had pretended the same thing as boys. The sun intensified and it began. Davy did not close his eyes and intended as hard as he knew how. He focused on the place and the time and the when of it. The trail of light energized and spun and leapt through Davy's pipe filling his sight and mind and his whole being with a binding flash of agreement. The pipe spoke its joy as the trail of time opened and coursed and fed through Davy. It wrapped its delicious warm direction around him and it spun him in golden light and it took him.

Davy thumped down hard, back at Charles A. Foster Elementary School, sitting rigidly in his seat next to the window. The classroom was an agglutination of itself shimmering in its gelatin prison. Tilt was motioning extravagantly and pointing and defying the laws of gravity in his posture as usual and Davy was not part of it and saw it and smelled the geraniums and thought nothing of it, that it was happening in a blur world. The wave of clarity approached like a typhoon and the shock-wave hit him and he made a loud start with both feet against the wooden floor and the entire class turned to the noise and stared at Davy. Tilt stopped.

"David! So. You have been gone since recess and now here you are. I have you marked absent and here you are. I did not see you come back in."

Tilt was beginning to doubt his sanity. An hour or so ago he saw a quick flash like the reflection of the sun off the mirror of a passing car into the room, yet there was no roadway on the east side of the building. He was sure the Pilcher kid was responsible and glowered at him.

"Stand!"

Davy stood and covered his holster with his hand as best he could and tried to ignore the slight tinkling sound emanating from his pipe. He massaged his left shoulder absent mindedly and then stood with his arms crossed awkwardly.

"What is your full name, please?"

"Pilcher sir. David Steadman Pilcher."

"Well. Mr. David Steadman Pilcher, you seemed to have gone missing at recess and now, now you show up like Orpheus returning from Hades without so much as a by your leave or I beg your pardon. Where have you been for the last hour? Where, pray tell us exactly, have you been Mr. Pilcher. We are interested."

Davy knew this would happen and he had prepared a convoluted and fully logical answer, but instead out popped, "Spain. I have been to Spain. er.. Sir." The class looked at each other and broke out laughing and sniggering, knowing this was big trouble for Davy. They could hardly wait. They all swung fast to Tilt and squirmed deliciously to watch the carnage. Mildred stayed looking at Davy all the while, scanning his face, surprised at the truth of it.

Tilt had heard many an excuse for why a kid was absent but this was a new one. He admired it. *Spain. Ha. Good one.*

"Well Mr. Pilcher, the next time you go to Spain do it on your own time."

The closing bell rang and the disappointed class filed out and Davy inserted himself into the stream so as not to be last in line and an easy target. He did not catch Tilt's eye. He was thinking the time in the gelatin in coming back was not so long as when he first stood on the deck of the Victory. He also wondered if he did get taken into the trail of the light, how big was the space. How many people could it take or hold or want. Did it have its own intention apart from his and it just permitted him to use the trail? Also, he seemed to get hit with the storm front of reality faster this time. And how is it I was on the *Victory* for about one week and I was absent here for just an hour!

From behind him he heard an amused, "Spain eh? Nice place I hear."

The next morning Davy was up early. He picked up his favorite pants from the chair on which he had thrown them and removed the belt with his pipe and its sheath and hung it in his closet. As he let it swing free on the hook he heard a small rattle. The button off Nelson's coat was still inside the pipe. He put the belt on the bed and opened the sheath and shook out the button into his hand. On the surface of the button was one small splash of blood. He thought of Spider and Bert as he walked to his dresser and cleared it off and put his stuff into the bottom drawer and closed it. He set Nelson's button by itself on the top. He turned it so the sun would bounce off the surface in the evening. He went to the closet and hung up the belt and as it left his hand there was a little shiver from it.

Davy left for school as late as possible. He wanted no facetious questions from half of the school about his 1-hour trip to Spain; bad enough the look he had gotten from Mildred and there she was, also late, about 50 yards ahead of him. He laid back, not wanting to catch up with her. They entered the classroom with Davy close behind just as the bell rang.

The day was an ordinary day and the geraniums reeked on and the dust bane oiled on and old Tilt gesticulated on. Davy perked up when he saw the title of today's reading on the board. The Tale of Two Cities. The dialects and formal descriptions were difficult for the class to read out loud fluently but when it came to Mildred, her face beamed and every word was beautiful. The class was mesmerized. The day at school dragged to a merciful end and Mildred and Davy walked out together, not entirely by accident. Davy had two books in his book sling for a show of doing homework and Mildred had not even gone that far. She was carrying nothing.

"Mildred, your reading was great. Have you read the Tale of Two Cities before?"

"Well, three times and I liked it as well every time. What a time it must have been. It was the best of times and the worst of times so to speak".

They laughed at her quoting of Dickens. She continued, "I would like to be there at that time to see the ceremony of the court and the dresses and finery at its best and the gardens in the Tuileries. From a distance I mean. Not the revolution and the guillotine and that. Had you read Tale of Two Cities before this week in school?"

Davy was pleased to be able to say yes, he had read it. He was extravagantly nonchalant about it and Mildred smiled her implacable smile. Every paragraph Dickens wrote transported Davy somewhere in his mind. He would really have liked to have seen how they did the guillotine but he kept his mouth shut about that. As they walked on together, they slowed in the sun and Davy learned Mildred's last name was Craft and she lived in the rental row houses about a mile past where Davy lived. Her mother had just gotten a job at Foster Industries three months ago and Mildred was so proud of her. A lump filled Davy's throat at what Mildred did not know. Davy did not tell her about Foster Industries' closing in six months.

Chapter 6: Spies

They walked west together along Grove Street through a cathedral of maples toward the sunny flat at the end of the corridor. Their route was lined on both sides with 60-foot-tall sugar maples touching to make a canopy. The breeze was up a little from the south-west and the riffled leaves overhead made uncertain shadows around them. The pavement was still wet from the mist off the Borstal and dry spots here and there kept the maple leaf shape where the wind had plucked the leaf. This year the trees had colored early and the hot September continued to intensify their brilliance.

Davy was trying to get his land legs and he was a little unsteady on his feet. The optical effects of the moving leaves did not help. He occasionally stepped off the side of the concrete onto the grass. Mildred noticed his erratic gait but she said nothing. They arrived at the old concrete bridge over the Borstal River where Davy usually crossed to go home. A concrete barricade stopped vehicular traffic at that end of the bridge and town road maintenance was long gone from it. Whatever would grow in the flaws and flakes in the concrete road surface or anywhere around the bridge was allowed to grow. Wild Thyme ran in every crack and it turned the bridge deck into a purple grouted mosaic. Blazing Star plants bloomed on both river banks and filled the air with vanilla and the Hyssop was everywhere.

Mildred inhaled the perfumes amid the drone of the honey bees on patrol. This was her favorite place, a place for thinking. She often poked along the far bank of the Borstal because the sun exposure was better there and the wild flowers were more prolific. Blue Francesca was her favorite for a bouquet as the blooms were large and they lasted better than most. Her mother liked them particularly. Mildred assumed Davy would cross the bridge and go home so she carried on. Davy pivoted quickly and locked into step with her. Mildred pointed with her eyes.

"Don't you live down there Davy?"

"Yes, a couple of blocks over, near the top of the bluff, but I can walk with you if you like." He was carrying his fake homework books which he never opened. "I don't really have homework to do."

Mildred suspected that about Davy and homework. They left the cutoff to Davy's street behind and headed toward the apartment complexes and row housing area where Mildred lived. He did not go to the newly built neighborhoods very often as they were farther away from the sea and nowhere near the dump where he loved to go. The smaller homes were immaculately neat and as the neighborhood graduated into multiple housing units, there were more and older cars parked in the street and more of the clamor of kids. Dogs barked over the way. The paving was new and in good shape and on this hot day there was the faint odor of baking tar.

Davy put his free hand in his jeans pocket to appear casual. "Mildred. Do you mind if I ask you one question? And don't be insulted."

She stared at Davy with a tutoring look an aunt might give. "Davy, how in the blazes can you tell me to agree not to be insulted when I have no idea what you are going to ask me?"

"All I meant was, I am just curious, not wanting to be rude. You know, just a question." She nodded and made audible air out of her nose as a sign of exasperation.

"Okay then. So Mildred. How can anybody ever name a girl Mildred. I have an aunt Mildred for Pete's sake. I mean did your father want Jennifer and your mother wanted Dianne and they couldn't agree so they compromised on Mildred? I can hear your father. 'Fine. But when she complains about 'Mildred', tell her she could have had 'Jennifer'."

Mildred laughed. "You know, it might have been exactly like that but I don't care a bit. I like my name. I don't know another Mildred and it sets me apart."

He was smirking. "Not that way, you jerk." She had known him two days and was calling him a jerk.

"It feels as if my name casts me back to another, nicer time. To a time when everyone was not so mean-minded and thinking only of how much they could get and families had dinner together. People talked to each other in person. I have been at school two days and I have had one conversation. With you, now. Every other kid has been glued to their phone."

She turned slowly to Davy and assumed the look of coming in for the kill. "Now Davy. My turn. I get to ask you one question."

"Shoot." said Davy, He looked at the sun and reckoned it was approximately eight bells. She stopped walking so Davy was compelled to do the same. *This seems serious Dopo.* Mildred stood square to him, face on and asked a question which was a demand.

"So how was Spain."

Davy's right hand flew to his side and it felt for his pipe but it was not there. He looked down quickly and blanched in panic he had lost it and then remembered it was hanging in his closet at home. He breathed out hard and wiped small beads of perspiration off his upper lip. He could not look Mildred in the eye. He said nothing and began walking with Mildred by his side. He took a couple of quick shuffle steps off the edge and back onto the sidewalk as he walked. Davy stopped and turned toward Mildred and said nothing but scanned her face for the mocking or derision to come should he share this with her. Neither was written there. She was waiting placidly as he rubbed the memory of his damaged left shoulder in nervousness.

"Mildred, I saw and did amazing things which are true and I don't understand and were wonderful and are impossible." He thought that covered it.

"I was in Spain. Honest. I did not make that up." He waited for the gibe but Mildred just listened. Davy went through the whole thing starting with Mr. Rickman's plumbing, Bert and Spider, and landing back with a thud into the classroom.

For one agonizing minute seeming to take an hour, she stared at nothing on Davy's shirt then looked up quickly into his face. Mildred remembered the leather sheath on Davy's belt. She almost shouted.

"Sea legs! Land legs! Sea legs! That's why! Of course! You were away for 10 days with the pipe on a rolling ship and you don't have your land legs back. Your walking muscles still have you on the ship!"

Davy nodded. That was so. He was still working on his balance back on flat unmoving terra firma. They walked on in silence, each of them thinking over the impossible trip, and arrived outside Mildred's building. Her family had a small row house and each house had a short walkway to the main street with two steps up at the building end and a small front porch. It was a simple rust brick building and the front yard had its own fern leaf maple tree. Davy saw the young maples were already making a nice row along the line of houses and the leaves sort of matched the brick. Mildred pulled her key from her pocket. She was not allowed to have anyone in until her mother got home. She said goodbye to Davy and started up her walk and froze with alarm at what she saw. Her front door was open and the screen door was slightly ajar. Her mother should not be home for at least another hour.

She rushed up the steps and Davy lagged behind not having been invited to go in. Mildred pulled open the screen door and ran in. Her mother was sitting at the kitchen table with her head in her hands. She was crying quietly and ignorant of the teardrops spotting her skirt. Mildred ran to her and put her hand on her mother's shoulder.

"Mom. What is wrong. What is happening?"

Helen Craft looked up and just shook her head and wiped her eyes with the palms of her hands. Still sitting at the table, she hugged Mildred with one arm and sighed, not wanting to tell the child who was already too serious and worried, her mother's job was gone.

"Sweetheart. I was laid off today. Not for a while but permanently. Not fired or anything like that, laid off. Mr. Gregious, the plant manager has decided to close the plant. All of it. I don't have a job now."

Verbalizing it made it worse and Mrs. Craft resumed her quiet crying. Davy had sidled to the door and Helen saw him there. Again, she wiped her eyes with her hands. "Who is this, Mildred?"

The small diversion of the youngster standing there made a recovery for her and she liked that Mildred had made a friend. Since the disappearance of Mr. Craft, a year ago, nothing had been normal and she hoped this one thing signaled the beginning of better times for Mildred.

"Who? Oh! That is Davy. Davy, come on in. Sorry. I didn't mean to leave you standing out there."

Davy came in tentatively, in and not in. Helen saw this and stood up and smoothed the front of her dress.

"Nice to meet you Davy. I am Mildred's mother, Mrs. Craft. You two go and sit on the front steps and I will bring out some drinks."

Helen needed to be busy with something right now. Mrs. Craft brought out the drinks and sat on the top steps with the two kids and Davy thought that was cool. She finished her lemonade quickly and left the youngsters to themselves and went inside to make some ham sandwiches with pickles, her daughter's favorite.

The lemonade was really delicious. It was not beer, but delicious all the same. Davy drank it thirstily but Mildred held her beading glass in two hands at her lap, lost in thought and not drinking anything. Davy did not know what to do.

"Mildred, I am sorry. I don't know what to do for your mom and soon my Dad will have the same thing." Mildred was nodding inside a vacant glaze.

"He has been at Foster Industries since before I was born and he will be laid off too. I think the plan for the final layoffs is for April, to shut it all down in April, so about six months and my Dad will be out also. Laid off. He says he knows what to do but I don't know what to do. I don't understand it. My Dad says they still have orders coming in and they build good machinery to clean up coal but still the plant is closing. He thinks if Mr. Foster were still here this wouldn't happen. It is Mr. Gregious, Bully Gregious who is making it close down."

"Bully? His first name is Bully? I already don't like him for closing the plant and he is called Bully? Two strikes and I have never seen him."

"I think his real first name is Melvin or Calvin or something like that. Melvin. It is "M. Gregious" on the company newsletter. His son goes to our school. Porky. Porky Gregious. The big kid who hangs out at the Coke machine. Not such a bad guy." Mildred did not know him.

Davy attempted to interject a positive note. "Mildred, what about your dad. Where does he work?"

Mildred turned to look at him and she understood he was trying. "Thanks Davy." She said it simply. "My Dad is missing." Davy waited.

"My father is a civil engineer. He went to Peru to help build a dam near a town called Quilombo, on the Urubamba river. He was the lead engineer on a project sponsored by the United Nations. He and a surveyor and a rodman left camp at 6:30 am and did not return. His papers marked the camp about 1000 kilometers by road east from Lima. Lima is on the Pacific Ocean coast, so they went in toward Brazil about 600 miles, into high jungle. I have looked at the map 100 times. Their walkie-talkies did not answer and that was the last anyone saw of them. It rained steadily for five days and it was as if they had never existed. There were no tracks, no calls from them and the Land Rover and surveying equipment never turned up. I know he is alright. I feel it. Somebody is stopping him from coming home. I know he is fine. Nobody is going to mess with John Craft. Nobody. Not my Dad."

Davy could see Mildred reinforcing herself and he felt for her. " How long ago was that?"

"13 months. And two days."

They did not speak for some time while they studiously crunched on the ham and pickle sandwiches Mrs. Craft had provided. She brought her eyes back from distant conjecture and looked directly at Davy.

"I am thinking of some way to contact my father. Nobody has been able to find him. I just don't understand how. Not yet. I have tried hard and I don't know how."

Mildred was disappointed in herself. She was working on doing something no-one had been able to do and yet she was beating herself up.

"Mildred, I think you are too hard on yourself about this."

"Well, .." She paused to think, not wanting to give away anything of herself. "This is so important to me and my Mum and I can't do it Davy. I can't do it."

"Mildred, wanting to be good at something and trying to do that thing well is fine. But be careful of what you demand of yourself. What you are actually doing right now is competing. Competing with yourself with no rules as to what winning is. No matter how that kind of battle works out, when you compete with yourself, you still lose. Seems a rough way to travel."

Davy could see Mildred was desperate. He thought there might be a possibility. In that magic day in the classroom when he had been absorbed or taken over by the pipe and the light, he had landed inside his imaginings about Nelson and the *HMS Victory*. He reckoned he had picked an arbitrary time, a time determined by his wished intention about a certain event. If he was included in that particular time, why could it not be for any time. Why not for a time and place including Mildred's father. And could the light accommodate more than just him or more than one person and did they all need to share an intention or could one of them run it for others? Davy didn't have it figured so he kept it for when he could turn his mind to it. He did not mention it to Mildred.

Mildred came out of the thoughts of her dad and drifted back to her mother's job.

"Davy, I don't understand. Why would the plant close? What would be better for the plant than having it keep running?" Davy looked stymied.

"I don't want your answers Davy, I am just rambling and thinking out loud. Just bouncing my thoughts off of you and listening to my own questions."

Davy felt somewhat diminished by the role. *Dopo, I think I have just become Mildred's Dopo.*

"Fine Mildred. I listen to things I say out loud all the time. I understand. Your questions are rhetorical." He did not mention Dopo.

Mildred looked at Davy in a pleased way. She knew the correct term also. She had not used it because she had become so accustomed to the need for dumbing down her vocabulary. "Indubitably." she said. They looked at each other and laughed.

"Davy, what could the bosses and the managers and owners be thinking. What could have made them decide this was right!"

"Actually, Bully Gregious is all of those things you mentioned. Boss, manager, owner. He is, was, a partner of Charles Foster. You have probably seen Mr. Foster's picture above the school office counter. He is the Foster who named Foster Industries. He dedicated the land for the school and he donated the land and built the library. He was an inventor and a sort of jack of all trades scientist but really brilliant. My dad says he has all kinds of different and really good patents. He has a big laboratory that only he used at the plant but it is locked up now. Steel doors and all that and with old style push button pad combinations and no one has bothered with it since he disappeared."

"Disappeared?" *Like my father.*

"Yes. About four or five years ago, he went into his lab to work one day, and he never came out. Dad told me all about him. I looked him up and he is, was quite." Davy stopped. He realized he had just used the past tense for the man who had disappeared as if he were dead. Disappeared like Mildred's father. She had not noticed.

Davy continued. "He is quite the inventor and he even grew up right here. My grandfathers, of both my Mom and Dad, went to high school with him. They said he was really not much interested in school and left early to do his own thing."

Davy had heard that phrase for the first time a few weeks ago and he thought it was the best phrase. Do your own thing. He is doing his own thing. He wondered if Tilt would go for it. *"Pilcher! What are you doing?"* "Sir, I am *doing my own thing.* "Maybe not.

"Davy?"

"Oh. Sorry. Yes. His name is Charles Abernathy Foster. That is our school. Charles A. Foster Elementary. The story is he saved a little money when he went out working and helped a young inventor get his project going for a share of the profits and away he went. He wanted 15% of the profits until the patent ran out but the inventor said, 'No, Charlie, I would have gone nowhere without your help. For life you get profits.'

"So, he got profits for life, and I guess he still gets some money from that. I know it is still being used. It is one of the things Foster Industries still makes. A coal cleaner. It is called triboelectric. It uses a static charge to separate things while gravity runs coal down a belt one way as the heavier stuff tumbles down the belt and the good clean stuff all cleaned drops off over the top. You need nitrogen so it doesn't blow up. Mr. Foster himself has dozens of patents. One I read about is really cool. Electronic storage in a hologram. No waiting to get things out or put them in. Take them out from any angle and put them in at any angle. You never have to wait for things in a line."

Mildred had no interest in any of this patent stuff. Her problem was jobs and what to do about it. "But Davy, how does Bully Gregious get to make these decisions. How can he just do this or that and take away thousands of jobs?"

"Hard to say. My Mum says he can't do it but my Dad said there is a rumor they found a letter in Foster's papers giving power of attorney to Gregious. That means Bully can do things just as if he were Foster. But I am not sure about that rumor of the power of attorney you know, what I just said. It might not be so. You know how rumors are."

Mildred did the valley girl voice. "Yeah. Rumors. I heard about those." They both laughed.

Mildred wanted to get it straight. "He makes all the decisions himself. "

" Pretty much I think so, but he has other people around him, and at least one all the time. A tall thin lady. An executive. The pale scary one. She has been with Foster Industries a long time. Bully got rid of most of Foster's executives once it was decided by Bully and his helper that Mr. Foster was not coming back. I guess it is just the two of them."

"Davy, imagine the discussions taking place to make the decision to close the Foster plant."

Mildred tipped her head back and looked down her nose and snooted her versions of two people with Princeton University accents.

'Here ah the annual reports Mr. Gregious. We ah in a profit position. We have more new orders than we can fill. Our research staff has jost oowon, the Nobel Prize for physics. Our alternative to fossil fuel for energy is finally perfffected and our workforce is the best and most effficient in all the world.'

She continued in her most imperious ivy league voice.

'Oowhat? Who do they think they ah, doing such things! Making profit and solving problems and winning awards! It is obvious to me we have no choice. We must close the plant.'

'My thoughts exectly B.G. I oowill get things rolling. Six months?'

'Six months.'

Davy laughed at the accents and Mildred's elevated nose but he understood and agreed with the premise. A business rationale did not seem to exist for the closure of the plant. There was another motive. What was Bully Gregious up to.

"Davy. I have an idea. Two ideas actually. Well, maybe three."

"That's all?"

"Yes. Have you ever been in the Foster plant?"

"Yes, I have been many times. They have an open house every year and my Dad shows me the changes and innovations and the like. Foster's private lab was off limits but I know where it is."

"Do you think you can visualize accurately where you have been in the buildings?"

"Yes, I can. I have not been there for about a year but I can see it clearly in my mind's eye. I know it."

Mildred was listening and not listening. She was thinking how lucky she was to have found this particular boy as a new friend in a new school within the first few days. He was clever and thoughtful and a reader. He wasn't egotistical and he was really nice. More than that, he was creative and funny.

Davy saw Mildred was not really listening to him now. He understood her worry. Her mom had just lost her job and her father was missing.

"Davy, what if we... you went back to the time they were making the decision. You know, be there when they were discussing the whole thing about closing the plant and eavesdrop on what they are really doing."

Davy flushed at the thrill of the idea and he imagined he could feel the pipe at home give a glimmer.

" I don't know. I have only been back and forth once. And it is not easy. I am not invisible you know. The place you land is real and the people are real and the hot water you get into could be boiling. It is not totally predictable."

"Can two people go?"

He didn't really know so he answered too quickly.

"It is too dangerous."

"For a girl?"

"Yes for a..." He thought he better rephrase this.

"Not for a girl only, for anybody. Anyway, what if only one can come back. I don't know all the tricks yet. I suppose when you ask whether two can go, you mean you are one of the two."

She nodded. Davy was by no means sure he wanted to share the pipe, even with Mildred. "Besides, how do we do it. Do you hold on to my belt or what."?

"That's easy, we would hold hands." Davy blushed and Mildred assumed control.

"Also, Davy, do you know how many meetings they have to have in a year? You know, their rules about having a meeting to discuss the business or the budget or a change on how they do things. A meeting where things such as closing the plant and laying off workers would be discussed."

"Actually, I do. Porky Gregious told me. It was about eight or nine months ago. His dad would always complain about the meeting. One meeting a year and his dad complained about all the work. Porky thought it ridiculous and laughed about it. One meeting and it was too much work for Bully Gregious."

Mildred was excited. "That is wonderful. The exact meeting date is already pinned down for us. Davy. We don't have the internet at my place. Do you?"

"Yes, we do. Why?"

"We need that report. You can go online and get the information."

"I could if Foster's kind of company needs to report, but you know Mildred, that isn't where the sort of thing we're talking about would have been discussed. An announcement to the public might have been made then, but the planning and the decision made by Bully would've been in private with his executive assistant or vice president or whatever she is. I have seen her at the open house and she scares the heck out of me but I don't remember her name. Something like Dragon or Wagon. What we really need to know is when their private meetings were held. The only thing I can think of, is security makes everybody sign in at the main floor reception kiosk, even the executives. There is no exception. If we could see the sign-in log that would be the thing."

Mildred was smiling. "Use the pipe."

Davy knew she was going to say that. He thought it was a good idea for two reasons. He wanted to experiment with the pipe again and as far as taking Mildred along, well he would think about that. At least they would not be landing among alligators or in the middle of a lake. Maybe, just maybe, another person, particularly somebody intelligent like Mildred, intending and focusing in the light on the same idea at the same time was actually safer and maybe stronger.

"Mildred, we will do it, but if I get caught in my Dad's plant, I am persona non-grata in the Pilcher house, forever."

Davy understood if he got caught it was not in his current real-life history and he would create a new stream of history from that point, but he did not want to be in trouble in any time frame. He looked at Mildred closely to see if she knew the Latin phrase 'persona non-grata' he had learned only last week. She nodded in understanding. *She knows it. Rats!*

Davy stood in his bedroom dressed in black. He buckled on his belt and tied the end of his sheath down like a gunslinger. The pipe seemed somehow innervated. He pulled on his maroon toque and looked in the mirror. He decided he looked appropriately burglarish and he was pleased at the look. They had agreed to meet Sunday at the foot of the pier, as far as possible from the throng on the promenade. If there was sun, then they would engage his pipe and hope for the best.

Chapter 7: The Vicious Scribbler

The wind had picked up and the gulls were hunkering down in the lee of the break wall, using the heat from the sun still stored in the rocks. The inbound waves hammered the break wall from the south and they made 30-foot geysers where they found a trough. The bay in the lee of the high piled stone was choppy and dappled with moving shadow and two wind surfers in yellow wet suits streaked across the surface, hiked out to water level. The rigging of the tethered small boats made wind chimes of the aluminum masts. Mildred was waiting in overkill mode on the foot of the pier opposite the entry gate to the yacht moorings. Not only did she have a pad for notes inside a plastic bag attached to her belt, but she was also wearing a red balaclava. She had socks over her shoes for quiet work.

"Mildred, you are conspicuous."

She looked. "I am incognito. Not conspicuous. If they see us, guess whose face they can recognize."

"Hello Davy," said Mrs. Williams, the woman who lived next door to the Pilchers as she strolled by slowly. She wanted to pinch Davy's cheek but he knew what was coming and moved away.

Mildred eyed her with her best clandestine look. "Who is that?"

"Mrs. Williams. She lives next door. She works the day shift at the plant." Mildred nodded. Davy sighed at his blown cover and conspiratorially he leaned in to Mildred.

"Ok. On Sunday, the best place to land in the plant offices is in the elevator corridor. It is out of sight from the reception area where the log book is and it won't be used."

"Where does the security guard stay?"

"Right near the login station at reception. The sign-in book is on a pedestal. We will have to wait to check the log book until he begins his rounds or uses the washroom or something. The elevators will not be running. If the book is a new one and it doesn't have the older dates, we will have to take the stairs to the second-floor offices and look there."

Mildred nodded fast in a continuing bob of agreement. Davy saw she was nervous.

"Flashlight!" said Davy. He had forgotten it.

"Check," said Mildred as she patted the flashlight in her pocket. He was quiet.

The pattern of the clouds running inland was making a sharp sunny break about every 15 seconds. Davy took Mildred's right hand in his and flicked open the top of his sheath and slid out the pipe. A gap was forming in the clouds as Mrs. Williams walked back. She looked at the youngsters holding hands. "Davy, you are so cute."

He could feel Mildred's nervous grip on his hand tightening with anticipation. In a few seconds the time was right and he swung the pipe up hard against his eye to get it perfect and they were gone with the biggest flash yet. Several people turned to see the spot but on a day like this the strobing clouds could play tricks on your eyes. The golden intention of the pipe swept them away and caressed the two of them to rest, standing in the corridor between two rows of elevators, safe inside the Foster Industries office building.

Davy was motionless. It was his third time riding the consciousness of the light. He was surrounded again by the miasmic shimmer of unreality but it seemed less dominant. He saw the shock wave of the present coming hard and he accepted the need for it when it hit and instantly he recognized the closed elevator door in front of him. Mildred stood beside him, facing him, her note-pad tucked into her waist band, resplendent in her red balaclava and shoes covered with brown socks. Davy watched and waited. Mildred saw herself wrapped in a viscid wall of glutinous unreality just as Davy had done on his first trail. She saw him, saw the elevators and did not relate to them, consider them or have a need for anything at all. All things were unconcerning and immaterial to action. She saw the pace of something coming fast and simply received it.

The wall of awareness hit her like the front of a typhoon and she said in a normal speaking voice, "Hello Davy," and she smiled beneath the balaclava. Mildred was ready.

Davy blanched and put a quick finger over his mouth. She put two hands over her own as if it could unring the bell. They heard nothing from the foyer. The trail with the two them had been perfect. In fact, thought Davy, it was somehow more definite. *Two minds may be better.* The trip had been perfect.

71

Davy took one step and his right shoe squeaked loudly. He stopped and listened for movement from the guard. Mildred did not say anything. He knew, fully formed under that balaclava, was the look. He took off his shoe and tied it to his belt by its shoelaces. The light was subdued in the corridor and they carefully peered around the corner toward the central kiosk where the guard should be. The guard was not at his station. *Must be on his rounds.* They listened for his returning footsteps and heard nothing. They ran to the log-in station with Mildred slipping and sliding in her socks on the terrazzo floor and she skidded to a stop against the desk. The name on the identifying security placard was 'Darryl Johnson'.

Davy jumped behind the pedestal platform and opened the heavy log book with a thump which reverberated around the empty lobby. They stopped and listened and they heard no action coming their way. The front page of the log book had five signatures, all from last Friday and that was it. He looked at Mildred and shook his head. This was not the book they needed. Her eyes went immediately to see where the stairwell door was located. Then they looked at each other. The offices would be locked.

Sharply, they heard the forceful click of a key in the security check-point wall-box just around the corner. They dashed to the refuge of the elevator corridor and Mildred crouched and shot past Davy and bumped against the wall. From that darkened vantage point they could see the small illuminated stairwell sign on the other side of the guard, next to the public washrooms. Darryl Johnson sat down heavily and opened a bag and pulled out a sandwich. He hummed as he teased out a pickle from his paper bag and adjusted his ample behind deeper into his seat. He hung his bristling keyring on its hook on the pedestal below the log book and began to enjoy his food. They watched, knowing they needed those keys if they were to search for the older log books. Darryl left the bag splayed open and got up and headed to the washroom. He took his keys with him and when he got back he hung them up on their hook. Security guard Johnson was careful. That complicated things.

They waited in silence. Davy gave the palms up shoulder shrug 'now what' sign to Mildred. She gave back the palms down push signal twice. 'Just wait.' The guard had finished his lunch and he got up abruptly and Mildred ducked back. He strode directly toward the elevator corridor. Apparently, he had heard them. Davy and Mildred looked right and left. They were trapped. They moved with their backs hard against the wall in the darkest corner and heard Johnson's heavy tread coming directly toward them. Johnson stopped as if to listen. He crumpled up his paper bag and thrust it into the waste receptacle and made the metal flap spin. He turned on his heel and went back to his spot at reception. The aroma of the exhaust from the paper bag was of chicken.

They began breathing again and Mildred peered around the corner at the guard. He had his head down and looked as if he were reading. Then they heard the sweet music. A small but sonorous snore was building. He was sleeping. They moved quietly toward the podium and the heavy ring of keys. Davy hobbled with one shoe on and one shoe off and Mildred shined the terrazzo with her skating feet. Davy held his breath and slowly and carefully lifted the key ring above the hook, allowing the full weight of each key to swing slowly to its lowest position so it would not jingle. Davy's theft was noiseless. He thought of the artful dodger. Together he and Mildred tip toed to the stairwell door. They pulled it open and slipped through without a sound. It was usually two hours between security checks so they had some time if Darryl Johnson stayed sleeping.

On the first stair landing, Mildred removed the socks from the outside of her shoes and stuffed them into her pocket along with the flashlight. Davy kept his shoe off. It was too squeaky. They climbed the stairs to the darkened second floor which was illuminated only by emergency exit lights Now the question was, where would the log books be kept.

Davy could not tell one key from the other in this light and they were not labeled. He and Mildred would have to risk the flashlight and then it would still be trial and error with which key fit what lock. They stood on the second floor at the other end of the corridor from Bully Gregious' office. Mildred held the flashlight shining on the floor and the reflection off the polished surface was enough. All of the doors had small rectangular glass windows at eye height. They shined the light through the window into the first room on their right and it had chairs and desks piled with what looked like old typewriters sitting on a table. One typewriter even had some carbon paper in it. *Cool* thought Davy. *Just like the old movies. Hard clicking mechanical typewriters with carbon paper. Neat.* Laboratory glassware was standing along one counter with extension cords and cans of chemicals, all in a mix together. The room was a combined storage room and junk collection. It was unlikely the entry logs would be there.

"What do you think Mildred?"

"Unlikely."

The next office had a simple "M.D." on the door in four-inch-high black and bold Old English script. They looked at each other with the same question on their lips. *M.D.? A doctor here at Bully's offices? Who knew!* Mildred shined the light inside. Blackout drapes kept the room in total darkness. The room contained a filing cabinet and a large desk and one chair. The corner near the back left had a dead Aspidistra in a rust red clay pot. The leaves had fallen and curled, left there unwanted and dead and scattered around its base. There was a large pitcher of water on the floor next to it but the plant had gone unwatered. Mildred bristled. The Aspidistra was called the 'iron plant' and was almost impossible to kill. Someone appeared to have worked at it.

Davy looked at the keys. The key hole size eliminated about half of them so he began trying the older styles. He was lucky. The third one fit and the door opened easily. The desk was devoid of paper and there was one paper in an outbox. It was dated four months ago and was covered with dust. The bookshelf standing against the entry wall had a handful of books, with most of them devoted to amortization tables, zoning regulations and tax codes. The rest of the shelves bristled with tubes for holding maps or architects' drawings. They were labeled with local street names and places. That was all there was in the room. Mildred tugged hard on the filing cabinet, expecting it to be locked but it was not. She looked at Davy with anticipation of what they would find. When she opened it, it was empty. There were no logs here. They closed and locked up the office door and moved down the corridor. The last office on this side was Bully's. The brass nameplate on the wall said 'Bully Gregious Esq. President, Chairman and Chief Executive Officer. Foster Industries.'

There were no lights on, but looking through the glass panel, the room was astoundingly bright. The floor was strewn with loose newspaper pages and a plate of unfinished food was on the desk. Above the desk on the wall was a large Foster Industries calendar with Bully's enlarged round face leering in the forefront, with 100 or so employees in reduced size smiling behind him. The rack-like shelving to the left of the cluttered leather topped desk was heaped with books of every kind. They tried Bully's door and it was not locked. The office was inordinately hot and stifling. Mildred spotted the thermostat and went to turn it down but it was off. Pyramiding above them was an enormous four-sided cathedral skylight with concentric rings cut into the glass of every panel. It was dizzying to look at and Davy felt as if he were under a magnifying glass.

"Those glass panels are all Fresnel lenses." said Mildred. "Terrific for collecting and focusing light." She knew they could not dawdle and she said no more but she was thinking.

On one shelf stood binder after binder of neatly labeled patent and trademark records. *This must have been Charles Foster's office before he disappeared.* On the left in a neat array of blue and gold leather binding, stood the entry logs they had come for. The neatly labeled and numbered books stood in order from the first one of 30 years ago and continued on in order. To the right of them, in disarray and loosely piled were the more recent ones. *The ones Bully was responsible for,* thought Davy. Together they lifted down the ledger from the top of the loose pile and put it on the floor, under the brilliant light from the Fresnel lenses. They sat beside it and Mildred excitedly opened the book. The two of them flipped to the back page for the most recent entry. *Last Thursday. This was it!* The book went back a whole year to the front page. It was possible Bully may have acted alone but his reputation was he did not have the intellect for it. If he had special meetings to get advice on the plan to close Foster Industries, the sign-in log might show it up.

Mildred pulled out her pad to take notes and Davy went through day by day looking for sign-ins which matched. They did not know who Bully might have met with but matching was the first thing. A pattern began to emerge. Repeatedly, the same vicious scrawl which almost cut through the paper of the log book had signed in close to the time when Bully signed in. The signature was totally illegible and it was always furious. Davy had not been counting the matchups as he whispered them for Mildred to record. They spoke so quietly to each other they were nearly inaudible.

"How many times Mildred?"

"Well, 37 overall, but before the announcement of the closing of the plant, I have only 19. Those two signatures, Bully and the scrawler, had 19 very close sign in times on the same day."

Davy's shoulders slumped. 19 trips with the pipe to spy on discussions. 19 times to hope not to get caught. Escaping detection was impossible. Just a matter of time. *I am a dead man if I get caught.* He looked up at the picture of Bully on the calendar.

"Wait a minute Mildred! Do you have the exact sign in times recorded as well as the dates?"

"Sure Davy. I recorded them as you read them to me."

"What ones are in the very early AM or late PM?"

Mildred ran down the list with her finger.

"One time only Davy. Bully and the maniac scribbler signed in within six minutes of each other at 11:43 and 11:49 PM on February 15."

Davy went to the Foster Industries calendar on the wall and flipped it back to February. Every page had Bully's perspiring face, leering out like a corpulent gargoyle.

"That must be it!" whispered Davy hoarsely. He tapped on the calendar.

"Those 11:43 and 11:49 sign-ins are on a Saturday night. The meeting would run into the AM Sunday morning. Just the one security guard enforcing the sign-in is here then. The cleaners don't even come on Sunday as witness to any comings and goings. Mildred, I think this is the time the mystery scrawler and Bully Gregious decided to close the plant!"

They hefted the book back onto the shelf and put it exactly as it had sat in its dust outline. Mildred was sniffling from the dust they had raised. She followed as they left Bully's office quietly and she locked the door behind them. Davy heard a balaclava muffled 'Rats!'. He turned and saw Mildred testing the knob of the locked door. They had found it unlocked and it had to be left that way.

Davy said nothing and grabbed the key ring and fumbled nervously for the older keys. He tried one, then the next, each one with a greater sense of urgency than the last, hoping but not knowing whether Johnson was still sleeping. After five terrifying minutes he succeeded in unlocking Bully's door and they left it as they had found it.

The two culprits hurried hot and worried down the stairwell to the lobby level. They remembered then the stairway door opened out toward the guard. Fearfully, Mildred cracked the door open, millimeter by millimeter. Darryl

Johnson was not at his post. They saw him not ten feet in front of them, his back turned toward them, mumbling and walking away from the washroom right beside them. *I could get fired. Never lost keys before. They ain't in the washroom. If them keys are not stuck in that last zone checkpoint box, I don't know where, I don't know where.* He passed by his desk and stopped at the pedestal log book. For the third time he looked at the empty key hook and continued shaking his head on the way around the corner to his last hope for finding his keys, the zone checkpoint box.

Davy rasped to Mildred, "Stay here!"

He ran and slid ten feet on his one stockinged foot and stopped with a bump overbalanced against the podium and looped the keys back on the peg and they jangled. With one shoe off and one shoe on he charged back to the stairwell door and started up the stairs with Mildred close behind. They entered Bully's office and closed the door behind them. They held hands and looked to the skylight and Davy sighted his pipe. As the energy coalesced, Davy hoped Mildred was thinking of the pier.

The intention from the light was focused and multiplied by the Fresnel lenses into something close to a thunder clap. Mildred and Davy were grabbed by a golden blender of spinning acceptance and freedom and a welcoming timelessness connecting them them to all things. They landed back on the pier facing the receding derriere of Mrs. Williams. They looked at each other and burst with a tension relieving laugh, feeling better than they had ever felt. In home time they had been gone one minute. At the Foster Industries executive suites, Darryl Johnson had heard what sounded like a thunder clap from somewhere within the building. He ran back to the reception area and saw nothing, except for the glint of the lost keys, hanging on their hook at the pedestal desk, just where he had hung them.

The weather forecast in real time was for brilliant sun for both today and through tomorrow afternoon with a guarantee of a hard squall and then a week of heavy rain starting tomorrow night. If they were going to go and check out the meeting of February 15th, they had to do it before tomorrow evening, or wait at least a week and they had no time to lose. If it rained or was overcast or dark at the other end, it really did not matter. They could wait for the sun. Ten days away was just an hour or so in real time at home. They agreed to meet after school at 3:15 the next day at the Borstal River bridge.

Mildred was there early. She had changed the color of her noise buffering socks over her shoes and she had retained the red balaclava. It was rolled up like a toque on her forehead but it would come down when the inner spy came out. Her notepad was in a plastic bag under her belt. Her flashlight bulge was obvious in her pocket. Davy arrived on time from the other end of the bridge and he saw her without her seeing him. Mildred was gathering some fallen Francesca petals to toss into the stream to watch them float and spin, trapped in the swirl of the eddies. Even with the vigor of the fallen petals exhausted, their blue color was still strong. The water below them in the stream was darker as the growth of the season had encroached along the banks to make a shadowed overhang.

"Oh. Hi Davy. I didn't see you coming. So, all set?"

Davy was all set but he had just had his seniority with the pipe taken away in one sentence. He was supposed to be asking the questions from experience, not the other way around.

"Yes. I am all set."

Davy turned to scan the sky and felt the wind was beginning to quarter more to the east. That was a sure sign the predicted weather change was coming on fast, earlier than promised. The gulls knew it first. For the last hour they had been riding the thermals up the face of the bluff and with a quiet purpose they were streaming inland to meadows and leeward protection, not willing to face this storm. It was going to be a heavy one.

The sky was bright but it was settling lower. A wedge of deep grey clouds was forming in the east and the angled leading edge chiseled into the diminishing light. Davy did not have much time to get into action. The cloud bank would soon be in the westerly line of site.

"Mildred, let's discuss our intended landing for the Foster offices. If the two of us intend it together it will be more reliable." Mildred took that as a compliment.

Davy suggested, "I am visualizing the storage room next to the M.D. office. You remember, the one with the stacked chairs and the old typewriters and the laboratory glassware." Mildred nodded.

"Yes, I remember it, carbon paper."

"Exactly. That is the room. We should agree to land about 11 o'clock. That will give us time to get to the right place to listen. Bully logged in about 11:45 on the night of the 15th." She nodded and checked for her extra pen in case the main one went dry. She had it.

Davy fixed his pipe on the hazing sun as they held hands on the Borstal River bridge. The storage room shot a quick flash of brilliant light through the glass window into the darkened second floor corridor and it bounced along the polished floor. The light had delivered its cargo of Mildred and Davy as intended on a sleeting February 15th at 11:00 PM.

Mildred stood about ten feet apart from Davy and she was facing the typewriters. Apparently, her intention had been slightly different. She reached out and ripped the carbon paper out of the old machine and stuffed it into the plastic pouch protecting her notepad. If there was something interesting on it, it could still be read. Old carbon paper had the permanent imprint of the keys which struck it and whatever had been typed there was easy to read. She sneezed hard twice as the dust she had raised began to settle and then she sneezed again.

"Sorry. Dust allergies."

As their eyes acclimated to the light, they could see a large wire screen in the wall near the ceiling. Mildred shone her flashlight there and saw it was a hot air vent. The heat was down and the fan was not running. It was cold in the offices and they sat down with their backs against the wall on the tile and hugged themselves to keep warm while they waited for Bully and his collaborator. Davy wondered if Darryl Johnson was on duty at the sign-in desk tonight. Mildred wondered what was written on the carbon paper and she itched to go after it with the flashlight right now. They were startled from their introspections by the slamming of a car door. It echoed around the empty parking lot and in through the hot air vent and two stomachs tightened. They listened for footsteps.

Bully Gregious unlocked the front main door under the watchful eye of the security guard, who was not Darryl Johnson, but one Frank Trotter. Heavily laden with a bulging briefcase, Bully nodded and walked past the guard and past the log-in book, getting out his key to unlock and activate the executive elevator to the second floor.

"Mr. Gregious. Sir." Bully pretended not to hear.

"Mr. Gregious. Sir. You have to sign in."

Bully turned and fixed the guard with his most exasperated look but he was not very good at it.

"Mr. Gregious, I will bring you the book."

Frank Trotter good naturedly lugged the log book to Bully standing at the foot of the elevators. As the elevator light brightened and the door opened, he signed the book and stepped into the car. The door closed and the guard noted the time next to Mr. Gregious' name. 11:43.

Davy and Mildred heard the groan and whirr of the elevator cables, the ding of the door opening and the footsteps of Gregious as he walked to his office. They heard the office door open and close behind him. *Ah. The meeting was in his office, not the other office.*

Bully flopped hard into his office chair and made a small 'oop' sound with his mouth. His girth had increased over time and it had driven the padding in his chair to parts unknown and now he hit hard on the wood when he sat. He pulled out the folder of documents to be discussed tonight but he left the elastic retainer in place over the flap. He wouldn't be allowed to run the meeting anyway so why bother. He was perspiring heavily despite the cold of the building and he was already soaked through at the small of his back. He had dressed with his best tie and shirt but as he looked down he sighed audibly. The tie was wrinkled and askew and he had done that just in the drive from home to here. His shirt was straining to keep him in and a pyramid of skin showed just above his belt. His sunburned belly was peeling and it was bright pink and bulging from the gaps between the buttons.

He and Mrs. Gregious had been on a two-week trip to the islands and now he was back and more stressed than ever from two weeks with his missus. She had made him slather the sunscreen on his face and to wear a straw hat against the sun. His face and head were as white as a lab rat and the rest of him was peeling and bright pink. He flew to the islands for one purpose. He did not give a hoot about the sun and the sea and the sand. He wanted simply to strut and display his tan when he got back and to show off he had been away, and blast it, he couldn't even do that.

His undershirt had crept up the incline of his belly and it was lodged in a discreet roll around his torso. The expensive grey light wool pants Bully wore were sticking like paint to his legs and bottom. Here he was, skulking in the middle of the night, holding a meeting for two in his own office and he was nervous. *Blast it.! I am the boss. How does this happen. It happens every time.* He sighed again.

Bully Gregious knew he would get clever ideas and hear strong proposals at this meeting. He also knew they would be heaped on him in the form of orders and hammered into him as demands and he would do the orders and agree to the demands as usual.

He heard a turbo engine whining in the distance and the occasional shriek of automobile tires taken to the edge of tearing. He began to perspire heavily and in dread, he looked hard at the door. He shifted his weight in his chair to find a stable spot and Davy and Mildred heard the objection from the straining wood through the air vent in the storage room. They also heard the same fast approaching automobile as it geared down and ripped around the corners. It entered the parking lot with a roar and slid to a halt with the tires chirping over the occasional bare spot of pavement not yet covered with sleet. The driver gunned the engine for ten seconds, forcing the revs higher until the car screamed like a Banshee and then cut the power. The car door thunked closed hard and the pavement seemed to relax. The new arrival keyed its way through the front door of the building and as the security guard recognized the individual, he blanched and implored Providence. *Please let me not have to ask!*

"Give me that book!", demanded the entrant.

Frank Trotter relinquished his grip and handed over the log-book quickly and the signing scrawl tore through three pages and the perpetrator tossed the pen and bounced it off the podium onto the floor and disappeared into elevator row. The guard heard the click of the turn of the key to activate the executive elevator and he heard the too familiar crack of a shoe kicking the elevator door for being too slow. The doors parted and the occupant elevated to the second floor and to the meeting with Bully Gregious. The security man retrieved the pen from the floor and in a shaking hand he attested to the time by writing 11:49 beside the torn and illegible signature in the log book. He signed off. Frank Trotter.

Chapter 8: The Forger

Mildred and Davy were keened with anticipation. They heard the whirr of the elevator and its ding as a second person came up to the second floor, left the elevator, stomped to Bully's office, entered without knocking and slammed the door closed. Through the connecting forced air vent they heard two thumps and a chair scrape across the floor and it was as if Mildred and Davy were right there in the office. The heating duct running between the rooms projected sound in both directions loudly and clearly. Mildred pulled her notepad from the plastic bag at her belt and cocked her head, getting ready to record. She clicked open her ballpoint pen. It sounded like a gunshot to her but no one else noticed the miniscule click.

The tension from the meeting in the other room was palpable through the air conduit. Bully was soaking wet and stuck to the back of his chair. The newcomer was at ease and sat fully upright in the opposite chair and gained the optical power advantage of height and spoke.

"Bully, you have a folio stuffed to bursting on the desk in front of you. Presumably it is something you wish to discuss."

The second arrival was still wearing her driving gloves as she set her thin folder on the desk in front of herself and smiled serpently at the Chief Executive Officer of Foster Industries.

Davy and Mildred's eyes widened as they returned each other's surprise. *The collaborator with the paper slashing signature is a woman!* Davy's heart sped up. *It had to be the executive woman, that Dragon, Draggle whatever person.* For the first time, Davy felt fear. Indeed, it was a woman, and not just any woman. It was the Drago, in the flesh.

That morning Malveena Drago had returned from the office of her handwriting expert feeling euphoric and satisfied. Their state-of-the-art forgery was absolutely perfect. She and the expert had worked together for months with energy and guile to fabricate the perfect forgery and they had done it. Computer assisted design had reproduced the crucial signature with the correct pressure areas on the strokes and every element of the flair and panache to irrefutably confirm the signatory. Each curl and dot and stroke was exactly correct as was the color of old ink designed to mimic dated documents. Neither a computer analysis nor the practiced eye of human expert handwriting analysis could recognize or accuse their forgery as a forgery. *Case closed.*

M.D. was pleased and happy with her work and she had decided to reward herself with some shopping. She was not deterred by the cold winter weather. It was the Ides of February and it was certainly portentous. She deserved this treat. What she had done today would set her up for life. At her meeting tonight, Bully would do exactly what she would tell him to do and that was that. She would relish watching him squirm as he operated out of his depth.

She walked contentedly past the old style narrow storefronts designed with their entry door side windows angled to increase viewing time for the passersby. People walked in those days. She enjoyed the old business section of town. The ornate lamp posts cast in the 1920's with fluted sides and Romanesque capitals still lined the streets and they spoke to a time when quality and detail were respected. The concrete sidewalks which had been poured at the same time were still in good shape.

As always, the second-hand shops had the detritus of lives displayed in their windows, offering it up to a whole new generation of fresh starts and little thrills. The dated clothing and pieces of history she found there pleased her. They were dissimilar and unplanned and many of them surrounded her in her apartment. Taken together they made a statement which she liked to think of as recovery decor. Malveena came here routinely to buy her clothes as she had for 20 years but now things were changing. The stores were becoming too clean, the bums she ignored on the street were dressed better, name brand chain stores were invading the old neighborhood to grab the suckers and now she was called chic. She hated chic. She had been funky and now she was chic. The whole area had become faux funk. She had become faux funk. Faux funky stuff was now made in China. In 50 years it might be funk, but now it was just faux.

She did find one real treasure. It was a Ronson Touch Tip lighter like the one Humphrey Bogart used in a black and white movie from the 1940's, called "The Maltese Falcon." Now that was funk. She had finished her luncheon at Bistro Cardinale and headed home to prepare for the meeting with Bully. The Meursault had been wonderful and she felt a little residual effect of the fine wine. The Meursault had no Grands Crus designation but she preferred it to the Montrachet. Her favorite came from the Côte de Beaune. Tonight, she had enjoyed a 2014 Domaine Comtes Lafon Charmes. It did not yet have its expressiveness to come, but it was pleasing.

She paid the underground parking and climbed into her Porsche 911 Sports Cabriolet and tossed her purchases onto the passenger seat. Despite the light sleeting outside, she put the top down. The aerodynamics of the car were so refined and the sweep of the wind over the windscreen was so perfect the cockpit would stay dry. She blasted the heater and she was cozy and comfy in Drago-world and Malveena felt strong against the gloom of the wet, dank February day. The street had not been touched by a plow and the deepening slush was turning to ice on the windblown road. She hammered the Porsche out of the underground parking and vaulted up onto the street and did two swinging fishtails before she settled into a lane. Every corner leading home to her apartment was a controlled drift and she increased her speed as she sensed the texture of the surface. As she downshifted through the hairpins her car was a monster made of silk and she was the match for it. She brought herself back down out of grand prix mode and cornered with just a small fishtail into the street where she lived. The Porsche had purred her to her apartment in record time. She peeled off her driving gloves and threw them on the entrance table. She reached into her bag and eased out and unwrapped the Ronson lighter and set it on the copper rimmed end table under her reading light. It was perfect there as she knew it would be. For lighting candles, the Ronson art deco lighter was definitely ultra-funk. She stepped out of her flat shoes and walked to her bedroom. *Now what to wear to knock Bully's socks off.*

Malveena was a statuesque 5'10" and she had an angularity of posture which exuded strength. Those who held a Carpathian obsession with gothic austerity might describe Malveena as beautiful. The whole Malveena package of pallid beauty and elegant carriage disarmed Bully and made him useless. He always swore it would not happen the next time but it always did. He was helpless in the presence of Malveena Drago. The late-night meeting time had been of Malveena's choosing. She had delayed her arrival as planned to drive up the anticipation and angst in Bully Gregious.

She slammed Bully's door closed behind her to set the tone and slid the soft

84

chair sitting against the desk to the side. She dragged the heavy wooden arm chair from the corner across the floor and screeched it into position across from Bully. Her chair was now two inches higher than his chair. Malveena sat and crossed her legs. She ceremoniously took off her driving glasses and put on her amber tinted reading glasses and fixed Bully with her green eyes.

"Bully, you have a folio stuffed to bursting on the desk in front of you. Presumably it is something you wish to discuss."

She smiled. It felt to Bully the temperature in the room had just gone down. Malveena's smile could do that. He scanned her as he melted in the leather chair.

"Well, Mal.. well, uh, this is the final offer we have from the Macao Casino Syndicate. They will buy all the voting shares of Foster Industries for this location. The price they are offering is an astoundingly good price. You will be rich. I will be rich. For their money, they get the land and buildings where the plant and the library are situated. Those will be demolished. They will have complete control of Foster Industries property."

Listening attentively in the storage room, Mildred gasped and the air conduit transmitted it.

Malveena looked for the floating thing in the air which had just suggested an intrusion. She held up her hand and Bully stopped. She listened. *Nothing. This building, so close to the river, there are always water sounds.*

She eased her tension a little and turned to Gregious. "Yes Bully, continue."

"The main casino will be on the property where the plant sits. They are calling it simply, 'Macau Casino Macau.' Parking will be on the library site once the buildings are torn down. They expect to begin demolition and construction next April."

Bully stopped and slumped into a pudgy sort of pout. He picked up his folio and tossed it back down on the desk disconsolately as if he were discarding the contents. He knew the offer was very good and Charles Abernathy Foster was not there to interfere, but Charles Abernathy Foster was also not there to supply the one thing Bully needed from him.

"So then, Bully dear, what is the problem?" Bully hated it when Malveena asked questions to which she already had the answer, knowing Bully knew she did.

"You tell me Malveena. Why don't you tell me!" He felt courageous and added a pout.

"Why Bully! Alright, since you ask so nicely, I will tell you. Foster has been gone and missing for four years and good riddance, but that does not yet constitute him being dead. So, Foster still has control of his shares for at least another three years or so doesn't he. He has the majority of the shares, doesn't he. The Macao syndicate must have those Foster shares to make the deal, mustn't they. You however, have not dealt with that little fact, have you. Your problem is entirely your own lazy fault, isn't it!"

Bully felt as if he were shrinking. He knew there was more coming and he just wanted to get it over with and go home.

"Malveena, why are you doing this? You handle the company books and ledgers. You authorize the new shares. You share with me the executive signing authority for share transfers. You know exactly the authorization we must have from Foster to do this deal and we don't have it. Please stop stating your mastery of the obvious."

Malveena was merciless. "You neglected to do what every other corporation or partnership or mom and pop business in the world would have done. Every corporation and partnership have a contingency for this exact situation, so don't give me the whining baby boy act, 'Oh Malveena, if only I had his approval, or ability to vote his shares, I could get the casino deal done and we would be rich.' You didn't make the paper Bully. You blew it because you were careless and now you are complaining as if it were bad luck. You need a power of attorney don't you Bully. A power of attorney which allows you to act just as if you were Foster and approve the casino deal. Isn't that so?"

Bully Gregious nodded. That was exactly what he needed. He knew she was right and that fact aggravated him even more. With a power of attorney, he could vote Foster's shares to accept the deal, sell the voting shares to the Macao syndicate along with all the others, close the plant and tear down the library and live rich and happily ever after. He looked across at the spectral woman he was so attracted to. He hated Malveena and yet he could not do without her. He had hated to do the hard day to day work also and he had made her indispensable and now he was stuck with her. *Worse than a marriage. Can't even divorce her.*

"Yes, that is so. I need his power of attorney."

She let him percolate for a bit. She stayed silent and made the beginning of the rictus she always made when she knew she was delivering the coup de grâce. She attempted to look coy. On Malveena coy took the form of a striking wasp.

"Bully, tell me. How much, what would you give, to have that power of attorney. This is a serious question so pay attention. What would you give Malveena if she could deliver you such power of attorney? 25% of your shares? 35% of your shares? What?"

He sat quietly and he was not surprised. The axe had fallen and it was somewhat of a relief. He knew something like this was coming and here it was. Malveena always had the answer and she always had the angle calculated. *How many of his shares. Well, there is no deal at all without the power of attorney.*

"5% Malveena, tops."

He leaned onto the desk and crossed his arms and tried to look tough as the perspiration began to pour off of him and a drop from his forehead ran down and off his chin and made a little splash on the desktop. Malveena stared pointedly at the water spot. She said nothing. She knew the next one to speak lost. Bully couldn't take it.

"Fine. Fine. Make me an offer."

Malveena calmly released the elastic retaining loop off of her manila pouch. She removed six documents and spread them across the desk top upside down so Bully could read them. The one closest to Bully stuck in the perspiration. There were three copies of Transfer of Shares to Malveena and three copies of a faded looking Power of Attorney done in blue ink. Malveena leaned in across the desk closer to Bully and allowed her blue-block reading glasses to slide down her nose and give him the full bore of her tiger eyes. She grabbed his cuffs on his crossed arms in her gloved hands so he could not retreat.

"Bully, those documents do not constitute an offer. They are the deal you will sign."

Bully swallowed hard and said nothing and remained transfixed by the green eyes.

"You will transfer to Malveena, one half of your shares. Those are voting shares." Bully nodded on cue.

"You will retain the other half of your shares. You will sign the transfer document right here and right now and I will give you the power of attorney you need, right here and right now."

She released him from her grip and leaned back and sat straight to her full height. She pushed her glasses back up on her nose. She gestured with a balletic extension of her right hand.

"See there, Bully, the POA from Charles Foster is signed. You see I have personally witnessed it. Pick it up and please check all the copies to satisfy yourself they are complete."

He did so and he opened and read each page carefully and he recognized Charles A. Foster's signature. He knew it well. Malveena had acted as the witness to Foster's signature. *How did she do it. How does she do it.* Bully continued nodding as each perusal he made confirmed what he wanted to see. Bully knew he was beaten but he had the Power of Attorney and he could not sign quickly enough. He took the fountain pen which Malveena proffered to him and he scrawled his name, fully in agreement with the transfer of 50 % of his shares to M.D. in exchange for the POA from Charles Abernathy Foster. They shook hands and Malveena with her gloved hand put the pen away in her folio. He gave one copy of the POA to Malveena and kept two for himself. They each kept copies of the share transfer agreement.

"Thank you Bully. By the way. The Power of Attorney you have agreed to take is a forgery."

At their listening post, Mildred and Davy were aghast. Mildred had never written so fast in her life. She had recorded every word of the entire conversation and this part was unbelievable. She finished it with three large exclamation points.

Bully blinked and prepared a laugh but he could see Malveena was entirely serious. "Yes Bully, the POA is a forgery. Also, the pen you signed our agreement with is the very same pen used on the forged power of attorney. Thought you might like to know. Your fingerprints are on the pen and all over the POA you kindly handled on every page. You may have noticed my gloved hands. No prints."

Bully Gregious said nothing. He stood and with the back of his fat thighs he pushed his chair away from the desk. He walked to the coat rack and took down and wrapped his long black wool fringed scarf around his neck. He stuffed himself into his fur collared winter coat, did up two buttons and walked to his office door and opened it and hesitated. He looked at Malveena without emotion, walked back to his desk and picked up his document satchel, stuffed the power of attorney into it and stepped through the office door into the hall, waiting for Malveena to turn off the light behind them. Malveena smiled to herself. She knew what Bully had wanted and she knew he would not refuse her. She was transported with her success.

In the storage room Mildred could tolerate it no longer. The dust and the wool of the balaclava were too much. She rolled her balaclava up onto her forehead in an attempt to breathe better. The air was filled with floating bits and she realized she was about to sneeze. She concentrated and denied it but it was coming. She put both hands over her mouth and buried her head against her two bent knees and the sneeze exploded. The choo of it cannonaded along the air duct and into Bully's office. Malveena was lost in her thoughts and Bully was still stunned by the events just concluded and he had turned his brain off and as far away from Malveena as he could get. He thought he heard a sneeze. It penetrated him as if from far away and he reflexively said "Gesundheit!"

Malveena had been swept away into her own thoughts and had not heard Mildred's sneeze.

"What?"

"Gesundheit."

"Bully, you are an idiot! You have just accepted a forged document designed to incriminate you which is covered with your fingerprints and as you are about to leave our meeting, you say to me, 'Gesundheit'? Are you stupid.?"

Bully shrugged and moved his eyebrows up and down and brushed at his tie which he could not find as it was under his coat.

"You sneezed and I said 'Gesundheit'. So what."

"I did not sneeze, you idiot. Pay attention!"

Bully shrugged again and looked at Malveena with his unthinking face. *Did sneeze, didn't sneeze, this is torture. Let me go home.* Bully began to speak when Mildred sneezed a sneeze for the ages and blasted it through the air duct and into Bully's office. Bully pointed triumphantly in the air in a gesture of vindication.

"There. What do you call that! So that is not a sneeze? Who is the idiot now!" He shouted 'Gesundheit' to the air duct and had his revenge on

Malveena.

Malveena shot bolt upright. *Someone is listening. They have heard everything.* She turned transparent and the rage in her eyes pushed Bully against the door jam.

"Gregious! Do you realize what they have heard? They know I forged the irrevocable power of attorney and they know you Bully, innocent Bully, are using it to demolish the worth of Foster industries to get rich. They know the International Casino Corporation is going to build a casino on the land. They know of the planned demolition of the library. Jail time Bully, big jail time. And you shout 'gesundheit' once again as a response?"

Davy and Mildred ran to the door and threw it open. Bully had Malveena cut off at his office door opening and the size of him in his great coat blocked the way.

"Move you oaf!"

He spun like a Michelin Man as Malveena pushed through and tore down the hall toward the storage room with Bully Gregious tilting along behind her and very close. Mildred and Davy burst out through the storage room door with Mildred careening in her stocking feet and they ran headlong into Malveena and knocked her down flat on her back and sent her glasses flying. Bully's momentum carried him into Malveena who was almost on her feet again. He bludgeoned forward and down they both went again. Malveena could not see without her glasses but she saw two smeared forms run around the corner in the direction of the back stairwell. One of them had a red hat and unbelievably seemed to be skating.

"Bully, quick into your office. They are going out by the back stairwell. They will have to cross the loading dock. Do you know or did you see who they are?"

"No, I didn't. They were a couple of kids. A boy and a girl I think."

They rushed back down the corridor and into his office with Bully wheezing all the way. Malveena ran to her purse and then to the window. Bully turned off the lights to cut down the glare and Malveena rummaged for her driving glasses while Bully pushed his perspiration drenched face against the glass as if it would help him see better. They stood beside each other and waited to see if the two eavesdroppers might emerge at the back exit.

Mildred skidded and bounced off the railings around every one of the six landings all the way down with Davy steering her when he could. The emergency exit door led to the loading dock and as they pushed through it at full speed the alarm shrieked. The motion sensing floodlights turned on and Davy and Mildred stood in what seemed to be broad daylight. Bully and Malveena were at the windows in the executive offices when the loading dock blazoned under eight spotlights and two small forms stood in the center with their shadows making pinwheels around them and the alarm screaming intermittently in the background. Bully said. "That kid," as he tap tap tapped on the glass with his greasy forefinger, making little scallop marks.

"Which kid?"

"The boy. I think I know him. I think he is in my son's class at Foster Elementary."

"Porky's class?" said the Drago with hope.

Bully, whose own given name was Melvin, corrected the 'Porky'.

"My son, Leonard's class."

As a kid, Bully was an insecure braggadocios bully and he had earned the easy nickname "Bully", which still hung around his neck thirty years later. He did not want his son to carry the name "Porky" for the rest of his life. *Maybe Leonard can ditch "Porky" if he loses some weight. Ditching Bully is not so easy.*

Malveena spoke clearly. "Bully. Snap out of it! What is that boy's name? Bully, pay attention, blast it! Those kids can hang us! Jail Bully. And you, your prints are on the documents. "

"His name is Davy for sure. Pilcher. Yes. His father works here. The boy is David Pilcher."

"Do you have a photograph of him I can use?"

"No."

"Not a class picture the boy would be in with your Lorky.. Pleon.... Leonard?"

"Er..yes. There is one on my desk." Malveena did not bother to shake her head.

"Good." She leered that they could identify Davy. "Get the photo for me before you leave. I will get his address from personnel records and that is the beginning. There is no urgency now. We know who he is and we will get his friend too. In fact, maybe we can still get them tonight." She jerked his sleeve.

"Come on Bully, we may still get them. Where the devil is the security guard!"

They ran down the stairs toward the loading dock. *Maybe the guard already has the little monsters, but it will be much better if I can grab them on my own.* Then something struck Malveena. *The alarms are working and all the doors are alarmed and motion detectors alert the guards to any intruder yet no alarm has gone off except at the exit to the loading dock. How did those two kids circumvent the security to get in here. It is as if they just dropped in from the sky.*

At the main entrance security desk, the zone panel beeped and lit up and flashed the schematic isolating the opened door to the loading dock. The claxon alarm continued its ragged wail and the guard knew immediately where the breach was located. The alarm for that door was coded with an interrupted claxon sequence. Each one of the twelve exterior doors had its own unique pattern of alarm tones to identify its location more quickly, anywhere around the building. Frank Trotter jumped up from the log-in desk and hesitated just for a moment, fearful of what he might have to deal with at the rear exit door. The loading dock was on his floor level and about 150 feet away. With sirens blazing in the distance, police cars promised to be there soon as they converged from all directions on the fenced property of Foster Industries.

Davy grabbed Mildred and pulled her to the edge of the dock. "Quick. Jump down and get under the overhang of the dock. Stay out of the light!"

They dropped easily down the four feet and into the shadow of the loading platform. The motion lights went out and they were in total darkness in the shadow cast. One sole light stayed on above the exit door. Davy edged up from the gloom bordering the platform and watched as Frank Trotter's fingers appeared at the loading dock exit. His left hand gripped the edge of the door and pushed it open very slowly. The bill of his security guard cap followed. The motion lights activated again and Davy and Mildred hunched lower into the depth of the shadow over the brink of the platform. The guard bent and placed a wedge into the door hinge to keep the door from closing behind him and he stepped onto the loading platform into the floodlights. His heart rate started increasing as he realized how exposed he was. *I am a sitting duck out here.* He froze at the footsteps behind him as Malveena Drago and Bully Gregious charged out of the open door onto the dock.

"Trotter!" bleated Malveena. "Did you see them? Do you have them?"

"I don't have them and I didn't see them and I don't know where they are or even the 'they' who you are talking about." He wanted no part of this frenzy. He added hopefully, "They are probably long gone." He wished it were so. He did not know it was two children he was after. He visualized ten marauding thugs.

Malveena was furious. "This entire property has contiguous seven-foot fencing on the periphery doesn't it?"

Frank nodded. "No breaks in it anywhere either," he added helpfully.

Malveena gritted. "Surely, they are trapped, aren't they?"

Frank tipped his head and raised his brows in speculation. "I guess so Miss Drago, seems like it if you think so."

Malveena put her head back and cackled as the light of the false dawn betrayed the contortion of her face. The malice in her voice turned both Bully Gregious and Frank Trotter to ice. She clenched her gloved hands and shivered and ground her fingers against her palms. "Then good, Trotter. They are trapped inside here. We have them trapped. I will grab the two of them and when I do, believe me, that will be the last of them. Rest assured, that boy has appeared in his last class picture or my name is not Malveena Drago."

Davy and Mildred heard every word.

Chapter 9: Into the Grave

Mildred and Davy listened to the conversation right above them between Malveena Drago and Frank Trotter. They were trapped inside the secure grounds of Foster Industries. There was no way they could get out. The security guard and Malveena were correct about that. Davy took a slow deep breath and thought back to the Victory. What would Spider or Bert or 32 pounder Gun Captain Watson have done in this situation. Coolness and patience and self-control in the face of danger wins the day. Mildred was petrified and shaking but she could feel the tranquility set in beside her and she trusted her amazing friend. Davy moved closer and whispered very softly.

"Listen Mildred, I have an idea. We are going to have to split up for a bit." Mildred started shaking her head. She did not want to be alone.

"No Davy, we will be easier to catch."

He spoke quietly. "Just listen Mildred. They are correct in what they said. We cannot get out through the gate or over the fence. So, this is what we do." He had a positive smile on his face in the dim light.

"We are going to go to the front of the building and then come right back here. You will stay low and tight to the back wall and in shadow until you get to the corner. You will then run all the way to the front of the building along the port side."

"What?"

He pointed to the closer left side.

"Along that side. I will run all the way to the front along the starboard side. That side." He pointed to the right.

"When you get to the front, start back this way and hammer and shake as hard as you can on the outside of the first exit door you come to. That will activate the alarm for that door. When the alarm starts, run to the next door and hammer on it as hard as you can and so on and keep moving along the side, coming back here. I will do the same on my side. Got it? The alarms will start going off like crazy, one by one. Each alarm will show a new spot of trouble. They will have no idea where we are. There will be 12 claxon horns all going off at once. It will be bedlam. It will be nuts."

Mildred wanted to tell Davy she knew what 'bedlam' was but she stayed silent. She liked the idea and hoped noisy confusion would do the trick. "Then what?"

"While Bully and the guard and the woman are running toward the alarms, we will be coming back here to the loading dock. We will go back in through the wedged open exit door and hide somewhere inside until we get light for the pipe. If it is a bright day tomorrow, we can get back to the bridge."

"Davy, no. My mother will be really worried for me to be out all night. She w.." She stopped in mid word and rubbed her fingertips on the wool at her temples. "Oh. Sorry. Well. I forgot. All night in this time will be about two minutes where we started from, won't it." Her balaclava got redder. She gave a palms up little mea culpa shrug.

Dawn was about an hour away and they needed the cover of the dark. They took deep breaths and ducked low and ran as hard as they could in a crouch and made for the front of the building. Mildred heard the first alarm go off on the other side of the building. At the first shriek of the new claxon horn, Gregious, Drago and Trotter froze in their tracks. Trotter shouted.

"They are at the front of the building, west side! Four blasts!" The three took off for the west corridor.

Davy heard the port alarm start. Good work Mildred. Six screaming blasts from the claxon started to repeat. His four blasts continued to repeat cycle after cycle of four.

Mildred heard Davy's next door activate. Eight blasts of the enervating jangle began their assault on Malveena's brain. They repeated themselves, revealing trouble at that specific location and the pattern continued. Four in cycle and six in cycle and eight in cycle hammered the air as Mildred activated her next door. Three blasts joined the others. The air was dissected with cacophony.

Frank had his gun out and Bully spun right and left brandishing his master key to shut off the alarms, looking for a key box, somewhere.

"Put that thing away, you moron!" screamed Malveena at the guard. Bully obliged with his key and wondered what he had missed.

"Not you!" screeched Malveena and with new permission Frank got out his gun again as the alarm signaling the next assaulted door burst into action. It seemed as if there was an army of intruders. The monitors at the front desk were screaming and the screens were blazing. Mildred and Davy arrived on the loading dock simultaneously as twelve claxon horns rose to the challenge and shattered the early morning with five hundred horn blasts per minute and lights began going on throughout the town. Davy and Mildred sped into the Foster Industries building through the wedged back door.

Davy knew the layout perfectly from his open house visits to the plant with his father.   "Follow me, Mildred!" He sped them directly to the women's locker room and past the array of combination locks hung on the daily use lockers and continued on to a row of empty and unlocked lockers at the back.

"Here, Mildred. They will not find us in here. Pick a locker."

She hesitated. So many of them.

"Pick one. Mildred, pick one."

She found a nice one and stood in front of it.

"Good. I will take this one right beside you." Only Mildred. He would not know what time the shift changed. He had forgotten a watch. Davy had planned to mix into the congestion of the morning shift arrivals and get out to the parking lot unimpeded and with any luck sight his pipe into a brilliant sunrise. Almost inaudibly, Mildred commented off handedly.

"Should I let you know when it is time for the 7:00 am shift change? My watch has a light."

Davy sighed a whisper. "Yes. Thank you." They squeezed into adjacent lockers and pulled the stiff squeaking doors closed from the inside and waited for footsteps.

Bully shut off the 12th and last zone claxon horn at 6:20 AM. All the exit doors had been found secure and locked. "Vandals," said Trotter. Malveena insisted the police check the integrity of the fence running around the grounds from its outer aspect. She did not want them running into Davy and his cohort on Foster property only to have them told interesting stories of pens and fingerprints and powers of attorney. She knew who the boy was and she would soon have his photograph.

The police scoured the exterior periphery and found nothing. Bully and Malveena searched for an hour inside and found nothing. Frank went back to his post. He ran the lobby surveillance video backward and then fast forwarded it. Nothing interesting was there. Davy and Mildred had never been in the lobby. He looked at all the stairwell videos. There. Two kids running down. He looked back farther on the tape and ran it at high speed. No kids running up. No kids in the elevators to the second floor. Only Gregious and Drago used the elevator. Two kids, running down the stairwell. Brats. Nothing taken far as I can see. No locks broken. Nothing broken. Little monsters. Probably sneaked up there during the day. Not on my shift so who cares, not my fault, not my problem.

He sneaked the tape into his lunch box and logged out at the entry panel. If there is any trouble, my tape will show nobody got past me on my watch. Nobody.

The dawn broke bright and clear. A hum of female voices began to percolate into the lockers where Davy and Mildred hid. Mildred was thinking this hour was the longest she had stood in one place in her life. Davy was thinking how they could look nonchalant walking out of the ladies' locker room. They needed to get into the throng of people coming in and filter through and out to the parking lot. Clicks of combination locks and nearby voices began to fill the locker room. Davy whispered to Mildred through the locker vent.

"Mildred, we have to go now. That is the next shift coming in."

Mildred nodded to herself in agreement. They opened their doors and Davy's hinges screeched. They stopped but nobody coming into work had the slightest interest. Davy and Mildred walked directly past three ladies who looked at them blankly and turned back to their conversation. Mildred and Davy picked up the pace and turned the corner toward the entrance door and ran smack into the arms of Mrs. Williams. She started and broke into a generous smile.

"Why Davy Pilcher. And your friend. Oh. You must be lost in all these people. Can I help you? Of course, I can. You two are so cute. Where are you going?"

"Hello Mrs. Williams. Uh, well, we are, uh, turned around, and m.. looking for the parking lot."

"Of course you are. Someone picking you up. And up so early too. How nice. Come with me. Wouldn't want you to get turned around again." She laughed her generous laugh and walked Davy and Mildred through the main entrance and past the door guard to the parking area. She shielded her eyes against the strong eastern sun. The asphalt was already warming.

"Well, must go, can't be late. Again." She giggled at herself and left the children alone in the sun and hummed as her shadow led her back to the job.

They rode the trail back on the light from the eastern sun. It seemed to Davy the light had its own understanding of his intention. He had not quite completed his full thought when the light took the two of them and there was the feeling of happiness in the taking as if there was a partnership beginning and not just a carrier.

As they came to themselves Davy was clear headed and aware almost immediately. Mildred took longer to escape the turbidity of the agglutination and reacted more as the slam of reality hit her, yet she came alive with a smile. They both had felt the difference. It was almost as if the light knew they were attempting to do something good. Would it resist if their intention was something bad? They did not know. What they did know was this Casino and Power of Attorney business was serious. What to do and who to tell. Who would believe them. Where would Mildred keep her notes. Should Davy hide his pipe. Were Bully and the boss woman and the authorities still after them or had they just forgotten about them and in fact, how could they even know who they were.

The black Porsche moved so noiselessly in low gear its engine seemed not to be running. It crept with intent like a big cat with the essence of the hunt in its blood. Draped into it and caressing the wheel was Malveena Drago, resplendent in new dark grey driving gloves. She had destroyed the pair she wore the night of the meeting with Bully. The new gloves held the wheel with their own texture and adhesion so Malveena's hands were fully relaxed and in position for action. Porky's class picture was propped up on the passenger seat. Two spots to the left of Porky in the same row stood a smiling David Pilcher, whose image was burned into Malveena's brain.

She liked this slow creep past Charles A. Foster elementary school. Malveena loved low gear. Low gear held so much upside potential for satisfying her fury. Her car was well known around town and nothing was made of her presence near the school. Davy and Mildred ambled slowly out the main front entrance. Mildred had taken to wearing old style heavy leather walking shoes and the red balaclava had become her standard attire. Davy had concluded he must have his pipe at all times. Somehow the pipe seemed to have spoken to that decision. They left under the watchful eyes of the portrait of Charles Foster and under the equally watchful eye of Malveena Drago.

Davy was telling Mildred about Mr. Mullett. His mother had told him last night Mr. Mullett had passed away two days ago and his funeral would be today at 3:30. Davy was sad over the news. Mr. Daniel Mullett had known Davy his whole life and often Davy bought a few candies in Mullett's general store just to see the neat old things Mullet had there.

Dan Mullett liked kids. He had time for them and every kid liked that. Davy's mom and dad had gone to buy candy at the same store when they were little and as far as his parents could remember it, the store was still the same today. The black and white diamond pattern floor tile still shone.

Licorice bits were four for a nickel when his dad was 13 and now they were three for a quarter. There were 48 large glass jars full of candies and Mr. Mullett always dropped an extra one into your small paper bag as if by accident. When he weighed his goods out on a scale he added a bit extra so nobody got short changed. When Davy went in there with his father, old Mullett would call his father "Harold" with a certain tone of discipline built into it, just like when Harry Pilcher was ten years old. Mullett made four fresh sourdough bread loaves by hand on the day he died. He was the happiest person Davy knew.

The Eternal Welcome cemetery was on Davy's way home. He knew most likely the cars and the whole procession would pass by Mildred and him and even though he liked Mr. Mullett, it made him uneasy to think about it. Nobody really knew how old Mr. Mullett was and the newspaper didn't say. Perhaps in the ceremony at the cemetery Pastor Reinhart would tell the folks the secret. Davy sensed a change in the general level of traffic noise and he turned around to look. It was just after three but the cars had their lights on and they were going much slower than usual.

Mildred knew. "Davy, they do that out of respect at funerals. Look there. You see how other cars have stopped and pulled over? All but that little black one anyway. Just for respect."

Davy had heard about something of that sort before. Yes. Out of respect. All but that black one which seems to ignore that and is going a little faster now. The funeral cortege had caught them up and was passing slowly. At a steady gentle pace, the vehicles proceeded in solemn order and began to turn left through the gates of the Eternal Welcome entrance about 100 yards ahead. The small black car coming along the shoulder sounded different somehow with the purr it made. Davy turned to inspect it. A ray of green-eyed hate lasered through the windshield and annealed him to the spot. He was transfixed and immobile under Malveena's glare. She threw open the door and shrieked as she flew out and lost a shoe onto the gravel shoulder. She twisted her ankle and staggered back against her car, ripped off her remaining shoe and threw it bouncing off her window.

"You two don't move a muscle.!"

In two strides she was beside Davy and the size of her hands seemed to grow as she reached for Davy's throat with the slow hypnotic pace of a snake. He could not move. Mildred charged forward and before the Drago could throttle Davy, Mildred kicked her as hard as she could in the shins with her heavy soled walking shoe. Down went Drago. Her car was still running and the door was wide open blocking the traffic.

"Run Davy. Come on.!"

Davy snapped to life and followed blindly. Mildred blazed the way and flashed through the line of slowly moving vehicles and crossed the road.

"Keep your head down Davy."

They ran in terror using the cars for cover along the line of the procession and into the cemetery. Malveena was on her feet and with a limp, sprinted hard across the gravel, tearing open her stockings and she did not feel it. She could see the road ahead on the other side of the gate and the children had not gone that way. They were in the cemetery. She was faster than they were and she too ran parallel but on the near side of the vehicles. They stopped to catch their breath and there, ten feet away between two cars was Malveena Drago. She snorted at them in triumph but the rear car moved up and blocked the space.

" Davy this way!"

Mildred pointed to a pile of earth 30 yards away and they stumbled and ran to it. At full speed they scrambled around to hide on the other side and down they went. They fell seven feet into four inches of watery mush at the bottom of the grave and landed on their backs. The flap popped open on Davy's pipe and his holster filled with water. They saw one large earthworm working its way out of the flat-cut earth wall about three feet up. Malveena Drago strode calmly to the edge of the diggings and looked down. She towered over them like a gaunt Carpathian colossus. Her stockings were torn and her feet were bloody. The welt on her shin had come up like a blue egg and her black eye makeup had run and filled the creases under her eyes. Davy was petrified, and pulling Mildred with him, he backed away from Malveena and against the one wall illuminated by the angling sun.

"I have you, you little monsters. Feeling clever, now are we? Hm?"

She jumped down into the grave. She went on her knees and crept toward Mildred as Davy reached for his pipe. He put it to his eye and the muddy water blinded him. He shook away the slime and grabbed Mildred just as Drago leapt. A blinding flash stunned Malveena as she lunged and slammed into the wall of the grave. She sat down hard in four inches of glue clay and looked amazed at her empty hands. The earthworm fell on her neck and she plucked it and held it between her fingers. The approaching procession had seen the flash from the pit. Their contemplations of the hereafter became visions of a crack into hell.

Arriving at the open grave, an ashen Pastor Reinhart peered down at the woman dripping in muck with black rivulets running on her face and holding an earthworm. Malveena looked like the devil.

"Don't just stand there you boob, get me out of here."

They dropped down a ladder for her and with complete aplomb she climbed out barefooted and dripping, as if the grave thing were something she did every day. She brushed herself off which did nothing to remove the mire. She angled her head high and blew a wisp of hair out of her eye, brushed it back with a mud-covered hand and hobbled to the road. Her shoes were there but not her car. Someone had stolen it. Malveena arched her neck back and searched the heavens and screamed like a tormented evil beast.

"I will throttle you Pilcher!"

Davy and Mildred were gone from Drago and out of the sodden grave into a welcoming vortex of golden safety warming them toward a curved horizon. They felt more than saw a blending roseate hue in the distance populated with bead like colors. They arrived still dripping wet on a worn yet spotless white diamond patterned floor not yet accessible to them but observable. Around them there was an array of multicolored glass surfaces which shimmered and shone and enticed with their curvature. The aroma of wintergreen berries permeated everything. Davy arrived in useful mode first and Mildred followed, almost as fast as Davy. Their wet clothing made muddy drip spots on the tiled floor. They sat down and laughed. There they were in Mullett's old general store, surrounded by 48 jars of sweet wonder. There were two small paper bags sat out on the counter near the scale, with one piece of extra candy sitting there, waiting to be added to the bag by mistake. Davy's eyes were moist. He had not intended anything but escape, but the pipe seemed to know where two youngsters might want to be.

Malveena settled into the bath and wiggled her sore feet as she relaxed in the warmth. She had lit the candles surrounding her with her Ronson Touch Tip and that made things better. The bath salts were expensive and aromatic and she inhaled the essential oil aroma deeply into her lungs as she slowly simmered down to a medium wrath. Drago was seldom confused but after today, she was confused. Those kids. They dropped into our offices as if out of the sky and today they vanished in a flash from between my hands, once again as if into the sky. And that Pilcher brat with his copper telescope or whatever and then gone in a flash. Phewt. Gone. I cannot work it through. I was careless as well. I must be more circumspect. It may not be wise to strangle a neighborhood boy in broad daylight at a funeral.

Malveena toweled off and put on her jogging outfit and her running shoes. She wanted to be at the office. Her feet ached and she gritted her teeth as she picked up the keys to her rental car. She knew she would not accept her own beautiful Porsche baby back even if they did find it. Someone else had driven it. The drive to her office in the yellow rental car was mortifying. Not one drift, not one grind, not one near miss or shrieking skid. What a world.

Malveena Drago tender-footed it to the accounting office on the second floor and once again pulled out a stack of the old Charles Foster records, with no idea of what she was looking for. The staff had left for the evening and she was alone with the books. She knew Bully would be somewhere in the building but with luck she would avoid him. It was the tenth time she had looked at this ledger. The numbers made sense, the auditing had been correct and the entries were specific and easy to understand but she did not understand them. They added up, but the items Charles Foster had added so lavishly to every building in his empire, in the six months or so before he disappeared, were unfathomable.

The books in front of Malveena showed Charles Abernathy Foster had demanded one skylight of his own design in every laboratory in all of his buildings and one in every office used by him in every one of the 12 plants in the Foster conglomerate. Bully' office has one of them and according to this ledger entry the laboratory Foster worked in right here in this building has one. She had never seen the laboratory. It had been locked since Foster disappeared. That idiot Foster spent $884,000.00 on skylights. Another $310,00.00 in the same span on something called Fresnel lenses. What the devil is a Fresnel anyway. She remembered her conversation at the time with the workman outside Foster's office, adjacent to her own.

" What do you think Mr. Foster is doing, Miss Draggle?"

" Not Draggle. Drago. Why?"

" I think the old guy is losing his marbles."

" Really? Why?"

" He is putting one of them things in every building he goes to in the Foster businesses. Do you know how many skylights he has installed in all his places?

"No, how many?"   " 21 so far,
and still counting, skylights just because he has a thing
for skylights. They look like those pyramids of Chops in Egypt, but hollow from the bottom with glass sides instead of stone. With rings inside other rings on the glass."

" Cheops."

" Yes. They are wonders. But I suppose it is his money, as they says, and he can do what he wants with it, as they says."

"Say."

"Say what, Miss Draggle? Well, say it was grandfather clocks. Could be it was grandfather clocks instead. Think of it. All ringin' and chimin' every 15 minutes all day every day. Me, I would rather have skylights."

Malveena ended it then but perhaps had she endured a bit more at that time she would know more now. She had terminated the painful exchange as rapidly as she could but now, she regretted it.

Every one of his installations is a stupid ugly enormous pyramid of plate glass with swirly circles. One in this laboratory too. His personal laboratory here in this building on the second floor. Is there new patent work half done? Something Malveena could call her own perhaps?

The prospects of the intrigue started a little buzz in Malveena.

Confound that fool Gregious for closing up the lab and only then realizing he did not know how to get back in, and worse yet he was totally devoid of curiosity about it. Blast the court for saying until Foster was declared legally dead in another three years, his private fiefdom was off limits. We shall see about that!

Malveena flipped to the inventory of Foster's laboratory Bully had done hurriedly at the time of Foster's disappearance. She knew it was incomplete as was everything Bully did, but it was still interesting. Item 9 was a Tom Ford tuxedo jacket with Jacquard stitching with a grey stripe.

This is too strange. He wore nothing but lab coats and jeans for twenty years and he leaves behind a very expensive haute couture dinner jacket.

The list had the standard burners, oscilloscopes, glassware and the like, but item 23 was particularly interesting and confusing. The notation said, '18-foot copper xylophone?' With a question mark. Did this mean someone else had doubt about the entry and notated it with a question mark, or did Bully not know whether it was an '18-foot copper xylophone' or not, when he did the inventory. The wanting to know ate at Malveena. Foster was no fool. Those skylight installations are not decorative.

The accounting office was across from Bully's and Malveena turned out the lights. She stood just inside the door and waited. When Bully was gone, she would go to the laboratory. Foster's keypad was old and it may give up its secrets to Malveena. Forty minutes went by and she heard Bully exit his office. He closed the door quietly as was his habit and he did not lock it which was also his habit. Bully's heel clickers disappeared in diminishing echoes down the hall and gradually he became inaudible. The security beeps of the key pad being activated told of the time of his leaving. Now she was alone in the building and the laboratory was at her disposal if she could beat the lock.

Malveena Drago kept the lights off as she left accounting in case Gregious looked back at the building. She stuck the high heels of her shoes in her waistband and stealthed along in stocking feet to avoid alerting the solitary security guard. She carried a roll of black duct tape. The floor was cold and the feel of it on her sore feet was good. She moved with her back pressed tight to the wall beneath the security camera for Zone 8. She put her heels back on to gain some height and slowly tore a two-foot strip off the duct tape. She twisted it to make it into a stiff wand, except for two inches at one end which she left intact. Still against the wall and below the camera, she stretched and draped the sticky surface against the lens and left it hanging there. The lens was blind.

She knew most secrets of the company and of Bully Gregious, but knew not an iota of the treasures she was sure were awaiting her in the laboratory of old man Foster. She was excited by the game.

Foster was still not declared legally dead and until such time, his laboratory could not be liquidated. It was locked and secure but Malveena Drago was clever. She had access to all company records. She had searched meticulously every invoice, receipt, voucher and supplier to the company from the very first day of operation. Davis and Sons was the one and only locksmith used by Foster Enterprises and old man Davis was dead. Davis junior was still servicing the company's security needs but he had been no help. The locks had been changed twice over time and Davis kept a backup key and code and security protocol for every one of twelve entry zones, with one exception. That was Foster's laboratory. Charles Foster had forbidden it and the code memorized by Davis senior had gone with him.

Malveena Drago had the security codes for general entry but no-one had the code to the C.A. Foster lab but Foster himself. The keypad was an antiquated four number style. It was also of the time urgency type. If all four correct numbers were not entered in 10 seconds, the keypad reset to try again. Three unsuccessful tries locked the lock for twelve hours before it could receive a number again. Malveena Drago had her work cut out.

She opened her cell phone and flooded the corridor with light and looked at the door that had witnessed the ruminations of the great man. The keypad was on the door and not on the wall. The lock had been there for eight years before C.A. disappeared and he alone had used it. The door was in a steel frame with steel bolts through the length of the door and through the frame both top and bottom. The door could not be forced and it was blast proof because of the dangerous nature of the work Foster sometimes did in his lab.

Malveena knew about numbers. When given a choice, a high percentage of men choose only one odd number in four digits. Very few men will put the same number next to itself. Very few men will use a three in a combination and more than half will use a zero. Most will pick a significant historical date. 1215 for the Magna Carta. 1066 for the battle of Hastings. Even then they lean toward sevens and twos and fives, but Foster was not most men. He would not do what most men would do.

Her cell phone lit up the corridor. It was too bright. She could barely read a number against the reflection off the metallic surface of the mammoth steel door. She slid the phone into the breast pocket of her silk blouse and the diffused light through the fabric was perfect. With her first glance at the raised metal digits on the keypad, she noticed it immediately. The pad looked as if it had never been used. Only numbers one and two were worn and had lost their gloss. That meant Foster used just two numbers to make up the four-digit code. He used 1's and 2's. She was getting there. Only six possible combinations. Malveena, you are fine. Then she realized. Six possible combinations but only three attempts before the mechanism shut down.

People use their birthdays in combinations. Charles was born on June 15. Not that. Home address. No. 15664 is his house number. What would be significant. Year of graduation from Southern Methodist University in Dallas Texas. No. Malveena had it. He was at university in the 1960's. The numbers were 2211. The 22nd day of the eleventh month. The assassination of John F. Kennedy. Oh Malveena, such a girl! She confidently and adroitly entered the 2211 and the pad was receptive to the depressing and she pushed the 'Open' key and waited for the bolt to move. The readout flashed four times and shut off. The LED readout said "Two attempts remain."

A bead of sweat started on her lip. She was sure she had had it figured. Had she missed a button in the reduced light? She knew she had not. Two cracks at it left. Think Malveena. What would make Foster happy to use just two numbers. Think. First patent! She retrieved her phone and searched the company data base. Not that. Nothing to do with those numbers in the patents. What. Wait.

Malveena ran in her stocking feet into the storage room beside her office and looked across the labels on the boxes of security camera footage. It was Zone 1 she wanted. The front entrance. She went through the box and found the one she wanted and dashed into her office and pushed the old DVD into her computer. She froze it on the view she needed and howled.

"Oowwweeeeeyesss!" She clasped both hands over her mouth to retrieve the howl from being heard downstairs. No action.

She flew and slid in her stocking feet back to the steel door of the laboratory. The combination was Foster's license plate on his Auburn. 1.2.12. She popped the combination in with rhythmic assurance and depressed the 'Open' key and waited for the bolt to move. The readout flashed four times and shut off. The LED readout said, " One attempts remain."

She could not believe it. Her underarms were wet and her heart rate was climbing. She scratched one of the itchy spots coming on her left arm and the sharpness of her nail surprised her as it abraded her skin. She peered closer at the keypad and cursed her 45th birthday. She swung the reading glasses hanging from her neck up onto her nose and laughed out loud with relief. A shard of her fingernail had broken off and it was jammed between the one and the two. She wiggled it out gently. Carefully she pressed 1,2,1,2. Open. The light flashed four times and turned green and the bolts ran steel on steel and opened. She had opened Charles Abernathy Foster's personal and private laboratory.

Drago pushed inward and the heavy steel door swung away noiselessly in perfect counterbalance as if there were no weight to it. The room was entirely interior within the building and it was windowless. Four enormous skylights pointed together in a pyramid at the four points of the compass and the skylight glass was made of circular Fresnel magnifying lenses. What a strange old buzzard. Malveena had expected the place to be messed and populated with Bunsen burners and flasks and test tube racks. There was none of that.

The wall directly across from the door to the laboratory held a thirty-foot-long floor to ceiling bookcase. A track traveled along the valence to support a wide stepped, wheeled ladder with brass handrails. The cabinetry was crafted from dark mahogany and it was completely filled with exquisite leather-bound books. Amazing. He has at least five thousand books here. Fresnel light bounced off the deeply embossed first letters of ten thousand words and as Malveena scanned their illuminated facets they formed a gibberish cipher that denied decoding. Every goatskin cover had been dyed a color to categorize its content.

Malveena stood within arm's reach and rubbed her hands across the spines of the beautiful collection. There were books on numismatics. I had no idea Foster collected coins. She pulled out a Spanish book and riffled through its pages. It was well thumbed with numerous pencil notations in the margins. She was surprised that only a few of the books were technical. Those were in deep green. Energy Grid: Harmonic 695: The Pulse of the Universe by Cathie.

Dickens and authors of his era were wrapped in dark brown with light brown lettering. Bleak House. Philosophical and religious tenets were grouped together in deep burgundy and gold. Schopenhauer. The Koran. The Power of Kabbalah by Berg. The art of war by Sun Tzu.

Grouped and colored in the deepest blue, almost black, and featured in the center of the collection were volumes of Masonic literature. They were Foster's centerpiece. The Builders by Joseph Fort Newton. The Dionysian Artificers by

Hippolyto Joseph da Costa. Duncan's Masonic Ritual and Monitor by Malcolm C. Duncan.

Malveena turned away from the distraction and walked back to the central lab bench. Its work surface was clear and polished and pristine and nothing appeared to be in use except for one very curious thing. Along the wall backing the full length of the center lab bench was what at first appeared to be a dazzling vertical xylophone. It ran for sixteen feet and stood tightly spaced like a line of polished pool cues in a rack. Malveena ran the light from her cell phone across it. Arranged in a row from largest to smallest and diminishing from the left by various increments were 192 different lengths of perfectly polished beautiful 3/4-inch copper pipe. Each pipe had the precise length recorded above it on the back board. The astounding array of glistening pipe was perfect except for two things. The 8-foot-long pipes on the left were pristine and polished. As the length of pipe diminished to the right, the pipes were increasingly fingered. There was green patina and general dullness and smudging of the luster as the length diminished. In the shortest range at the right, the pipe surfaces were obliterated with fingerprints from much handling. Most strange however, was the fact two pipes were missing. Such care had been taken to display and arrange the copper xylophone, yet two pieces, marked on the backboard as 152 millimeters and 203 millimeters, were not there. The board behind the empty slots revealed abrasions and chips in the paint, so something had been there at one time and removed and replaced many times. Malveena knew very well Charles Foster was a careful and fastidious man. Things did not go missing. If those specific pieces of copper pipe were not there, it was by his design.

She turned off her cell phone light and sat down on the lone stool, puzzled. Pieces of pipe. Ordinary copper pipe, but well fingered and Foster kept or sequestered two pieces. So, he did not consider it ordinary. Very odd. Wait. That monster kid. Pilcher. Was it not something like a pipe at the cemetery? He vanished when he held to his eye.. a copper pipe? Pilcher, Pilcher, Pilcher!

Chapter 10: Bully on a Ledge

Bully and Lucretia Mae Gregious sat watching their son Porky as he pondered his mathematics at the kitchen table. Bully gazed at the boy disinterestedly and Lucretia scrutinized him with something less charitable. Lucretia had spent 20 minutes explaining the simple mathematics problems to Porky and there he sat. His pencil had not moved in 10 minutes and he showed few signs of being alive. Lucretia scanned his profile from the side and shuddered at the three-inch roll of fat hanging over his belt and he was 13 years old. She hated Porky, he was just like Bully. He looked like Bully, he walked like Bully and he was just as stupid as Bully and now she had two of them. A big Bully and a little Bully. She had hoped by now she would have only one Bully and big Bully would be in the big doughnut shop in the sky but not so. He was still kicking. She struck again.

"Porky, you will not get that math homework done by sitting and looking at it. Do it."

" Lucretia, give the kid a break. He is just thinking about it."

" Bully, he is not thinking about it, he is thinking about nothing. He is sitting semi-comatose."

Porky heard nothing but he heard everything. He heard the insults and he heard the distaste and disappointment emanating from his parents. He had had enough of this stuff and one day he would have a chance to get even. He looked at the paper in front of him with indifference. Nothing on it meant very much to him. He was still on the first problem. He was asked to find X. He looked at the equation. There it was. X. What was so tough about that. He circled it.

The telephone rang and Bully waited but no one moved. On the fourth ring he struggled up out of his armchair and splayfooted to the phone. At least the phone call spared him the endless dialogue with Lucretia Mae.

"This is Gregious."

"Bully." It was Malveena Drago. Bully mouthed the word 'Malveena' to Lucretia. Lucretia said very loudly, "Tell her to get stuffed."

Malveena heard the comment clearly. "Bully dear, tell the missus I wish her well. Or something rhyming with that." Bully wanted to, but he didn't.

"Bully, get a pencil. I need you to get something for me. Pay attention. Write this down." He scuffled to the kitchen table and snatched Porky's pencil and returned to the phone. "Oh wait. I don't have any paper." He snaffled the sheet Porky was working on and came back to the phone and rustled it as evidence he was ready. Malveena had expected nothing more.

"I need 10 pieces of ¾ inch copper pipe, 8 feet long. Have them delivered to the office building and put them outside the door to Foster's laboratory. Call me when they are there. You be there too and bring a pipe cutter with you." She hung up.

Bully knew better than to ask. He had no idea what was going on but apparently, he was going to be part of it.

" So, what did Dragon Lady want?"

Bully pretended he didn't hear. He dialed the warehouse at Foster Industries.

"Hello Chester, this is Gregious. I need some things delivered to the office building. ¾ inch Copper pipe. Have it?" Chester did and for Mr. Gregious he would dig it out. "Good. I am coming now to supervise." Bully had not written down Malveena's demand he bring a pipe cutter and it was gone from his mind.

The deluge from Lucretia began anew.

"Bully, it is 8.30 pm and because Malveena demands it, you are going to a warehouse. You should be here with your wife and family. Tell her that. Also tell Palezilla when she has some spare time she should spend five or ten years in anger management therapy."

Lucretia spat out the 'that' to emphasize it and wriggled at her good zinger. Lucretia didn't give a fedoo whether Bully stayed home or went out, she liked laying the guilt trips on him. If her life style continued, Lucretia didn't really care if Bully ever came back. She still had Porky to hector. There he was, looking at the empty kitchen table in the same dull stupor as when Bully scrounged his math paper to record a phone message.

"Porky, you are hopeless."

Porky felt hopeless for sure. His mother hated him, his teachers despised him, his father was absent and he had no friends at school. Maybe Davy. Davy never made the fat jokes or the sweat jokes the way the others did. 'What's fat and pink and wet all over?' 'Porky in a math exam.' *Hilarious. Trouble is it is true.* Yes, Davy Pilcher was his one friend for sure.

Bully clickered his car unlocked with a toot and opened the door. The driver's seat was deformed down on the left corner from his weight and he had owned his C-class for barely four months. It seemed the seat belts were defective too. He had needed to re-size them twice in the same four months. He buckled up and sucked a quick breath as the cold buckle slapped onto his belly where his shirt had strained open. He signaled left and pulled out into traffic. He was on the road at the command of the Dragon Lady but the stress had dropped off him when he had closed the door on Lucretia. *Lucretia's restaurant was closed. No more hot tongue or cold shoulder.* Still, in the contest for Bully's humiliation there was little to choose between Lucretia and Malveena.

Chester was waiting in the glare of the loading dock with 10 pieces of ¾ inch copper pipe, eight feet long, ready for 7:00 A.M. delivery. Bully supervised it with approval. He called Malveena back and said simply, "7:00 a.m. at the laboratory." *That was efficient.*

7:00 a.m. at the Foster offices gleamed bright and cloudless and the day was warming nicely. Bully and the Drago arrived at the entrance to the parking lot at the same time and Malveena hammered the accelerator and cut Bully off. Her new Porsche was vicious but her tires were not yet hot. She spun easily with the slickness of cold tires and she made a full doughnut so Bully had to cut the wheel hard to avoid her. He parked as far away from the entrance as he could, against the wire Frost fence at the end of the row of light standards. So far, no dents no scratches in his nice silver Mercedes. Bully trailed Malveena into the building.

They elevatored up to the second floor and Malveena swept along the corridor past their offices on the left to the lab on the right with Bully in tow. Her copper pipe was tied with plastic ties in a bundle outside the door. Malveena kept her driving gloves on. She strode to the door and typed Foster's password into the stiff old keypad and Bully heard the security bolts disengage. She swung the heavy counterbalanced door open and pointed at the bundle of pipe for Bully to pull it inside.

"Whoa Malveena. This lab has a restraining order against entry. You know that! The court has ruled. No entry until Foster is ruled dead. Three years yet. Count me out." He backed up making a baseball umpire's safe sign.

Malveena snarled. "Gregious, you are in this up to your neck so dispense with the heroics. If we don't hang together on this, we will hang separately. Or rather, might I remind you, it is you alone who will hang separately. The sole fingerprints on the forged power of attorney are not mine. They are yours. Bring that pipe inside."

Bully hated Malveena but at the same time he also envied the steeliness of her resolve and her decisiveness. He said nothing. He grabbed the plastic tie with both hands and dragged the bundle of pipes into the laboratory. Malveena swung the door closed and it made a well fitted leak proof thunk.

Refractions and concentrations of light bounced all around the room from the Fresnel lenses which made up the panels of the skylights in the ceiling. They made it astoundingly bright in the lab, even at that time of the morning. The brand-new copper piping scintillated like a bundle of jewelry. Malveena stood in front of the xylophone-like array of copper pipes Foster had mounted along the wall above his lab bench. She was not sure where to start or what to do.

She pulled her Rostfrei stiletto from her hip sheath, folded it open and cut the plastic ties to free up the pipes. She placed an eight-foot length of pipe on the bench and rubbed her gloved hands together to help her think.

"Malveena. That knife. I don't think that's legal. Is it?" Bully did not know what the law was but he wanted it to be illegal just because it was Malveena. Malveena wasn't listening, she was looking at the pipe.

" Why on earth are you carrying a switchblade?"

" Because it matches my shoes Bully. It matches my shoes." Malveena could shut down the rationality of any conversation with a fork of her tongue.

Malveena was looking carefully across the row of Foster's pipes. Some of them had been fingered more than others. The shorter ones were corroded and dull from the oils and acids of the hands that had played with them. The cut ends however, were shiny.

"Bully, the ends of the pipes have been cleaned up with an emery cloth or a piece of sandpaper. I should have asked you to bring some emery cloth as well as the pipe cutter."

Bully went white inside but he didn't show it on the surface. He was good at covering up his omissions. Malveena was equally as good at interpreting his demeanor.

" Bully. You didn't bring a pipe cutter did you." Bully shook his head. It was much easier than explaining.

"Start looking in the drawers. You start at that end."

Malveena started at the left and Bully at the right and they worked toward the middle. Malveena found some emery cloth in the second drawer and Bully had no idea what he was looking for. They met at the center drawer and Malveena saw Bully had closed the previous drawer with a pipe cutter in it.

"Gregious. Do you have any idea what you're looking for? You just closed that drawer with a pipe cutter in it." He opened the drawer and pulled out something that looked as if it could cut something.

"Give me that."

Malveena took the cutter from Bully and fitted it around the first piece of pipe she had set out on the bench. *What could be so hard.* She picked an arbitrary place as a test spot and tightened the knurled end to bring the blade against the copper surface. She swung the cutter around the pipe and it made a beautiful spiraling mark and traveled up the pipe about four inches. The pipe was not cut, just marked.

"Bully, I can't turn the blade in hard enough to cut. You do it. Try again on that piece I just messed u.. tested."

Bully could not believe it. Something Malveena could not do. He smiled despite himself. Bully stepped in and pushed the pipe securely into the cutter and turned the knurled knob. He could feel the cutter blade move into the copper. He swung the cutter once around the pipe, tightened the knurled end again and swung the cutter and off fell a perfectly cut piece of pipe. He could not believe it. He looked at the pile of copper pipe on the floor, just waiting for his expertise.

Foster's bench had a millimeter rule running its full length. Bully put his cleanly cut end at zero mark and said to Malveena, " OK. Where do I cut?"

Malveena saw the shortest five or six pieces in Foster's collection were the most used. Also, there were two pieces missing. The lengths of the missing pieces were marked on their mounting board as 152.4 millimeters and 203.2 millimeters. A difference of 50.8 millimeters. Malveena decided to cut ten pieces and that suited Bully fine. Bully's fine point felt pen marked the pipe cleanly but he could not see the pipe surface well enough to measure correctly.

The room was so bright and the light coming through the many Fresnel lenses was so pure and intense the multi-directional reflection from the copper was blinding. He leaned down close to the pipe so his head made a shadow and still it was difficult. He borrowed Malveena's blue-block reading glasses and that did the trick. He soon had eight pieces of ¾ inch copper pipe cut, ranging in length from about 20 inches down to about six inches. He and Malveena sat there with their emery paper and cleaned up the ends.

It was just 10:30 in the morning and the laboratory was blindingly bright and already hot. Bully was very pleased with himself and he lined up the pieces he had cut. *So now what.*

Malveena wondered the same thing Bully did. *So now what.*

She thought she had seen the Pilcher kid hold the pipe to his eye or maybe up to his face. *Why not start with that.* Malveena picked up the longest piece of pipe and put it to her eye and looked through it around the room. It was amazing how it made you focus on a small spot. She swung it to the center of the Fresnel lens above her and a blasting spiral of repressed intention rocked her so she did a stutter step with both feet and bent her knees and stabbed a hand out for balance. Malveena recovered her posture and put the pipe back on the bench as if it were radioactive. She looked up at the lenses above her as if they were to blame for her little jig and felt a pain in her eyes from the intensity of the light. She picked up the next shorter piece of pipe and handed it to Bully.

"Here Bully. You do the next one."

"Nice try Malveena. I am the pipe cutter, you are the pipe looker. Go girl." He felt cool.

Malveena sighed and looked at the remaining seven pieces. *Blast that rotten little Pilcher.* She picked up the next shorter pipe and put it to her eye looking at the floor. Gingerly she sighted the pipe degree by degree closer to the edge of the Fresnel lens and then she swung it full bore into the light. She had her feet farther apart and she was well balanced. The light spun through and seemed to pull at her a bit and made her vibrate. There was something generous about it. *This isn't so bad.* She progressed through ever decreasing pipe lengths until she got to the eight inch one. *This is one of the lengths which was missing.*

The temperature of the laboratory was approaching 100° F. Bully was soaking wet and even Malveena was perspiring. The brilliance of the light concentrating and coalescing around her was overwhelming. She put the eight-inch pipe to her eye and swung it directly into the center of the brightest lens she could find. A typhoon of light blasted into Malveena looking for an intention to fulfill. The pipe was not quite right to engage the consciousness of the trail but it was close. The energy and the wanting of it grew in her and she would not release her fixation on the light. There was a surge of color and hope and welcome and it knocked Malveena flat on her butt. Bully reacted to help her but too late.

Malveena was wild eyed and excited. She flew to her feet and snatched up the shortest piece of pipe and crowed almost maniacally,

"Bully, you won't believe this. I don't believe this. Never anything like it. I felt elevated or something, like the air being the most clear I have ever breathed."

Bully moved close to Malveena. She could get hurt if the pipe really nailed her. And there he would be. Trying to explain away an unconscious Malveena to the security guards and why he was in Foster's lab despite a court order to the contrary. What was he doing with all these pipes and how did Malveena get that pipe shaped cut under her eye. He did not intend to go out on a ledge for Malveena. He put his outstretched hand firmly on her left shoulder to support her.

Malveena did not notice Bully's hand as she placed the six-inch pipe over her eye and moved it closer until it contacted. She took it in both hands and put it to the light. The light answered the call and flowed into Malveena in total perfection and enveloped her. It swathed her in a golden benevolence and began to gather and gather and Malveena began to shake. Bully put his other hand on her right shoulder. The goodness and the sharing and the full commitment of the caress disarmed her. She felt as if she would fall but she did not. She was taken out of herself in freely given acceptance and the light took her hard in its embrace. The flash of intention was enormous and Malveena was in the trail of the light. But she was not alone. Bully Gregious was with her.

They arrived standing with Bully holding tight to Malveena's shoulders, with both of them immobilized in an agglutinated mass which had a texture close to acrylic. The consciousness of the light had contrived a destination from the contrary and fleeting intentions of their two conflicted minds. Bully had been totally mindless and was looking off into space when Malveena communed with the light. Malveena was conjuring nothing more than a wish to recreate the recent experience of elevation. Immobile and helpless in their mucilaginous restraint, they saw dimly through a thick unforgiving gelatin, far into a distance which seemed exaggerated and limitless. They accepted the far horizon and thought nothing of it other than they observed it. It posed no threat, it carried no concern. They were not required to react but only to be and see and deny engagement. They were benign and they waited. Malveena was the first to feel a change within the impenetrable plastic. It began to take on a shimmer which moved not within it but of itself. Malveena sensed the medium was thinning in front of her and she had no consideration of what that meant. Coming toward her with great pace and increasing clarity was a wave of blistering cold and it struck her into reality with the slap of a winter's day. She threw her arms back in panic. From behind her came a pathetic high-pitched whimpering. Bully had made his escape from agglutination too.

The ledge was no more than five feet wide. Bully was standing behind Malveena with his back against a granite wall towering into overhang 4000 feet above them. Chiseled deeply into its face, with wings spread, the wall had a full-sized petroglyph of a condor, the ruler of the upper world. The carving was deep and the chiseled lines were cut perfectly to exactly the same depth and with an identical bevel as if they had been cut with a laser. Malveena stood in front of Bully no more than 18 inches from the edge of a precipice. They had landed on an undermined shelf tipping down and away from them to their left and it hung 12,000 feet over a dark and tumultuous river. They stared west into the chasm as the increasing wind carried the mocking *hut hut hut hreek* call of condors throughout the canyon.

They shivered at 12,000 feet in a cold early morning in the Peruvian Andes. The steam from their breathing went to nothing in the shadow of the massif glowering over them. A small aquifer had broken out of the rock face just to their right above them and it wetted the surface where they stood. It carried an oozing sludge which ran past them and accelerated along the tilt and over the edge to the valley two miles below them. Frozen with fear, they stood perfectly motionless. Despite that they began to move subtly left and down the gradient toward the brink. Influenced by the tilt of the shelf and the clay substrate of the aquifer slicking the surface, they were moving. They slithered inexorably toward the abyss. Malveena acted quickly and worked the blade of her stiletto into a crack in the shelf and braced up against it with her foot. *Why is Bully here wherever the blazes here is. Why am I not here on my own. It was I who held the pipe. Ah. Now I remember. Bully had a hand on my shoulder, no, a hand on both shoulders. So, we were taken away together. Hmm. Those little brats. They traveled together. But they went exactly where they wanted to go. How did they control that?*

Malveena gathered herself. She was breathing too fast. She began slow diaphragmatic breathing to regain her equilibrium but she could not ease off. They were at an altitude of 12,000 feet and she was not acclimated to the reduced oxygen. Bully was wheezing heavily behind her. He had jammed his loosened belt buckle over a small projection in the rock face and tethered himself there facing inward, staring glumly at the enormous carved bird. For the moment they were staying put. From behind them over the shoulders of the shelf, streams of sunlight ran out of the valleys to the east and painted paths into the canyon in which they found themselves. Westerly, the morning sun gilded snow-capped pinnacle 8000 feet above them.

Malveena estimated it was about 10:00 AM. Their ledge was about 30 feet long, tapering narrowly at the ends and concave at the back midpoint. They were at its deepest concavity. Given that and the overhang shading the sun from behind them, she estimated it would be at least 2:30 PM before sunlight reached them. *That blasted pipe got us here and it bloody well better get us out.* She had it tucked in her waistband. From behind her a quavering and petulant voice bounced off the cliff face.

"Malveena, I hate you for this. I hate you a lot. What the devil were you thinking? You take us and put us out here on a sub-zero ledge? If you had asked me where I wanted to go, do you think I would have answered 'ledge'?"

"Bully, don't blame me. I did not intend to take us anywhere. The light sucked us through this pipe and planted us right here. And who asked you to come anyway!" She touched the pipe and it quivered. "It was not my choice."

"Malveena, that is not so. You could feel it just like I could feel it. It was practically asking us where we wanted to go. I was thinking of nothing in particular. But you. What were you thinking of to get us stuck out here on a ledge? Are you nuts?"

Malveena stopped and her eyes widened. Bully was so stupid, sometimes he was brilliant. He had put his finger on it exactly and she had even said it herself. *I did not intend to take us anywhere.* She had not intended it. Intended. Could it be that simple?

"So then Bully. If you could feel that question from the pipe. 'where do you want to go?', what was your answer? Tell us Bully. Tell me and the pipe why we are here." It quivered.

Malveena had felt the question from the light also but she was not admitting it. She had been thinking of the amazing feeling of spiritual elevation she had experienced with the eight-inch pipe. When the pipe took them, she had been imagining soaring. So here she was. Bully remembered his exact thought. A ledge and Malveena. So here he was.

The breeze increased from the north and the temperature was dropping. The shape of the concavity was accelerating the velocity of the wind along the ledge and it was picking up water from the aquifer and spraying in on them. They were very cold and they were losing their concentration to keep themselves stable in the flowing muck.

"Malveena, we're going to die here. My hands are frozen. I can't hold on here very much longer."

"Yes Bully. We have to get off the ledge somehow."

Malveena scanned their choices. They could not go up and they could not go down. The south end of their perch was slick and rounded and was separated by one careless step from the rocks 12,000 feet below. *Someone has gotten up here and carved out that bird. There must be a way.* With her arm extended fully, Malveena felt through the ooze with her hand and found the next crack in the stone toward the north. She gripped it with her fingernails and down on one knee she pulled her stiletto out and worked it into the fissure five feet to the north. She was now about ten feet from the north end of the ledge and about eight feet from Bully. From that position she could see the ledge was not as narrow at the north end as she had thought. It seemed to cut back into the face of the overhang. If they could get there they would be away from the drenching of the aquifer.

Bully whimpered, " Malveena, please don't leave me."

"I am not leaving you Bully."

"Thank you Malveena."

Bully rotated in place to watch her. Malveena put her foot against her stiletto and laid down in the mire and spread herself as widely as she could, fully extended. She ran both hands in a circle under the sludge, sweeping as far as she could reach and feeling along the surface. She found another split that would take her knife. The ooze was running fast at that spot and she knew if she did not get the knife locked in on her first try she was over the edge. She reached back, wrenched the stiletto out sharply and drove it hard into the new crack. She missed and chipped out the edge of the small fissure and she began to slide. She strained to force the edge of the blade cross ways against the stone to gain traction and her feet began to swing around behind her and off the edge. As she felt herself going over, she made one last thrust and the Rostfrei stiletto found the spot and lodged firmly in the crevice. Malveena pulled herself to it and scanned the terminus of the shelf. There certainly was a flat spot cut back at the end of the ledge. It was dry. She was now about 12 feet from Bully and she could not go back.

" Bully! How long is your belt?"

" What?"

" How long is your belt?"

Bully knew it was 50 inches but he always said 44. "44 inches. No wait. 50 inches."

This was the first time Malveena was pleased at Bully's girth. She put one foot against the knife handle and with all her strength she pushed off to the flat cutback and scrambled onto it. From her vantage point, looking south, she could see only the surface of Bully's belly. She took off her belt and tied it tightly through two loops of her pants. She stored her knife sheath and the pipe hard against the wall. She took off her slacks. She estimated Bully was 12 to 15 feet away. *Tied together, his belt, my belt, and my two pant legs should reach that far.*

"Bully listen carefully. Now pay attention. I am going to throw you my belt attached to my trousers. Take off your belt and tie it to my belt. I am going to pull you across."

Malveena swung the makeshift pants rope out to Bully and it landed about four feet short. He reached for it and fell with a belly bounce onto the growing river of sludge, two feet from the edge. He was done for. Without a thought he began to fish flop. *Help if salmon can help do it help, so help can I.*

It was something the petroglyph had never seen. Bully flopped like crazy and front crawled in a frenzy of ninety strokes per minute. He made five feet of headway but every stroke also moved him closer to the chasm. The buckle end of his undone belt was dangling over the edge as he upped his stroke rate. Suddenly Bully stopped gaining and he realized he was stuck against Malveena's knife. He bent a knee and put a foot on it, and rocketed off the knife toward the safe spot. The handle of the knife snapped off and flew over the edge. Malveena grabbed Bully's freezing hand with her own freezing hands and pulled him in. They were limp with relief in the safety of the alcove. Thirty seconds later they heard the ping of the knife handle as it struck an outcrop a mile below them. Bully wondered what the sound would have been like if it had been him.

They hugged each other. Malveena looked into Bully's face and she saw relief but something else too.

"What is it Bully?"

"I lost my belt."

Malveena pulled her pants back to her through the slop. She wrung out her clay sodden pant legs as best she could and tied them around her waist. She had lost her knife so she put the pipe in the sheath and cinched up the belt. She and Bully were out of the wind and out of the spray from the aquifer yet they were still in deep shadow. Malveena knelt and felt over the back of the small platform. It was a step. The way down from the north end of the ledge. The steps were cut leaning into the face of the cliff and for the first time Bully and Malveena felt they might survive.

The stairway followed the natural arc of the root of the cliff face and it swung back south-west as it approached the river. Bully and Malveena took turns leading as they clambered down. The riser height in the stone stairway was about 20 inches and every step down tore at their leg muscles and their backs. They worked their way down for two hours and they were exhausted. They arrived at a wide landing where they agreed to stop for a rest. Malveena hoped they might gather the sun in a couple of hours. They laid on their backs, cold and wet and looked at the high blue perfect sky. Bully closed his eyes and fell asleep immediately. Malveena did not disturb him. As terrible as this event had been, the mystical energy flowing from the earth fortified her like nothing she could remember. She drank in the clarity of the air and fell soundly asleep.

Malveena startled herself awake. She sat up sharply and covered her eyes against the glare of the sun. Bully was already up and he had his pants off drying them on the warm rock.

" Oh, sorry." He scrambled to put his pants back on and beltless he held them up with his left hand. "I did not want to wake you."

Steam was coming up from the river below and the full heat of the day was heating up the stone. The condors above made perfect circles at the limits of Malveena's vision while flies droned around in puny imitation.

"Bully we have the sun. So, this is how we do it. I'm going to sight this pipe and think about going back to the laboratory. I believe the way this works is you should think about going back to the laboratory also. I take that back. We both need to intend to go back there. Intend to go there Bully."

Bully was swatting at the flies. They were not bothering Malveena but they seemed to like Bully. He smacked one on his wrist.

"Get over here Bully! Put your hand on my shoulder. I'm going to the sun right now."
Malveena put both hands on the small pipe. She held it lightly and like a delicate instrument. Bully put his hand on her shoulder. Malveena placed the pipe to her eye and gave herself up to the light just as Bully removed his hand and swatted at the fly biting his neck. The golden sun from the sacred valley of the Incas took Malveena. She was imbued with a force and a purpose and an acceptance she had never known. She traveled to the stars and touched and brushed all there was and landed softly at the edge of the laboratory bench of Charles Abernathy Foster. She and Bully had been gone for three minutes.

Malveena was heavily restrained and immobile inside a scintillating mass refracting an spinning the light like a mammoth gemstone. The Fresnel lenses above and around her gathered up the brilliance and from a million angles bent it through the envelope of gelatin. Malveena observed the laboratory. It meant nothing, it meant something, it was there and she was there, and it required nothing from her and it possessed nothing particular for her. She gazed off in complete peace and watched without judgment as the wave of today's reality swept over her. Malveena was joyous. She had done something fantastic.

"Bully, I could never imagine something as spectacular as this. What an experience!"

She was not surprised Bully was speechless. She turned to speak with him again and there was no Bully. The laboratory was locked, Malveena was in the laboratory, but not Bully. *Good grief! That idiot! I tell him to hold on and he lets go. That idiot! Wherever that place was, I have no idea where it is. Bully Bully Bully. Oh. Bully. You moron. The power of attorney. Only you have it. Blast you Gregious!*

Malveena was stumped and she sat down with her back against the face of the laboratory cabinet. She flipped the copper pipe end to end in her hand while she thought. *I got back here by intending to be back here. Maybe if I intend to be with Bully that will happen. Hmm. What if Bully has fallen off the mountain and is in the river. Hmm. Well Mr. Gregious, here I come.*

She landed back on the same stone platform from which she had left. A semi-solid shimmering agglutination constrained every impulse of thought and motion and removed her need for decision. She was in a strong suspension but it finished its work faster than the last time. She embraced the harsh transition into the new time and steadied herself on her feet. *Now to find Bully.* She turned into the strong sun and there he was. He was lying on his back with his legs crossed with eyes closed and a smile on his face. She was pleased to see the slob.

"Bully."

Bully Gregious languished for a moment longer before he opened his eyes. He was not sleeping. He basked in the sun and breathed in the best air he had ever breathed.

" Hello Malveena. Wie geht's."

Malveena fisted her hands onto her hips.

" Get up and come over here."

Bully obeyed and came and stood near Malveena. She turned him around and grabbed him by the collar. Pure light honored the pipe and with an intention and consciousness honed by the eternal magic of the sacred valley, Gregious and Drago returned home.

That evening, a cold glass of Montrachet bent the light from the candles around Malveena's bathtub and bounced it around the room. The ambient aroma of the essential oils conflicted with the bouquet of her marvellous white wine but times were tough. Her tub water was very hot and it steamed the room. Malveena felt satisfied. She melted deeper into the water and lifted up a leg and watched one toe go up the faucet. She sat her copper partner beside her on the tub ledge and warmed in the gloaming it threw onto the tile. She was sure she had the pipe business all worked out. *Now I have that little monster.* She knew she could intend to be where he was at any time as she had done with Bully. *The time has come for that Pilcher kid and his slick sliding red hat little sidekick.*

Chapter 11: The Bastille

Davy and Mildred were worried and uncertain. They had no idea of what Malveena and Bully might be up to. Mildred had her written record of their fateful meeting and Davy was a witness too. So, what to do about it. Who could they tell and who would believe them. They did not know if they were in real danger, but a cloud of foreboding moved with them wherever they went. Their anxious minds turned every step they heard and every shadow they saw into Malveena Drago. They expected to be throttled around every next corner. To quiet their minds, they withdrew into their own company.

They subsumed the reality of the meeting they had witnessed by immersing themselves in fantasy. They read every book they could find. As with everything they did, they turned it into a contest. With great intricacy they hashed over and dissected every book they had read in common and agreed they would anoint one book as the best.

Davy chose his best book on the basis of what would make the most interesting and exciting destination for his pipe. In his mind, his first choice was unquestionable. He did not need to write anything down.

He pontificated. "I have the best book Mildred. There is no question, so you might as well agree in advance. Your arguing about it will do absolutely nothing to improve your book."

Mildred had chosen a winner within her own list by attributing a score and value to each book she read. She had then set up a decimal system which she marked on the spine of her books so no matter how many books she read, there was a place for them by a number in order of her literary preference, not by alphabet. She would never have to reorder Mildred's list. She showed Davy her arithmetic calculations and spread out her graph of the relative values of her top 63 books.

From somewhere in the empyrean came, why am I not surprised.

Mildred heard something but she had not caught it.

"What did you say Davy?"

"Oh. When I saw your list, I was not surprised. I knew you would have a list. But lists don't make a winner."

Mildred slitted her eyes. Dopo cowered. "What's wrong with a list?"

Davy backtracked. "Um.. nothing. I just knew you would have one. We do things differently that's all. So, what's your book?"

"Well after careful consideration and absolutely irrefutable analysis, my book, the book, the most excellent book is.."

She turned and raised one eyebrow. "Are you ready?"

"Mildred."

"Ok. The Tale of two Cities." Davy burst out laughing. "That's my book too. Who would believe it. We agree on something!"

The Tale of Two Cities begged to be read aloud. It had great characters and great accents from the 1700's in England and France. They agreed to read The Tale of Two Cities aloud to each other in alternating chapters. Davy would start. One chapter each and that was it for that day. Every day they looked forward to the next day and the next two chapters. Davy knew that was how Dickens had sold some of his books. A chapter at a time. People had lined up to buy the next chapter.

Davy spent a lot of time at Mildred's house. He got along well with Mrs. Craft and he knew she liked him. The three of them were much at ease with each other and Mrs. Craft enjoyed every moment of their reading. She was happy the two of them were content with her company and she was oblivious to the dilemma they endured.

"Davy, I love to hear you do the English accents. You amaze me. Why, it is as if you had been around common speaking English folk in a previous time. However do you do it!"

Mildred joined in with batting eyelids and a devil's smile. "Yes Davy, however do you do it!"

"What chapter did you just finish, Davy?" asked Helen Craft.

"Chapter 26 Mrs. Craft. Charles Darnay and Lucy Mannette are newly married and they are visited by Sydney Carton, who has taken on an air of fidelity."

"Well, good for him."

Mrs. Craft turned up the sound on the flash drive in her Bose player. Out belted Creedance Clearwater Revival with Proud Mary. Why Mrs. Craft. The music was new to him and Davy loved what he was hearing. He looked over at Mildred. She was doing a little bop move. Why Mildred.

"Mrs. Craft, what is that music?"

"That was recorded live at Woodstock, Davy. 1969." Janet had a look of happy nostalgia on her face. She and her husband had played the Woodstock recording often. What could be wrong with peace and love and 500,000 young people looking for what they believed was freedom. Davy had never heard anything so good. He put Woodstock on his mental pipe list. He looked over at Mildred and she looked back. She would put it on her real pipe list.

They broke their rule and they read alternating chapters after chapter to each other, enthralled by the book and its characters. The last chapter arrived too soon for them while at the same time it arrived at the perfect time. Mrs. Craft had foreseen the dilemma about to arise and headed it off. Davy had read the first chapter in the book and Mildred the second and so on and therein was the problem. There were 45 chapters. Davy got to read one more chapter than Mildred, and Helen Craft knew exactly how that would sit.

"Alright you two, I see you are on the last chapter. It is my turn. You listen, I read."

Mrs. Craft read the 45th odd numbered chapter, 'The Footsteps Die Out Forever' to Davy and Mildred with an extraordinary sense of pathos and drama. Her voice spoke the words of the book directly to their hearts. They were heartsick at the sacrifice of Sidney Carton in giving his life for the woman he loved. As the pathetic and noble words spilled out, Davy's eyes welled and a large quick tear rolled down his cheek. Mildred was glad it had not been her.

'It is a far far better thing that I do than I have ever done. It is a far far better rest I go to than I have ever known'.

Davy brushed the tear and did not rush it. It seemed fitting. Mrs. Craft sighed with the beauty of it. Mildred was quiet and said nothing to embarrass her friend as she got up and gestured for Davy to follow her to the front steps to sit down. The concrete had been soaking up the sun and the steps were warm. Mildred sat pigeon-toed and looked at the recently planted maple trees. She thought by this time next year they might give shade. The whole epoch of the French Revolution was a thing they could not believe could happen. Surely it was a product only of the fertile mind of Charles Dickens.

"Davy, could what Dickens wrote about really have been that way? The guillotine and the crowds and the lot?"

"I don't know Mildred, but he was not many years removed from that time when he wrote the book. There were still old men and woman around who had been there."

About half way through the book Mildred had downloaded a hand drawn and stylized map of Revolutionary Paris at the library. She knew the cross streets, where the main buildings were and she traveled to and from them in her mind with every line Davy read. Davy enjoyed that Mildred and her mother were so enthralled by the book. He felt the same way and he admired Mildred's studiousness and her interest in learning the layout of the city.

"You know Davy, I would like to go back there. To see the finery of the court and to see one of their grand balls, maybe even dance er...to see the Tuileries in full bloom and beauty, maybe even to listen to the philosophers such as Montesquieu and Voltaire. Not to see the Bastille or the guillotine or the sans culottes, the poor clothes-less ones, but the artistic parts. The softer parts."

He nodded. He would like it for Mildred to see that. For himself he was thinking more of the soldiers and how they would be mounted in battle dress on their fine chargers and the rowdiness of the crowds they controlled and, in the background, even the creak and whomp of the guillotine. That would be something from a distance on the outskirts of the crowd and it wasn't real in a way. He nodded to himself again at that. Mildred saw the nod and that he agreed with her.

"Davy, it is a sunny day. And I have my map and my notebook." He was already looking at the angle of sun and what sort of cloud cover there was. It seemed they were thinking the same thing. The pipe seemed to agree with the idea and it gave a little pulse even though he had not yet finished formulating the where and when of it to himself. *Dopo, I am imagining things about my pipe.* Dopo wondered.

"Davy, if you and I went there for a day, how long would we be away?"

"Just a few minutes Mildred, I think. A few minutes." Tacitly they had agreed. They would go to Paris.

"Where do you think we should arrive Mildred? Somewhere safe but not too far away from the Tuileries or the Bastille? You know your map of Paris from that time, so somewhere on the outskirts of the activity but where we could get the flavor or the feel of what happened? It can't be like Dickens portrayed it anyway, but the safer the better."

"Well Davy, how about the Tuileries? Maybe it will be easier to hide in there if we have to hide? According to my map those places you mentioned are not very close to each other. Between the Tuileries and the Bastille is about five or six miles. That is a long route to travel without cover. If we landed somewhere like the Tuileries, we would be between the Jardins des Champs-Élysées on the west and the Louvre which is a mile or so away on the east. We can go from the Tuileries to wherever else we want to go."

Through the screen door Mrs. Craft heard the kids talking to each other about Paris and where they would like to go in the city. She sighed to herself at the beautiful imaginings of the two youngsters and she was sad she had had the delights of such fantasy drained from her. *I agree with them. Paris would be a wonderful trip.* Listening to the ingenuousness of youth diluted her worries for a time. That day she had received a letter from her missing husband's employer notifying her in six months his salary would terminate. *I am sorry to inform* you that... She had just lost her job and in six months there would be no income to carry the household. She had read the letter to Mildred and now she regretted she had done it.

Mildred and Davy decided they would leave from the old bridge. In lockstep the two stepped intrepidly off the front stoop with images of Paris guiding them. Mildred shouted back to her mother.

"Mom, we are walking down to the bridge. We shouldn't be long. Maybe an hour or two. I will bring you back some flowers."

"OK Mildred. Have fun. Bye Davy."

They walked quickly to the bridge over the Borstal river. The Blue Francesca was well past its time and some maples were beginning to drop leaves. Along the banks near the bridge Mildred would still find full bloom evening primrose and purple morning glory to make a nice bouquet for her mother. If pressed Davy could sometimes identify a rose. The sky was high and cloudless. It was a pristine day and the sun was magnificent and penetrating. Mildred patted her notebook and street sketch in the plastic pouch on her belt and took Davy's hand as he sighted to the sun with his pipe. Thoughts of the Bastille, the Guillotine, the horse guard and the mob coursed through his mind. Mildred swirled on the dance floor in her light blue gown showing her white crinoline. She peeked coquettishly from behind her fan at the powdered wigs and fine hosiery of the gentlemen.

Davy stood perfectly still and captured the sun. Oddly, he felt a slight delay in the embrace of the light. It was as if the light doubted their intentions. The energy of their gathering seemed harsh. For the first time the spin of the pipe seemed dizzying rather than caressing and helping. The form of the travelling did not seem smooth and clean but rather abrasive. They landed together still holding hands and stayed locked in the mass of gelatinous restraint for what seemed an hour. The agglutination was not clear but had moments of shadow playing a cloud within it. The arrival into reality was soft. They stood looking at each other and felt a little unfulfilled.

The day in Paris was overcast and the intermittent rain had stopped but the residue was dripping from the trees above them and making them wet. They looked around. They were in a small perfectly rectangular copse of manicured trees. The trees were large and sparsely leafed. They were intended to be trimmed up for easy walking beneath them but that had been neglected and they hung low. Mildred was disappointed at where she stood. There are no crinolines here. There are no posters of coming events, no happy laughter from a cafe. This is not a ballroom. She did not know the leader of the Revolutionary Citizens Committee, Robespierre, had banned dancing.

Davy was disappointed at where he stood. This is not the Bastille. Where are the horse guards? Where is the rattle of the drums?

Subconsciously they each had intimated their true intentions to the pipe and their intentions were different and conflicted. The pipe landed them in an improvised location of its own choosing. They had not focused on the same intention either in place or time. They had allowed their minds to drift to each of their own preferences and because there was no agreement they had achieved neither. Davy realized too the pipe had picked its own destination. It was not he who controlled the intention, but rather it was the consciousness of the light that controlled the intention.

It was very cold and Davy's shoes leaked. The grass was damaged and trampled and it held remnants of a recent snowfall. A skin of ice marked the puddles. It was near freezing and they were underdressed. Mildred was wishing for her balaclava. The rectangular copse of manicured trees stretched 100 yards deep behind them. From it they entered an enormous circular plaza where an elaborate fountain sat dry and glooming. It was the centerpiece of the corridor leading east to the Tuileries and to the massive front wall of The Tuileries Palace. The fountain was made with a sixteen-foot-high green and gilded striped pedestal supporting a dish spreading 20 feet wide. Seated figures in traditional Greek posture ringed the pedestal and looked frigidly into the distance. Their gilded hair sat on black marble heads with their onyx bodies swathed in deep green chiseled drapery. Their stone eyes looked to their former

132

glory as the rain drenched them and made them clean. The eastern exit from the Jardins des Champs Elysees became the entrance to La Place de Revolution. Mildred had memorized her downloaded drawing of Paris but she had no idea where they were. The scale and size of their surroundings confused her.

"Mildred, where are we?"

Mildred looked around. She pulled her map out of her plastic bag and unfolded it. "I am not sure. From this angle nothing looks the same as on the map."

Davy understood. "What is your best guess?"

"I think we are here." She scrabbled across the surface of the map with a finger. "I think we are in the Jardin des Champs-Élysées. Made by Marquis de Marigny. He was the brother of Madame Pompadour and.." Mildred felt rather than saw the exasperation on Davy's face and suspended the tour. They could see their breath as they exhaled.

"The lines of trees run that way." She pointed past the fountain down a wide boulevard. They saw they were being examined by the passersby as they stood and deciphered their drawing. Davy and Mildred walked quickly to the fountain and Mildred stopped to get new bearings. She looked down at her map and then pointed to the right.

"There Davy. Over the river. That building with the Spires. That is in the part of the city called the 6th arondissement. I think we are in the 8th arondissement. If those three large Spires are the Benedictine Abbey of Saint-Germain-des-Prés then that is the hill of Montmartre, which is one of the highest spots in the city, and that is right here." She tapped the plastic cover.

"You see over there how the land slopes down and away from the abbey and is so low sometimes it floods there." Davy saw the meadows running toward the Seine were browned by recent high water.

She continued. "Those towers there. Those squared off kind of blunt towers. That is Notre Dame cathedral if I am reading the map correctly."

Davy had expected Notre Dame would have high ornate spires. Mildred relaxed somewhat as she began to make sense of the map. She looked around to find more bearings. An old couple had stopped and they were staring at them. The couple were emaciated. They had rags wrapped around their feet against the slush and they ogled the shoes they saw standing at the edge of the sparse winter woods. Both the man and the woman wore soft Phrygian caps emblematic of their allegiance and adherence to the cult of the Jacquerie, and both wore suspicion of the strangers on their faces. Davy and Mildred felt acutely how incongruous they were in this place. They were obvious. They were dressed oddly, and they were demonstrating to the world they could read. Mildred closed her map and pointed with it down one of the tree lined spokes leading away from the circular plaza. "That is the best way I think."

"Fine." Said Davy, and they started off quickly but their haste had made them interesting. The others moving through the plaza wore wooden clogs or no shoes at all. Mildred had on her stout leather walking shoes and Davy wore sneakers at which every person stared. Mildred wore jeans, and new jeans at that, with a knife edge crease ironed in at her request. She was the lone female in pants. They each had a belt of leather. Not one person they could see possessed a belt. Davy motioned for Mildred to follow him and he led her back thirty or forty yards into the trees.

"Mildred, we are stupid. We should have thought of this. We look like aristocrats. Shoes, belts, new cloth. We are asking for a problem."

He bent down and picked up some soil and began to rub it into his shirt sleeves and pantlegs. He ground the mud hard onto his sneakers. He slipped his belt out of its loops and fastened it around his waist inside his pants and did it up. His pipe and belt were out of sight. He waited for Mildred. She held a handful of cold slopping mud and she looked down at her jeans and shined shoes.

"Mildred?"

"These are new jeans."

"You need to tone down your appearance."

"But, they are new."

Her shoulders slumped in resignation. Mildred looked down again and closed her eyes as she rubbed the pale beige mud into her jeans and finished by muddying her shirt and shoes. She inadvertently wiped a tickle spot on her face and the smudge was a nice touch. She draped the plastic pouch holding her notepad and map inside her waist band. Davy led the way again within the woods. They agreed to rest there twenty minutes to dissipate whatever curiosity they might have aroused in the onlookers. They emerged from the woods fifty yards closer to the east exit leading to La Place de Revolution. The old couple had not moved on. They were speaking with a fellow in a red hat and animatedly pointing at Davy and Mildred.

Mildred had figured out their location. They were just west of the Place de Revolution in one of the large rectangular groves within the Jardins des Champs Elysees. The exits leading off to the right and down to the Seine River were barricaded and they could go nowhere but forward. The people in the plaza seemed to be gathering and coalescing and forming a stream moving east along the Champs Elysee. The stream moved inexorably forward as it gathered momentum and swept the sans-culottes along inside it. Davy and Mildred would have preferred to go back to the shelter and privacy of the woods from which they had come. To do that against the tide would expose them and place them in great danger.

"Davy, this is a bad idea." Davy nodded. It was indeed a bad idea to be anywhere near this throng.

"Mildred, we need to get away from these open spaces and into the smaller side streets until we can find some sunlight and get away from here."

They stood alone in the ancient city, unprepared for the weather and for the ferocity of the world. They had expected to arrive in warm weather. They had expected to see the gaiety and light of Paris. They were trapped in an uncertain time and they feared the worst.

Davy and Mildred hurried east on the boulevard of the Champs Elysee. Mildred wanted to go to the right to the south to escape from the congestion building around them. They picked up their pace walking toward the Place de la Revolution but they did not seem to be staying ahead of the crowd. It was the first time Davy had felt any fear coming from Mildred. A light drizzle began as the cold skies darkened. They began a trot toward the Palace of the Tuileries whose frowning wet face they could see about half a mile ahead of them. The surface of the cobblestones was slick and warn smooth and they could not get traction in the slush as they slipped and slid attempting to go faster. They burst from the end of the tree line confining them on both sides into the 20 acre Place de la Revolution. The entire area was dyed purple from the barrels of spilled wine brought there daily by horse-cart. Purple rivulets ran everywhere between the cobbles as the intensifying rain washed the wine from the surface and into gutters that streamed down to the Seine. Hags intercepted the flow and collected the swill to bottle up and sell. In the center of the enclosure stood a wooden platform. Leading to it were wooden twelve-foot-wide, open-backed stairs with railings on each side, rising to eight feet above the ground. At the far end of the platform which was surrounded by a railing, stood the towering monument to the revolution. It was Madame La Guillotine.

Mildred stopped and clutched Davy's arm without speaking. They resumed walking but shrunk inside at the sight of the guillotine and what it represented. A huge clamoring throng, pushing and chanting, streamed into the plaza on their immediate right. The crowd had nothing to its name but hate and it rampaged on, looking to devour whatever displeased it. Steam rose off the sweating bodies that bullied and berated and herded en masse 20 or 30 well-dressed families with their children. They were corralling them to the Bastille, 5 miles away.

In growing panic, Davy and Mildred began to run and in doing so they made themselves something to chase. They saw escape on either side was made impossible by the large moats surrounding the space. Eight or ten young marauders, led by a frail youth in a red Phrygian hat, took up the pursuit of the running youngsters. The Jacquerie was eager to add to their haul of despots, young or old. The pursuers were gaunt, emaciated and starved and they could not keep up with the pace Davy and Mildred had set but they were not concerned with that. They knew the warrens and the shorter paths and they would follow at a distance and at their convenience they would cut off Davy and Mildred and take them.

Davy blew on his hands to warm them and put them on his ears. He checked his belt had not worked its way up to expose the pipe. He looked at Mildred and he saw she could not choose which way to go.

"Come on Mildred. Run with me! Straight ahead."

Davy did not have a map to guide him but right now they needed speed. The posse behind them saw what Davy and Mildred were doing and they positioned two chasers to follow behind and the rest peeled off to the right. They careened into the first alley and down the incline to the Quay des Tuileries on the north bank of the Seine River. They ran parallel with and about 50 yards away from Davy and Mildred, intending to intercept them at Pont De L'Egalite, about half a mile ahead. The youngsters sped through the ornate gilded gates of the Tuileries. They raced around the octagonal lake in front of them ignoring the ring of Grecian statuary populating the circumference. On both sides, acres of beds of annual flowers were dead and brown and their sodden remnants were beaten flat by the rain and snow. The ornamental trees were ragged and unkempt and the gardens were woeful in the downpour. Mildred saw they were blocked ahead by the five-story wall of the Palace of the Tuileries and led Davy up the steps to the right and along the southerly terrace, going east toward the Louvre. *I see light in the palace I bet they are dancing right now spinning fluttering fans looking coy flicking curls and here I am running in the freezing rain from a mob wanting to cut off my head.* Below them to the right they saw the Seine and the Quay des Tuileries running beside it and it was not more than a few yards from them. Mildred worked her map out from her plastic bag and scanned it quickly. They were on the right track for getting south of the Seine and away from the terror. Mildred saw the Pont De L'Egalite ahead of them leading south off the Quay des Tuileries just below them and into safer territory.

"Look there! That is Pont De L'Egalite! That is the bridge we need." Mildred recognized the profile of its ten stone supporting arches just as her Visitors Guide to Paris had shown. Davy knew there was nothing she had not studied before the trip.

They turned right and ran downhill along the narrow Allee de Diane onto the Quay and as they cleared the retaining wall in full flight, Mildred smashed her shoulder headlong into the chest of the leader of the Jacquerie and knocked the small man flat on his back. As he fell, he flailed out and snatched Mildred's map from her hand and clutched it like a treasure to his chest as he rolled away. His Citizen entourage was thirty yards behind him and streaming fast to the fray.

"Quick Mildred!"

"But my map!" she shrieked.

"Forget the map. They are upon us!"

"Spy, spy, spy!" shouted the small man as he got up pointing at a running Mildred. He turned importantly to his comrades who were now arriving at his side.

"Look here Citizens, a map. A map I wrestled from that spy."

The gang stopped, impressed, and fondled the map, marveling at the texture of whatever the plastic cover was. The map is written in English. Surely a spy. Dirty English spy! They had something of value in their hands and they were satisfied with it. Someone would give them a reward for chasing down a spy.

As she and Davy sped south across the Pont De L'Egalite Mildred smiled. A spy they said. Me? Why yes, I am!

The river Seine moved away to their right in its semi-solid torpor and sludged its way through the pouring rain toward its estuary in the English Channel. Mildred had memorized the map from a perspective above the city but now that she was immersed in the buildings and the crazy quilt streets, it was difficult. It seemed to her the streets of Paris had been spun into a map by a master spider, a builder of grand and perfect concentric webs. Then somehow revolutionary malice froze the spinning stiff, and dropped and fractured it into a thousand shards, each of which was unrelated to the other. They led nowhere and everywhere and Mildred sped on looking for something familiar from her memory.

The Pont De L'Egalite led south to Rue du Bac she remembered. That was still too active a place and too close to the guillotine. Now what are the east-west cross streets. Mildred and Davy fought their way against the throngs heading for the Tuileries and the daily entertainment. Forty barrels of free wine would be delivered to La Place de la Revolution within the hour. Mildred thought the next cross street was Rue Ferneuil but it was not. It was Rue Bourbon. She could not get it in order. They continued south against the tide of humanity pushing north to the action. Mildred began to worry as she and Davy continued south. They came to the next intersection. Ah! This is Rue Ferneuil. They carried on together across Rue De l'Universite which was wide and teeming with sans-culottes. They ran steeply uphill to the east into a strong headwind and into sheets of horizontal sleet. The Abbey of Saint-Germain-des-Prés towered 200 feet above them on the right. The rubble of the recently destroyed pillory prison of the abbey lay strewn in tumbled heaps. Davy and Mildred continued to work against the tide and the numbers streaming past them were diminishing. They were chilled and shivering with the wet but they could not stop.

The map was gone from Mildred's head. "Davy, I don't know the directions. All the streets look the same."

"It does not matter a bit Mildred. When the rain stops and we have some sun, we are home again. Don't worry."

So be it. The slanting sleet was turning to rain. They slowed their pace and walked on looking as bedraggled as those who passed them in the other direction. The road terminated in a T at Rue Seine. They chose the southerly arm of the angled cross street and emerged into a square where seven spoked streets led at irregular angles in every direction. They chose one which seemed to travel south-east. The angles had confused them and they were actually travelling north-east. They came to a sign which said Rue Jacques. They

thought they were heading east now but in fact they were headed due north.
The pedestrian traffic around them had diminished to next to nothing. On
their right stood Notre Dame. It was ugly and glowering with its truncated
square topped towers. Out of compulsion they continued to hurry and hoping
to find some shelter from the cold they crossed Pont Notre Dame and entered a
morass of alleyways that carved narrow canyons out of the endless shops and
flats. They arrived at the entrance to an alley called Place Mibau. Davy pointed
at a recessed door ahead of them in the lee of the storm and they ran into the
shadows. Davy bumped directly into the large orange belly of a well-dressed
mud-spattered gentleman with a florid face.

"Well. My word. Pleased to meet you." said the gentleman. He spoke with a
clipped English accent. Mildred and Davy exhaled, waiting for their eyes to
adjust to the gloom.

"Who are you?" blurted Mildred with her chin stuck out and without
apology.

The gent smiled at the two youngsters standing in front of him, who were
soaking wet and shivering. "Well well. I am called Mr. Scrivener. Most
appropriate too. My name is my calling. Randolph, Arbuthnot, Scrivener,
correspondent for the Times of London, at your service."

When they burst into his alcove he had been making notes on his folio
which he now had under his arm. He wore a loose straight cut coat which was
bright red with eight brass buttons leading up each of his lapels. His wide cuffs
had two brass buttons and on each side of his loose coat was a large, flap
covered, bulging pocket. Bits of orange lining hung below the margin of his
coat which terminated at his knees. His white linen cravat was adorned on the
ends with a fringe. It was tied loosely about his throat so its tightness was
unlikely to contribute to his florid face. He was not wearing a wig. He wore a
large beaver felt hat cocked on three sides. His waistcoat was bright orange and
made of silk brocade. It opened with a vee below his stomach and strained at a
fatigued button. He wore bright red spatterdashes covering his legs down to his

low-heeled black shoes of soft leather closed with white buckles. Everything was covered with a pale mud spatter.

Davy and Mildred had never seen anything like it and they stood open mouthed before Mr. Scrivener. He saw them eye his writing. He tapped it. "Ah! Well you may wonder why I stand here writing on a day like this. This," he tapped again, "must go post-haste to my newspaper in London. Shall I read a bit to you? Hmm?" He wanted to hear how it scanned.

Davy nodded for the two of them. It would be a good idea to know what was going on.

Mr. Scrivener began. "This is what will appear in the Times of London in two days.

'Execution of Louis XVI King of the French.

At six o'clock on Monday morning, the KING went to take a farewell of the QUEEN and ROYAL FAMILY. After staying with them some time, and..'" He saw the look of disbelief and fear on the faces of the children.

"You did not know! These are terrible times."

Davy interjected. "Sir, can you tell us. What year and month is this?"

Scrivener did not answer. *Who are these strangers who do not know such a thing?* He looked at them for a moment longer and realized the rain had stopped and the air felt lighter. He pulled on his watch chain and withdrew a fat day-date watch and rubbed it on his sleeve to clean the lens.

"It is January 22, 1793 if I can read this blasted thing. Make the numbers so small. Well. I am off. I have to get these scribblings to the packet ship before nightfall. Good luck you two."

He strode out of the doorway holding his hat on his head with one hand and his folio in the other and turned southward, the way they had just come over the Pont Notre Dame. Davy and Mildred moved deeper into the recessed doorway. They slid down inside the alcove with their backs making wet marks against the closed door and hugged their knees for warmth.

"1793 Davy. They executed the king yesterday. The Terror is beginning and here we are in the middle of it. This is like being chased by Malveena Drago."

"Worse Mildred. She does not own a guillotine."

Mildred heard the distant sound first. It bounced around the alleyways and returned to bounce again. Davy heard it growing a few seconds later. It came from the south. The low pitched wooden clatter began to bounce and roll and build from the distance like the first thunder roll of an impending deluge. Wood striking stone, first a few clacks then more, then the deluge of hammering angry feet as the mob burst around the corner onto Place Mibau. The clacking of the wooden sabots on a thousand feet underpinned the roar of angry voices that grew to win the battle of tumult. They snarled their way past Davy and Mildred, intent on the twenty or thirty prisoners they beat and herded ahead of them. It was the mob from the Place De la Revolution tormenting the wealthy families on the way to the Bastille. Davy and Mildred flattened against the door in the alcove. The red blur of the same small Jacques whom Mildred had knocked down flew past the open doorway followed by his cohorts. The mob rushed on past them in a stream and the noise began to diminish and it was quiet. Mildred and Davy looked at each other knowing the worst was over and they smiled.

Suddenly a red Phrygian hat thrust itself into their doorway.

"Look here Jacques" said the man under the red hat back to his henchmen. "I see two chickens for the pot which the Citizens Committee has missed. You there." He stepped to the center of the doorway and opened his two hands toward them invitingly.

"Little sweeties. Come with us. You have a date with a friend of ours, I think. Come little dears. Have your shave with the national razor." The crowd laughed at the wit of the man under the red hat. They gathered around the opening at the doorway. They eyed Mildred and Davy who were wearing trousers. The cloth looked new and they were wearing shoes. Red hat's thugs were growing angry. Red hat resumed his presentation, designed to impress his coterie.

"Little dears, you have just missed your friends. They are a little ahead of you. Let us see if we can catch them up."

142

They grabbed Davy and Mildred and threw them into the muck of the refuse on the street. They picked them up by their hair and the seat of their pants and kicked them ahead. The Jacquerie pushed them up through the throng until they reached the front where the 20 struggling families staggered on. Their children had ceased to cry and they hung to their mother's skirts and their father's hands.

The drunken horde gaggled on, driven by a collective fury not understood by the furious. They entered Rue Antoine and the echo of the tumult weakened in the wider street and the mood was lighter now that the rain had stopped. The throng approached the Bastille. Davy and Mildred were numbed by cold and exhaustion. Their disbelief at the circumstance was etched on both children's faces. They shuffled on in silence ahead of their captors, mixed in with the twenty families, all to meet the same fate. They saw monster Bastille and five of its eight turrets as they turned left onto Rue Des Tournelles. It sat drowning in an eighty-foot-wide canal. It was built on a former swamp and a sickening methane gas smell permeated the dankness. The ringing of heavy bells tolled ten and Davy turned to the clock on the west tower of the Bastille. It had two chained prisoners carved into its face. The gate to the outer entrance on Rue Des Tournelles opened and swung back with a thud against the wall. The weight of pressure forward squeezed them through the street door and across an outer court which narrowed again to a drawbridge. They jostled over it, crossed the second drawbridge over the moat and into the Bastille.

The corridor was surprisingly bright. Light from the courtyard on the right fought through slits in the wall and illuminated the floor and showed up three open doors in the left wall. The prisoners were pushed one by one into each of the rooms with about 20 misfortunates in each room. Families were allowed to be together. Davy and Mildred were driven into the last of the three cells nearest the guard station. Mildred allowed herself to be swept along without complaint and tears began to roll down her cheek.

"Mildred. Don't worry. We have the pipe. The minute we have sun we are gone home."

"It is not that at all Davy. In seeing these poor families, I was thinking of my dad. No one knows where he and his men are. He could be in some place just like this one. Just like this. I fear it. How can he get out and come home?"

The prisoners were neither afraid not angry. They were not frantic nor combative. A gentle resignation had replaced those first emotions. A gentility had settled on them which brought guilt and shame to their captors. The door closed and the weight of noise disappeared in the distance. The cell walls were twelve feet thick and slits for light from ten feet above gave a forlorn finality to the stone. A surge of brightness came and went. Mildred whispered. "Davy. It looks as if it is brightening up."

Davy had seen the same thing. He felt a little energy from the pipe. "Yes. We need to wait just a bit."

The clock struck 10:30. Five bells thought Davy.

The eyes of the prisoners had acclimated to the reduced light and they had made small groups to be near their friends. Among them was the Marquis de Comte d'Artois, the brother of Louis XVI, the king of the French. The throng pressed itself more to the back of the cell than the space dictated and that puzzled Davy. He left the thought alone and enjoyed the small measure of privacy given to them by the distance of this separation. Davy and Mildred were just inside the door opening and listened to the guards.

"So Demolins. How goes the battle with you, eh?"

"Me, Citizen Pageau, a battle? Not much of a one hunh? Just business as usual. Mother is kissing many a pretty neck. Even some not so pretty. Ah well, someone has to die for someone else to live. Today D'Artois and the last of the D'Artois will embrace Mother Blood."

They both laughed in a drunken way. Each carried a half empty skin of Muscadet and the spilled residue of an early tug at the wine showed like blood on their shirts. Their job was not one for sober men who could see the fallacy of the raison d'etre of the whole mess.

Davy and Mildred looked back from the door to the families and the bewigged elderly huddling in the corners. They wondered which one was

D'Artois. They saw a mother scavenging patiently for lice in her son's hair. There was a lack of any fear or desperation. The pipe travelers drew some peace from the example. The clock struck 11:30. Seven bells.

Rhythmic and measured footsteps approached and the click of steel shod heels bounced down the corridor. Must be soldiers thought Mildred. They heard a scurry from the two jailers and they rattled at the door with a key. The multitude shrunk back and Mildred and Davy stood up in anxiety. Demolins stepped inside and scanned the lot with his glazed besotted eyes. He opened a toothless drooling smile and called with as much authority as he could muster.

"Marquis de Comte d'Artois. Come!"

Marquis de Comte d'Artois stood erectly and without fear. His hair was powdered and he was dressed in a dark green great coat, beige waistcoat and black breeches. He was not tall but he exuded stature. His wife the Marquise stepped forward and took his arm and together they walked forward serenely, yet they seemed to make haste. She spoke in an even unquavering voice.

"Let us go then. I believe our date is set for 12 noon."

Demolins thrust a quick hand to the doorjamb to stop them.

" Ah. Such a rush. Do not go empty handed. Let me retrieve your valuables for you."

He walked past them and pulled forward two pale and helpless children. He led them gently to their parents' hands. "Here. They will be better with you than left behind."

Subtle scuffling at the door revealed a military escort waiting in the corridor. The Marquis spoke to Demolins in a direct unemotional way and without rancor.

"Citizen, are you proud of the Terror? Proud and sure what you do here is correct?"

Citizen Demolins responded placidly with the words he heard every day on the street and they were words he believed.

"Terror is nothing more than justice; prompt, secure and inflexible."

The Marquis looked at the other man's face and he did not understand a blind adherence to such perversion. Holding hands, the couple and their two children were led away to the execution cart by a guard of eight soldiers. Through the open door Citizen Pageau croaked.

"Two more. We need six for the cart. Hurry it up." The crowd shrank against the back wall. Closest to the door were Davy and Mildred. I see. Be back as far away from the door as possible.

"You two." Mildred and Davy stood alone within Demolins' grasp. Demolins grabbed Mildred by the scruff of the neck and reclaiming the viciousness cowed by Marquis de Comte d' Artois, he threw her out through the cell door onto the stone corridor and tore the knee of her new jeans. She was furious. Davy attempted to intervene and they kicked down and booted him along the vaporous corridor toward the increasing light signaling the loading area for the fatal tumbrel. Pageau waited there. The four Aristocrats were in place and eight guards in formal parade regalia sat mounted on enormous war horses snorting and stomping in complaint against the lack of action and the percolating methane gas.

Pageau watched Davy and Mildred emerge from the gloom with Demolins whacking them from behind and he chortled. "Well, look here. Two more pretty necks to add color to the gutter."

Pageau put his veined bulbous nose one inch from Davy. He smiled a smile of hate at the richness of the boy's garb.

"There will be such a fight over those trousers my boy. However, you, I believe, will be looking the other way."

He smirked knowingly over to his pal and they chuckled at the little joke and Citizen Pageau began his shuffle back to his post at the cells. Demolins prodded the two kids into the back of the tumbrel They would be tipped out first and they would be first to the scaffold. Davy climbed up. As Mildred stepped up behind him something caught Demolins' eye. A quick shimmer bounced off the top of Mildred's plastic pouch protruding from her waist band. With avarice he ripped at it and pulled it out. The transparent pouch was a wonder. He had

146

seen glass and he had seen cloth, but this. It had no warp or weft and it was transparent. It was riches. He pulled it open and removed her notepad and threw it into the small puddle surrounding the tumbrel wheel. Mildred watched as the ink from her writing began to color the surface of the water. She was aghast at the loss of her pad. In a panic she rasped to Davy.

"Davy! He took my notepad. The bag. My notepad. All the notes on Malveena and Bully. In the pad. Gone."

Davy looked at Mildred and tipped his head in sympathy.

"Yes. I saw. Don't worry. Don't worry about it Mildred. Just think good thoughts and relax."

These few words terrified Mildred. Davy was trying to pretend things were good. That things were all right. He thinks we are going to the guillotine. She began to sob and caught herself and turned angry. No. Not me and not Davy.

The clock struck seven bells and Davy was not afraid. The Marquise had said the executions were at eight bells. 12 noon. It was 11:30 so they had thirty minutes and the cloud cover was thinning a little bit although the sun was not yet useful. The day was brightening and it was still close to freezing. The crowds were not deterred. They were waiting eagerly at the last exit gate onto Rue des Tournelles outside the Bastille. It soon proved not to be an advantage to be in the company of the brother of Louis XVl. The masses pressed around the tumbrel, cursing and spitting, wanting to tear or bite or cut a piece from the monsters in the cart. All therein were guilty of the same unnamed miseries and all must suffer. The guards looped their enormous horses in and out and bunted a wide swath against the spectators to keep the route clean and their cargo intact for the spectacle to come. The Marquis and Marquise had pulled the four children including Davy and Mildred inside them and they did their best to protect them from the mob.

The guillotine and its platform were about five miles west in Place de la Revolution. The route there from the Bastille was along the string of Quays running uninterrupted from the foot of Rue Petit Muse to the Quay de la Conference. Once there they would enter the south gate opposite the Pont de la

147

Revolution and move directly to the guillotine. The throng was already there by the thousands and clamoring for justice. A battalion of soldiers was there as well. The Marquis was a big fish. Forty barrels of free red wine had arrived two hours ago by wagon and the cobbles were running purple. The day seemed warmer. Souvenirs such as small guillotines were big sellers and locks of hair purported to be from executed aristocracy sold well too. Guillotine earrings and bracelets were everywhere. Steeped in wine, justice and fraternity, the people sang sweet republican songs of mayhem and revenge under their soft Phrysian caps.

The tumbrel had reached the Louvre, about a mile from the final destination. Mildred saw lights in the Louvre Palace. *Hunh! Another ball flirting dancing may I have this dance mademoiselle I am sorry my card is full oh how droll you are monsieur.* They had just passed Place Mibau where they had run into Mr. Scrivener and Davy smiled at the memory.

Mildred looked over. "What?"

"Scrivener," said Davy. Mildred smiled.

Davy was not afraid. He was thoughtful. I wanted to see the horse guard and the mobs kept at bay but not from this side of the horses. He was on the way to his end and there was so much left undone. Mildred's father was missing and he was probably a captive like them. They needed to free him. Bully and Malveena had to be stopped and now the notepad was gone. The plant was closing and Mr. Foster was missing and he could help if they could find him. Davy's dad and Mildred's mother would be out of work and they would have to sell their houses. The library was to be torn down for casino parking. Malveena was after their skins and here they were riding a tumbrel on the way to the guillotine. What a mess this is Dopo. Dopo concurred.

Mildred interrupted his thoughts. "Davy, I have to ask you. Now. What did you feel. I mean what was all around you in the floating. You know."

Davy knew what she meant by all around. It surrounded him from the first. He thought for a minute.

"You know Mildred, it was like a source of pure goodness. You know? It was like getting caught in a draught but not the same. It did not come in the window from somewhere and blow over you and go its own way, it made you part of it and took you. It helped you in a golden warm and special way just for you, you know?"

Mildred looked at Davy with a sublime peaceful face and turned away. "Yes, that was it exactly." They were quiet in in their own thoughts and somewhat in each other's thoughts too.

The heavy square tumbrel horse ignored the incline and trundled up the slope and tipped onto the flat of the Place de la Revolution. A barrage of brilliant color hammered Davy and Mildred's eyes and jangled their senses. The sullen monochromatic trip through the cold wet city was expunged. The cavalry controlled the space and it moved at a measured pace in a widening circle to force back the clamoring crowd. Their horses had begun a sweat and they glistened despite the dull light. The lieutenant of the horse guard pivoted perfectly on his horse holding his position to the right of the guillotine. It was he who would give the signal for the drop of the blade. A huge 2-foot red plume arched back from the left of each gold combat helmet and bobbed in time with the trot. The helmet was secured by a wide gold chin strap and a black plume curled forward in the Roman style. They sat on black saddles over red blankets and were uniformed in black with gold stripes running down their pant legs. Their jackets were tight and black and they wore high necked red vests cinched at the waist with a 3-inch-wide red belt. 12 Brass buttons led down the chest to a large gold buckle. A wide gold strap buckled over a shoulder and under their sword arm which had a red cuff above a white leather glove. Battle sabers were held at a 45° angle, ready for action. At the foot of the steps leading to the guillotine was a squad of blue clad infantrymen. Their black knee-high leather boots were mirror polished and the white crossed straps on their backs were immaculate. Their guns were primed and eager to fire.

Four blue and white clad drummers stood erect below their tricolor cockades and continued their percussion facing directly to the guillotine. Opposite them

149

was the Lieutenant of the Execution. He held in his left hand the rope he pulled to the release the blade. He watched and waited for the Lieutenant of the Horse Brigade to give him the signal to act by sweeping downward and pointing at him with his Sabre. The Lieutenant of the Execution placed his back against the platform and faced the drum corps. He would not watch the shave of the National Razor.

Above, one break appeared in the clouds. Some blue sky showed and closed but no-one saw it. The clatter of hooves on the cobbles was constant and rhythmic and hypnotic. The drums and trumpets were deafening and they flattened the senses. Davy scanned the gloom in hopes of the sun. As he looked up, one taste of light pierced the changing clouds as a tease and then it retreated under cover. Then he saw them above and he knew, but how long would it take. Gulls. Seagulls were in Paris and floating over the Seine. The weather front was leaving and the gulls always understood it before it happened. They were already riding the changing thermals. Open sky was happening somewhere and eventually it would be there too but how much time did he and Mildred have. The thunder of the bells at the Abbey of Saint-Germain-des-Prés began pealing the first of twelve. 8 bells. The watch was over.

The trumpets blazed in the Place de la Revolution and the rattle of the snare drums made hearts beat and the crowd went mad. It was the time of execution.

The cart carrying the prisoners approached the steps leading up to the platform and stopped. Mildred and Davy clutched each other and each of them wept. At this momentary lull, a crone, half dressed and besotted, broke through with maniacal fury. She slashed with her bony taloned hand at anything D'Artois. She latched onto Mildred's hair and tore a clump from above her ear. Mildred shrieked and put her hand to her head.

"I got one, I got one!" screamed the hag. The crowd roared its approval and it spat toward the six captives. Through the disorder a shirtless small girl approached unnoticed with a bauble proffered in her outstretched hand. She came to the edge of the cart and offered it to Mildred who had her eyes closed. Davy smiled and took the small effort of sympathy from her.

"Thank you."

It was an earring in the shape of a guillotine. He reached under his waistband into his leather sheath, dropped in the earring and left the flap open.

The tumbrel had split the squad of infantry into two ordered ranks. It tipped down abruptly to the back and spilled out its passengers in a heap and the crowd roared their enjoyment of the indignity. The cart-horse moved away the second it felt the release of the weight and left a sticky double wheeled track on the wine-soaked stone. Special boxes with ornate balustrades sat fully occupied by those capable of paying for tickets to the best seats. The rabble watched from 50 feet away.

The elevated platform had eight open plank steps with a railing on each side. On the platform a priest waited and two Citizens stood at the blade to assist with positioning the prisoner. The executioner had arrived early in order to strut. It was he who would dispatch the Marquis de Comte d'Artois. Two burly Citizens manned the foot of the stairs. They grabbed and held Mildred and Davy securely. Both children were too overcome and stunned to resist. Under her breath Mildred said only, "Razor. National Razor." The Marquis de Comte d'Artois also spoke. Calmly and with a tone of final relief he said, "Madame la Guillotine."

Davy and Mildred attempted to ascend the stairs together and they held hands.

"One at a time my fine little chicken," said the guard as he jerked Davy and Mildred apart and cuffed Mildred back to the base of the stairs. With his bad teeth and drunken shark eyes he smiled sardonically at Davy as they moved up the stairs and along the platform. He and the executioner exchanged sullen "Jacques." A few gulls swooped through looking for a handout and fled from the noise. One even had a few red feathers on its chest.

Davy was removed from the reality around him. The bells of Saint-Germain-des-Prés had stopped their death knell and the time had come.

His mind was happy and clean of worry and he carried an intrepidity of innocence. He looked back at Mildred at the base of the steps, standing there alone in stoic defiance. The sweating war horses continued their hypnotic trotting dance over the cobbled track and he felt his knees go down, solid on the platform and he saw the head stock swing up and he felt it swing down and nestle on his neck. He gazed his last gaze and it was beautiful. White and red chested gulls swooping past, the light gleaming off the golden helmets, the sabers flashing in the sun...

He thrust his hand into his sheath and whipped out his pipe. The guard to his left smashed the copper thing from his hand, propelling it in a fast spin against the platform. It bounced six feet in the air and spun like a propeller and shone like a thousand gems as the sun caught its sheen. The two guards at the base of the stairs were watching the sport on the platform and did not watch Mildred. They were accustomed to placid docility from their victims and they did not expect this child to bolt. She was up the steps before they could move and dived for the pipe that was spinning like a top, two feet from the blade of the guillotine. She thrust the pipe to her eye, and made a deep cut with it. She stretched for Davy and grasped his ankle. Bleeding, she held on with all her might and rolled over to the sun. The Cavalry sabre dropped and the Lieutenant pulled the rope and the blade hurtled to its target and a blinding flash stunned the crowd. The impact of the heavy blade echoed off the cobblestones but there was no satiated roar. The executioner looked down at the quiet blade shining at the closed headstock and nothing was there. The two D'Artois were gone.

The fire in the pipe roared like a blast furnace and covered Davy and Mildred with safety and smooth acceptance. They goldened home with a blessing from pure intention and they were warmed and caressed to the old bridge over the Borstal river. The miasmic unreality was quick to leave Davy and he looked for Mildred. She was still its prisoner and she had not yet cleared the agglutinating mass. She was lying on the ground with a death grip on his ankle, holding Davy's pipe in the other hand clutched to her hair.

Mrs. Craft looked out the screen door and saw the two young friends walking toward her. Mildred had forgotten about the bouquet of wild flowers from the banks of the Borstal. Davy seemed to be examining Mildred's hair at the side of her head.

"Hello you two. Davy what are you looking for on Mildred's head?"

"Lice" said Davy. They all laughed.

"You are back earlier than I thought. Where did you go?"

In unison they said, "Paris."

Helen Craft shook her head, knowing better than to expect a straight answer. Mrs. Craft said to both of them. "Fine. I don't suppose you have done your homework."

Chapter 12: Tilt Is Recruited

Davy was up early and he was looking forward to seeing Mildred at school. He pulled his belt and pipe down from the hook at the back of his closet and a rattle in the pipe reminded him. The little guillotine earring was in there. Davy undid his belt and put it on the bed with its sheath and opened the flap and dumped out the earring. It was small and intricately carved and it was a perfect little guillotine. He looked at it carefully and thought sadly of the shirtless waif whom had given them her sympathy at the tumbrel. He sat the earring on his dresser top, to the right of the shard of Nelson's medal. Spider.

Davy walked into the classroom five minutes before the opening bell. He was still hearing the clatter of the sabots and the roll of the drums bouncing off cobblestones. *Dopo, my ears are still ringing.* Dopo did not hear what he said. Davy stopped in the doorway and inhaled deeply. The dust bane wafted its oily perfume throughout the closed hot room and the reek of geraniums was the best thing he had ever smelled. It smelled like a homecoming. He said Hello to Mr. Tilt.

"Hello Mr. Tilt. Hill."

No-one ever said hello to their teacher and neither did Davy but today he did. Tilt looked up and angled out to test gravity as he watched Davy standing closely beside his seat. What was that kid up to.

Mildred was already there as usual and she was tapping on a notepad with her pen and wearing black circular spectacles.

"Mildred. I did not know you wore glasses."

Mildred looked at Davy as if he were an idiot.

"I don't", and she returned to her notepad.

"What do you mean you don't. You are."

"I am not."

"Mildred! I see you. I see them. How can you say you do not, that you are not wearing glasses!"

Languidly, Mildred scratched an itchy spot at her eyelid the easiest way she knew, by putting her finger through the lens opening and rubbing her eyelid.

Davy blinked. "You don't have any glass in there."

"Correct." She scratched the other eye the same way with a finger through the opening for the lens. "Hence I am not wearing glasses. I am wearing frames. Pure frames. I like the look of them and I never have to clean off my fingerprints."

"Mildred. Really. That is like saying you bought a car without an engine and the big advantage is you don't have to put in gas."

"Precisely." Mildred responded with a nod as if he not only agreed with her but had proved her point. That was as deep as Davy wanted to get. The pad on Mildred's desk seemed to be a bullet point reconstruction of the conversation they had overheard between Bully and Malveena. Good idea.

It was the morning of the term exam on European history and Tilt had his papers ready to go as the bell rang. The squeal of skidding feet turned everyone's head to the door. Porky Gregious arrived as if shot from a cannon and he skidded his way to his seat, covered in perspiration. Mr. Hill gave Porky the Tilt look and Porky chameleoned to deep pink. As he watched, Davy inadvertently remained standing.

"So, Mr. Pilcher, you are standing. Sir David, I suppose you are standing in order to elucidate some exotic travel you have made. We remember the last time. I believe it was Spain." He turned to the class. "We all remember that, don't we?"

They did and they sneered. They had been cheated of watching Davy in trouble.

"Where is it this time then?" Mr. Tilt looked at the class as an invitation to share his bit of fun. Porky joined in by clapping his hands, happy to have the focus elsewhere.

Mildred had not been paying attention. The 'Where is it this time then?' question pulled her out of her reverie. Too quickly, too strongly and in perfect unison with Davy she said 'Paris'. They all stared. Mildred wiggled a finger to an eyelid through a lens hole and Davy stood with exaggerated aplomb. Tilt half believed the two of them. Maybe more than half.

" Ah! I believe Paris is nice this time of the year." He waited for them to respond but they did not. " Sit Davy."

It was not a difficult exam. It was his attempt at stimulating interest in a subject which taught much and was first in Mr. Tilt's heart. The class was finished the test in good time except for Davy and Mildred who were scribbling furiously when time was called. They were not children looking to pad an answer, they were spilling out knowledge.

Tilt walked home under the enormous and heavy brown chāta he carried against the sun. Thirty years ago, a friend in India had given the umbrella to him as a gift and despite its weight he had it with him always when he walked. Tonight, he also carried two examination packets. He had seen the faces of Mildred and Davy as they worked on their papers. He was sure he was fantasizing but he had to satisfy himself.

The kettle worked up to a boil. He walked into his den with the steaming brew and sat behind his scarred desk. It had been around the world with him. He had not repaired the corner splintered by a stray bullet in Afghanistan. The desk had saved his life. Behind him on the wall was a series of discolored photos made pale and rippled by the heat and cold and wet of the jungle and the desert. He was built for that life and it claimed a part of him which longed to pump his blood.

He sipped his Chai tea slowly. He read and re-read the papers. He had never read as detailed and intimate a description as Davy's commentary on Admiral Nelson and the action on the Victory. The almost identical exposition done on La Belle Epoch by Davy and Mildred was without equal. He sat quietly studying the grainy residue at the bottom of his stained teacup and pondered the impossible. He doubted the fantastical conclusion at which he had arrived. He would speak to them about it tomorrow. They must talk.

Tilt spent a sleepless and excited night. At the end of the following day, he collared Davy and Mildred as they left his classroom.

"You two, please come and see me. Just for a minute."

They entered his office with caution. It was stuffed with worn and fingered books from floor to ceiling, some of them in piles defying gravity much like himself. He gestured for them to be seated opposite him. The chairs were deep brown polished leather and slippery and over time the leather had stiffened and contracted from little use. The padding was bunched up at the back and Davy started sliding forward and jammed his feet down to stay fixed. Mildred sat pigeon-toed in total comfort and removed her frames and held them elegantly to the right as she had seen done on a magazine page.

Tilt unfolded himself from his chair and walked to the door and closed it. He returned to his chair and sat down with his hands hanging loosely inside his legs and he allowed them to dangle there. He scanned the faces of the children sitting opposite him, looking for the subtle muscle activity which betrays falseness. He saw none of it. He looked down with a solemn face trying to penetrate the fog of impossibility which covered his desk and confronted his intellect. He believed these children implicitly. The old man's voice was softer than they had heard it.

"This will not take very long. First, your examination papers were astounding. Thank you for those. Your insight to and accounts of both Nelson at Trafalgar and the apparently shared perspective on the horror of the Parisian Jacquerie were tops. Better than I have read anywhere. It is as if you were there. In fact, I believe you were there. Don't say anything. I don't know how you do it and I don't know why you do it but I know why I would do it. I cannot imagine the richness of choice and the delight and satisfaction to speak with Aristotle, to stand on Ararat, or to run with Tecumseh. Think of it. The Oracle of Delphi. Imagine, just imagine for one moment, walking through the war room in a fog of Churchillian cigar smoke or standing side by side with Motecuhzoma against the Spaniards."

Tilt's whole being longed for a return to the fray. He glowed with the fervor of his longing.

"The prospect is more than I can fathom."

He abandoned his zeal and became serious.

"You should understand I have spoken to no one of this and I shall not speak to anyone with regard to it. Now, please tell me I am not wrong."

Davy and Mildred did not say a word. They had not expected anyone to take them seriously even though being taken seriously was what they wanted. If they could really convince Tilt, they had an ally to go after Malveena and Bully and stop the plant from closing. They exchanged glances. They needed to confer.

Mildred knew exactly what to do. She put on her frames to impress with her seriousness and spoke quietly. "Mt. Til.. Hill, sorry. Mr. Hill, may Davy and I have a moment alone?"

He raised and lowered his right bushy brow in half a second of surprise. "Of course. And by the way, 'Tilt' is fine. "

He stayed seated and they looked at him and waited.

"Oh, I see." He got up and stepped outside and closed the door behind himself and stood in the corridor. Amazing. They have just tossed me out of my own office.

Inside Tilt's office Mildred leaned to Davy. "Davy, this is really good. We want his help to convince people and we don't want him to tell on us either. We can kill two birds in the bush."

Davy angled his head at Mildred. She was the master of the mixaphor. She continued unfazed. "He talked about Aristotle and Ararat. He talked about the Oracle of Delphi. It is simple. We will take him."

She smiled at her own brilliance. She loved the conniving. Davy sat back in a posture of reflexive refusal, after all it was his pipe. Also, Mildred seemed to have forgotten on their last escapade she had come within two minutes of having her head cut off. As the possibilities impressed him one by one and removed his resistance, he saw the genius of it. Tilt cannot reveal the consciousness of the light and its communion through the pipe without also confirming what we said was possible and what we overheard was real. 'Indeed yes, the kids could certainly penetrate the security at Foster Industries and get in and out in a flash of light.'

"Mildred, that is brilliant." She knew it was. "Let's get him back in."

Davy jumped to Tilt's office door and opened it. Tilt was sitting against the far wall with an idyllic look on his face. Davy said nothing as Tilt came in, when he realized he and Mildred had not agreed on a destination.

Mildred took over. "Mr. Hill, Mr. Tilt. We are undecided and we are not sure what we will do about this, but I tell you now, you are not wrong." Davy and Mildred rose together and said a simple "Goodbye." They left without haste and Freddy, Hill, Tilt, watched them go. He was already making travel plans.

Chapter 13: The Ghoul at Woodstock

Davy leaned over the stone bridge railing and looked down into the water of the Borstal river, waiting for Mildred. The water was clear and shallow and hypnotic as it looped its gentle way down to its estuary two miles south. As usual he was looking for bass around the weeds in the shadows of the bridge pilons and as usual he did not spot any. A small school of fingerlings showed silver and panicked at his shadow and fled into the reeds. There was a light wind from the southwest and it carried singing to him. Mildred waved hello to Davy as she approached and he waved back. Mildred seemed to be practicing some kind of dance step as she walked and she was turned a little sideways as she stepped to the beat, off the road and up onto the bridge. She was in a semi bop mode and was singing something Davy thought was Proud Mary. She closed her hand and put it to her mouth, pretending she was holding a microphone.

"But I never saw, the good side of the city, till I hitched a ride on a riverboat queen."

"I like that one. Creedance Clearwater Revival, right?"

"Yep. My mom was just playing the Woodstock album again."

"Woodstock. We said we were going to go there didn't we. These days I would go anywhere just not to be here. That Malveena is nuts and I think she is serious. I'm going to get a rear-view mirror."

Mildred laughed. "Not a bad idea. Where will you attach the bolts?" They sniggered.

Davy was nodding. "I think we should go. It was a lot of fun in those old days I think. Happy people and good music. Can you imagine Malveena Drago at Woodstock? Mean, pale and raging?"

"Enough with the Malveena. I think we should see Woodstock as soon as we can. CCR. Remember, time and tide gather no moss."

Davy blinked a couple of times. He could not argue with that. Little Dopo shook his head.

Mildred carried on. "By the way, sorry I am late. There was a fence in the way and I had to climb over it."

She was later than she had expected to be. Her latest route through the fields was slower going. It was the first time she had used it and there were some burdock burrs sticking to her pants. She brushed at them but nothing came off so she began picking them one by one.

Mildred had taken to developing new routes to and from school and to and from the bridge. She was not going to let Malveena Drago have her way. Mildred had calculated combinations of paths she could take through various fields, down particulars streets and then alternative paths through wooded areas so she would use the same route only once every 43 days. Malveena would not find any habitual place to nab Mildred. Today she had traveled by the Borstal woods. There were 36 appropriately spaced trees on the side she entered. She used a different numbered space every time so no tell-tale entry would be trodden down. Weeds and grasses and the like would have time to regrow. When crossing planted fields, she used a different angle and a different exit point for each trip. Nothing was trampled enough to make a trail. She changed the times she agreed to meet Davy as well. Her route along the river was different every day also. If she were throttled by Malveena it would not be because Mildred had been predictable.

The two friends walked 30 yards or so back over the burm at the river bank into a circular clearing. In case Malveena was patrolling they were not visible there from the bridge. They surprised a flock of gulls tucked away from a storm the birds knew was coming. Davy and Mildred agreed from then on, they must meet at the woods or in a similar spot away from dangerous eyes.

Davy flipped open the sheath covering his pipe and pulled it free. He put out his hand to join with Mildred and she did not react.

"Can I do it?"

" Do what?"

"The pipe of course. You know, make it go."

Davy had never considered this. It was his pipe. He had a look of stupefaction on its face.

"Make it go? It isn't a question of making it go."

He was buying time to think of a good reason to say no. He was about to embark on some circuitous logic but he stopped. Maybe that is not a bad idea. Mildred did use it once and she cut her eye. She should have more practice. It would be good if she didn't have to worry about it. Davy relaxed and looked directly at her which he seldom did.

"You know, I think that is a good idea. Good." He looked at her again. "You cut your hair."

Mildred had cut her hair very short three days ago and Davy had just noticed it. She was not surprised at that. Davy never noticed anything, but she was surprised and even disappointed at his quickness of agreement she could use his pipe. *I have constructed elegant rationales and I have perfected them in their most persuasive forms to evoke a positive response and he didn't let me use them. Well I shall save them for something else.* He handed off the pipe to Mildred and she was not nervous. She took his hand in hers and leaned back to the sun with the pipe at her eye. A galactic flash of gold spun them through the stars and coddled them softly onto 600 acres of rolling farmland near a place called Woodstock New York.

Davy stood immobile and looked down at the sea of oozing muck flowing slowly over the tops of his shoes. It had slimed through his socks and he found himself wiggling his toes to squish the ooze a little and test the reality of the gunk. The flash from the pipe had been enormous and the time in gelatinous suspension of non-involvement had shortened from minutes to just a few seconds. Mildred stood next to him in the slop with his pipe in her hand and held Davy's hand in an iron grip with the other. He saw she was still separated from the place and the time and had not yet received the blast of consciousness which would make her real. She had made the trail fewer times than Davy and she was still waiting for her clarity. He waited protectively and stepped a little closer. Mildred started hard as the wave of today hit her and her arms shot out to her sides for balance. She did not seem to be able to move her feet. She smiled quickly as she entered reality and saw Davy and then stopped smiling just as quickly. It was pouring rain and cold. They were up to their ankles in mucilaginous clay. Her polished brown walking shoes were below the surface. They each took two sucking steps toward each other and wondered if they had made a mistake. Lying next to Davy on her back in the mud was a girl in a tie-dyed shirt. She was looking directly up into the rain with a smile of total bliss and contentment. She laid there half buried in the mud. They looked at each other in disbelief. So this was Woodstock. Davy took back his pipe.

They stood motionless in the pouring rain and looked around slowly. They saw an enormous natural amphitheater shaped like a bowl in the middle of a sloping field. Around them, behind them and before them sat, stood, slept and danced more people than they had seen in one place in their lives. Mildred extended one arm and prodded Davy slowly and got feedback. Yes, he was solid, this was happening and here they were. And no music.

They began to explore. Mildred walked behind him to use his tracks to protect her shoes. They had no idea of where they were going, lost in the half million. They came to two wooden signposts nailed to a tree. Written in chalk on one of them was 'Groovy Way' with arrows pointing two ways. The other sign was equally unhelpful. It said 'Gentle Path'. Below that was an arrow pointing left which said 'High Way.' Mildred suggested they investigate 'High Way' but Davy could see no apparent road and he shook his head. Ahead of them was a toothless man in a Smokey the Bear outfit who warned the crowd if they made trouble they would be doused in fizzy water.

Davy walked around the corner of a bright yellow tent and thumped into a tall dude with spangled white pants, carrying a guitar. At the impact the dude dropped one of his guitar picks and swiped at it and missed. Davy picked it up quickly and handed it to him.

"Keep it Kid. I have a hundred of them. Plus, I am not going on until the rain stops. With all those wires and all that water, a cat could get electrocuted."

He laughed and tousled Davy's hair and walked past with a little jangle, moving in time to the music in his head, humming something. The pick was embossed with a JH entwined. JH thought Davy. Well. Not knowing who JH was, he dropped the small plastic pick into his pipe sheath. He watched Jimi Hendrix disappear around the corner of a green tent and he mimicked the walk. Mildred was watching Davy.

"What are you doing? You don't usually walk like that."

"No, but I'm going to from now on. I like it."

" I would not do it if I were you." She left it at that.

Mildred dropped back a bit and Davy practiced the walk as they moved on but somehow, he could not get the hang of it. He would turn his mind to it another time. The two stood quietly among half a million people but they did not go unnoticed.

The man was soaking wet and his tie-dyed shirt was skintight from the rain. His long grey ponytail hung limply and water dripped from it down his back. He stood 50 feet away, his iceberg blue eyes riveted by what he saw. Quietly he watched. He angled around to get a better look and then sidled back to a position out of their view. He saw the girl wore Hilfiger jeans. He was sure the boy had a Nike swoop on his shoes and if the man was not mistaken the boy had a small alligator on his shirtfront. With a troubled mind he began to rotate the signet ring on the third finger of his right hand slowly, brushing his fingertips over the worn compass and square and it settled him. What on earth are you two doing here. They were out of the time and they were on their own. He moved to about ten feet above them on the side of the hill. He moved down closer and hung back until he saw them squeezed to the margin of the crowd. He turned sideways to keep his footing as he short-stepped carefully down the incline and reached level ground three feet behind them.

Two strong hands grabbed Mildred and Davy by their shirt collars and jerked them off of their feet and dragged them backwards. They made a trail of four neat furrows with their dragged feet and the slime built up and ran in at the heel and filled their shoes as they flailed with their arms. Two large footprints separated their furrows and they heard puffing breaths of the exertion in dragging them uphill. They squirmed but could not get free. Abruptly, they were stood up and spun around. "You two. What are you doing here!"

They were speechless. Davy realized with a rush of adrenalin they did not have tickets. He looked up at the large man standing slightly above them on the slope with hands on his hips and concern on his face. He was not angry. He was perturbed.

"Well.., you see, we..." Davy stopped and stared at the piercing blue eyes in the face in front of him. He looked at Mildred. She was blinking and she was frightened. Davy looked back at the big old man.

"You are Charles Abernathy Foster. From the painting. Foster, on the wall."

Davy looked away from the blue eyes to the tie-dyed shirt, the open-toed shoes filled with muck and the long pony tail in Foster's hair.

"But different" added Davy.

The grey-haired man was startled and laughed altogether but he did not deny it. "How in the blazes do you know that?"

"I see you every day at school. Hung on the wall. Your eyes. It is you isn't it!"

Foster smiled at the question. "Well, young man, it is true, I am certainly me. And you are also correct in that I am Charles Foster. Now my turn. Who are you two and how the blazes did you get here."

Davy explained the pieces of pipe Mr. Rickman had cut, the treasure trove of books in his father's small library, daydreaming in class about the battle of Trafalgar, looking through his pretend telescope and just like that he was on the deck of the HMS Victory. He had no idea why it worked.

The storm clouds above rumbled with thunder and a chant went up: 'No rain, no rain, no rain.' Thousands began to sing 'We shall overcome'.

Charles Foster glanced toward the singers and then back at Davy.

"So, you found in one lazy schoolroom gaze, by accident, what it has taken me thirty years of experimentation to determine. You are a marvel. Would you like to know how it 'works' as you put it?"

Together their eyes opened widely and in unison they said "Yes."

"This is the key to it. Light has a consciousness and intention of its own and it acts faster than the speed of light." He gave them a moment to hear it.

"Davy, when you arrived on the deck of HMS Victory, it was exactly as you intended. It was not after the battle was done that you landed on the deck or before the ship was launched. The light already knew whether you were arriving exactly as you intended. Its consciousness had to scope out the situation before it arrived there as light, to be sure it was OK to land you there. It was sure the situation was correct before it landed there. It has to make up its mind whether your intention is satisfied, faster than it delivers itself and you there. You see? It had already intended itself there and confirmed the correctness of the situation before your intention took you there at the speed of light."

They were not sure.

"You have traveled here, you rode the trail as you put it. But you now know the light had already intended it and you simply participated in its intention. You did not create it, you participated. The light already has an intention for every place and every possibility. I did not say for every time as you probably noticed. Intention obliterates time. That is why there is a derangement in the relationship between how long you are away when you ride the trail, let's say 10 days, and the fact those 10 days represent only 1 hour away from home. Do you understand? The light has a consciousness of everything. I do not say "everything" loosely. I mean every and all things for all time."

Mildred and Davy looked at each other. They did understand. They were astounded by what they understood. Charles Foster could see wonderment on the faces of the two children listening to him.

Mildred asked. "So that means we have no choices? That everything is already determined?"

"No, it is just the reverse. You may choose to intend a certain thing or never intend that thing, but the consciousness of the light has already prepared the intention for anything you might choose. It may be used by you, it may not be used by you, your choice. Whatever you choose, the consciousness of the light has already intended that very thing and all things and you just have to ride the trail." He saw their uncertainty.

"There is a book you might read. If you read it and really think about its contents, it will answer most questions you will have about, well, anything." Davy and Mildred looked at each other. Mildred hoped she got the library copy first.

"It is called the Dancing Wu Li Masters."

Davy gasped. "My father has that book. I see the name every time I go to his study. Orange cover with a wheel of legs like spokes going around an open center. Right there beside Man and Superman."

Mildred pursed her lips. Again, he has the book.

"Good. One last comment. There is something much larger. There is a larger consciousness the light is part of. The photon, the particle, however they describe light these days, has to know everything everywhere ahead of time. It must be conscious of every choice, everywhere and for all time. If you intend to go to Oslo Norway it has to know exactly what exists in Oslo to place you there correctly in the present. If you trail back to an earlier time in Oslo, it must be conscious of exactly what was there then and what existed, or if you take the trail to years ahead, it must be conscious right now of what will happen then and there in the future. If not, it could not satisfy your intention. But not just with you. It has to have a consciousness of every possible intention, of every individual, through the entire universe, now, before, and forever."

Foster put out his hand to Davy. "May I see the pipe?"

Davy clutched his holster. He had never surrendered it to any adult and he was wary, even of Charles A. Foster.

"Uh, not, not right now." Foster was impressed with the caution of the young man.

"Well. That is understandable. Look here. This is the one I use."

He drew a pipe which looked identical to Davy's from his zippered front pantleg pocket. He held it out to them with his pipe resting across his two open hands. Foster's pipe was greened and dulling from handling, with the patina leaving just a few areas of brilliance on the surface.

The smell of cooking beans was everywhere and they were hungry. They heard a stumble and muttering as a careening young man wearing clay thickened sandals staggered at them and bent his face over Foster's outstretched hands and stared at the pipe, attempting to focus. His headband was askew and it had slid down at an angle to cover part of one eye. He had seen many pipes and he was sure this was a new high waiting to happen, and all shiny too. He toted a soggy book which he attempted to keep dry in an armpit. He looked up at Foster. Foster looked important. He could tell. Another autograph from somebody who is important. He whipped out the wet book and offered it.

"Hey man, can I have your autograph?"

In a slight of hand magician-like move, Foster had the pipe back in his pocket and zippered in one second. Rather than refuse the autograph and make an explanation, Charles nodded once with a smile and pulled his pen from his left shirt pocket. Davy noticed the beautiful old-style nib pen with the Foster monogram done in gold script on its top as Foster prepared to write.

"That is a beautiful pen Mr. Foster."

"Thank you. It is my favorite. I always use it for important things. Important things such as signing this gentleman's autograph page."

He turned to the young autograph hound and to a page full of wet bleeding signatures. With a flourish and a couple of arm pumps to get his non-existent shirt cuffs out of the way, he brandished his beautiful signing pen and scrawled a deep signature into the autograph book.

"Cool. Thanks dude." He left one sandal behind in the slime and staggered on in search of the next somebody.

"Mr. Foster, why are you here?" asked Davy. "Why in this crazy place with all the rain and the sludge and the wasted people?" Davy had picked up on the jargon and threw in wasted for hipness. Charles Foster smiled.

"Well Davy, for a simple reason which may surprise you. I simply wanted to see Janis Joplin. I saw videos of her, I have listened to the energy of her music and I just think she is special. I never saw her at the time. She only lived to 27 I think it was. So, I intended and focused and let the light take me and here I am. Along with another 500,000 Janis fans, I am waiting. And you? "

Davy felt sheepish. "Creedance Clearwater Revival."

Foster just nodded. He understood. Mildred had not been listening.

She was watching the stage where there seemed to be some renewed activity. Maybe a band was coming on but more likely one more request for patience and a promise things were about to happen. The crowd did not care. The existence of this event was an entertainment of its own and a statement of the times all in itself. If a band was coming, sometime, anytime, they would wait. They watched the stage. A gaffer tied down a cable and exited stage right. They cheered.

Davy was uncomfortable he had not told Mr. Foster the other reason for being at Woodstock. Anywhere was better than in the grasp of Malveena. He wanted to disclose everything. Charles Abernathy Foster was here for music and nostalgia and not for the heavy news of things back home. Still, Foster was the victim of a forged power of attorney, Malveena was involved in it all and who knew when they would fall into her clutches. This was the time to reveal all to the man in the painting.

Davy began a torrent.

"Mr. Foster please listen. You have to know this, you should know what is happening. First came the notice Foster Industries was closing next April, a few weeks ago Mildred's mother was laid off permanently."

He pointed.

"That is Mildred, her father is missing. Malveena Drago and Bully Gregious are fiddling with their shares, his shares your shares, all shares I think but they can't do anything without your power of attorney so they forged one and a casino is taking the property and the car park is going where the library is and we have to stop it you can stop it."

Davy took a deep breath, preparing for his next stream of consciousness.

"Slow down Davy. We have plenty of time. Don't forget a day here is just a few minutes back home."

Davy described their detective work and the eavesdropping through the vent, that they recorded the actions of Drago and Gregious and that Malveena heard them and about their narrow escape from her at Mullett's funeral. Mildred jumped in. "And the Jacquerie took my note pad at the guillotine." Foster did not ask.

Davy and Mildred were vibrating with emotion. Charles Foster understood they were excited to see him and they would ask him for his help but some overarching worry was showing through from them. Foster could see they were wanting something else. They were scared.

"Now slowly Mildred, tell me what else is happening."

"Malveena Drago is trying to kill us."

Foster's face did not betray surprise but it seemed to toughen at the mention of Malveena.

"That is bad news. Malveena is a different animal and a very clever and vicious one. I believe it will not be long before she understands the use of the pipe. She may understand it even now and she is a woman of action." Foster scanned the hillside as if he half expected to see her. Mildred and Davy nodded fast and emphatically at Malveena being a different animal.

"Mr. Foster, we try to stay in the open where Malveena has to be careful about going after us. There are always people around school as witness and she really does not know where we kids go otherwise. But suppose Mr. Foster, she had her own pipe. She could just chase us, no matter where we were. We couldn't hide in the woods, we couldn't go anywhere without her being able to get us."

Mildred became more worried as she said the actual words she had not wanted to face. It had the same effect on Davy. They reflexively moved closer to each other.

Foster saw this. "I understand your concern. There is one thing though. The consciousness of the light understands these sorts of things."

Mildred spoke quietly. "I don't understand what you mean Mr. Foster. Sorry."

"It is like this Mildred. The light's innate purity has a built-in filter against mean-mindedness and malice. There are all possible intentions for every person for every circumstance for all time, but the consciousness and intention of the light does not treat all of them the same. A good intention or a curious intention is treated very differently from any intention which means harm. Mean mindedness is not rewarded."

Davy and Mildred were hopeful. The three of them walked through the crowd as they talked. Mildred looked down at her brown walking shoes and wondered when she could clean them.

"Suppose you are trailing within the custody of the light. It is much like riding a subway train. You're not really part of the train but it is taking you where you intended to be and it surrounds you safely and you are passive within it. You have your own little area with some people seated before you closer to the front and some people seated behind you farther away but all going to the same place, so they have a similar intention. Let us say it is the light which runs the train. It won't allow a destructive passenger onto the train who might damage something or interfere with the other passengers. But that bad intentioned passenger is determined to do his damage anyway so he hangs on to the outside of the train. He wants to go where you are going. He presses his face against the glass as the train moves through the tunnel. He cannot reach you. He puts his ear to the glass to hear what you say. He hears it dimly. He sees you faintly with poor definition. He is going where you go but he can't quite connect with you. Understand? You sense he is there and he knows you are there but he does no harm."

They thought they understood and they nodded pensively as they reflected on it. Mildred voiced it for both of them.

"So, if Malveena comes to us that way she can't kill us?"

"If she comes, that way, she cannot hurt you. By the way. In your description of your experiences, you say you have 'used the trail.' Do not use the term

171

again." Foster's tone was stern and he had not made a suggestion. He had given an order.

The two friends were relieved somewhat but something had been implied and left unsaid. "That way" carried the ominous implication of there being another way in addition to 'that way'. It must have something to do with 'the trail'.

Davy pulled up abruptly and put his arm out to stop them walking. He pointed down.

"Mildred, isn't that the same tie-dyed girl lying in the same place in the mud. She is still looking up into the rain with that smile on her face."

"Bad trip." said Mildred.

"She fell? Why doesn't she just get up then. She doesn't seem hurt. She is smiling." Mildred and Foster exchanged the 'he is such a boy' look. Foster elaborated. "LSD Davy. Lysergic acid diethylamide. That kind of a 'bad trip'."

"Oh." Davy had no idea what they were talking about. Mildred did not know what to do about Davy.

Pilcher brightened. It had just occurred to him he and Mildred might have an option to nullify Malveena. Why can we not go back in time and change who Bully hires for his assistant and then there would be no Malveena. "Mr. Foster, can we go back in time and change things?"

Charles Foster was expecting that question. "Yes and no. Let's see. Do you know who Genghis Kahn was?" Mildred did and Davy did not. Mildred wet her finger and drew a one in the air. One for Mildred.

"Genghis Khan was a war lord around 1200 I think the date was. He conquered most of the known world and eventually made the largest single empire in history. Let's say you went back to those days and locked him up when he was a boy before he could fight his wars. Everything resulting from those wars, right down to today would be changed. But not really."

"I don't get it." Davy was puzzled.

"When you changed that one thing, you locked up Genghis Khan, you started a new history right then. You began a completely unique line of events

172

from then on, two parallel histories running side by side. The new history where you changed things, would go forward following its own new path. No Genghis Khan. That has nothing to do with the history we experience where indeed there was a Genghis Kahn. That history is unaltered and runs forward as the history that you know. Nothing in the real life you know at home would be different.

Davy saw the sense of it.

'You can't take away what has happened, you can only make something else happen in addition. So, getting Malveena fired from her job in the past or locking her up, which I would enjoy seeing, that would begin a separate parallel stream of new history, but it would not eliminate her in your real life. Who knows how many such parallel histories are running side by side."

Davy wondered. Could stories of ghosts and the like be attempts by travelers like Malveena to enter one stream from another. He would turn his mind to it at another time. Right now, he needed help and he was with a man who could give it.

"Mr. Foster, what are we going to do about Bully and the closing of the plant?"

Foster stood erectly and looked off into space over Davy's head. "I am not sure. It is complicated. Also, I have appointments."

"Appointments? We must stop Bully and Malveena!" Davy was astounded at Foster.

"Davy, I am here and not at my plant because this is where I choose to be. From here I have a date with Napoleon on the island of Elba. Following that I intend to visit Nikola Tesla in New York and that is just the beginning. I am not coming with you. I am out of it."

Mildred was aghast and her voice broke. "That is not fair! How can we come and find you again? We need you!" Davy remembered his uncle telling him a fair was where they judged mincemeat pies. That was the only fair.

Foster stood firm. "You know how to find me wherever I am. If you come with good intention we will certainly meet again. Goodbye." With that, Charles

Abernathy Foster turned and walked up the hill looking for a solid spot with a good view of the stage. They watched Foster diminish in the distance and they were distraught. They could only trust and hope he knew something they didn't. Davy and Mildred had been left on their own to deal with Malveena.

Malveena Drago was not a patient woman. The sun was up and the pipe beckoned to her. It was as if she and the pipe had consulted and they had agreed. She went to her filing cabinet and pulled up the class photograph of Porky and Davy which Bully had given her. She looked at Davy and consolidated his image in her mind. She pulled on her leather boots and stomped them to get them comfortable. She pulled on her driving gloves and looked at her hands. These will do nicely. Throttling gloves. She stepped onto her twelfth story balcony and sighted to the sun with the image of the little monster burning in her brain. The pipe warmed to its task.

From the quadrillion intentions active at that millisecond it began its conscious collaboration with the sole intention satisfying the need. The hue of the light embroiling the pipe was darkling. There did not seem to be the welcoming joy she had felt before. There seemed to be a sullenness in the glow of it as it enveloped her. An occasional string of gold spun through the envelope which then became sublimated to an achromatic steel greyness. Malveena drank it in. It was perfect.

She landed up to her ankles in the trampled bog of Woodstock. The dimmed light of the dull day barely penetrated her viscous cocoon. The wind blew the rain around and ignored Malveena. There was no headlong thrust of energy to strip away her torpor. Instead, a gargantuan black and swirling cyclonic funnel streaked to her and tore away her suspension and drove her down on her back into the sludge. Malveena laid still in the mush, waiting for reality to clean up her view. She stood slowly and swiped irritably at the fog hanging around her. Water seeped into her leather boots and it felt as if it were unreal water belonging somewhere else. The rain struck and stung her but it seemed as if it was not part of the real rain. She smelled the pot and saw the cook fires but it was as if they were inserted and not really on the wind and in her nose. She shook herself like a dog and looked around blearily. I have piped into this mess to deal with the two brats and they better be here. Malveena saw Davy and Mildred standing not fifteen feet away and they were looking directly at her without a qualm. It was fogged and hazy near them and she strained to see them well. The weather will not protect you. They were not running. Showing brave will not help you. She flexed her hands and tightened the wrist bands on her throttling gloves.

There was a break in the rain and Davy looked up to see the weather. A thousand feet above a large whirl of gulls tested the barometer. They were familiar and beautiful and timeless. He was sure they had their own gull way of intention.

Malveena crouched and made three quick strides and reached to grab Davy by the shoulders. Her footing was bad in her leather soled boots and she somehow missed the mark and slid past as she screamed Pilcher! Davy shivered at the sudden coldness. The Drago slid to a stop, nose to nose with Mildred. Mildred ignored Malveena. She looked blandly into Malveena's face as if she did not see her. Malveena was furious. This brat is wrapped in fog and pretends she does not see me. Malveena swiped to knock off Mildred's balaclava and she missed. She thrust her hands to Mildred's throat and grasped nothing. Mildred walked ahead unimpeded feeling somehow soiled and stood beside Davy.

Malveena fell to her knees and punched a hole in the mud with her glove. Somehow, she was here and not here, close yet so far away and the brats were impervious to her. She inhabited some dark unfocused realm which kept her apart. Malveena stumbled dimly down her own thick river of clay and climbed blurrily up her own stairs and onto a stage. The crowd noise floated oddly to her from the huge amphitheater. She seized the microphone and threw her head back and shrieked the fury and futility of her confoundment to half a million people. The microphone feedback was a tormented electronic scream unlike anything ever heard. To a person, 500,000 people turned to the stage and it seemed a dim shadowed energy moved off. Cool. Smokin' microphone feedback with nobody on stage. Strange to see that bit of fog,

It was the Sixteenth of August 1969 and it was the second official day of the Woodstock Festival, just outside the town of Bethel New York. The weather was decent now and the bands started early in order to placate a restive half million stoned and hungry patrons. Most had not paid a ticket. Davy Pilcher and Mildred Craft and Charles Foster were about to hear what they came for. The enormous crowd buzzed expectantly as the hum of warming equipment spread excitement through the fields. Stage lights came to life and the energy picked up. The Grateful Dead came on at 10:30 PM and finished their set a little past 12:00 midnight. Their stage was immersed in water and the band got electrical shocks when they touched their strings or used a microphone throughout their whole performance. At 12:30 AM Creedence Clearwater Revival took the stage and the kids were in heaven. Mildred bopped full on and Davy spasmed and they sang their lungs out to 'Green River', 'Bad Moon Rising' and 'Proud Mary'. It was wonderful. Right on the heels of CCR came Janis. Foster had worked his way to the front. Joplin sang eight songs and two encores. Charles screeched his way through 'To love Somebody', 'Summertime', 'Try Just a Little Bit Harder' and 'Kosmic Blues' and his throat was never so sore and he had never felt better in his life.

Malveena haunted the festival like a disembodied ghoul. She thought she saw the bands but she could not see them. She thought she heard the music but she could not hear it. She was on the outside of the subway train with her face pressed against the tinted glass, deaf to the voices and never able to enter. Only the sun could relieve her of her torment.

Chapter 14: Poisonous Gases

The morning was a cool one. Mr. Tilt looked at his row of sickly geraniums shivering along the east window ledge. The light was not good for growing them and the room stayed cold. He began at the back of the room and one by one he slammed down the heavy wooden window sashes to stifle the keening wind. The students dribbling in to take their seats paid no attention to him. As childish as it was, Tilt exorcised his frustrations slam by slam and began every day with a cleared mind. As Davy entered from the west side of the school, he heard the concussion of the heavy frames slamming down. He walked past the portrait of Charles Foster hanging stolidly on the wall above the office reception counter, Hello Mr. Foster, and carried on. His Jimi Hendrix guitar pick rattled in his pipe and when he got his jangle just right, the rattle stayed on the beat. Tonight, he would set the plastic JH pick on his dresser beside Nelson's medal and the guillotine earring.

The school day ground down. At 3:45 PM, Mr. Tilt concluded his daily harangue and dismissed his class. He spat on the floor and threw a little scoop of dust bane on it. That day the floor looked more like the Andes than the Apennines. He had not gotten around to squashing them with his boot. As the mob pushed its way out he put his head in his hands and closed his eyes. He did not notice Davy and Mildred remaining behind, sitting quietly in their seats. The last few days had seen him descend more and more into himself and he had become disconsolate. Nothing had happened with Mildred and Davy and he was sorry for that. They owed him nothing and he was sympathetic to their dilemma of fraternizing with him. He rubbed his eyes and sighed and stood with a stretch which cracked something in his neck. He worked his head in a circle and it cracked again and it felt better. He opened his eyes at a rustle and there they were. The three exchanged looks and Davy spoke.

"Mr. Hill, Sir, Tilt, Mildred and I have decided. We three," he nodded at Tilt, " are going to Greece. To Delphi to be exact. We thought you would like that. There is the symposium held there which includes major philosophers and then there's the oracle. That is the plan, although so far, no plan has been exactly what we had expected. So, we are ready to go in 1 hour."

Tilt felt a weight fall off he did not know he had been carrying. He was overcome with a million imaginings. He blurted out his first thought. "Before I go I have to feed my dog."

Mildred responded. " We have about one hour of sun left Mr. Tilt. We have not traveled with lower light levels than that and we are not going to risk it."

Mr. Tilt looked the two children over carefully. They were dressed as they normally were, but in Greece their garb would be indicative of the slave class. Individuals of status wore a chiton made of much fabric secured by a braided belt or an anamaschalister, a leather strap which crisscrossed at the back and clasped at the front. None of us will fit in. We will appear both foreign and not of the patrician class. We will be ignored or outcast, or worse, treated as escaped slaves.

"Davy, Mildred, please come and sit just here, nearer to me and we can chat. I will tell you about the Greece of that day. Please do not protest as to its fairness. Greece was built on a very strong hierarchy of status. Male adults and particularly those philosophically or politically active held the highest status. Male boys were considered the next most valuable." The heat was rising in Mildred. She knew exactly where this was going and her face was reddening.

"The third level of importance was held by foreign women and female children. Below that level was the slave class. What we are wearing today would brand us all as slaves. We must dress the part in order to pass inspection unmolested." Mr. Tilt saw they were not pleased with this turn of events but they were listening.

"Mildred, in order to be included in things you must dress like a boy. I see you have cut your hair short. Very nice." Mildred put on a sourpuss and crossed her arms.

" You will wear a tunic-like garment called a chiton. It hangs to just below the knee and is made of light linen. It is clasped with a peronai or big clasp at each shoulder. And sometimes a sash or girdle is worn."

178

"I want a pattern around the edge. And green peronai."

"Um, I will see what I can do."

Davy looked at Mildred. Perhaps the way to handle Mildred is to dress her up.

"David, you are tall. You will wear a longer chiton made of heavier linen secured by an anamaschalister. That is a leather strap crossing your back and tied or pinned in front. A la Mildred, you will have a brown border on your tunic. You will not have a hat. Mildred, you will be hatted with a petasos to disguise you better. A flat felt hat with a wide brim." He hoped that would do the trick. If not, Mildred could not be included in the society of Delphi.

" Over my own chiton, I will have a heavy woolen cloak called a chlamys which is worn by military men. It will be royal blue. I too will have my peronai and a wide sash." Tilt intended to have his chiton shorter than normal. He had scars residual of his military action and he wanted to show them off.

"So that is it. What do you think?" Davy thought perhaps another choice of destinations could be made but Mildred was visualizing her pale green chiton and matching peronai and her jaunty felt hat.

"Great" said Mildred.

"Excellent" said Tilt.

Nothing said Davy.

It took Tilt two weeks to gather the paraphernalia and it was perfect. They dressed up in the washrooms at the school and the three had a good laugh at each other. The scars from Tilt's military action showed purple and elevated and they ran like a road map along his bony legs. Mildred looked boyish in her petasos and Davy looked sheepish wearing what he felt was his dress.

The sun bounced around the school quadrangle and shimmered off the glass of the windows surrounding the enclosure. It was private and sheltered and it was the perfect departure spot.

Mildred spoke. "Did you feed your dog?"

Tilt nodded. "Yes. Kibble." Davy did not have a dog and kibble was Greek to him. He opened his sheath and put his pipe to his eye. "OK Mildred, hold my hand. Mr. Tilt, hold Mildred's hand. Get ready, 'cause Delphi, here we come."

Proclus the philosopher walked studiously down the long gentle decline of the ravine toward the small grassed peninsula ahead of him. The demeanor with which he approached the private gathering was critical to him. He did not look at his feet despite the fact the ground was irregular and sloping away from him. It was unseemly for a renowned philosopher such as himself to be concerned about such things. The wind at his back was steady and it gusted occasionally, rushing his decorum and pushing him down the hill a little faster than he wished to go. His shadow danced around him as his loose ankle length garment caught the wind. He was wearing his best pure white chiton embellished by an intricate red border, secured by a red braided belt, tied off with a large tassel which swung nicely. Over his chiton he wore a heavy himation secured at the left shoulder by a large red peronai, his favorite and most beautiful pin. The heat of the day did not demand a himation but style did. A small leather pouch was attached to his belt by a red string tied in a simple bow. The pouch was full and it swung in time with the tassel. Little gifts can do no harm.

Trailing red headed goldfinches piped him along his way. Despite the heat of the late morning sun, mist from the valley below rose in the distance. The Castilian spring water in the irrigation channel ran along at his left hand, louder here where it steepened to speed downhill. It originated high above and broke out between Parnassus and Mount Kirphi. From catch basin to catch basin it filled the valley with green. It widened a few feet at the base of the down-slope and ran slower beside the narrow grassy shelf and tumbled over the edge of the plateau. Because of it, Pleistos Valley below was fertile. Behind Proclus, Mount Parnassus rose to eight thousand feet where it joined three massive snowcapped peaks. Proclus stepped onto level ground and assumed his most thoughtful posture.

In the tidy glade made by the olive trees ahead of him, seats at today's symposium were already occupied. Set out on the left, a long low wooden table displayed three large amphorae, one for each wine to be served. Dartis the steward had set out eight kantharoi and eight kylikes. Either the kylix or the kantharos was a suitable cup for the wines warming nicely in the intensifying sun. He had been fortunate to acquire three exceptional vintages and he was pleased. The first to be served was the Athiri. It was the prince of white wines from the island of Santorini. It was a low acidity wine and it soothed the stomach. It was conducive to mellowness. The second serving was to be the Assyrtiko. It was an amber ripe wine which fostered acerbic commentary. The philosophers drank this with much relish. The third and most important was the red Kalambaki. It was deep and brown-red from the Aegean island of Lemnos. With this wine, men visited Olympus.

Dartis had chosen traditional and strategically embossed red and black kylikes. He would fill them perfectly with the red Kalambaki and present them with great care so as not to expose the scenes depicted on their broad shallow surface. It was only as the wine was consumed the images seen there would reveal themselves. From such surprises the gods whispered to the ears of men.

Five couches were set in a circle in the shadow of five ancient olive trees. Despite their age the trees were still fully leafed and they provided a gentle dappled shade for the thinkers. The circle had no head of the table and all those who sat within it were equal. Wine was consumed equally, time for speaking was allotted equally and as philosophy came under the power of the grape, inhibitions were lost. The fellowship of the symposium created strong bonds.

Beyond them and by himself sat Artimes the scribe. He sat downwind of the conversation to ensure he heard it well. To avoid eye contact he sat with his back to the speakers as was the custom. He waited faithfully for instruction. He looked away from the plateau and out over the spires of cypress trees separating one olive grove from another in the valley. He could see the fig trees now that the fruit had begun to brown and the birds were after it. Against the gusting wind Artimes pinned his sheets of papyrus to a plank he held across his knees. The papyrus would not tolerate extraneous marks or blemishes to be forced upon it by the gusts. The symposium could rely upon a perfect record of the

181

dialogue and trust the beauty of his script. Artimes was the collective amanuensis for the three of them and it was an honored position coveted by many.

Proclus approached the small group in a detached manner. He was not at ease and he struggled to conceal the fact. The symposium was not by invitation. One could come to the great men and join their discourse at one's own peril. If one could demonstrate adroitness of presentation and a suitable level of intellect and philosophical depth, one was rewarded. One was asked to sit. Simply that. To be asked to sit was all. *Sit Proclus. Sit fellow. Do be one of us. Steward. Bring sweet Proclus some wine. No no, not that one, the Ambrosia. The best for our Proclus.* He was angering himself at how they made him feel. These presumptive judges. Who are they. These great men, these great thinkers. This Plato, this Aristotle, this Socrates. I Proclus am their equal. I am their superior in all ways. Yet they have anointed themselves. They have made a little club. They have declared it to the world they are great and the world believes it. I do not believe it, but I must have their club.

Proclus stepped out of the sunlight and into the shadow of the three great men. The steward had begun to serve the wine and he carried a kantharos of the sweet Athiri white wine to Plato. He held the deep cup by one of its high vertical handles and with a deep bend of his back he offered it. Plato accepted the wine with a tilted nod. The sun had warmed the silver container filled with the Athiri and he held it against his cheek. A little light eluded the olive trees and bounced off a silver nymph. Looming behind Proclus were the Phaedriades, the shining ones. The pair of cliffs rose 700 feet vertically like two enormous mirrors. Their white surfaces reflected to the harbor-city of Kirrha 15 miles away on the Gulf of Corinth. They were so dazzlingly bright in reflection that Plato saw only an approaching faceless silhouette against them.

"Proclus. I thought it was you. I recognized your gait as you came down the hill." At one-time Proclus was a student of Plato but the thinking of Proclus had not matured as he aged. Plato eyed the bag swinging at Proclus' hip. "You are back so soon and I see you have brought us something." Plato was hoping for Pasteli. It was his favorite chewy sesame seed candy.

" Yes. I have brought a gift. I was remiss in not doing so when I was here yesterday. Some baubles you may have use for. Trinkets."

He moved his hand smoothly to his pouch and undid the tie but it snagged. His easy pressure on the string did nothing until the tension gave way and it shot small gemstones out of the pouch and sprayed them at the feet of the three great men. One shot high in the sun and splashed into the cup of the white Athiri wine held by Aristotle. The wind picked up as Proclus knelt to recover them and it whipped his chiton over his head. He fought to see what he was doing as one by one he picked up his gems and returned them to his pouch. He dumped the stones onto the couch next to Socrates to display his gift and two of them bounced onto the grass. He left them there. Plato fixed Proclus with a look of dismissal.

"Yes Proclus? I believe we have detained you too long."

The three great men got up from their places and walked together to the edge of the plateau. They looked into the valley to clear their minds and make them fresh.

Proclus said nothing and turned into the north wind and away from his chagrin. He stepped slowly, waiting for the call back but it did not come. Disappointed once again, he began his stomping angry trudge uphill. He had worn the heavy himation as a cloak in the style of the day and he was drenched with sweat. He tore at the peronai to release the garment and his chiton fell down around his waist. He stood there bare chested as he shook and cursed the heavy linen himation and the startled finches made red and yellow starbursts.

Aristotle stood at the edge of the plateau and breathed in the scent of the valley below. He smiled at the conversations of the birds surrounding him and at the water sounds in the irrigation channel. He was lost in the magic of the rising mist but something in the sounds was slightly different. Water was shooting out of what appeared to be a crack in the catch basin above the front lip of the main trough and it had undermined the support of the spillway on the face of the cliff.

" See there." Aristotle was equally at home in the realms of mechanics and mathematics as he was in the contemplations of the universe. He pointed with a stab to where he saw the growing waterfall escaping over the edge of the conduit. It had worked a few stones out from below the support. The largest catch basin in the entire irrigation system fed it. It collected the full volume of the Castilian spring which drained the mountains. Melt water from the snowcapped peaks above joined the flow and built with the rainwater. It had been a wet year and the system was engorged. Aristotle punctured the air with his rigid forefinger in a staccato repetition.

" Look down there. Look at the way the surface of that plateau runs. Its natural slope is to the west toward the temples. If that catch basin collapses, it will flood and destroy the temple of Apollo and much of the valley and perhaps the Pythia with it."

Plato and Socrates were interested and not interested. These physical things were impossible to decipher. They believed Aristotle was correct, they would give that to him, but undebatable propositions were nothing to them. Certainly, the loss of the Oracle, the Pythia, was a concern, but she was a favorite of the gods and if they did not protect her, then who were Plato and Socrates to interfere.

Aristotle insisted. "Plato, is it not Matesic who is tasked with this. Matesic the engineer?" Plato was not listening. He knew Aristotle was probably correct but it was nothing to him in the larger scheme of things.

" Plato. I have seen you in his company, this Matesic. You must send someone to him. This is urgent."

Plato nodded. " Yes, I will. Today." He said the words but they were gone from his mind as he looked south. The shine on the water in the gulf of Corinth bounced to him as the waves moved. Aristotle leaned out as far as he dared and watched a freshet from the cliff face finding its way southwest. His concern was interrupted by a sound behind him and an explosion of startled finches.

A blast of consciousness cascaded through Davy's eye and the other two felt the surge. Together they were shot in a flaming tubular arc as if from a bow. With a residual shimmering amid a blinding flash and a crackle of electric discharge, they landed forty feet behind Plato, Aristotle and Socrates. They looked directly downhill to the symposium and the backs of three standing men. Davy had come back into reality with a small shock wave and he was bright. There was a subtle smoking around his feet as he secured his pipe in its sheath. Mildred was stirring beside him and Tilt stood holding her other hand like a granite statue. The crackle of arrival caused Socrates to turn around to them. He said nothing in greeting and walked back to his seat. The other two joined him. They had not heard these fellows approach them but what of it. The tall and martial one wearing the military style chlamys was frozen to attention as military men often were.

The Tilt statue clutching Mildred's hand gradually humanized and its first awareness was of birds flustering behind it. Tilt turned and saw a shirtless Proclus with his head down storming up the hill and stirring up finches with every stomp. Tilt spoke to no one in particular. "Who is that man?"

Socrates answered as the philosophers seated themselves. "Sir, that is Proclus. He aspires to sit at our symposium. There you see some of the trinkets he has brought to curry favor." He gestured dismissively to the small array of stones strewn on the couch opposite him. "He comes often but he is not thoughtful. He is like a moth returning to the flame."

Mildred shook her head.

Aristotle observed it and he was interested. "So, boy. Tell us your name. You seem to disagree. Do you have some thoughts on it?" Mildred's subterfuge in dressing as a boy had been accepted. Without missing a beat Mildred said, "I am called Mercutio and I do not agree."

Plato knew the derivation of the name. "Ah! A Roman." He looked knowingly at his two compatriots. "Perhaps Rome can teach us something yet." They laughed together at the absurdity of it. Addressing Davy, Plato asked him, "And you boy, what is your name?" Davy answered haltingly, "David..us. Davidus. Sir."

Plato nodded and turned to Tilt who was towering and mammoth in his military chlamys. "And you sir?"

Tilt stood erect and strong with the mien of a warrior. "Tilt," he said in his most martial speech. Plato saw the scarring on his legs. "You have seen action."

"No. I have seen victory." The three wise men liked what he said. Athens was not all philosophy and higher purpose. It was a warlike state before all else. Davy and Mildred saw a man whose mettle they had not known.

Aristotle turned his attention back to Mildred. "Young Mercutio, please tell us of the moth."

"Yes. Thank you. You have deemed yon Proclus to be unthoughtful and have likened him to the moth. One cannot say that of the moth. He is perhaps more thoughtful than most."

Davy and Tilt looked at Mildred. She was like an onion. Layers upon layers.

"The moth is us. He is the inner me, the inner you, the inner all of us."

The three great philosophers were unaccustomed to this personalized style of argument and they liked it. Tilt too had been a sucker for maladjusted spirituality his whole life and here he was standing before Plato, Aristotle and Socrates. He wanted to hear this as much as the symposium did.

Mildred began again. "Tell me. Is it not true that when you look at the flame of a candle something comes over you which influences you to contemplate? Is that not true? Do we not contemplate the heavens in the flame?"

They nodded in agreement.

" What is it which pacifies us in the flame and puts such a spell on us. We sit and we stare and we feel we are part of it and that it keeps some beautiful thing there for us."

Tilt and Davy and the symposium nodded. They had all felt exactly that.

" We do nothing more than find our inner moth. Our fantasy of flight and spiritual centering and worth through purification by fire are represented in that little candle flame. Just as we search for the peace in it, the moth searches for the same thing in his primordial simple moth brain. The candle offers us a peace which externalizes us to the chaos within the flame and gives us the choice, the choice to enter or not, while knowing we might perish if we do but we still can't ever totally reject the lure of it. We too, like the moth, have the need to push at the edge. We want the experience and the exhilaration of new margins without experiencing the consequence, just like the moth."

Tilt was enraptured. He considered himself a guest of Mildred and Davy and thanked their generosity of spirit for including him. Also, he was a guest in the presence of great men and a guest of the time. He wanted to spit somewhere but he thought it might be misunderstood.

Mercutio held forth. " You see, like the moth, we have dual contradictory natures, each striving to emerge."

Mildred stopped there and dropped her head and slid her lens-less glasses frames down her nose so she could look over the top. She had seen people do this for emphasis. She wanted the listeners to appreciate the vocabulary.

"He singes his wings yet he swoops back to experience it again. That is what we do. We are singed yet we swoop back to experience it again. We want the experience until we get it, then it is too late not to have it. We watch and we watch, looking for the way, looking for what lies hidden. That is the human dilemma. We burn, but despite that, we look for something good in it all. And you know what, you know what is the most amazing thing? If we look the right way, we find it. No, the unthoughtful Proclus is not like the moth."

The three wise men were fascinated by this young Mercutio's perspective and by his exceptional mind. Aristotle and Plato tipped their heads at exactly the same time and at exactly the same angle to indicate their consideration of the matter. Pupil and teacher had learned well from each other. Socrates noticed Mercutio looking at the gem stones strewn on the couch beside him. A few stray shafts of light picked up their scintillation. "Mercutio, would you care to choose one for yourself? You may if you wish. Choose and be welcome to it."

Mildred looked at Tilt for approval and Plato saw the look.

"Mercutio, I see you request permission."

" He is my teacher."

Instantly, the status of Tilt was elevated. He made a very proper miniscule nod of acknowledgment that it was so. Mercutio stepped to the couch and picked up one diamond. It was not the biggest nor was it the smallest. She suspected it was some sort of test to see whether she would take the biggest one. She selected the second largest stone and held it up to the light. The three travelers were upwind to the symposium. Mildred spoke to Tilt under her breath but the philosophers heard every word clearly.

She whispered," Mr. Tilt, this is peppered. Full of black things. See?"

Tilt took the stone from Mildred. He held it up and looked between the olive branches and spoke under his breath, but too loudly all the same.

"These peppered things are called inclusions my dear. They are little bits of carbon that didn't get quite the right amount of pressure or heat or their timing was bad in emergence from their primordial pipe. If you pardon the expression. They are often considered flaws or blemishes but that is entirely wrong."

Mildred did not like the flaw business.

"They are much like people. They are formed by what is around them and they develop certain characteristics."

Theatrically he held the gem in two long bony fingers and reached for the sky. He arched his back and extended his arm to the height of eight feet and extended his other arm in a balletic posture so that his chlamys draped his statuesque pose. The refracted scintillation from the diamond played colors on his face and chest.

" This my dear is perfect. It has a pattern which has never been and will never be duplicated. It is unique among all things and has a worth in and of itself and it does not need the approval of anyone. It is its own thing, a perfect entity and a statement of the wonder of its creation. You my dear are exactly like this. A diamond beyond compare and a unique perfect you." With a generous face and a sweep of his arm toward an empty couch Aristotle said, " Mr. Tilt, sit."

Mr. Tilt assumed his full 6 feet 5 inches and breathed in the glory and wonder of it all. He heard the birds, he felt the warmth of the sun, and he was close to the marvels of Delphi. This was where he belonged and he had been spoken to by Aristotle. But he did not sit.

"Sir, I am protector of Mercutio. Until he can do so, I cannot, will not sit."

The request of Mildred to sit had been intended as Aristotle's next words. "Do not trouble yourself with it. Mercutio, please do sit." He gestured across all the couches with a sweeping arm. Mercutio sat.

" Thank you. I will. After all, time and tide gather no moss." They looked at Mercutio. They had no idea what she meant. They did not understand metaphorical speech. They did not write it nor did they speak it. Mercutio was speaking beyond their understanding. Davy marveled. *Dopo, they are actually considering that.* Dopo was considering it too.

Tilt stretched his long arm across the couch and returned the two-carat diamond to Mildred. She did not look at it but handed it to Davy. Without thinking he fished under his chiton, flipped open his sheath and tinkled the diamond into the pipe. He snapped the flap closed, patted it and covered up with the chiton. Aristotle glimpsed a brief shimmer of the end of the pipe but said nothing. Could it be? May such wisdom at such youth be god given? He saw Mercutio and Davidus with new eyes.

Proclus had reworked his chiton and he had attained the height of the ridge when he heard the sudden panic from the birds flushed by the flash at Davy's arrival. He looked back at the symposium and there were now six. He strained to see them. How have they gotten here? They did not pass me on the path. There is one path only. Have they come from the gods? Are they in fact gods themselves? Who could it be. A god with two children? He did not dare to walk back yet he wanted to do so. He watched and waited in the distance. The wind had reversed and it was carrying intermittent snatches of the conversation to him. Sit? Did I hear sit? No, it cannot be! Yes! That huge one just sat. Yes!

189

That tall one has been asked to sit. Proclus watched in agony. The assembly appeared to be listening attentively to one of the children. I do not believe it. He too has been asked to sit. The wind was stronger now and he had heard it correctly. Certainly, they have come from the gods. Only they would be asked to sit after descending to favor the great philosophers. I must see. He took three steps and stopped abruptly. Proclus, restrain yourself. Gods may be seated there indeed, but indeed the gods are fickle. They can turn you to stone. Worse than that, they can make you poor. He told himself he no longer cared for the symposium. Along with the chaff from the olive trees the wind blew Proclus up the ravine.

The increasing wind brought some pleasant coolness with it from the sea. Plato began to plumb the air around him with his eyes and inhaled slowly through his nose to confirm what it carried. Socrates felt the change on his back as the draft streamed up from the terraces to blow his long hair forward over his right shoulder. A sweet cloying smell began to flow across the narrow platform and Tilt cleared his throat. Blossoms of.. no, not blossoms only. Mildred coughed. Socrates and Plato exchanged glances as they inhaled the vapor and Socrates nodded. "Yes. She is in communion today. I warrant the gods have much to say."

Davy was standing alone. All the others were seated and that was fine with him. He was sure he had no sagacity to offer. Aristotle spoke.

"Davidus, your friends are remarkable. You and they must converse often, what do you say to that?" Davidus looked down and then directly up at Aristotle with a confidence belying his age.

'Well. I understand that you three," Davy looked them over, "must do or think in a bigger sweeping way. You are Philosophers. You look for wisdom and you wonder about the origin of things. You are also getting older and the feeling of largeness helps when you get old. It is less tiring than a thousand little things."

The three smiled at the youth of Davidus. Socrates responded for them in good humor. "Yes, we are old, but we stand now in a place which is a wonder.

190

The wonder is that one stops getting old at a certain point. Getting old is just for young people, not for we three, we are already old. Once one is old, one is old and one stops the getting of it. So, you see, we are released from responsibility to age. Our minds are free for greater things."

Davidus considered that. A delicious smile crept onto his face and beamed out. He got it. What a great way to go through life. He thought maybe he should pick a younger time when he got there to be old but would he even know it when he was there. He liked Socrates.

"Davidus. Continue."

"I know It has a special feel for you to sweep along with a big concept but what I believe is this. Many smaller things, taken in full energy and total commitment, when added up to a whole, construct their own larger concept. They force the thing out of theory or cerebration and hammer it into life. It is real then. Sweeping things embraced without commitment to the smaller things never amount to much. That much I know."

Davy had learned much from his time on the Victory. He was pleased he could use "cerebrate". Mercutio had her look of implacable knowingness making what Davidus had said seem to be a mastery of the obvious. The three Greek sages took this to mean it was a common thought in the sphere of these two children and they marveled at it.

"Davidus, sit. Choose a stone for yourself."

Davy did not want to copy Mildred so he picked a red one. It was a flawless three carat ruby and in the late morning Grecian sun it was at its most beautiful. He felt under his chiton, opened the flap and dropped in the ruby. It played a little tune on the sides of the pipe as it settled. Aristotle had watched carefully. Davidus has understood the most valuable of the gems immediately. These are children of the gods.

Aristotle smiled at Tilt. "Are all youngsters from your country so gifted and contemplative?"

Tilt in all modesty answered, " Only those who find themselves under my tutelage sir." Aristotle nodded. He knew what it was to have been tutored by fine minds. He also believed he now knew what it was like to be tutored by young gods.

Socrates called out. "Dartis. Wine for Mercutio. Wine for Tilt and Davidus. Bring the Kalambaki."

With great care Dartis set the red and black kylikes in front of Mercutio, Davidus and Tilt. They were filled so completely only the meniscus kept them from overflowing.

It was the first time Mercutio had had wine. She watched to see how the others managed the wide and shallow two handled kylike. The beautiful vessel held the red Kalambaki and its bouquet swam through the glade. The first sip was not pleasant for Mildred but the little spin from it was. Davy was fine with it and approached it gingerly remembering his experience on the Victory. Mr. Tilt drank judiciously all the while peering through the depth of the wine waiting to uncover the mystery of the image concealed there. He was in paradise.

It became apparent the three philosophers were approaching their wine at exactly the same pace. They watched each other in agreement to be sure they had harmonized it. They scanned their guests and the look seemed to gather the three newcomers into the tempo of imbibing. It became apparent too that philosophy was not for teetotalers.

Mildred was enjoying herself. The breeze was wonderful and the day was wonderful and the small water wheel turning in the irrigation channel was wonderful. It had been built by Aristotle to attract the hummingbirds which flew through the spray it threw up. Mildred put a thumb and forefinger through the opening in her glasses frame and cleaned the lens. She was sitting with a pleasant smile as she moved her head and body in a slow clockwise rotation. Aristotle saw that Mercutio had caught up to them.

"Fair Mercutio. Have you anything else you wish to share with us, that you wish to explore?" It took Mildred a minute to recognize she was the Mercutio to whom Aristotle was speaking. The philosophers thought she was considering her response. From somewhere she heard herself say one word. " Oracle."

The three sages were surprised and they thought perhaps they had misunderstood her. Plato asked again. " Mercutio, is there something you wish to explore?"

Again, Mercutio managed to blurt the one word. " Oracle." Mildred looked at Tilt and Davy and began to nod along nicely to the beat of the music only she heard.

Plato nodded too but at a more sedate pace. " I see you commune with the Oracle. You should go there now, you and your compatriots, while the affinity is strong. Come." He led Mercutio to the edge of the plateau and pointed to the right.

"That is the stairway down. You will find the Pythia attended there as this is the seventh day of the month. May you commune with her and may you find enlightenment if it is the wish of the gods."

Plato released Mercutio's hand and clasping his chiton to his chest he walked back to his wine. Aristotle watched them leave and understood. He understood their need to communicate with their fellows. They would do that at the temple of Apollo with the intercession of the oracle. He felt elevated having had their company.

Mildred looked at the wide shallow steps snaking their way down to the right and terminating at the Temple of Apollo. The stairs mystified her.

"Tiltus, I don't know nothing about this. Oh. Duggle nebbative."

Tilt took her hand gently and steadied her. " Come Mercutio, we will go together." Mildred looked around to find Mercutio.

The stairway to the main plateau was exposed fully to the sun and the stonework radiated heat. The flagstones were not mortared and several joints were washed out by growing rivulets of water running across them. Along the west side of the stairway a little stream gathered pace and scoured a bit of the soil out and enticed it to leave. The monuments below glistened back to the sun. The path curved to the right and it worked very gradually to the main plateau on which stood the temple of Apollo. Therein and deep below the surface resided the Oracle, the Pythia.

Tilt, Davidus and Mercutio were feeling fine. The youngsters were tipsy but Tilt was not. He was responsible for his charges. As he walked toward the temple, Tilt remembered the aroma and the blossom which made it. The cloying semi-sweet perfume blowing through the symposium was oleander. He had a faint reminiscence of nausea when he smelled it. As a boy in Suffolk they had three colors of oleander in the garden. One of them had made him feel dizzy and nauseated when he got anywhere near its blossoms. Laurel his Gran had called it. That is what he smelled in the olive glade. But there was something more complex in it. Something he could not identify.

They crossed the expanse of the courtyard and a small rivulet of water was outpacing them. It ran ahead along a joint in the paving and it accelerated down a hole it found against the foundation.

" Tilto, Tiltus, it went right down that hole." Mercutio was amazed at the racing little stream and she made a tiny circle with her finger to copy it.

" That is not surprising. This whole area is honeycombed by seams and voids in the rock. This is limestone. It is soft and over time the pressure of the water from above has scoured out caverns everywhere. Surface clefts in the rock are all over the place. They drain the water away through a thousand subterranean tunnels."

Davy heard the cries above him and he looked up. The gulls were flying very high and that presaged a storm. The thermals streaming up the plateaus of Parnassus gave them tremendous lift. Davy envied their view to the Gulf of Corinth. Their droppings were everywhere but as Davidus, Mercutio and Tilt approached to within fifty yards or so of the temple of Apollo, there was nothing. It was as if there were something unhealthy or dangerous to avoid and the gulls would not fly there. That worried Davy. The gulls knew what they were doing.

Tilt had been lost in thought. The mixture of smells at the symposium had eluded him, but now he had it. When he was a boy they made him have his tonsils out. That was it. It was that anesthetic smell. He thought they had used ethylene or some such agent. Yes, that was it. Ethylene and oleander had come to him on the wind. Tilt recalled ancient Plutarch had named these very vapors the "sweetest and most expensive perfumes". Tilt could not agree.

Mildred was coming back to herself and she was feeling no wrath of the grape. She had abandoned the Mercutio boy walk and was more relaxed. The statuary and the beauty of the architecture surrounding her made her speechless. Located in front of the Temple of Apollo, towered the Altar of the Chians, made entirely of black marble. Surrounding it and leading to the main entrance were dozens of priceless votive statues. Not even such perfect targets as these could lure the gulls into proximity with the temple. Mildred felt nothing from the sweet miasma emanating from the temple and she was getting used to it. She wondered why Plato had referred to 'Pythia' and not to 'Oracle'.

" Mr. Tilt, what is Pythia. Plato said ' The Pythia'".

"Mildred, that word comes from very ancient Greek. Myth has it that here at this spot the god Apollo slew a monstrous python. Its decomposing body left a sickly-sweet smell supposed to be the cause of the gases at the temple even today. That is the myth. I think it is something else though. Literature says entering the inner sanctum brought its priests into ecstasy and madness. There is certainly something else."

Davidus had a question. " Mr. Tilt, what did Plato mean by 'this is the seventh day'? It seemed important or significant to him."

" It is very important Davy. It is central to the amazing history of Greece. The oracle was a highly revered and important priestess of Apollo. Approaching the seventh day of each month she fasted for several days. Then, two oracular priests lead the oracle down one of many tortuous sloping natural rock tunnels to deep within the temple. On her own she then descended deeper into the 'adyton' which means inaccessible. In a delirious and frenzied trance, she received knowledge from the spirit of the god Apollo, which she then dispensed to the supplicants who consulted her. That is the history and it is more than legend. It was recorded by countless eyewitnesses over many centuries."

Ten high risered steps led them to the mammoth open door at the central chamber of the temple. On both sides of the entrance, rampant unicorns pawed the air. The main area of the temple was not large but the structure was surrounded by 180 thirty-foot-high Doric columns supporting a peaked roof. The facade bore a frieze depicting ancient velour. As they entered the dark interior they saw the circular wall of the essential chamber of the building was decorated the same way. Natural limestone made a floor and at the center, a large sloping crater revealed natural rock openings to several tunnels. The odor was stronger now and the sweetness seemed almost pleasant. One of the tunnels was illuminated by torchlight and they made for it. In their heart of hearts as they had approached the temple each had wondered whether this was a wise course. Their discernment seemed to have softened under the exposure to the gases.

The light was bad and water dripped from the ceiling. It was wet underfoot and the worn path was slippery and smooth. The wet limestone slurry on the low ceiling brushed its mixture of chalk and soot onto Mr. Tilt's hair. Drafts began to be move slightly faster from every direction and the torches responded uncertainly with a crackle. Davy thought the storm portended by the seagulls must have arrived. The influx of air to the tunnel seemed to pressurize it and it heightened the claustrophobia. The tunnel continued its downward slope and all along the way side tunnels branched and those tunnels branched into more tunnels. Looking back at them, each one looked identical to the last. Some climbed, some went deeper into the mountain. Eons of water working through the soft spots in the limestone had made an unfathomable honeycomb below Delphi. Outside on the heights of Parnassus the storm had struck. It was a heavy rain squall building into a torrential downpour. The catch basins were straining.

The water streaming from the ceiling of the tunnel had increased and there was half an inch or so of flowing water around their feet. The inflow and back drafts from the increasing wind velocity of the storm blew out some of the torches. From the passageway ahead came the smell of many torches burning and their glow bounced down the corridor. There was an overwhelming increase of gas yet they welcomed it.

196

Davidus led them into a small brightly lit cavern whose walls were covered thickly with soot. Mildred felt the surface and the black greasiness smeared onto her hand. She tested it between her thumb and forefinger. A myriad of torches revealed the ceiling as higher there and running away in every direction were more tunnels. The floor was riven by a deep narrow cleft surrounded by freshly cut boughs of white, yellow and red oleander laurel. Seated in the center of it all on a high three-legged stool straddling the cleft in the rock was the Pythia. Her ageless face was covered with a purple veil which she proceeded to remove. She was dressed like a youth and she wore a short white chiton with a simple green border. Beside her and on either side of the cleft sat two solid gold eagles emblematic of the authority of Zeus. With her left hand she chose from her table the laurel leaves within which lived the essence of Apollo. With her right she lifted a shallow bowl of holy spring water into which she briefly gazed. Her head swayed rhythmically and her eyes rolled as she inhaled the spirit of Apollo and the sacred pneuma emerging from the fissure below her. Tilt and Mildred and Davy stood transfixed at the sight of her and without discernment and by leave of the sacred pneuma they joined her in her trance. They closed their eyes and took in the oleander and drank the sweet mist issuing from the cleft and waited for enlightenment.

Engineer Matesic tied himself with his belt to the olive tree closest to the edge of the Plateau. Rainwater from the mountains was raging down the ravine and past him at knee depth and its full weight was bearing down on the weakened catch basin. He had been summoned to deal with a problem but he had been summoned too late. The rain was coming horizontally from the north and visibility was impossible except for the fork lightning which froze its photos in the sky. He leaned hard against his belt and hung out over the edge as far as he could and what he saw was catastrophic. The catch basin was an enormous natural limestone formation which had been used for centuries. The brilliance of the lightning strikes illuminating the surface of the stone showed him what no natural daylight could. Two intersecting seams in the limestone made a V on the valley side of the basin and one of the arms of the V was opening. The shudder shook the roots of the tree anchoring Matesic as the thirty-foot-wide section of stone failed and loosed the first one hundred thousand tons of water into the valley. Matesic put both arms around the tree and closed his eyes and thanked Zeus he had worn a belt.

The thunder of the water mixed in with the thunder of the gods as it hurtled toward the sacred temples and the valley below them. Its enormous mass drove a compressed wall of air ahead of it that furled into the sky above and shot down through the clefts along the walkway and blasted into the tunnel of the Pythia and extinguished the torches. The water driven wind brought darkness with it and it also brought the water.

Deep underground the high pressure of the incoming air dispelled the gases surrounding the Pythia. Tilt had been affected least by it and he was the first to sense danger. Mildred and Davy were holding hands and together they were returning from the netherworld. They looked to Mr. Tilt immediately. He had become the leader. They failed to understand the rumble which surrounded them. It seemed impossible but it sounded as if a storm was approaching inside the tunnels. The first water began shooting down from the ceiling in the tunnel to the right, just ahead of where they had come in. There was a pulsating sound from somewhere high above as the water pushed through some perfect tunnel and activated a harmonic node. The Pythia who was now partially resuscitated began a disconsolate moaning. Davy gritted his teeth at the caterwauling. Dopo, go smack her one. Dopo stayed where he was. He was afraid of the dark.

Tilt had no idea which way to head. The blackout was total but they had to get on the move. They were at the lowest point and they needed to go up or drown.

"Here. Mildred, take my right hand. Davy you take Mildred's right hand. I will lead."

In total darkness Mr. Tilt struck out to find the way he thought would lead back up the tunnel and away from catastrophe. He took two steps and he could feel cold water pushing against his leg. It was not heavy but it was steady and it

198

was already above his ankles. Mildred's brown walking shoes were a foot underwater. *Hmpf. I just polished them.*

Tilt felt his way along the wall and he came to an opening. He did not think that was the one. They went on for twenty yards or so and he felt another opening. He stopped and stood trying to work backwards in his mind the route to take them out. Suddenly the front of a heavy stream hit him. The face of it was about two feet high and Davy and Mildred struggled to stay on their feet. The water was up to Mildred's waist and rising. Much of the water was snow melt. It was near freezing and the muscles of all three were slowing and weakening from the cold.

Tilt rejected the turnoff and he stayed straight on. A new flush hit him from the left. He put his hand down and felt some flotsam with what seemed to be bark and leaves. That most likely came from across the plaza. That was a promising direction,

" Mr. Tilt."

" Yes Mildred?"

" I have this soot on my hand."

Tilt could not believe it. These two never failed to amaze him. "Mildred, do you think this is really the time to complain your hands are dirty? You think we might have other things to think about? Such as being surrounded by poisonous gas in a subterranean maze filling with water?"

" But Mr. Tilt. The soot is from the walls. We are going by feel. You are tall enough you can feel the ceiling. If it has oily greasy soot, then there have been a lot of torches lit there and it may be the way usually used in and out. I think if you feel no soot, that means the way is wrong. That is all Mr. Tilt."

" Mildred, just kick me."

" I would love to Mr. Tilt, but the trouble is I never learned how to kick when I was up to my waist in ice water." Despite the circumstances the three laughed at that. Before the laughter had stopped echoing in the channel a heavy thrust of water tore down against them from the left. It had greater speed which meant its angulation was likely up not down. He stepped toward it and felt up to the ceiling and it was covered with a slick oily residue. He rubbed his nose in satisfaction and striped it black with the soot.

" This way." They could hear bubbling and tumbling above below and all around them as the water fell over a thousand ledges and pushed air down a thousand tunnels. Mildred was up to her chest and she was struggling despite holding Tilt's hand. She was becoming stiff from cold and fear and the tears streamed down her face but she did not make a sound. The angulation was slightly up and the floor was slippery here. The strength of the flow was increasing against them. Tilt did not want anyone to fall and be swept away. "Mildred, grip your hands on my back pockets and hold on. Davy, stand behind Mildred and hold onto her belt. I will push ahead and break the force of the water. You two just hold on tight."

Mildred was doing her best but the water was at her neck. She had to tip her head back to keep the water out of her nose and she was panicking. Tilt heard her and was about to pick her up when he saw the light up ahead.

"Hold on here we go!"

Tilt stretched his bony legs and in three racehorse strides he was out of the tunnel and the three of them stood there soaking wet and laughing with relief in the center of the temple of Apollo. Shivering, they straggled to the height of the doorway and looked out over the plaza. As far as the eye could see in every direction it was a lake. Twenty-Six votive statues to the gods held their laurel wreathed heads above the water as they glared at the flood with their dead marble eyes. Fourteen shorter gods were not so observant. A thousand gulls dotted the water and skreeked their approval. Not one of them was within fifty yards of the temple. Mercutio and Davidus looked up at Tilt. His soot blackened aquiline proboscis was a thing of beauty.

Davidus, Mercutio and Tilt had been spared drowning by the fact the ten steps leading into the temple protected the entrance with a fifteen-foot barrier. That barrier was now being overcome. The waters from the heights of Parnassus flowed slowly and gently past them and with relentless disinterest they filled completely the tunnels leading to the Pythia. The water rose another six inches and then, satisfied with its work, it withdrew. It drained off to the west and scoured its way through the graperies there. From the open doorway they examined the cliff face below the promontory where the symposium was. There was an enormous void where the failed catch basin had been. A small waterfall fell over the ragged lip of its remnants and into the spillway below. They heard shouting. At the edge of the plateau directly above them they could see a man gesticulating and pointing. Engineer Matesic was already hard at work.

Davy broke the silence. "Mr. Tilt. Sir. Do you think the Pythia survived?"

" I do. Davidus." They all liked that. " I am sure she survived. There were tunnels all around her to lead away from there. If she was out of her trance as we were leaving then I am sure she is sitting somewhere wet and aggravated and asking why me, but she is fine all the same."

The collaborative intention of the light was strong. The three of them landed in the school quadrangle amid startled gulls that squawked up and away from the apparitions. A gentle blender of golden light spiraled around their edges and brushed them back into the world. Dimly, Mr. Tilt saw himself reflected in the glass. He did not know it was him and did not care about it. He enjoyed the glutinous suspension and the lack of responsibility to act. He was in a wonderland of pleasant observation and he didn't care if he left. Davy and Mildred blended back into reality one after the other and waited for Tilt. He came around with a beautiful face. They greeted each other.

"Tilt, Mercutio."

" Mercutio, Davidus."

" Davidus, Tilt."

They left the quadrangle and walked home. Davy opened his leather sheath and dumped the ruby and the diamond onto his bed. He liked his ruby and he would give Mildred her diamond at the first opportunity. He walked to his dresser and placed two gems beside Nelson's gleaming coat button, Jimi Hendrix' guitar pick and the perfect little guillotine earring. The early gloaming streamed in over his shoulder and struck the gems on the dresser top with soft light. It scattered a million moving diamond and ruby scintillations off Davy's bedroom walls. He sat down on the bed and mulled over the situation.

Greece had been very worthwhile. It had made a staunch ally of Mr. Tilt. Tilt now knew the travel by Davy and Mildred to the storage room in Foster Industries was a plausible thing. Now they had a reliable adult who could support their story. That was fine, but otherwise few things had been resolved. The plant was still going to close. Mildred's mother's job was still gone. Her father was still missing or captive and they needed to deal with that. His father was going to lose his job. Mr. Foster had not agreed to come back and help. Bully and Malveena still had the forged power of attorney.

Malveena. Malveena is still out there and determined to throttle us. At Woodstock, Foster told us she was a woman of action. No kidding. If that is a woman of action, spare me from women of action.

Chapter 15: Janet And Helen Rock All Night

Janet Pilcher needed a shower. She had taken three appointments for job interviews that day, and they were located diabolically as far from each other as geographically possible. She had dressed in her best and most business-like outfit to be as presentable as she could manage but it had not gone well. The weather forecast had missed the temperature by ten degrees and a day forecast as cool was sweltering and she was drenched. Worse, the low heeled black pumps she chose for the day were designed for admiring and standing, maybe even a little dancing, but not for appointment trekking. She had cuts at the back of both heels within fifteen minutes and after another ten minutes a blister began peeling off the bottom of her left big toe. Janet had not worked outside the house for ten years and if she could find work, any work, she would take it. The mortgage did not care whether Foster's was closing. The mortgage had its own needs.

She and Harry had sold off their lone car and banked the cash before the small local used car market was glutted. A thousand other families would soon be thinking in the same way. Harry managed the two-mile walk to and from Foster Industries easily. He left for work earlier in the morning and they set dinner a little later for a relaxed return home.

Janet sat on the front hall bench and worked her shoes off over her cuts. She de-stressed for a minute and did cross handed kneading of her eye brows for 20 seconds. It helped. She sat alone in the house and tried to recall whether there was any epsom salts to soak her feet and if there was, where it was. Despite being alone, as she hobbled along to the kitchen to put on the kettle, Janet 'ouched' out loud with each step. She picked her large mug from its hook beside the stove and dropped a teabag into it and waited for the whistle of the kettle. I should really give away my teacups. Her mind wandered to her son as she relaxed and stepped out of her skirt. He was a changed boy over the last few months and not just because of his growth spurt or being a few months older. The kettle screamed at Janet to do something. She pulled it off the burner and poured the water over the bag. With her skirt over her arm she carried the brew up to the shower and started the water running.

Davy had worn his pipe to school as he always did these days in case he and Mildred needed a quick getaway from Malveena Drago. So far, he knew of three black Porsches just like Malveena's in town and he flinched at the sight of any of them. He worked his way home from school along the back lanes and through the back door into the kitchen. The shower was running upstairs and it made its usual chatter in the pipes. That must be mom. It was too early for his father to be home. He walked upstairs and tossed his jacket onto his unmade bed. His mother had shouted "Make your bed Davy!" as she left for her appointments but he had not done it. He slid his pipe out and put it on the bed and gazed at it. It had regained most of its sheen and it looked fresh, much like the first day he got it. His fingerprints were hardly visible. It is as if it is getting ready for action. He did not want it. Davy seized it without doing up the flap and hung it on the hook inside his closet door and left it swinging there. He was not sure he wanted to use it again. Dopo, I am done with using the trail of the light. Dopo doubted that but he said nothing to Davy about it.

Davy sat on the edge of his bed and looked around. One by one he had denuded his father's library of its books and he had them piled neatly on the floor against the sides of his dresser in the order he had read them. It struck him he had no real books of his own. Yes, he had his baby books and the like but the important stories of the real world came from the bookshelves downstairs and they were what he wanted.

He bounced down the stairs to his father's small office, ritually skipping the second step from the top and the second step from the bottom because they creaked. Davy smoothed his right hand along the oak railing and swiped it off with a flourish at the end. He closed the office door behind him and sat cross legged on the floor. On the third shelf was the gold and black embosser. As a young man Harry Pilcher began embossing page 150 of his books with "Property of the Pilcher Library." The embossing stood out in shallow relief so when Davy got to page 150 he would rub a finger over the nubbles in the paper. Harry no longer bothered to emboss but Davy knew when he had his own books, he would do the same thing his father had done.

The small cozy room quieted him. His shoulders began to fall in relaxation and he absorbed the safety of his familiar sanctum. Davy smiled at the gaps he had made in the shelves. It was quite an accomplishment. The little library was a gold mine of the mind and it was where he wanted to be yet it was also the catalyst for every pickle he had put himself into. He came there knowing today he would be intrigued and stimulated by some new book. Even the covers intrigued him. Davy was not only a prodigious book reader, he was a co-author. He created his own imaginary extensions of thought, of dialogue and outcomes. He wrote his own phantasmagoria right along with the author. He retained every word he read and placed it spatially on the pages in his head.

Previously he had leafed through Treasure Island and it seemed a little juvenile. What spoke against that was his father had kept it. Then there was Plato and The Republic. He had skimmed that also and it seemed really dull. He knew Plato and that explained it but his father and mother decided on keeping that one too. He rocked forward on his knees and pulled down 'Thus Spoke Zarathustra' by Friedrich Nietzsche. Beside it was another teaser by George Bernard Shaw. 'Man and Superman.' Superman. That is more like it. Davy put back Zarathustra and opened Superman. The water stopped running upstairs and he did not notice.

Janet had finished her shower and she felt human again dressed in a loose jogging outfit. Her slippers were killing her feet. She had intended to go with Harry and Davy down to the boardwalk for fish and chips but not now. She was sore and tired and if they went they could bring her something back. She thought she had heard Davy come in.

"Davy!" Davy did not hear her and he did not answer. He was now the captive of Superman.

On sore feet she shuffled gingerly to his room to look for him and his jacket was on the bed and his closet door was open. On his dresser top, the brass button with the gold crown embossed on it was no longer alone. It had companions. She walked over and picked up an earring. A little guillotine. "Cute". Beside the earring was a monogrammed guitar pick, and two glass stones. The things kids will collect. She picked up the ruby like stone and held it to the light and looked through it. It was absolutely perfect. She put it back on his dresser and in that light, she saw how professionally it was cut. Davy, Davy. Janet walked to close Davy's closet and saw the pipe hanging there exposed under the open flap. She laughed to herself. What a kid. Some kids want clarinets, others want bicycles or iPods but his favorite is a copper pipe.

Still smiling she reached in and holding the sheath immobile, she pulled out the pipe. Funny how it hefts so nicely and it fits my hand too. She had seen Davy sight through his pretend telescope and she wanted to do it. Janet moved to the doorway and listened for signs of Davy and she heard nothing. She stepped back into the room and held it to her eye and tracked across the window. It was so interesting taking smaller areas and looking closely at them. She moved across the jungle wilderness of the maple tree at Davy's window. The sun was ten seconds away from the sill. She scanned to the window ledge and the sun caught the pipe. It began a subtle spin and the air heavied and warmed and the lure began and she dropped the pipe, petrified. She had just felt a welcoming stream of ethereal gold and it had scared her.

The front door opened and Harry Pilcher came in with a big hello. Both Davy and Janet heard him and shouted back hello. Each heard the others. Quickly, Janet put the pipe back and snapped the sheath closed. She hung it back on the same hook and as she shuffled guiltily to the top of the stairs. Janet could smell fish and chips. Right behind Harry was the delivery man.

" Ah, that was good timing."

Harry had called from work for delivery of the fish and chips. He paid the man and added a smaller tip than usual. With the rumors of plant closure, the man was getting used to smaller tips. Harry turned and spoke to Janet and to Davy who was coming into the hall carrying a book.

" I know we talked about going down to the pier and getting fish and chips but I am just too tired. I hope you don't mind." Harry saw Janet seemed relieved at that. She was coming down the stairs holding the railing with both hands to take some weight off of her feet.

" No, I don't mind at all. In fact, I was going to beg off. My feet are terminally sore. I walked two hundred miles today. That's about sixty-six miles per appointment. Nobody knows the troubles I've seen."

" Good one mom."

Harry got some plates while Janet fished for the cutlery and Davy attacked the package. One by one he tore open the cartons and the smell of the French fries and vinegar made him realize how hungry he was. At school he had had no appetite for lunch. A tired Harry put a hand on Janet's shoulder and kissed her on the cheek as he sat. Davy liked to see that.

Janet Pilcher turned inquisitionally to Davy. " So Davy, how is Mildred? I met Mrs. Craft at the Credit Union and I understand you and Mildred have been frolicking on the left bank. Janet said one sunny afternoon when she asked you where you and Mildred had been, simultaneously the two of you answered 'Paris'." His mother did not leave him with her eyes. Since she had not finished her sentence with a question Davy risked not answering. Helen realized her mistake.

" All right David. When I ask you where you have been, you say 'out'. Translated, does that mean, " I am not telling you where I have been?"

Harry wondered what this was about and on a different page he looked back and forth between them.

Davy thought. How do mothers know how to do this. The Spanish inquisition should have used mothers. He was trapped. If he said no, then why didn't he just tell her where he was. If he said yes, then where were you that you can't tell me about. There was only one way to handle this. He was going to try it without committing himself.

" Yes, we did say we were at Paris. Nice place Paris. Maybe nicer than Trafalgar. Although I suppose Woodstock could be considered nice too although maybe not so nice as Greece. Very nice, that Greece. Warm, occasionally wet you know."

Janet had no idea what just happened. She blinked her eyes as she shook the vinegar onto her fries. Harry knew what books Davy had been reading and understood his fantastical imagination. He remembered the same excited fascination he had had with some of those same books and the swashbuckling adventures they had conjured. David was his son.

" Well the next time you go to Greece, let us know and we will wait dinner. Also, David, after supper I want to have a little chat with you in my office. It won't take very long."

Janet thought. Good. Harry will straighten him out.

Davy thought this was getting serious now. His father would pin him down. He wanted to get out of there and he wolfed down his fish and chips.

" Um, may I be excused? I need to, uh, make my bed."

Harry nodded that he could be excused. Davy made a beeline upstairs. He had just volunteered to make his bed and now Janet was really suspicious.

Recently she had asked Davy where he had been. Old Tilt had asked Davy the same and he had answered glibly to both of them, "Spain." She was not sure but she thought Trafalgar was in Spain. "

"Harry, do you know where Trafalgar is? Davy mentioned Trafalgar."

" Yes. It's on the coast of Spain on the Atlantic Ocean side, not in the Mediterranean. Very near the Straits of Gibraltar. That's where Nelson fought against Napoleon's fleet in 1805 I think it was. I have a good book about it if you want to read it. I'm sure it is one of those Davy has read. It has joined the pile in his room. Why?"

"Nothing. Just wondering." *Spain. It is not possible. What I am thinking is not possible.* She did not convince herself to leave it alone.

Davy flopped down on his bed and laid on his back looking at the ceiling. He kicked the unmade bed clothes out of the way and thought about the pipe. These days he could think of nothing else and what was more worrying was the fact that now if he were separated from his pipe, he became anxious and uneasy. In addition, he now had a willing collaborator in Mildred to share and intend with and to create a much stronger trail. He had hoped the pipe might help provide solutions but it appeared he was wrong. Because of it he had created an implacable enemy in Malveena Drago who was working on using his own discovery of the pipe against him. He rolled over on his right side and saw the closet door was closed. He had not done that. He swung his feet over and walked to the closet and opened it. His belt and sheath were still there but the flap was buttoned down tightly. He had not done that either but he did not care. As far as he was concerned it could stay buttoned up forever. He knew Dopo would understand. Dopo was quiet on the matter.

The following day, Davy had breakfast with his father. Harry asked him how he liked 'Man and Superman' and Davy nodded with moving eyebrows to imply the book was fine. He recalled a phrase from it. 'Life contains but two tragedies. One is not to get your heart's desire; the other is to get it'. The pipe was teaching him the truth of that all too well.

Harry left for work and Davy walked out with him. It was very early for school but Davy wanted to walk and to think. He ran into Mildred who was restless also. They walked on to school together not really knowing the time and they were the first two into the classroom. Mr. Tilt was there early as well and they greeted each other. " Mr. Tilt." "Davidus." " Mercutio." That was it and that was what the three wanted. Tilt looked to see whether Davy was wearing his belt. The day at school passed interminably and all Davy could think of was his pipe.

He was not alone in that. Janet Pilcher could think of nothing but the pipe also. She wanted answers. The line of interesting baubles on Davy's dresser top had grown and boyish collections were fine, but the oddity was as his collection of small items grew, none of the pieces seemed remotely related to the others. And her little boy was becoming a different person. Yes, he was growing up, but that was not it. He had become wary and secretive and perpetually serious. He seemed unable to be childish now. She made her decision. She walked up to Davy's room and snatched up the Nelson button and his red stone from the dresser. She scrolled on her cell phone, found what she wanted and called Karl Richter.

Karl answered on one ring. " This is Richter."

Janet also had no time for small talk. " Karl, this is Janet Pilcher. Can I see you this morning?"

" Janet! How nice to hear from you. What's up?"

" Not much, but if you have time today would you look at some things for me?"

" Your timing is good. If you can get here within the hour I can help you out. After that I am in meetings all day."

" Thanks Karl. I will be there in 10 minutes."

The Museum of Antiquity was about four blocks away and Janet thought she could walk there in ten minutes despite her sore feet. She arrived right on time at Dr. Karl Richter's office. He was the curator of the museum and the only one on staff who had been educated locally. He and Janet had been high school chums and they were still friends although they saw each other seldom. He had his head down and he was looking at a coin with his five times magnifier.

" Hi Janet, come on in. Sit ye doon. What do you have for me?"

Karl Richter was not up on his small talk. Janet reached into her purse and pulled out the tissue she had wrapped Davy's button in. She put the button on the desk and Karl was not particularly interested. He had seen 1000 buttons

209

from 1000 uniforms and one more button really was one button too many, but Janet was his friend. He picked up the button and put it under his glass with a sigh then sat bolt upright.

"I don't believe it. Where did you get this?"

Janet answered as ambiguously as truth would allow. "I got it from an old desk."

"Well, what you got is a treasure. Astounding! This is very valuable. This button is one of Nelson's, worn at Trafalgar in fact. One set of engraved buttons was made for him in 1803 with his initials and the date. See, the small engravings?" He held his magnifying lens over it. Janet saw it clearly. H.N. 1803.

"There is one set of these buttons in the world and there is one button missing from that set and this is that very button. How did you come by it?"

He watched Janet's face and realized she had no idea what she had and obviously did not even know where it came from. Janet asked quietly. She had to be sure. "Where is Trafalgar?"

"Oh. Spain. On the Atlantic coast of Spain." He put his glass down and sat back.

"Janet, how did you come by this? A thing like this is not found in old desks. This is a 'lock it in the vault' item." She just shook her head.

"I see. Do you have more of this kind of thing?"

Her face was elsewhere as she thought about Davy.

"Oh. Sorry. No. Maybe. Yes, I do but it is not a button."

She picked the button up and stuffed it back into her purse and pulled out the other tissue and dumped the red gemstone out onto Karl's desk. He looked at it, disappointed it was not another thrill.

"Hmm. A gemstone? Sorry, that is not my area. Wait a second." He punched the intercom button.

"Roger."

"Yep."

"Got a minute?"

"Yep."

"Good. I will be right there. I am bringing a friend with me." He released the button.

"Janet, come with me. Roger Witty is the guy to look at this. He is

210

downstairs. He should be able to help you."

There was a distinct sulfurous smell in Roger's lab. Roger had been doing titrations and acid testing for so many years his damaged olfactory receptors could no longer discern whether there were ambient gases around him.

"Roger, you need to increase the volume of your evacuation hood. This place could asphyxiate an elephant."

" Oh. Well, not surprised." He shrugged and wiped his hands on a lab coat grimier than his hands. He walked to the hood and punched the button and the fan ramped up.

" Have something interesting for me?"

Janet held her hand out to show him the ruby sitting on the Kleenex. He went to a drawer and fished out two white cotton gloves and a gem cloth, a jeweler's loupe and a pair of tweezers.

"Let's have a look."

He took the stone and as he walked with it he came to a preliminary conclusion. It looked like a ruby.

"This is not the best time of day to be looking at a ruby if that is what it proves to be. At this latitude, eleven in the morning is the truest light for a proper examination." They went to the end of his bench and he sat on his wheeled stool and turned on his color corrected light. He placed Davy's red stone on the table of his phase contrast microscope and focused it. He focused to and through the stone several times and nodded.

" Thought so. Nice ruby. Better than nice." He rotated the stone slowly with the tweezers and hunched to it looking through the microscope.

" Beautiful table. Absolutely precisely cut." He turned to the color corrected light and held the stone in the tweezers against it.

"Wonderful. Eye clean and there is virtually no extinction."

He turned to Janet and saw no understanding and turned and saw the same thing on Karl's face.

" No extinction means the cut is so precise that when light reflects through the facets and up through the table, which is the top flat part, the light does not bounce around and cancel itself out and leave a shadow. It is most unusual to see a ruby cut so well as this one, with so little extinction."

The gemologist moved his stool along on its rollers and placed his gem cloth on the scale. He hit the tare button and set the scale back to zero. Roger set the ruby carefully on the platform and the red numerals showed 0.627 grams. He tapped his hand calculator to convert to carats.

"Excellent. Just above the number. The stone is 3.125 carats. If it showed 2.999 carats it is worth about 20% less. Just above the magic number and really good." He put his loupe down with a satisfied finality.

" I am very familiar with this stone. Not this particular one but with its characteristics and origin. This is the top of the line. There are no inclusions. Not one. There are no feathers, little weak spots, and it has not been filled, nothing has been faked. I'm sure this is a Mogok ruby. From northern Myanmar."

He turned to Janet. " If you own this, you are lucky woman. This type of stone was the most prized by the ancients and it is prized even more so today. At auction this stone would start the bidding at about $80,000 per carat. So, you have a nice little rock worth at least $250,000."

He pulled out a small cloth bag from his junk drawer and dropped in the ruby and swung the bag to Janet.

" This might be better than the Kleenex."

She and Karl walked in silence back to Karl's office where Janet said a dumbfounded stumbling goodbye. Her footsteps echoed off the museum floor but she was deaf to them. She walked home and went directly to Davy`s room and placed the button and ruby back on the dresser about where she thought they had been. Two astounding priceless articles had been sitting there like junk. She could not fathom it. Quickly she walked to the closet and removed Davy's pipe from its sheath and stuck it in her purse. There was someone she needed to speak with.

Helen Craft walked around the house throwing open window after window in an attempt to get the paint smell out of the room. She enjoyed painting but the smell of the latex paint made her dizzy and she was trying to blow it away. The landlord had gotten her some touch-up paint and there had been enough left over to freshen up the living room side of the wall which separated it from the kitchen. She had paint spattered on her face as she usually did before she got the feel of the roller. More paint was not always better.

Under an uncertain cumulus sky, Janet Pilcher walked toward the Borstal river and the Craft's row house. She could see the four-foot-high wild lobelia from 100 yards away. Its blossoms swathed the entire riverbank in a brilliant deep red and there was enough of a breeze to make them shimmer. She crossed the old concrete bridge through a flurry of cabbage butterflies that appeared and disappeared as the moving clouds covered then exposed them. They fluttered in contrast against the lobelia and the bumblebees continued their rounds along the bank. Squadrons of blue skimmers helicoptered low over the surface of the water and sped downstream looking for tidbits. The sight and sound of the life on the water gentled her. She asked herself why she did not come here more often. She ignored her sore feet and picked up her walking pace. Her purse swung rhythmically against her thigh and the pipe tapped a reminder it was there.

Janet looked forward to seeing Mildred's mother. They needed to compare notes. As she approached the Craft residence, a soaring rock ballad accompanied by crowd noise rang along the street. As Janet got to the front door of Mildred's house the place was jumping. Janet listened before she knocked. Ah! She joined in to hum an out of tune melody line of 'Don't Stop Believing' by Journey. She knew every note, every word and every breathing spot of that song and of every song Journey had ever sung. She knocked hard on the front door trying to overcome the volume of the band. *Wow. Mildred really has it blasting. Wonder where her mother is.* Janet had walked a long way to see her and she would wait.

Inside the house, Helen Craft was singing along too as she cleaned the paint from her brush and roller and ran the hot soapy water down the drain. She thought she imagined a knock and doubted it but walked to the door just in case. "Streetlights, people, Livin' just to find emotion Hidin' somewhere in the niiiiiiiight." She wailed it at the top of her lungs a full third of an octave under the pitch and knew it was perfect and felt great as she approached the door.

No-one had come to answer the door and Janet was moving to the music and began to sing along also. "Streetlights, people, Livin' just to find emotion Hidin' somewhere in the niiiiiiiight." She wailed it at the top of her lungs a perfect fourth under the pitch and knew it was perfect and felt great. Helen opened the door and put her head back at the same instant Janet put her head back and the two of them let it rip. They both heard the screeching from the other one and stopped and looked at the person in the doorway. They looked at each other and they ran their eyes from top to bottom and back down to the bottom again. They did not know why they did it and they both recognized they had done it and they burst out laughing. Helen Craft had her hair back with a ribbon and a small halter top and torn blue jeans. She had paint on her face and paint on her running shoes and looked frazzled. Janet wore a black skirt and black shoes and a white blouse and looked frazzled.

" Mrs. Pilcher. Come in, please come in. Let me turn down the music."

Helen walked to the Bose player and turned down the volume. It could still be heard faintly.

" I apologize for the racket. It is the live album from Philadelphia. June 5 1983. Journey. 90,000 people outdoors on a summer's night. That kind of concert is something I never did and I have always wanted to do." She laughed.

" I guess I should apologize for my singing too, but what the heck. I belt it out along with the band and I just feel liberated. I know every word in every song Journey ever sang."

Janet could not believe it. " Call me Janet, please. As you heard I do the same thing." They laughed again and all embarrassment was gone.

" I love to sing with that band and I know I'm nowhere near the notes but I don't care. It's the thought that counts." They laughed again. Mrs. Craft gestured to the kitchen table as she walked to the kettle and felt the side of it. She cranked up the heat and opened the tin of tea bags. She got down two mugs and plopped in a tea bag each without asking.

" I'm glad to see you Janet. This is perfect. I just finished cleaning up after painting in the living room and I was about to have some tea. Sorry for the paint smell." She scanned Janet's face and beneath the pleasantry she saw determination.

"I think this is only partially a social call. I see "mission' written on your face."

Janet sighed as she nodded and hoped she wasn't always that transparent. She knew she was carrying an unpleasant demeanor these days but she couldn't put it down. She put her purse on the table and it made a clunk from the pipe. Janet sighed again and pulled the pipe from her purse and set it down and it did a neat single full spin. She looked down at the pipe.

" That, is partially why I wanted to come and speak with you. The other part is how my Davy is behaving and I wondered whether Mildred was the same. Davy is a fearful boy. He's lost in thought but not in a youthful imaginings way. He has stress in him. When he leaves the house, he stops in the door jamb and scans his field of vision. It is as if he's looking out for something or he thinks he's under surveillance or some such. He's taking longer and longer to get home from school and when I ask him about it he just says he is using more interesting new routes. He is not himself and his new self is an uptight worried little boy."

Helen nodded. " I see some changes in Mildred also. She has always been so fastidious about her clothes but she comes home covered in burrs with little catches and pulls in her clothing as if she's been caught on barbed wire. She says she's picking flowers but I don't think that's it. When she dresses in the morning it is almost as if she were preparing a disguise."

" Helen, when you ask her where she has been, does she deflect your question and give you what seem to be sarcastic or flippant answers like Moscow or Paris or Spain or the like?"

" Yes, she does," Helen's voice showed defeat. She was on her own without a job and week by week she drained more of what remained of her small savings. She and Mildred had always been close and sharing and now Mildred confided nothing. John Craft was missing and she carried great guilt that in her heart she feared he was dead.

Janet's feet were still sore from her blister walk and she kicked off her shoes and got some relief. She admitted she had been snooping in Davy's room. Helen nodded as if that were a normal practice, so what. She recounted her visit to the museum to Helen. She told about authenticating the little artifacts Davy had on his dresser and how they matched the places he said he had been. Helen got up, poured the water on the tea bags and brought the mugs to the table. Neither of them said anything but just sat and watched the steam rise. Janet reached and picked up the pipe.

" Then there is this thing. It scares the wits out of me."

Helen did not understand. " It is a piece of pipe. What's to be scared."

" It's what it can do that scares me."

The Bose player had reached " Don't Stop Believing" from the live Philadelphia concert and they looked at each other and smiled at how great it sounded.

" Yesterday I took this pipe to the window and looked out with it like a telescope and when the sunlight came in, it spun and it lured and it wanted to take me someplace. I knew if I was really thinking of somewhere I would've been gone in an instant. I felt a warm and wonderful and inviting escape coming from that pipe and it shook me up and I got scared. I dropped it like a hot potato."

"Don't Stop Believing" swam laps in their minds. On and on and on and on. Helen looked incredulously at the pipe. Janet stood with it and shuffled in her stocking feet toward the window. "Come on, I will show you exactly."

Helen got up and neither of them realized they were moving exactly in time with the music and both would rather be in Philadelphia.

" This is what I did." Janet wanted to demonstrate the event of the previous day but she also feared she would. She trembled as she held the pipe to the window and Helen stood close at her shoulder as witness. The wind was picking up and some clouds were breaking. Shadows from the billowing cumulous moved across the flower beds below the window and teased them with a bit of sun. Janet was not looking at the flower bed. She had sighted her pretend telescope on one particular cloud and she followed it as it became a gargoyle and then a rose and then it blasted wide open and the sun welcomed Davy's pipe.

Spun gold consciousness overcame her with its warmth and its enormous integrity startled her and she made a little " unk" noise and went rigid and into a sway. Helen reacted and grabbed her to stop her from falling and the light had both of them. The throbbing harmonic within the pipe endorsed the tempo of the music in their heads and it spun them beautifully into a rhythmic goldness. The strength of their dual intention was large and the embracing honey sweet channel through which they moved was confident for them and protective of them. They gave themselves up to its leading tones and landed without concern, worry or care among an ecstatic crowd which insulated them from a critical world. They stood beside each other in a delicious agglutination. They heard the murmur of thousands of people and they did not have to act and they looked around in total acceptance of what they saw, with no interest in how they were part of it. They observed the sweep of searchlights move across a thousand faces and they waited for clarity to release them from passivity. They saw the storm of consciousness coming at them through a jello telescope and it hit them hard and made them into themselves with a rim shot.

It was a very warm night for June in Philadelphia in 1983. The humidity was off the charts but it seemed to waft the pot nicely. They had arrived 20 rows up, just off stage right in JFK stadium in Philadelphia. From that angle they could see the technician for the drummer hunkering down adjusting the bass-treble balance on the monitors. Janet and Helen made an odd couple. Helen had a paint spackled face, she wore blue jeans with a tear in the right knee, a small halter top and sneakers. Her hair was tied back with a green ribbon and with her slender physique she could pass for a kid. Janet was in her business attire wearing a straight black skirt, a conservative high necked white blouse and subtle makeup. She could pass for Helen's maiden aunt. A maiden aunt without shoes. The shoes were under Helen's kitchen table.

Mildred walked into the kitchen and got out two glasses and put them on the table. She walked to the refrigerator and pulled out the milk and poured some for Davy and her. She noticed a pair of shoes. Odd. Mom doesn't usually leave stuff around. Well she is getting older. Maybe she just forgot about them. She did not attribute anything to the two warm mugs on the table. Mildred hit the front screen door with her hip to open it and let it slam behind her. She sat down on the stoop beside Davy and handed him the glass of milk.

Twelve Searchlights looked for infinity but they had to settle for playing across the low cloud bank. The throng was primed and it felt like heaven to them. 25,000 cigarette lighters were lit one by one to become new stars in an inverted dome of the sky created in the bowl-shaped concavity of the open-air stadium. The believers had made a cosmic creation of their own, a rock galaxy appearing from nowhere to share its light and life and burn bright for one brief night. The back of the stadium had a better angle and they saw the show was beginning before anyone else could. A wave of sound rolled forward from the back and it built and grew and broke like a wave against the stage. By the second soaring bass guitar chord, 90,000 people knew the song. Janet and Helen were one chord ahead of them. 'Chain Reaction' took off like a rocket and the lead singer took over their world. The show moved forward with clockwork precision as the seventy technicians and support staff made it perfect. 'Still They Ride' followed 'Send Her My Love' followed 'Line of Fire'. Janet and Helen sang

217

every song and felt every hurt and lost every love right along with the band. In 'Don't Stop Believing' the guitar player started his solo accelerating riff and the crowd screamed as one in their common familiarity with the music. The lead vocalist handed off to the crowd as he pointed the microphone to them and shouted " Sing the song," and ninety thousand of them sang. They sang deliriously in love with the band and each other for being there. A constant hum of adulation and joy filled the stadium. Janet and Helen were sixteen again and the youth coursed through them. When the band began the first chords of " Forever Yours Faithfully" the mood of the stadium changed. There was a warmth that came over it and the band was into it like never before. Around the stadium eyes welled as the song's message of a promise of fidelity moved their collective spirit. Tears streamed from the eyes of Janet and Helen. Helen for her missing husband and Janet for her hardworking man. At the end of the song ninety thousand people stretched their arms high above their heads and applauded as if they had never applauded before. When the concert ended it was like a broken heart.

There were one hundred climactic explosions and the stage went dark. It was the first time Janet realized she'd had no shoes on. There was also one thing they had not counted on. Sunshine was hard to come by.

The lights began to ratchet down tier by tier within the stadium. The roadies were scrambling to pack up the monitors and get back on the road after a beautiful concert and a job well done. The technician for the drummer began packing the huge kit as if it were fine crystal. Janet and Helen watched happily as the beautiful June evening contracted around them into a frigid night. As their eyes acclimated to the diminished light they saw the stadium was still half full. Thousands were staying. There was no show on stage but the afterglow kept them there. One by one the cigarette lighters were shut and in their place ten thousand ends glowed like so many fireflies. Everyone was happy. Janet and Helen were cold. Janet's feet were freezing and she found a piece of cardboard to keep them off the concrete. Shivering, they huddled into each other in their seats and as the stadium continued to empty, the wind could make a longer sweep and it got colder. A young man wearing a red white and black fringed poncho stopped and looked at them. They looked pathetic.

" Here." He took off his poncho and handed it to them. He spoke to Helen.

"You and your mother need this more than I do. Peace." Janet was going to complain and thought better of it. It was a fair trade.

First light showed against the upper deck on the west side of the stadium above and behind them. Colitas were strewn everywhere on the concrete walkway. Janet had nothing to bring back as a souvenir so they were it. She picked up two of them and put them in the pipe and stuffed its ends with a hot dog wrapper. She handed the pipe to Helen and she pushed it down into her jeans pocket. The cleanup crew had begun just before dawn. They sang as they pushed the brooms along toward Janet's section. The two women climbed the forty rows to the top and waited for the sun to come down the next ten feet. Mother Janet and daughter Helen stood ready, willing and able. They held hands and Janet swung the pipe to her eye. The two colitas were still inside and they spun like a blender as the force of the intention ramped up. The ladies floated safely away within a crooning smooth dynamic envelope and traveled around a million circles of fifths in perfect approving harmony, oblivious to what they saw. They landed back in the kitchen exactly where they had left, tight against the window sill. Helen did not absorb that the lawn needed watering and Janet saw Davy out front and had no thought about anything at all. They were dispassionate observers with no requirement of any kind for anything for any purpose. Dimly they saw something approaching them and that was fine, it was not their responsibility. The resuscitating release washed against them like a slow lapping wave and they focused on the street. Together they breathed a slow satisfied relief.

From the front steps Mildred picked up something in her peripheral vision and turned to see Mrs. Pilcher and her mother standing there looking out. Apparently transfixed by the view, they were immobile. Funny. They must have come down the laneway and in through the back door. That was one of her new routes.

Mildred and Davy got up and wandered inside to say hello to their mothers. Helen heard the screen door and snatched the pipe and stuffed it into her pocket. One of the joint ends fell on the floor and Janet put her stocking foot on it. The kids walked into the kitchen and their parents were both looking a little stunned. She saw Mrs. Pilcher was in stocking feet and standing with all her weight on one foot. So those are her shoes under the table. Why on earth would she go out walking around without her shoes. Mildred assumed the mother role. "Where have you been?"

Janet and Helen were not used to this. They blurted out in perfect unison, "Philadelphia."

Mildred's face went white. Davy grabbed at his hip but his pipe was at home. They said nothing and did not dare even to exchange a glance. Then Davy smiled. Ah. He got it. They were getting even for the times Davy and Mildred had answered like that. We say Paris, they say Philadelphia. Even Steven. He smiled at Mildred and she gained some color.

Janet and Helen walked coolly back to the kitchen table. Janet had her toes curled up to trap the piece of the joint and every step made a little round wet spot. She slipped her shoes back on and squeezed the juice around as she forced in her foot. It felt good on her blister and their tea was still warm. Davy and Mildred knew old ladies behaved in strange ways and this was confirmation. They went out the back door and stealthed through the back lanes on their way down over the bluff to the pier. The tide was out and Mildred had concocted a kite. They were going to try to fly it and besides Davy needed the gulls.

Helen extracted the remaining joint and handed the pipe to Janet. Helen held the souvenir between her fingers and waggled it to indicate she was keeping it. Janet smiled and nodded. Hers was stuck to the bottom of her foot.

At home, Janet Pilcher was deep in thought. She returned the pipe to Davy's sheath. She put the squashed colita on top of her dresser, starting her collection. She was not sure how to handle this.

At home, Helen Craft was deep in thought. She put her souvenir on top of her dresser. She had traveled to a distant location. She had seen and spoken with the people there. Could she do something like that to find John.

On his way home, Davy Pilcher was deep in thought. His mother and Mrs. Craft had behaved oddly. Philadelphia. What if they were really there. "What do you think Dopo, maybe that explains the closed flap on my leather sheath." Dopo was deep in thought.

"Maybe I should talk to dad about this."

Chapter 16: Snakes and Crocodiles

Harry Pilcher sat on the front hall bench and tightened the bow in his shoelace as Davy came down from his room and bounced toward the front door.

" Davy, I'm walking up to High Point Garage on Fraser street. I think you know the owner, Mr. Singh? I have a meeting with him about a part time job. We can walk together if you like. I thought you might want to watch the mechanics. Maybe they will give you some pointers."

Harry wished that was the case because personally he was hopeless when it came to fixing his own car. With a little luck he could tell whether his engine was running. He also knew where to put the gas in. That was the limit of his mechanical capability and to him automobiles were one of the mysteries of the universe.

Davy thought a walk to the garage was a good idea. He had already decided he owed an explanation to his father of his antics with the pipe and the problems with Malveena Drago. The time just never seemed to be right. He still had not decided exactly how he was going to describe the phenomenon of the pipe. It might be easier to slip the topic in while they were just walking along together. *"Dad, you should see the view over the bay of Corinth,"* or maybe, *" The Tuileries are beautiful when they are not cutting off people's heads,"* or maybe, *"What a laugh it is Dad, to see Mr. Foster standing up to his knees in mud at Woodstock."* Perhaps not. Davy grabbed his jacket off the hall tree and swung it on over his head in tacit agreement the walk was good with him.

" Better keep a weather eye dad, the gulls show the glass is falling."

Harry knew what he meant but his boy certainly had an interesting way of saying it. Harry grabbed his umbrella.

High Point was one of the older areas in town and Fraser Street ran east and west along the crest of the bluff, and it delimited the slope up from the sea. The warm updrafts were strongest there and high above the intersection, thousands of gulls tested the wind in happy conversation and adjusted themselves to the low-pressure front moving in. Mr. Singh had owned High Point Garage for over twenty years and he was Harry's mechanic until Harry sold the family car. From

221

the door of the north car bay you could see the end of the pier and a bit of the marina. It was rumoured a high-rise condominium complex was planned for there and Davy wondered where the gulls would meet if that happened.

Harry and Davy walked up to the Parts Desk beside Mr. Singh's office and waited for him. His door was missing and the work area was a shambles in the middle of renovations. On the back wall at the parts department of the High Point garage was a large calendar showing a beach scene in Australia and from it a bikini clad surfer girl flashed her chicklet teeth. Davy had never seen such a girl. The stepladder the electrician was using to replace a light fixture was tight against the calendar and it blocked part of the printing. All Davy could see was " Australia" and a capital "B" and another capital "B" right below it and in the vee of the ladder was the tanned queen of the universe. Davy saw his father watching him look at the calendar and he blushed. Harry said nothing.

From close by came the sinister whine of a highly tuned sports car shutting down. The door slammed furiously and clacking heels stalked and stomped away from the service bays and echoed throughout the garage. Davy stiffened and moved closer to his father and sidled into a parallel profile to hide himself. Without moving his feet, he craned through the glass panel in the door separating the work area from the parts counter. There in the third service bay to the right, sat a gleaming black Porsche. It was the same model and year as Malveena's. Harry saw Davy coming closer into his peripheral vision. Davy was shaking.

" What's wrong Davy? You are trembling." He put his arm around him and pulled him closer.

" Nothing dad. Just a little chill."
Davy looked back at the reception area and Malveena was not there. He ran his eyes along the walkways between the grease pits and she was not there either. *This might be the right time to tell Dad. He did ask. No. He has troubles of his own.* Mr. Singh saw the two of them standing at the counter and waved them into his office.

" Harry, David. Have a seat. David. Why so serious?" He smiled and turned to Harry and gestured to Davy. "Ok to talk?"

"Yes, fine. It's good Davy is in on this. So, when do I start?"

"First day, Wednesday evening, 8:00 PM. 4 hours a night, 15-minute break after 2 hours. From then on three nights a week, Monday, Wednesday and Friday. Pay every two weeks with standard deductions. Will that work?" Harry nodded a yes with a relieved smile. The garage owner had been very generous with his time. Harry appreciated it and he did not want to abuse the cordiality. He stood and shook hands with Mr. Singh.

" Thanks, Adeeb. I appreciate it very much. I will be here on time."

Harry ushered Davy out with his hand on his back and with concern over his boy's nervousness. Davy leaned a little into Harry's hand, shrinking from the impending collision with Malveena. He strained a look at bay three and astoundingly it was empty. No Porsche, no Malveena, and his dad had just gotten a part time cleaning job. Things were good. It was sprinkling rain as they walked out onto the street unmolested and they shared the umbrella on the quiet walk home.

Porky Gregious careened around the corner into the classroom and slid the last five feet and semi-crashed into his seat. He sat on the other side of Mildred from Davy and they seldom spoke to each other in class. Unaccountably, Porky was there early. He was so accustomed to being late and doing the frantic scramble to his desk, he had forgotten there was another way. Davy looked over at Porky who was already perspiring. Porky was smart enough, he just froze up and got nervous at the wrong times. Recently he had found a quiet place to get away from the jibes and the fat jokes, and that place was the library. He had become a good reader and he remembered what he read. Every day he was there reading diverse things. Porky was a surprise waiting to happen.

" Porky, you read about Australia, occasionally don't you?" Porky nodded yes but he was suspicious. Nobody engaged him in talk unless there was a zinger coming after it.

" Porky, yesterday I saw a calendar in Singh's garage with a picture of a beach in Australia but the name was partially covered up by a ladder. Two words, each word starting with a 'B'. The rest was blocked out. All I could see was the beginning of the two words. And a beach." He did not mention the surfer girl.

" Australia? Two Bs and a beach? Easy Davy. Botany Bay. Very famous."

"Botany Bay?" *Of course.* Davy knew that name. "I think the first settlers went, there didn't they?"

"Yes, something like that." Porky nodded slowly in agreement and said no more. He was not going to get trapped into some kind of ridicule. *I suppose first settlers, if you call convicts settlers. Then there are the Eora the Gweagal and the Bidjigal. Aboriginal tribes who were there already. Nobody talks much about them.*

On the way home, all Davy could think of was rolling waves and chicklet smiles. He bounced up the steps to the front porch and pinched a bean. His mother was sitting reading in the little bower made by the scarlet runner bean vines. Davy had used up all his internet time for the month so he asked his mother. " Mom, Botany Bay. Australia, right?"

"Yes Davy. Thousands of people were transported there from England. Many unfortunate Irish and some Scots and Canadians as well. It was a very hard life for them even if they were lucky enough to survive the voyage. Yes, fortunate to survive."

"Mom, do they ah, surf, there in Botany Bay, do you know? "

" I don't really know, but well, it is a bay, so I guess they could. Why?" Janet knew something was up with Davy.

"Just curious. I saw a picture of a great beach and I think it was there."

That was enough for Davy. He thought about it for a few days but he had already made up his mind. He was going to Botany Bay, the land of white beaches, breaking waves and surfer girls. *Maybe I should take Porky. No. Porky's mother makes him wear corduroy pants. Perhaps Mildred? No. I know Mildred would not enjoy it. Her balaclava would be far too hot and besides, you have seen one beach, you have seen them all.*

At the end of the week the renovations were done at Singh's garage. The workman folded up his stepladder and put it under his arm and hit the freshly painted door frames with the ladder only twice on the way to his truck. The wonders of Australia held forth from the glossy calendar on the wall of the parts department. The sun sparkled on the sea, the perfect teeth of the surfer girl sparkled, and the silver sand of the beach ran up and faded into grass covered dunes; but it was not the sand of the famous Botany Bay. It was the sand of the famous Bondi Beach.

Davy fished into his mother's rag bag of discarded clothing. He searched through and found his favorite old blue jeans and black shirt tangled together. The old reliables were badly wrinkled but they were clean and they had that just laundered smell. He held them against his face for a few seconds then pulled them on and they felt good. He realized this was the last time he could do this. The shirt was two inches too short for his arms and the pants were three inches too short for his legs and his right pocket was worn white from the constant swinging of the pipe sheath. The tear at his left knee was a nice touch. He knew this outfit would be a big hit with his mother. He looked like an apprentice scarecrow. *Good huh Dopo?* Dopo just shook his head.

The red sweep hand of the too large kitchen clock quietly ticked off the seconds. Its initial aggravation had become a steadying reliable part of the home. Janet looked over her budget sheet and sipped her glass of hot sweet Vietnamese che. She had ordered it online from Philadelphia. She heard her son coming down the stairs and waited for his jump to the floor to avoid the squeaky stair tread. She was not disappointed. Davy swung around the newel post and made it creak and headed for the kitchen. Janet watched Ichabod coming toward her, all ankles and wrists. He walked past her to the refrigerator and grabbed out an apple. He slowed to get the reaction. "Good Lord Davy," was all Janet said and she went back to her budget sheet. Davy laughed to himself as he slipped his belt through the loop on his pipe sheath, cinched it up and strolled out and down toward the beach. He made his way downhill to the sea through a warren of side streets, staying away from the main thoroughfares. As he wound his way down and through the small houses, he saw more 'For Sale' signs were showing up. The town was worried about Foster Industries. A flock of vocal companions spun their perfect circles high above him and followed along in support. He wondered whether they had relatives in Australia he could say hello to.

The pier was very crowded and he was pleased to see that. Given Malveena's intent, the more people around him the better. Among them was the omnipresent Mrs. Williams.

" Mrs. Williams, is it possible you actually live right on the pier?"

" Oh Davy, you are so funny. No. Just wish I did. I love the gulls, I love the sky, I love the smell of the kelp. I just love it. Don't you just love it?"

Davy did love it but he had exhausted his gushing quotient for the day so he smiled and nodded and turned up the pier toward the marina. Mrs. Williams watched him go. *He looks so skinny. So, so, ... poor. I will get him some new pants.*

Davy was excited. This was the first time in quite a while he was traveling on his own. Small guilt niggled at him about not taking Mildred but he knew exactly how it would be if he did. Balaclava or not the duck lips would be hard at work. Anyway, surfing was something you did on your own. He had never done it but it looked like fun. He visualized himself hanging ten in a monster curl then paddling back to the shallows in perfect control and walking on shore with his rad board under his arm as he flipped his hair back off his face and flashed a crooked smile with his straight chicklet surfer teeth.

The cloud bank was opening and he could see it would be a few minutes until he had reliable brightness. He leaned back against the wide wooden railing with two gulls sitting three feet on either side of him and they didn't move a feather. He assumed his cool surfer posture and practiced saying 'dude' with every possible elongation of the 'u' and placed different emphasis on each of the two 'ds to make it real. He decided to scan an interesting cloud shape and to wait for it to blossom. He scoped the cloud and thought idly of the comments of his mother about the hard times for the Irish in Botany Bay. *Perhaps I should have invited Porky. Porky knows about Botany Bay and it might be better to have company.* The slow-moving cloud dissolved suddenly and with a coronal burst the intention within the light caught Davy completely off guard and transported him. The consciousness spun around him with a strong golden shimmer. It carried Davy warmly and rotated him slowly counterclockwise and deposited him down under.

Davy landed on firm turf, stuffed into neck high bushes covered with past ripe blackberries. As he swayed in a gelatinous torpor, the sweet red juice daubed his clothing. He felt punctures from the blackberry thorns on his uncovered ankles and wrists and he was unconcerned with them. He was divorced from the need to act. A low belt of bright green, salt cedar bushes ran away along the elevated sand bank to his right. Just above the high tide line, patches of golden rod swarmed with fritillary butterflies and the beauty of them did not register with him. Quickly, the Australian heatwaves melted away the congealment which trapped Davy and with a furnace blast of consciousness he arrived in his chosen reality on the bank of Botany Bay.

Wild blackberries were everywhere and Davy was trapped in a copse of them sitting on a narrow plateau which fell abruptly to the beach. A million thorns hooked into his clothing and pierced his ankles and wrists and he could not move. Already he was feeling the burn of the sun on his bare head. The blackberries were dense and covered with half inch thorns. He was surrounded by them for fifty feet in every direction except on the seaward side where he had about eight feet of thorns to fight through. From there into the soft sand of the beach there was a ten-foot drop Davy could not see from his vantage point inside the bushes.

The wind was against his right cheek and he heard commotion coming from that direction. People were coming, two by two with a strange gait. They were dressed brightly in black and yellow, some in gray and white and a couple of them wore red and white tunics. They carried something over their shoulders. *Paddle boards.* No, it was something else. *Glinting.* The string of forty men plodded closer and Davy's heart sank as he realized this was a convict work gang. They carried picks and shovels and heavy hammers. They walked along the flat of the wet sand where it was easier walking and they swung their feet in a short rhythmic stride to minimize the leg irons cutting into their flesh. Most of them wore their irons on the outside of their trousers. The ones dressed in yellow and black looked almost canary like or clown like. Their colors alternated in a harlequin like mismatch with large white arrows running up their trouser legs. Two Marines in stained red and white tunics guarded them with muskets and a warder with a cudgel followed behind. All men wore wide brimmed hats or floppy long eared woolen toques. Their jackets were short with six buttons and their trousers buttoned up the sides so they could be removed without taking off the leg irons. A few of the men were nothing but boys like Davy and some were aged, leather skinned skeletal wrecks. *Davy you idiot. You didn't bring a hat and you are here in what is probably 1820. All you had to do on the pier was focus, but no, you were thinking about settlers and Porky and your mother. Porky of all things.*

Davy's stifled the urge to call out to them. He decided this was not a group to surprise. The latent fury of a beaten cur hung over these men and he did not want to be the object of its release. Two besotted guards staggered and herded them along with mindless monotony. The last thing Davy needed to risk was a confrontation with drunken marines carrying muskets and looking for new blood.

He had been there for just a few minutes and the sun was already burning his forehead. He attempted to duck to make himself less conspicuous and as he did so, one hundred thorns tore at his clothing and into his skin. The prisoners were now about fifty yards to his right and moving closer to him as the beach curved in toward the small bluff. He pivoted to see his shortest escape from the thorns and it was toward the sea. He stayed low and began to lean into the bushes. They tore at his skin and they yielded only when they tore him. He made slow headway but he was gaining. All the men except for the cudgel warden had passed him when the final restraining face of the bush gave way and he burst forward and stepped into the air and somersaulted onto the beach. He let out a startled shriek and landed on his feet with one thorny blackberry bush tentacle still holding tenaciously to the seat of his pants.

Marine Sergeant Smits was on the near side and he spun toward the yelp. He went into a crouch while he fully cocked the hammer of his musket. The far side marine shouted "Sit" and the men dropped like stones. They had tasted the butt end of the gun stock often enough for being slow about it. Smits shouted, "Oy! That man!", and pointed at Davy with his musket. All eyes turned to that man.

That man stood with a dazed expression and looked fearfully at the black hole making the end of the Marine's musket. Davy was bleeding profusely from his hands and wrists and ankles. The blackberry juice had stained him a bloody red from top to bottom and his clothing hung in shards, the old fabric torn easily by the thorns. The marine was twenty feet away and he edged forward with his gun sight keened on Davy's chest. He examined the hapless culprit. He saw the fear and he relished it. The culprit was pale. *S'been out of the sun. Confined, maybe solitary. Bleedin' from his ankles and wrists. Some'ow e's gotten manacles off and e's tore the flesh doing it. Well I got 'im anyway but we baint taken 'im wiff us. We has eight miles to slog to Port Jackson and now we's behind time.* He pointed at Davy and barked at the warder with the cudgel.

"Burridge. Take this muck back to barracks. Get 'im set up with slops and get 'im out of 'is rags. Make sure the slops is canary. 'E's 'scaped from somewheres."

Smits approached to within an arm's length of Davy and thumped him hard in the gut with his musket stock.

"You. Go with Burridge." He tilted his head to reference the warder. The far side marine swept the seated convicts with his fully cocked musket as Burridge hurried toward Davy, smacking the palm of his open hand with his cudgel. Davy attempted to step forward to go with him but he was held in place by the thorny branch attached to the seat of his pants. He could not obey the order. The marine swung his gun around and drove the butt end hard toward Davy's face just as the tension on the blackberry vine let go and Davy fell flat on his face in the sand. The blow just grazed his right ear. Burridge strode forward and jerked Davy to his feet and shook him and rapped him on the left ear with his cudgel. The marine sergeant said nothing and looked at Davy's face closely. He would remember this one. He turned to Burridge.

"Burridge, get moving. Turn 'im over and catch us up on the double. Don't play about."

Burridge pushed Davy ahead of him along a trackless route. The footsteps of the chain gang had disappeared into the sea and Davy had no idea where to go even though he was leading. From behind, Burridge whacked Davy on his elbows to steer him. Left right left right they walked. A pair of green plumed blue-bellied parrots followed along and whistled in a sweet duet. They swirled up with every whack and settled with a soft whistle anticipating the next one. Davy ached everywhere and the sun burned him relentlessly but he still had his wits about him. If he could get a few feet ahead of Burridge he would sight his pipe to the sun and be gone. He subtly increased his stride and gained about three feet. He flashed his hand to his sheath and stumbled in disbelief. There was nothing there. His sheath was gone and the pipe with it. The blackberries had ripped it off when he vaulted to the beach. Davy emitted an agonized groan of disbelief. Burridge whacked him hard on the right shoulder.

"Shut your trap unless you want more. When I speak to you, you answer. If I doesn't speak to you, you keeps the trap shut. Savvy?" Half paralytic with panic, Davy croaked a submissive "Yes."

Over the brow of the hill Davy saw the clock face of Hyde Park Barracks in the distance. His left ear was bleeding and swelling and his arms were numb from the hammering of the cudgel on his elbows. The rips and tears in his shirt finally separated and it split open at the back to reveal hundreds of bloody rivulets. Davy and his shepherd arrived at the barracks. It was a hulking and gloomy four-story stone building which seemed to identify with the lot of the convicts. The surround of the barracks was a high brick wall and they entered through stout folding doors fashioned from red cedar slabs. Burridge propelled Davy forward across an immaculate wide cobbled courtyard by poking the end of his cudgel into Davy's back. He said simply "Canary" and shoved him into to the arms of two convict constables and he spun away to catch up with his gang.

The constables looked at the boy with his torn shirt and ill-fitting trousers and his swollen ears and shook their heads. They turned him and saw the deep lacerations in his skin.

" Lad, you need something on those. If they get infected in this heat you are done for." The scrape of shovels echoed off the stone walls as the horse manure brigade harvested the fertilizer for the convict garden.

David Pilcher stood naked in the infirmary of Hyde Park Barracks at Botany Bay Australia in the year 1820. He was in shock and in his hypnotic floating netherworld they were basting him with a sticky brown paste made of emu bush leaves and tea tree oil. All the pain was gone from his skin and much of it was gone from his battered arms and split ears. In two days every scratch would be pink and healing. The ancient aboriginal treatment guaranteed there would be no infection. His state of mind was recovering its stability. Davy's slops sat on the floor beside him. There were two sets of clean clothes for changing twice a week as issued by the Commissariat and there was a spare set of trousers given out at the order of Governor Macquarie for clean church going on Sundays. Beside the clothing sat a bag and bedding and a buckled strap to carry it all. As marine Burridge had ordered, his slops were yellow and black like the ones he had seen on the chain gang. One pant leg was black and the other was brilliant canary yellow. The jacket was the same. Running up each pant leg was a series of white arrows pointing upward. His ridiculous and garish uniform mimicked a court jester and it was intended as a public humiliation to have to wear it. Its implication was lost altogether on Davy. This was the garb of a repeat offender. He was a canary man.

Davy pulled on his brilliant yellow and black uniform over the sticky ointment and it stuck to him in fifty oozing places. Davy shook with anxiety as the same two constable convicts escorted him to the third floor of the barracks and stood him in front of a hammock. The sight of it carried him back to his time with Admiral Nelson on the HMS Victory and he smelled the gunpowder and he felt the roll of the deck and a great tranquility came over him. His breathing slowed and his heart rate slowed and his musculature relaxed and he was beyond the pain and he was at ease. The trustees were astounded at the sangfroid of this frail damaged lad.

" Listen boy. This here hammock is yers. Until ya get yer name sewed inta yer slops, wear 'em all. They be hooked otherwise."

The senior constable unfolded a paper and held it against a post and handed Davy a pencil. " Make yer X here on the line. This be yer receipt for slops." Davy took the pencil and signed his name with a flourish. The constables walked off and left Davy standing alone. They said nothing but they knew few convicts who could write and none of them was a canary man.

Along the length of the prison dormitory ran four stout wooden rails, with two rails on each side of a narrow central corridor. Ten large windows ran the length of each wall and three larger windows ran across the ends of the space. They made the dormitory bright and they made it hot. The temperature on the third floor was more than 100°. The building was made to house 600 men but now it held 1100. Hammocks were hung between the rails at sixteen inches from hammock to hammock. Davy was suddenly overcome with the need to sleep. He began to unlace his shoes when he remembered the 'hooked' warning against taking his things off so he did them back up. His arms were stiffening from the cudgel blows and with extreme difficulty he rolled into his hammock. He was dead to the world within thirty seconds with his extra sets of trousers clutched to his chest.

He was awakened by a punch to the shoulder.

" Lad! New chum! Get your bleedin' boot off my kip." Davy sat up with a shot and retracted his stray leg. He had covered himself entirely with his pants and when they fell away the boy who had punched him went white. Every new man was labeled a chum but this was a canary man. And he had punched him when he was asleep. Surely violent revenge would come his way when the time was right.

A loud bell rang out from the courtyard. The 20 or 30 men in barracks paraded out quickly past Davy and gave him a belligerent eye. *Another bloody*

231

canary man. Davy swung down awkwardly from his hammock and stood on unsteady feet. The sound of boots diminished down the stairwell and Davy raced to catch up. He kept on toward the sounding bell, hopping along and pulling on his two extra pairs of pants. His pain was tolerable now and with great effort he was able to work into the line. The men surrounding him were tough as nails and they had been made that way by life and death experiences. He feared he did not have the stuff for it. Through no fault of the pipe he had lost it and yet he felt abandoned by it. He had always had it as a backup and now he was on his own. *Dopo, if I die here, my mother will kill me.* Dopo agreed that was about right.

One by one the convicts from Davy's floor formed a tight line as they descended the stairs to the courtyard level. As they stepped out of the door into the cobbled courtyard they put on their floppy hats and formed into a smart two by two column. The bell continued to peal its call to labor and the echo bounced around the quadrangle. Davy did not know where to go and he wanted to ask, but the pounding bell resonated so loudly it erased all speech. The eastern half of the courtyard was still shaded yet the air was still and stifling and it promised to be a cooking day. The convicts had come grumbling from the mess. Their perpetual breakfast was a gelatinous slop called hominy, made from maize. The coarse grain concoction was the same food as given to the pigs and the men hated it. It became remotely palatable by the addition of berries in season. Today they had blackberries and currents added to the slop. Every day a picking party of convicts was led by aborigines from the Gweagal or the Bidjigal tribes to scavenge the bushes for berries. No one had reported finding a copper pipe.

The mustering for work was done according to uniform. In a tight line at center left were the tradesmen. Carpenters, quarry men and blacksmiths dressed in white pants with blue tops with six buttons and they held a high status in the Botany Bay convict society. On the far left in the front rank, four aboriginals stood at rigid attention wearing unlaced boots and loose blue pyjamas. Each of them gripped a thin seven-foot staff sharpened at one end. As soon as they left the parade ground they went barefoot and slung their boots over the thong around their waist carrying their woomera and tucker bag. They were trackers and hunters and they had their own special pedigree. The rest of the men were general laborers and those that denied having any specific skill. They dressed in white pants and pale gray shirts without buttons.

Assembled on the far right stood sixteen men in two rows of eight, separated by fifteen feet from the rest of the convicts. They wore the demeaning uniform of the yellow and black jester. They were the despised Canary Men. Davy's yellow uniform showed he belonged with them and he shuffled along and stood at the end of the line and spaced himself out to where he thought he should be. They stood in good order and quiet, but the guards prodded them with cudgels and threatened them with what was to come next. Some were military deserters, others just recalcitrant malingerers but all were prone to violence. They were held in contempt and feared by both convict and guard alike. These were the troublemakers. Now Davy was one of them.

Marine Sergeant Smits stood atop a small two step stand so the prisoners could see him. He was a small man but his stentorian voice commanded the space.

" Burridge. Take that lot to the pier." He pointed to Davy and his thugs with his right arm extended and his index finger waggling at the chaff.

"Take three Marines. Muskets primed and full cocked. Lead with Simon and Chukker to clear the brownies. No irons. They'll be working at water. If they get out of line, shoot them."

Burridge took over. " Squad, wheel right."

Davy was at the end of the line which made him the lead man and he didn't know it. *Wheel right.* He looked to his right and there was no wheel. He looked to his left and there, marching on the spot, were sixteen men looking at him, looking through him and looking past him and expecting him to lead them somewhere. Burridge screamed " Halt!" He stormed along the yellow line from the rear, bullying the men aside one after the other, as he shouted their names. " Sturgess." With a pull to the left. " Crick." With a push to the right. " North." With a push to the left. He manhandled the men along the line progressively faster and rougher until he got to Pilcher. There were two hundred men mustered there and Pilcher was the only one without a name sewn onto his uniform. Burridge opened his mouth to berate the man by name only to find a no-name in front of him. He spun Davy around to look at his back and still no name. He grabbed Davy by the collar and threw him in line behind Crick. " Alright Blank, wherever Crick goes you stay behind him." The line formed again and it wheeled right and out through the front gate with twelve hours of exhaustion ahead of it. Sergeant Smits spoke in a low voice to Burridge as he passed by. " Keep your eye on Blank."

The canary men were the first to be marched to work and they would have the longest day. If the job was dangerous or heavy or impossible, it was they who would do it. Smits hammered them with exhaustion, danger and heat. He made sure they endured the worst Australia could conjure. Depleted men were less trouble. Davy was one of those to be depleted. This day they would labor at the edge of a festering marsh where a misplaced pier needed repair. Storms had undermined its supports and boulders were to be dug and moved and placed in the water around the posts.

The track to the small pier was seldom used and it was neglected and overgrown. The small dock had been placed incorrectly and the shallowness of the bay made it impossible for anything but shallow draft tenders from the British provisioning ships to approach it. Burridge with his cudgel and a lobster-back marine with a fully cocked musket brought up the rear of the column. Two Marines walked right and left midway to the column with four convicts behind and four ahead of them. Davy followed third from the front on the left behind Crick as he had been ordered. Behind Davy was a man called Dobber. At the head of the column two aboriginals who answered to Simon and Chukker broke the trail and in wide arcs they swept the mixed grasses ahead of them with their staffs.

"Psst. Crick. Why does Chukker have that little wooden paddle hanging there on his back? And what did Smits mean? Brownies. What's brownies?"

" Boy, what Chukker's got there ain't a paddle. It's a woomera. That Chukker, 'e grips the end of his staff in woomera and 'e 'urls it like a bleedin' javelin faster'n a musket ball. Never misses. And brownies? Brownies is snakes, lad. Big fanged, fat, brown, kill ya for fun, poisonous snakes. Keep an eye out." Crick chuckled to himself. He knew any self-respecting brown snake would be half a mile from here with the racket the work party was making, but he wanted to take the mickey of the new chum Blank.

Davy heard a rustle on his left and he sidled right and got an elbow for his troubles. The group trudged along the track for 200 yards when Simon thrust

234

his staff in the air above the whole column and shouted "Wallawa." Movement stopped. In a flash Chukker laid his staff horizontal in the woomera and with a single great stride he loosed the projectile and Davy heard the swoosh of it as much as he saw it. It stuck in the grass forty feet away with its free end vibrating from the impact. Chukker bounded to it in two seconds and hoisted a fat writhing brown snake six feet above his head. Crick grumbled to himself, shaking his head. *Some snakes have no self-respect. Them brownies. They's fast and slithery and they chases you down and strikes you again and again, not just oncet. They makes yer blood ta go thick and then you go stiff like. No second chance with them killers. Dead it is.* Chukker seized the impaled snake and snapped its length from the tail like a bullwhip and broke its neck and stuffed it into his tucker bag. It was a fine meal over a fire.

The gang shuffled down the shallow incline leading to the bog laying between the grassland and the sea. The meagre onshore breeze brought the telltale smell of the marsh to them. The guides led the small party on an approach to the pier which minimized the hydrogen sulfide and methane percolating from the mire. They had seen the seizure, coma and death the gases could deal to a careless man. The verge along the edge of the low bluff was populated with many pale green broad leafed low bushes, each about three feet in diameter. They grew clustered tightly together, impeding the way through the marsh and to the sea beyond. Simon held his staff pointing to his left, barring the way through the bushes. Chukker did the same and they made a 14-foot barrier with their staffs. Chukker's face threatened impalement to anyone who went near the bushes. Davy spoke over his shoulder to Dobber.

" Dobber, why don't we just go through there? It's a lot shorter."

" Spurge. That be spurge. One touch and then one wipe of the eye with a hand, yer blind. Black night blind. The sap o' the spurge's what does it."

Dopo this is a nightmare. We haven't gone a mile and there is a snake that will kill you for a hobby and a plant that will blind you just for the fun of it. What a place. Dopo gave a little shudder and he agreed totally.

A roiling cloud of midges swarmed over the track to the left which was the only way forward. The men pushed through, swatting madly at the flies and feeling nothing but in ten minutes the stinging would begin from countless bleeding bites. They emerged from the bog onto a pristine wide soft sand beach.

235

Thousands of black and white, orange beaked pelicans beat across the bay at surface level, splashing with their wing to panic the fish into schooling for an easier harvest. On the prisoners' right was Blasted Creek, a soft banked black water creek which wasted its nutrients into the sea. The fresh creek water flowed lighter than the salt water and on the surface, it made a shallow fan with its color until it dispersed. In a low spot on their left, they saw the pier. It was surrounded by sea grass and it sat in a depression scoured out of the beach by the surf. Davy saw it leaned starboard. Davy heard a splash and turned sharply to the right but there was nothing to be seen at the creek.

The convict gang moved along to the base of the small pier and saw the last storm had exposed the rocks they needed and there would be little digging. They stacked their shovels and pry bars against the ramp at the pier. Simon and Chukker were puddling the surface of the water near the pier with their staffs and making little splashes. Davy watched and shook his head. He spoke to Dobber as together they struggled to lift a boulder.

" Dobber, I don't even want to ask you this, but why are they whacking the water?"

Dobber laughed. " Just for you, boyo. They're chasing away the stone fishes. They're a mite testy if ye steps on 'em."

"I suppose if you step on them, they turn you blue and stop your breathing."

" Nah. Nothing 'orrible as that. They stops your heart." Dobber enjoyed the banter and fingered his gold earring. Davy was not in the least surprised at the heart stopping and in fact he had expected something worse. Dopo wondered what that might be.

The heat was terrible and the men struggled with the work. They could manage the weight of the small boulders they stacked against the pier base but the footing was treacherous. Green slime covered the bottom and slicked every step. Isolated stones from previous stacking tripped them up and the men slipped on the slime and went down hard, hurting themselves. There was constant movement of sea grasses around their ankles and their legs and every man felt every touch was the first embrace of something lethal. They sloshed in the seawater knowing later that day they would dry their salt encrusted clothing by wearing it. To remove it and hang it meant losing it. Lobsters covered every inch of the shadow made by the dock and were more slippery than the stones.

Again, Davy heard a large splash back to his right. At that moment Simon shouted "Pukpuk. Birrie!" and pointed with his spear. All the men stopped and turned to the pointing. A huge scarred crocodile had entered the water out of the cover of the mud bank at Blasted Creek and was pointing his snout toward the dock. Ripples in the water adjacent to him showed where a larger beast had dropped off the shelf and likely had made the splash which alerted Simon. The enormous male weighed one ton. Ahead of him a flotilla of juveniles sped with silky tails and spreading wakes toward the scrambling workmen. Floating beds of blue water lilies betrayed their routes. From fifty feet away, the green vertical iris of twenty crocodile eyes calculated the perfect angle of attack. Five men were up to their waists on the slime covered rocks at the deep end of the pier and they tried to haul themselves up. Twelve others slithered and slipped and splashed their way out of the shallows and up the beach side ramp to safety. From the bushes at the base of the pier an old beast that had been sleeping in the sun came to the noise. He was scarred and torn from his battles with the world and he had seen much in his seventy crocodile years. These puny interlopers were nothing to him. Right in front of him was Sturgess. Sturgess was mired helplessly on the beach where the sand was deep. The crocodile was ponderous and his size made him seem slow but he was not. Sturgess tried to extricate himself but he fell and fell again in the soft sand. The old beast dragged forward implacably and gained on him. Burridge and the three marines shouted for the men on the dock to get down and they fired on the croc. It ignored the plink of the musket balls against its armor. The smoke and smell of the powder and the noise of the firing increased the panic of the men and they froze from action. Davy raced to the end of the dock and ran down and grabbed a shovel. He threw it like a spear to Burgess who caught it in midair with both hands and smashed it with all his strength against the snout of the crocodile. It stopped the brute for a moment and using the shovel to gain traction Sturgess pulled himself up and forward and he scaled the ramp. Davy ran to the shouts coming from the water. He attempted to help pull Crick up but in Crick's panic to escape the marauding teeth he pulled Davy off the dock. Davy went head first under the water at the deep end of the pier. He pushed off the bottom and frog kicked to a supporting post. He attempted to pull himself up but he could not do it with the weight of his extra wet clothing. Hands over the sides pulled and

237

strained and all men were up except for Davy who hung from the dock with his feet dangling in the water. The largest juvenile attacked him with his jaws agape, ready to twist and tear and drag his quarry under the bank of the blackwater creek and drown him there. Davy hit himself in the nose with his knees and the boys spun him up like a ball onto the sun heated planks of the dock. Davy stayed curled up. The crocodile closed hard on an oak cross-piece and slaughtered it just as the instructions from dim millennia told it to do.

In a collective bravado, the prisoners took off their yellow and black jackets and flapped them derisively at the crocodiles and it seemed to work. The crocs swam in wider circles away from the pier and worked their way out a hundred yards or so where they feasted on the fish driven there by the pelicans. The marines fired a few parting shots, not wanting to be left out.

Davy lied on his back with his eyes closed. His heart was slowing down and the sun felt good on his face. He was wearing three pairs of pants filled with brine and if he took them off someone would steal them. All the men faced the same dilemma. They would dry everything on their backs. Sturgess shook Davy's shoulder. " Thanks mate." Davy nodded his head in acknowledgment. He had to think. He had expected about now to be hanging ten and even if he was half that good, hanging five on a surfboard. He had not even seen surf let alone surfed. Then today, he had come close to being eaten by a crocodile. He had avoided the most venomous snake in the world, he had been within yards of a bush which could make you blind if you so much as sneezed at it and he had walked in water filled with fish that could stop your heart. What was worse, he had lost the pipe. And the day wasn't even over. Even so he was less concerned with Malveena. At least she couldn't come here and get him. Then again maybe she could. Foster had intimated there was another way to commune with the consciousness of the light. Blast that crazy determined woman. If there is another way, she would be the one to find it.

Chapter 17: Which Wolf Will Win

Malveena rested her head against the rim of the bathtub and waited patiently for the last drop to fall from her wine glass. It landed on her tongue and she rolled it around and closed her eyes. The 2013 Monthelie 1'er Cru les Duresses had become her favorite white Montrachet and that was the last drop of it. Misguidedly she had given Bully and Lucretia a case of it for Christmas. She doubted whether they could appreciate its excellence and Malveena intended to get it back from them. She blew out the candles surrounding her bathtub and stepped out of the tepid water and wrapped herself in her dressing gown. She auto dialed Bully and put him on speaker so she could do her stretches. After three rings Lucretia Gregious picked up the phone. Bully called from the bedroom. " Whoever it is, tell them don't they know it's midnight and to call back in the morning."

Lucretia saw Malveena's caller ID too late to avoid speaking with her. Breathing was loud over the speaker as Malveena did her stretches. Lucretia welcomed her with her most cordial salutation.

" What!"

"Lucretia dear. I thought I might stop by in a few minutes and borrow the Montrachet."

" What's that?"

Malveena was unsurprised. " Wine dear. Vin extraordinaire. White. Do you know where it is?"

" Oh that. Bully put it under the bed."

Malveena did not mind that. Under Lucretia's bed would certainly be a cool place. Malveena arched her back and punched the cell phone *off button* at the same time as Lucretia hung up on her. Montrachet was ten minutes away. She smiled and reflected that in another time, it might not be wise to ask someone named Lucretia to supply you with wine.

When Malveena arrived at Bully's front door it was 12:30 AM and Lucretia had set the Montrachet outside. *Fine. Easier all the way around.* She hefted the case and it came up like a feather. She put it down and threw open the cardboard flaps and there was one remaining. She snatched out the single bottle and kicked the empty carton up against the door. She walked back to her Porsche, placed the wine carefully inside the seat belt on the passenger seat next to her French rack and pinion corkscrew and burned rubber down the street and onto the river road that led to Foster Industries. Old man Foster's laboratory was consuming her. She had to have his secrets.

A gentle drizzle began and Malveena cranked up the volume on Shostakovich piano concerto number 2 and increased her speed. The score was frantic and searching and it spoke to her. Her speed compressed the road into tighter bends and Malveena geared down and accelerated into controlled drifts through every hairpin. She geared down again and as she came out of the drift she forced a fishtail to the brink of a spin, straightened out the back end and reduced the torque and approached the offices. She entered the gates to the Foster parking lot and goosed the black Porsche into two complete three sixties on the wet pavement and slid to a crooked stop in her reserved parking spot precisely as Shostakovich concluded. Her recent failure at Woodstock still gnawed at her but it had taught her something. There was more than one way to participate in the intention of the light and she would find the right way or her name was not Malveena Drago.

Gripping the neck of the Montrachet bottle in one gloved hand and her rack and pinion corkscrew in the other, Malveena walked past the dozing security guard. It was 1:00 AM and he was soundly asleep. She did not want a record in his entry log so she moved past him quickly and padded up the stairwell to the second floor. She made no telltale elevator noise. She was violating the court order to restrict the lab from entry and she wanted her little visit to remain private. She had at least six hours to work undisturbed in Foster's lab.

She punched in the security code and listened for the sound of steel. The vertical bolts retracted and the heavy counterbalanced laboratory door swung open quietly. The lights were off in the laboratory and she left them off. The Fresnel lenses in the skylight picked up the halogen light from the parking lot and bathed the room in struggling amber. She leaned with her back against the opposing cabinet and stared at Foster's copper xylophone while she stripped the lead foil wrapping from the wine. Expertly her rack and pinion marvel withdrew the cork from the bottle and she held it to her nose and it was fine. She set the wine on the laboratory cabinet in front of the copper pipes and threw a fastball with the cork and bounced it off the wall.

So many things made no sense. Charles foster was his own man and if he decided to kick over the traces that was one thing, but to leave no record was not what the man would do. Malveena had known Charles Foster for twenty years and she knew him well. He was a meticulous and compulsive recorder and a business man. He made exhaustive notes of every aspect of every idea down to the finest minutiae. There was nothing of value he would not have recorded meticulously with an eye to its commercialization. Malveena was certain too his ego would not allow him to go without leaving some grand memorial behind. Charles Foster was not the vanishing type.

The lab glassware was stashed in the cabinets below the workbenches so she looked for a small Erlenmeyer flask for her wine. The amber light was weak but she was long armed and lithe and she felt in the shadows of the first cabinet and moved her hand along the back wall, feeling for glassware. There was nothing. She reached into the second cabinet and jammed her hand hard, a foot short of the depth she had expected. She risked using her cell phone light in the cabinet, hoping the lenses would not magnify it out to the street. As her eyes accommodated, she saw half a dozen spotless Erlenmeyer flasks lined up in a neat row. She reached one out easily and set it up on the counter. Then she understood why she had come up short and hurt her hand. She put the rest of the flasks on the bench top. The left panel inside the cabinet showed a faint line in the paint from something which had scraped the wall. It was not a random irregular scarring, but a perfectly scribed arc. The back panel was made to swing down and it had scored the side wall.

"Charles, Charles! You are such a boy. Anyone else would use a simple fireproof safe, but you, you have to have a hidden compartment."

She crawled half inside and looked at the upper surface. It was covered with fingerprints and one small area was smudged like the paint around a light switch. She probed the area with her fingertips and immediately she felt the depression. The release button made no sound. The back wall scribed a perfect arc as the flap brushed against the paint and it chattered open. There in perfect order and in Foster's own hand were twenty-four consecutively numbered and labelled, fixed page black binders. They dated back 25 years. Now she was getting somewhere.

She reached for the white Montrachet and the clean flask and kicked off her shoes. She sat down and wriggled into the corner of two cabinets beside the binders and curled her feet up underneath herself. She poured 125 ml of the marvelous white wine into the Erlenmeyer flask and settled in to study Foster's notes. Malveena was alone in the laboratory but she had her best friend from France to keep her company. She might even get some Erlenmeyers for home.

She selected a binder at random and opened to the first page. It was not dated and the first entry was strung out and it seemed to be gibberish. It went on and on until six pages later a period denoting the end of the sentence showed up. Malveena supposed Charles Abernathy Foster could give lessons to James Joyce on the finer points of streaming one's consciousness.

' 3048 some action remeasured correct open minded better than urgent 3556 less than focused 4064 luxless slow back suspension interminable more ..." *Give me a break! What the devil is this nonsense!* She was familiar with dangled participles and misplaced modifiers but this was ridiculous. She looked inside the front and back covers and again at the label but there was no reference to any particular experiment. *Charles Charles.* In the dim light of the laboratory, the pale lead pencil nonsense rambled on for 48 pages and she read every word.

Malveena bounced the notebook across the garish halogen lit tile and it ricocheted to the door. Bruxing her teeth, she opened the most recent binder. It contained only a few pages but it was more of the same. More hard-to-read pencil and more unfathomable discontinuity.

'2032 bright and energetic pulsing to beats teasing to motion some encouragement 1524 yes yes yes two times 1524 angry Bully clouded darkening uncertain spin outside outside no touch no presence...'.

Malveena stiffened her spine at the last phrase. *Outside outside. No touch no presence. That was me at Woodstock. Clouded darkening uncertain. That was me. That was it. All of this is certainly about that bloody pipe.*

She drained her wine and poured 250 mls of the Montrachet into the flask and put the book on her crossed knees in a lotus position. A false dawn began to bleach out the halogen light and it made it easier for her to read Foster's pale hand. '1524 positive effective high intention small miasma no judgment all is well followed Napoleon had gone consummatum est patent pending'. The last phrase concluded in the middle of the page without a period. *So.*

Consummatum est is it? Big help. Malveena smiled at the addendum of
'patent pending'. *Always thinking.*

On the last page, with a strong hand in blue ink and in perfect cursive
writing, Charles Abernathy Foster revealed his discovery for the ages. He had
dated the entry.

'I have demonstrated ineluctably that something which I shall call intention
(Int) is faster than the speed of light. That 'something' is accessible by us all
through a perfect harmonic volume. I have found that perfect harmonic. It is
found within the cylinder 15241905ATM49816168. Consider this to be my claim
of priority. I shall file provisional patents.'

Malveena shook her head in bewilderment. A long alphanumeric string was
supposed to explain something. It was 4:56 AM and the false dawn had
collapsed into a stone sky. Malveena had no one to call but Bully Gregious so
she did. She speed dialed and she waited. Bully was dead to the world in his
usual apneic asphyxia. Lucretia woke after the second ring and looked over at
the clock. Only one person would call at this time of morning and that would
be Malveena. She could rot for all Lucretia cared. Porky woke up and the
phone continued to ring. He ambled to the phone and answered it with a sleepy
hello. Malveena thought she was speaking with Bully and she gave him
peremptory orders as usual.

" Now listen carefully. Pay attention. Write this down.
15241905ATM49816168. Got it?"

Porky wrote furiously and he managed an 'Ungh' in respose.

" Any ideas?" Porky recognized Malveena's voice and he recognized
something else too. " Hi Miss Drago. This is Leonard. You know, Porky that
is."

"Oh. Sorry Porky. Can you get your dad please?"

" Sure, Miss Drago, but you know, I recognize some of that stuff."

"What?"

" The last part. The ATM49816168. That is an atomic mass. I read it in the
library last month. Atomic mass 4.9816168. Approximate of course. Copper."

Malveena listened carefully. Copper for sure. She looked back at the long
string and recognized the first four numbers as having been set apart several
times by Foster.

"Porky, or do you prefer Leonard?"

Porky had never been asked that question. "Um. Well, I like Leonard better than Porky." *No, not Leonard. Too angry motherish.* "Actually, Len. Lenny. Yes, that's it. I prefer Lenny."

"Good. I like Lenny too. Lenny, do the first four digits mean anything? The 1524?"

Lenny searched his memory. "1524 doesn't mean anything to me except the Scottish Parliament said James V could govern and mathematician Adam Ries published his book on algebra. One thing though. If numbers like that are separated, it is often the intention to multiply them. That's a big number. Unless you stick in decimals of course."

Malveena wanted to kick herself. *Of course, stick in decimals Malveena, you idiot.* That was it. The pipe length she had cut was 152.4 mm. "Por..Lenny. You are wonderful. Smart as a whip. Thank you so much Lenny. Love ya. Wake up your mother for me, would you?"

Lenny could not believe it. He had a feeling explore him he had never felt. No one had ever said he was smart and certainly no lady had ever said love ya.

From the bedroom Lucretia shouted. "What are you doing Porky? Who is that on the phone?"

"Sorry if I woke you mum. Just a friend."

Malveena took a big swig of the Montrachet. She should have it warm more often. Her pipe length was correct but so what. How you used it to get where you wanted to go was the question. She returned to Foster's last record with a renewed enthusiasm. There was a single sheet of paper inserted loosely inside the back cover. It read "Addendum" and the increased slant of the pen strokes on both sides of the paper indicated rushing.

"My name is Charles Abernathy Foster. I am 72 years old and I have been blessed. For 25 years I have worked incessantly to develop explore and refine that which I have now done. I have just completed my forty-eighth sojourn into a realm which is the greatest gift the universe can bestow. I have been privileged to participate in a stream of sublime consciousness. It is a stream from which we are all invited to partake. It is a surrounding entity which has existed for all time, exists for today and exists for all time to come, should that be our choice. My choice. Your choice.'

'It is a simple thing yet it is complex beyond our imaginings. I have learned both to my chagrin and to my immense satisfaction there is nothing which is not available to us if we intend to participate in its attainment. Physicists will rationalize this, theologians will challenge this and generals around the world will attempt to militarize this. Let them. They will fail in their endeavor because to succeed requires graciousness. Let their frozen disciplines corrode them. They are not equipped to enjoy the golden consciousness offered to them for their taking. Their meanness disqualifies them."

Malveena was offended at the requirement of graciousness. It was as if the universe had conspired against her. She was certainly physically gracious in her statuesque posturing but a grace of character eluded her altogether. She did not like her prospects.

"Beside me on the bench as I write my conclusions, sits a copper pipe. It is not just any copper pipe. It is my permit to enter the cosmic continuum. It is a willing partner of all light that exists. It gathers light from stars beyond the stars and from a billion ageless suns and it makes me a partner. It allows me my choice as to where and when and how I enter the time and space within the surrounding continuum, provided my intention is uncritical and devoid of malice.'

'The pipe is my conduit through which I am invited to participate by intention, I repeat, by intention, in an eternal consciousness which exists just for me. But I am not unique in this. A consciousness has been prepared uniquely for you too, whoever you are, reading these notes. It exists for you for any time, for any place and for any need should you choose to participate. It is your choice, it is my choice, whether we participate in that existing consciousness. It is something we carry with us like a ticket for a train. We may choose to go on the train or not but the tracks for that train going to any intention of our choice were laid long before we had a ticket. And that ticket is an open ticket, one which is honored for all time and the consciousness of the light knows what is at the end of the line. The ticket is printed by your intention. The character of that intention determines whether your journey is a good one. Benevolent attitudes and generous intent will keep you on the right track."

Malveena was pouting as she read. *Where's the fun in that. Who the devil can have any intention that is uncritical and isn't basically devious.* There was

245

half a page scrawled on the back side of the loose sheet.

'I have had the good fortune and the misfortune to have done it both ways. All intentions, good and bad, have a path which already exists in the consciousness of the light. Participation will not be denied you but your outcome will reflect the character of your intention. Gracious intentions of goodwill and honest inquiry will land you in good stead, at the right time and place, in safety and at peace. Angry, mean minded or devious intentions, and even more hazardous to you, unclear intention, will expose you to peril, discomfiture and a netherworld of isolated ghostly meanderings. I have experienced them both. The choice was mine. The choice is yours.'

Malveena wanted to smack Foster. *Now he tells me. Running around Woodstock in a fog screaming my head off soaking wet and covered in mud for days on end and now he tells me it was because I had a bad attitude. Next thing I know, he will suggest anger management courses as a prerequisite to pipe ownership.*

'I have recorded and explained enough. I may not be believed despite my proofs. Whenever you are reading this, I will not be available. I am meeting with Napoleon. I intend to join Churchill in the war room. I intend to partake in ceremony at the temple of Motecuhzoma Ilhuicamina. I do not intend to return. Good luck and if you are wondering, patents are underway. I am off to Lahore for drinks with Rudyard Kipling."

Malveena was displeased. The key was to approach the intention of the light as a passive recipient as if one were immersed in a Zen mindless suspension. No angst, no anger, no agenda and no nefarious purpose. It was the worst thing Malveena had ever read. Who would want to go through life with no angst no anger and no agenda. How the devil can I clear my mind of the Pilcher brat to follow his trail when my intention for following his trail is to put him out of his misery.

Maybe sweet Lucretia was right. Anger management classes. How ridiculous. Psychologists.

She had a surge of nausea.

Pah! What a racket. Still trying to find themselves and getting paid to do it. Years of piddling through fuzzy edged abstruse meanderings of other confused psychologists who were likewise trying to find themselves. People who could never manage to do anything practical and by default fell into fluffy curly edged trying to find myself ten hours a semester courses and now they are psychologists. And now they hold themselves out as experts to tell me what I should manage. Pah! Blast!

There were six registered psychologists in the area and Malveena chose the first one at the top of the list. She thought it must be a joke. The name was Dr. Amber Glass. Malveena hammered the number keys on her cell phone and dialed the office. On the seventh ring a voice practiced in the art of disinterest answered and introduced itself as Miss Claire. Malveena wanted to vomit. She overcame the urge and took an appointment for two days hence.

She hopped into her Porsche and peeled out onto the street for her appointment. She was wearing a track suit and her hair was tied back off of her face. She had taken extra time with her makeup to achieve the high cheek-boned pellucid look which pleased her.

Malveena was towed into the consultation room of Amber Glass. Malveena would not have been surprised if the windows had been tinted that way. She was sure the woman's real name would prove to be something such as Penelope or Francine and to be cute in the way of soft Berkeley edged thinking she had called herself " Amber". On the wall behind her desk were her diplomas and her given name was indeed Amber. Malveena wondered whether her siblings were called 'Shot' or 'Depression'.

The furnishings in the room were seriously wonderful. Matching art deco floor lamps stood in two corners of the room. Malveena had seen those for offer at Sotheby's for $3000 per lamp. On the left was the most beautiful Biedermeier round topped mahogany sewing table Malveena had seen and she was very knowledgeable in the field. That was a $6000 table. So it went with every mahogany treasure and every piece of art in the room. Minute by minute as she waited, there was much more anger for Malveena Drago to manage.

Directly behind Amber Glass' chair was a framed homily in large stylized type. Malveena was not wearing her reading glasses but she could still read it clearly. It was a tale she had seen before. It was meaningless then and it was not new to her now but it was staring her in the face and it was something to read while putting in time waiting for the shrink.

Two Wolves

An old Cherokee chief is teaching his grandson about life:

"A fight is going on inside me," he said to the boy. "it is a terrible fight and it is between two wolves. One is evil - He is anger, envy, sorrow, regret, greed, arrogance, self-pity, guilt, resentment, inferiority, lies, false pride, superiority, self-doubt, and ego.

The other is good - He is joy, peace, love, hope, serenity, humility, kindness, benevolence, empathy, generosity, truth, compassion, and faith."

"This same fight is going on inside you and inside every other person, too."

The grandson thought about it for a minute and then asked his grandfather, "Which wolf will win?"

The old chief simply replied, "The one you feed."

Malveena finished the simple story quickly and it affected her. She had not been in the office two minutes and she was already forced into an uncomfortable place. She was a thoughtful person but she did not like to be maneuvered to think about things she had not chosen. She feared she felt a pulse.

Amber Glass came through the door from behind Malveena and closed it with a small click. With long quiet strides she stepped behind her immaculate desk and as she sat she reached across to shake Malveena's hand. There were no coffee cup rings on the polished leather top and the only papers in the room were those Ms. Glass carried with her.

Amber was immaculate in her at attire. She was pale, tall and gaunt. She had highlighted her cheekbones with her makeup and she had a pellucid Carpathian look which implied an older soul. Malveena was put off guard. It was like looking into a mirror.

"You must be Malveena. I am Amber Glass. I feel as if I'm looking into a mirror."

Malveena started a small nervous laugh and let it fall away. It was as if her mind had been read.

"Malveena. That is a new name to me. Is it your real name? Or have you substituted it for something like Penelope or Francine? That is what most people assume I have done. But my real name actually is Amber." Amber smiled and Malveena was quiet. She hated that she liked this woman. "Malveena is my given name." She was being one upped at every turn.

Amber Glass got right to it without a motherly smile or an ounce of Berkeley edged jargon.

" Nice to meet you. Malveena, why have you come to consult me?"

Malveena spat back. " Why don't you tell me, Ms. mind reader."

" I see. Anger management. Good. That's what I do best." She did not give Malveena an opportunity to interject.

"Did you drive here today?"

Malveena nodded.

" What kind of car do you drive?"

" Porsche. 911 Carrera S. Black. Turbo 420 horsepower."

" Perfect car for you. So, coming here you hammered it around the corners, beat every light, downshifted and spun to a stop in my parking lot. Am I right?"

Malveena nodded one millimeter.

Amber stood up and walked to the door. " Come with me. We are going for a drive."

Malveena led obediently to her Porsche. " Malveena, you will drive, I will be your passenger. Do you agree to follow my instructions? I'm sure this is a new role for you. Do you think you can handle it?"

Malveena was stymied. This Glass person was good. She had assessed Malveena very well. She understood Malveena was not built to admit she could not handle anything. That being understood, the next choice was to agree whether or not to follow instructions which any rational person would agree to do. Malveena nodded twice, under internal protest.

Glass began her instructing. "Good. That's settled then. Go where you want to, but stay in the downtown core. I will give you suggestions when the time comes. "

Malveena was eager to leave the office but she had not expected to have someone with her. She started off from her parking stall with a side slipping four-foot burn mark and shot away toward the downtown core, along Strathmore Boulevard. Malveena was watching the sequence of the traffic lights ahead of her and she dropped into second gear to beat the red she anticipated on the third light. She timed it perfectly, entered on a very deep amber light, beat the red and smiled at her control. Amber glass was a quiet relaxed passenger.

"Malveena, just go back around that same block please." Malveena was puzzled but she did so. She made four left turns back onto Strathmore into a different light sequence. She stayed in third gear as she anticipated less need for acceleration as she approached the second light. She ran the intersections again and once again Amber asked her to go around the block.

Malveena looked over. " What is this?"

" Slow down for this light." The light was about 300 feet ahead. Amber did not look at Malveena.

" But it is green."

" Yes. Slow down for it."

Malveena slowed down but as she approached the stoplight, green turned to amber and she popped the clutch and gained the other side of the intersection with dense red glinting off her back windshield.

" Do the same circuit again Malveena. Same block. This time stay slow, approach the yellow light slowly and get caught by the red light."

Malveena knew she had heard correctly but she was not sure she wanted to play this game. Amber knew it and beat her to the punch.

" I will guide you again and we are going to get caught by the red light at every intersection. Time your gear action and your pace so we sit at every light. Do not challenge the light."

Malveena had agreed earlier she could handle this. She was not sure now whether she could. She turned hard left onto Strathmore and a string of green lights beckoned her to begin a grand prix. Amber heard Malveena's leather driving gloves squeak under increased pressure on the wheel. At the first traffic light Malveena miss-shifted down with a grind and stuttered into the left-hand turn lane. The light turned red and she dropped her head in resignation.

They continued the routine for an hour. Malveena was a quick study and soon she timed her baby to enter the yellow light safely in the left-hand turn lane and to submit to the fascism of the light. She was beginning to feel less homicidal. Malveena reappointed twice. They spoke of childhood, aspirations, wishes, disappointments and temperance. Malveena was ready.

Malveena and Bully returned from lunch and arrived at the parking gate at the same time and Bully waited for the inevitable cut off, hard braking and mandatory collision avoidance. Malveena slowed down and waved Bully to

250

enter the parking lot first. She went directly to Foster's laboratory, closed the door and stood directly under the mammoth Fresnel lenses. She gripped her copper pipe. *Now. I must clear my mind. Think of the trail. Do not think of him. Or her. Just the trail. Be kind. Have a Zen emptiness. Think of the entity created by the uniqueness of the boy. Intend, intend, intend to join the indelible evidence of his passing. Open consciousness is all. Focus on the thing which is the trail.*

It was 2:00 PM and the sun was blasting. She sighted the pipe to the light and spread her feet for balance against the impact. Her mind was clear and uncluttered and the pipe seemed to be assessing the focus of her thought. She thought of the trail. She thought hard on the entity created as a permanent and indelible record of the boy passing through. She acknowledged the boy was unique. *The trail is all. Think of it only. It will take me. Don't think about how it will take me to the boy. I will just think of the trail the little monster made. I won't think of how I'd like to liquidate him when I get off this miserable trail. Intend intend.*

The pipe responded with a hard, counter-clockwise swirl of fragmented brilliance and it vortexed Malveena away. It spun with a hum and traveled in a perfect whirlwind track along the indelible trail of David Pilcher. Predictably and in consideration of Malveena's bitter relapse into attack mode, the consciousness of the light did not track where Pilcher was at that moment, but rather, where Pilcher had been.

The water was not cold but it was up to her waist. She knew she was standing in water but nothing was required and her view into the shore was unimpeded and unremarkable. A confining waterfall of gelatinous wash fell over her and it shimmered like a heat wave. It made no splash but that was no concern of hers. She waited patiently for release from it. The gelatin became steam as it disappeared into the heat and Malveena blinked into a full down under sun.

She had arrived standing up to her waist in silted seawater, directly opposite a dilapidated dock surrounded by sea grasses. On the left a black water creek fingered its silt into the shallow bay. Straight ahead the pier was surrounded. Five, one-ton male crocodiles sunned themselves not thirty feet from where she stood. Fifty feet away on the left, two smaller ones slicked forward just under

251

the surface and spaced themselves wider to cover the territory around Malveena. They were the females and they weighed about five hundred pounds each. Two males downwind on Malveena's right flared their nostrils and scented toward her fear pheromones. Malveena looked around for her way out. Behind her was the cascading surf and the incoming tide was forcing her ever closer to the shore. The implacability of the sun added force to the reality of her situation. The closest escape was the small dock. She scrambled toward it through thigh deep water and her splashing attracted the full attention of every somnolent beast. Their reptilian brains reacted with a speed belying their mass and they flashed into the water. The surf became a formless maelstrom as excited juveniles joined the game and thrashed toward her at attack speed. She dived for the little dock, pushed up off the sandy bottom and pulled herself up with her hands. She rolled onto the deck as a swinging head buffeted her leg and snagged off her right running shoe with a razor-sharp tooth. The weight of the flailing crocodile crushed one of the supports and tipped the platform down to the left so it touched the water. The largest and oldest of the crocodiles reacted slowly and with primordial coolness he pointed away from the prey. He had lived to be this big and this old because of his guile. Languidly he left the water and as he dragged his two-thousand-pound bulk to the land side of the decayed pier he scoured a wide furrow in the sand. His victim was on the pier and his ilk had command of the water. He walked his slow bow-legged walk. He did not understand haste. The rest of the pack swam in close circles and they shuddered the pier with occasional contact. Malveena could hear the tail of the ancient croc thunk across the spaces in the planking as he came up the ramp. He was 20 feet away. The tie on Malveena's pipe string had swelled in the salt water and it bound on itself and it would not slide free. She fumbled for the pipe as the oncoming brute raised himself and dropped the full weight of his body onto the pier. The impact of the behemoth splintered the platform and crushed 15 feet of the landward side of the dock, cutting off escape. Wood shards scattered onto the water where the jaws of the circling gang splintered them, their bloodlust driving them to frenzy. The old crocodile pushed on his tail and he leveled himself onto the remains of the pier. With patient deliberation he swung his dripping snout to within four feet of Malveena and an eternal smile confirmed the kill to come.

Malveena took the monster by surprise and with one athletic leap she jumped as high as she could over his head and landed between his shoulders. Her wet single shoe slipped and she fell on her back, back to back on the mammoth crocodile, jarring the knot free and she swung the pipe to the sun. The crushing jaws were instantaneous as they writhed backwards and snapped closed on a blinding flash. The pure Australian sun shone down on the crocodile, its seventy razor teeth crushing nothing but sunlight. The outwitted ancient beast thrashed in impotent fury and ripped apart the dock. Malveena screamed her way into the streaming consciousness along a thin febrile track which held no intention except escape to anywhere but there. A chaotic barrage of fragmented ideas rocketed out of her subconscious. Her terror stripped her of pretense and exposed her to the light as a writhing encyclopedia of hostility. She had no place in the consciousness of the light. A homogeneous dimness surrounded her in total silence. She saw everywhere and saw there was nothing as she coasted alone. There was no horizon to define an axis. She was motionless like a fly trapped in amber but unlike the fly she was aware of her horrific entrapment. Malveena was gone from the pier, but where Malveena swam was nowhere.

Chapter 18: Musket Balls and Killer Convicts

Simon and Chukker led Davy and the canary men away from the crocodile infested pier and back along the path through the low-lying bog they had crossed on arrival. Above them, the high pitched unh unh of a squadron of pelicans announced their final approach to the estuary. Davy was exhausted and he neither heard the birds nor saw the strobe of their passing shadows on the muck. He stayed in line and the land led them down into the toxic methane bog at the base of the incline leading back to the barracks. The hydrogen sulfide was strong that day and the poison gases concentrated in the wet depression seared their lungs with every breath. Total exertion at the dock had left Davy weak and his first quick exposure to the gas dizzied him. For a man to fall here meant seizure, coma and death. Two lines of stooped yellow and black harlequins drove themselves on to save their clown lives. The acidic residue from the ambient gases mixed into their sweat and burned their skins. Davy gripped the back of Crick's jacket. Dobber held onto Davy's back. Every man along the line held fast to his chum and pushed ahead, hoping for good air. The men had not been shackled for the work in the water, yet from muscle memory and mindless routine, they bowlegged along in a measured step which protected their ankles from imaginary iron cuffs. The Marines trundled along apace with their muskets primed and fully cocked, ready for action. Their orders were to shoot any man who left the line and they fully intended to do it.

Simon was barefoot in the vanguard. He chanted a low-pitched mantra in his native Bidjigal as he swept the grasses around the path with his staff and chased away the snakes. Chukker was Bidjigal too. He maintained a subtle crouch as he moved forward. If a brown snake showed up, he was ready and his spear was poised. The column could see a disturbance in the bushes ahead to the right just before the turn up the incline. Simon and Chukker did not falter and they moved toward it undeterred. They both knew the noise. A huge wombat waddled into Simon's path and stopped. It raised its fat brown childish head at him and continued on unimpressed. At another time Chukker would have speared this and tucked it away for supper.

They made the flat at the top of the hill and saw the Hyde Park barracks standing a thousand yards along the track. That day it proved any place can become home. Marine Sergeant Smits saw to it the men got water and he sent them to their hammocks to rest. That day they would work 10 hours instead of 12. The clock above the front door of the barracks struck six times as Davy rolled into his hammock. Four bells. He had tied his shoelaces through two buttonholes to his jacket and tied his jacket in a knot around his waist. He wanted to dry his slops but he did not want them stolen.

Davy melted into a full deep sleep just as one of the convict trustees sidled through the barracks door to Davy's hammock and poked him hard in the ribs. He carried a bundle with Davy's new slops and he whacked them into Davy's belly and ordered him awake.

"Get up and get out of them canaries. These'r yers. Has yer name sewed in."

He struggled awake and obediently peeled off his salt encrusted clothing. He ached everywhere but his cuts and abrasions were healing well and pulling on the new slops was comfortable. He had dry clothes and his name had been sewn in to discourage stealing. He examined the needlework. It was neat and it was spelled correctly. It read 'BLANK'. From then on that was him. Convict Davy Blank.

Morning came without mercy. At 5:30 AM a tolling bell from the courtyard jolted Davy out of a pain filled sleep with its call to muster for the day's assignment. He dressed and shuffled stiffly to mess with the rest of them. He sat with the canary men and looked down at his plate which oozed with quasi solid corn slop called hominy. He imagined himself back on the Victory. What he saw before him became salt pork, peas and oatmeal, with butter and cheese. Davy proceeded to fill himself and he did not complain. From the corridor, heavy chained footsteps approached and entered the mess at the point of a bayonet. The hum of conversation dropped to nothing as a sudden quiet pervaded the room. Davy watched the two marine guards opposite him stiffen slightly and heard the click as one of them full cocked his musket. The late arrival came from behind Davy on his right. A heavily built coyote like man snarled his way into a heap beside him and sat noisily on the bench. He was labelled Kelly. Davy looked at him, then looked away quickly but he was drawn back to the man's face. It had the bright green and yellow flecked eyes of a predator. They were coyote eyes. The coyote man wore the yellow pants of a dangerous offender. He sat with his shoulders rolled forward and elbows out like a cur protecting his bowl. He finished his food first, despite having arrived last to table. Belligerently he slid his plate away across the planked wooden table and spattered blobs of wet hominy on the men around him. He spun in his seat and swung his legs over the bench to face the door. In the spin he elbowed Davy on the same ear Burridge had split open with his cudgel and started it bleeding again. Davy clutched it quickly and Kelly looked at him, satisfied to see blood seeping from between Davy's fingers.

Dobber whispered at Davy's shoulder and pointed cautiously to Kelly with a finger extended into Davy's peripheral vision. " Davy lad, watch 'im, 'es the 'ardest case there be. Be careful of that lot. Look around you Davy. Look at all these lads in the black and yellow clown suits. The canaries, they call us. We are the rough boys, the hard cases and thugs and the like. Some of us came here that way and some of us got that way just by being here. But not Kelly. He was made bad. Plain vicious to the bone. He can take you down and he'll skin ye if he can. And I means it true with his knife."

"You lot!"

Sergeant Smits rattled the windows with his bellow. He levelled his musket with malice and touched the point of his bayonet to the chest of the seated Kelly. He smiled at Kelly, daring him. He and Kelly were old acquaintances from troubled times. Smits turned away from the hate in Kelly's animal eyes and swung his flashing bayonet along the length of the table.

"First ten. Treadmill."

Davy saw the hardening of the men's faces but not a word was said. The treadmill was generally assigned as a punishment detail. Who did what to merit punishment for the group was a mystery to all of them. Crick leaned over and whispered to Davy. " 'Tain't so bad Blank. Least no irons fer the day."

Two Marines gunstocked Crick to the back of the line and together they manhandled the new chum Kelly to the front to keep an eye on him and to have a better shot. The order in line was now Kelly, then Davy Blank, followed by Dobber. Guarded by four marines the troupe arrived at the treadmill where they were unshackled.

Smits hardened his voice.

"Kelly! Climb up there to the right end. Stand still and hold the wheel steady. If you play about I will shoot you. The rest of you fall in line beside Kelly. Blank! Don't just stand there, climb the wheel."

Davy scrambled up as best he could and stood left of Kelly on the same horizontal plank. The rest of the men followed one by one and spaced themselves out holding onto a shoulder height wooden rail not attached to the wheel. Convict Blank had seen treadmills at the gym but this was something else. It was about thirty feet long and built like a paddle wheel on a steamboat. All ten men stood side by side along the same plank. Davy looked down the row and saw the men gripping the horizontal fixed rail more firmly with both hands.

"Dobber! What am I supposed to do?"

Before Dobber could answer Smits gave the order. "Ready, now push! Push off the rail, you men!"

The huge grinder creaked into motion and the horizontal plank fell away from Davy's feet and he clutched the rail in panic and hung in midair. Kelly smirked at Davy, knowing the lad could be mangled in the mechanism if he fell. The next plank rolled down and hit Davy in the shins. The one above it rolled down in turn and he stepped up to save himself and he stepped up again to save himself from falling into the gears below. The leg drive of the men was moving the wheel down step by step. It was a never-ending stairway. Davy got into the tempo. Hold on, step up, push down, step up, push down, don't fall, push down. As the pace increased the creaking became a hum and the mill commenced with grinding. The treadmill was built outside of the perimeter wall of the barracks next to the storehouse for the Indian maize used to make hominy and cornbread. The treadmill was used to grind it. Small independent farmers brought their grains and for a fee the prison ground them into coarse flour.

The canary men worked in the shade of a canopy. The Australian sun beat down on it and it began to cook. The only air moving was what they pushed with the spinning of the treadmill. In an attempt to save their energy, the men did not talk for they knew to become fatigued or distracted could be fatal. The work was strenuous, mindless and monotonous and it was in the monotony where the danger lay. One lapse in concentration or one step short of the next vane could lead to mutilation. The prisoners continued holding on and they strained with their legs and gripped with their hands for twelve hours in a repeating sequence of forty minutes on and twenty minutes off. They were on the treadmill for three days. On the fourth day the punishment at the pleasure of Sergeant Smits ended. The men had concluded the exercise had been for the benefit of Kelly and they blamed him.

A Saturday of washing clothes and drying them on their backs culminated with mandatory witnessing of the flogging of 'Frankie the Poet'. Convict Francis McNamara had dared to compose doggerel which criticized his warders. Sunday was church services and clean shirts, and Monday they returned to work. The canary men were sent three by three to softer jobs of things done in the season. Chukker led a trio to comb along the beach and scavenge anything useful the tide might have produced. Led by Simon, Kelly and Davy and Dobber were put on the detail of gathering blackberries for the tables of the officers. Should there be extra blackberries they would be mixed with the hominy for the prisoners. One marine guard trailed them with a primed and fully cocked musket. Kelly saw the marine's uniform was new and it had not been faded by the sun. Simon saw something also. "Yin-ban," he said immediately. Afraid. Kelly nodded with the perception of a sociopath. The man is pale and unfit and he is already perspiring. He is not an old hand.

His name was Calvin Reynolds and he was freshly arrived from the snows of Quebec. Simon examined Reynolds. "Dalgool-Bumma," he opined. Fat man. Dobber wondered whether that was an observation or menu planning by Simon.

Simon had his boots off and slung around his waist and he did not seem to feel the heat of the sand on his bare feet. He was ordered to show trooper Reynolds the safe trails so he led the way slower than was his habit. Simon had his woomera with him and a small bag of pituri which trailed a vanilla like odor wherever he went. He had made the pituri himself from young shoots of the pituri bush and from ash of the gidya tree. The soldiers knew gidya as 'whitewood'. The pituri shoots were those which sprouted after running fires had ravaged the older branches. The combination of pituri and gidya ash lasted for months and made a stiff gum of which two or three chews was enough to help suppress fatigue, hunger and thirst. Twenty chews of the same gum ensured a long sound sleep. Pituri was a potent soporific. Simon was preparing for a walkabout and the pituri would be with him for hundreds of miles. If he went far enough west he would harvest and make more.

The blackberry bushes which had scourged Davy on the first day were about one thousand yards from the gates and that was where the five men were headed. They had no gloves against the thorns and they were expected to fill the bags they carried. The growing offshore wind trailed sand off the low bluffs to the right and the deepening beach was heavy slogging for the trooper with the musket. It was a particularly hot morning and he began to fall behind. Simon slowed the pace to accommodate him. Kelly hoped for more space. Davy hoped he might find his pipe. Dobber hoped Kelly would not kill anyone.

The new marine had not made two hundred yards and he looked for some shade. Surrounding a low spot at the edge of a creek ahead, he saw a few dense green bushes clustered to make shade between them and he could sit there. He was hot and he was hungry. For breakfast they had made him eat pig food hominy goop and now a vanilla smell from somewhere made him ravenous. They stopped opposite the bushes and young Reynolds made for the shade. "Sit," he ordered. They sat on the beach and looked at each other expectantly as Reynolds searched for a good spot in the bushes. Davy could not let it happen so he spoke matter of factly from where he sat.

" Not there. Not the place to sit, among the spurge bushes. They make you blind. The sap you know. Blind as a bat." He laid the words out casually in contrast to their import, showing he was wise in these things. Calvin Reynolds shot up and away from the spurge bushes as if he were on fire. His mother had told him not to go.

Simon reached into his bag for a piece of pituri and chewed it. Reynolds spotted him and pointed. " That. What's that you are doing there! You're eating." Simon removed the pituri from his mouth. He was accustomed to offering a friend a chew and it was intended to be passed around for all to have a couple of chews. Reynolds was not a friend so Simon pulled a strong fresh pituri from his pouch and offered it, all innocent like. It seemed to be food and Reynolds went for it. He popped it into his mouth and Kelly shouted to stop him from swallowing it.

" Wait lad, that's for chewing, sergeant sir, not for swallowin'. Just chew it a bit. Like Simon does. Energy in it. That's it. Just chew it." Kelly understood the full effects of Simon's herbal concoction.

Trooper Reynolds chewed like never before. He could not believe the vanilla and something else even better. He was far less worried now about these canary types sitting across from him. All he had needed was a little food. Why, he should take off his shoes. He proceeded to do so and began to sing. " Farewell Spanish ladies..." and he couldn't remember the rest of the words so he closed his eyes to think of them. In thirty seconds he was sound asleep in a seated position with an easy smile on his face.

"Wee-gee," said Simon. Weak.

The trooper had one shoe off and the other one unlaced and his Ozymandias musket was beside him and submerging itself beneath the lone and level sands. The barrel was filled and the flintlock mechanism was useless. Dobber put his finger to his mouth and made a couple of down pushes with his palms to encourage patience. They waited a full minute and then they were sure. Their guard was in a deep drugged sleep. Kelly stepped close between Dobber and Davy. He looked Davy in the eye and turned the same look on Dobber. " She's time ta scarper. Me an' Dobber," he presumed Dobber's acquiescence, "we's for it. Are ya in?"

" Scarper?"

Dobber nodded reluctantly so Davy nodded too to be agreeable. Davy had no idea what 'scarper' was, but his answer was 'I'm in." Whatever this scarper was, he was in.

Dobber turned Davy's shoulder and looked him in the eye and spoke seriously to him. "Understand lad, ya knows this is a lurk."

Davy thought, Lark. Fun. Good. About time. He did not know 'lurk' meant illegal. He did not know scarper meant running away to be hunted down with dogs and likely shot, or to be thrown into solitary confinement; or if the regiment was bored, likely hung but only after the appropriate lashing. Dobber looked at him as if surprised at his choice but he buttoned his lip. Simon looked into the distance.

Kelly stooped and filled his hands with sand. He looked malevolently at the sleeping soldier which puzzled Davy but not Simon or Dobber. Dobber stood

260

quickly and Simon thrust his staff between Kelly and the hapless marine. Kelly threw down the sand in disgust. They would be sorry they did not let him smother the soldier.

The wind was picking up as Davy and Dobber dragged Calvin Reynolds up the bluff above the high tide line and stuffed him out of the sun among the low cedars. He would sleep there for a day. His track in the sand blew away in the cross wind. Simon nodded to the right toward the sea and the growing tide and said quietly. "Won-gee." West. They were not expected back to Hyde Park barracks for six hours. Simon hoped that was enough of a head start. He knew Smits was willing to spend his life tracking them down.

The tide was sneaking in and they ran in the shallows westerly along the beach to cover their tracks. The three convicts churned along behind Simon who tempered his easy stride to keep the group together. The way along the beach was impeded by a scalloped string of thirty or so fingers of land stretching into the sea grasses in the tidewater on their left. Their tops were covered in cutting brambles and low bushes. Simon scrambled on over them to reconnoiter the way ahead. Davy stepped out into the shallows to skirt the first outcropping and Dobber grabbed him by his shirt collar and jerked him back. "Careful there in those weeds Davy. There be sea snakes."

Kelly chimed in. " Yas. Worst ones there. The yellow belly is the snake what hides in that kind of sea lettuce. Bait weed. Snake'll run away, but if yez surprises it and it fangs ya hard, yer kissin' Mother Carey. Dead as a door nail."

Davy sighed. Well that's nice isn't it Dopo. Another thing to kill us. Dopo did not consider it nice and he did not appreciate sarcasm.

Dobber shook his head at Kelly's ignorance.

"Says you Kelly! That yellow belly takes as long's six hours 'till ya croaks. The beaked one's worster in these here waters. Beaked sea snake'll stop yer breathin' right fast. Makes ya sick right off, then that's it. Better have a short prayer ready, cuz ye baint havin' time fer a long one. Beaked snake, that's Mother Carey for sure.

" Mother Carey? "

" Heard of Davy Jones? Davy Jones locker?" Davy had. He nodded yes.

"Mother Carey, she's Davy Jones' gal. The chanty goes. ' Mother Carey she's the mother o' the witches and all them sort o' rips.' Then I thinks it goes, 'She lives upon an iceberg to the nor'en and her mate is Davy Jones. And she combs the weeds upon her forehead with poor drownded sailors' bones.' There's more to it I reckon."

One by one they climbed up and over the fingers of land, staying away from the sea grasses. Davy was more agile and he took the lead. The outcrops and the elevated sand bank running along to their right were becoming populated by taller bushes with hand sized trunks for easy gripping. Davy thought they might travel more easily in the sparser vegetation and he reached for a trunk to pull himself up. Dobber tackled him and threw him down.

"Not that one lad. Don't touch it. Gympie Gympie. Freezes up yer nerves. It'll kill ya right off but if it don't kill ya, ya wish it had killed ya. Months o' pain nothin' can harness."

The small peninsulas became less frequent and the sand became more powdered and the sound of the waves changed as they entered a wide cove. They dropped over the dune starting the turn of the bay and beside them a rhythmic rolling surf pounded the shore. They were on a wide beautiful arcuate beach with forty-five seconds between each wave crest and an offshore wind to steepen the face of the troughs. It was absent seagrass and the sand was pristine from the constant wash of the rolling surf. A surfer's paradise.

"Kelly. What is this place? Where are we?" Davy knew this was the beach on the calendar in the parts department.

" Bondi Beach lad. Bondi."

Davy saw Simon in the distance coming back to them. The fugitives walked forward together for a mile or so and Simon gestured them to a halt. He walked directly to Kelly, spun him around and tore the name patch off his jacket. He did the same to Dobber and Davy and he ran off. Kelly said nothing. That Simon would be a tough nut to crack. Simon moved ahead for a hundred yards, tearing and dropping bits of coats onto the sand. He established their scents on the beach. When the dogs came it would take them hours to sort it out. He left nothing of his own. He returned through the shallows and faced them and beckoned them forward. He pointed to his left where a small stream glistened. Its banks were congested by spindled deadwood washed up by seasonal flooding. "Goon-ga". North.

They followed Simon blindly and picked their way along the congested creek bank until Dobber and Kelly agreed to collapse.

"Allawah." Rest, sit down.

They drank from the shallow stream which was surprisingly cold and rested in the shade for a short five minutes. Simon shared around his pituri chaw and it helped them ignore their fatigue. They splashed through the shallows and across to the east bank of the creek. The stream ran north and intersected with a low limestone bluff where the pressure from a subterranean river shot water out of a seam and made the creek. The rock bluff blocked their path north. Along its front and running away to the east was an impenetrable grove of dense, ten-foot-high red leafed photinia bushes. A pale green ground cover of low bushes filled the spaces in the grove and ran with the photinia for several hundred feet. The men began to skirt to the right and they heard a grunt. Simon pointed to the low green ground cover. "Goo-da-ra." Dog. The pale green bushes were dog bane. Tracking dogs would go nowhere near a trail touched by dog bane.

Simon steered his charges tight to the wall behind the photinia. They edged along the rock face, walking on the dog bane and pushing the branches ahead of them. Progress was slow and the brambles striped their hands with cuts. They emerged from the cover of the vegetation onto a narrow beach. Simon pointed to his left and sped ahead barefooted, splashing his way through the shallows of Bondi Lake on their right and onto a mixed pebbled beach which squeezed them back against the low limestone bluff on the left. As they ran, the bluff continued to grow in height and angled against them to diminish the beach to a four-foot-wide trail. The fugitives showed in dark relief against the pale thirty-foot-high backdrop. Simon had trapped them against an impenetrable limestone wall. He was fifty yards ahead of Davy. Dobber and Kelly followed another twenty yards behind that. Davy shouted back to Dobber. " Hurry. He's going to lose us. Come on Dobber!"

From ahead came the cry. "Yappulun gumirri!" Simon pointed to his left and disappeared. Davy panicked and strained to pick up his pace to catch up but he was weakening and he could not. Without Simon they were finished. From behind him, Dobber was waving his hand at Davy. He was so out of breath he could not speak. He fell down totally exhausted and rolled over onto his back with a groan. Kelly sat down puffing beside him. Dobber tipped to his knees at the water's edge and cupped his hands and drank from Bondi Lake. They were near the subterranean springs feeding it and he thought he could hear them laughing.

" Davy lad. Yappulun Gumirri. Yappulun Gumirri means 'enter the hole'. Simon has found something."

The three arrived together at the spot where they had last seen Simon. He was waiting for them in a cleft and apparently refreshing his memory of the small cave which opened into the limestone. He thrust his staff up within the shadow and rattled it around. A tornado of twelve-inch-long, grey headed flying fox bats streamed out and ricocheted off Davy and Simon and squeaked away complaining in fifty bat jargons.

Simon grinned. He remembered it now. "Beelara-attunga-tandara-quidong." The place of the echo is here, a good high place to camp.

Simon ducked into the aperture and they followed his steps in the dim light. They could hear water running hard somewhere in the limestone and its echo was amplified in the cave. The floor lost its fine sand as it angled up toward the light and they scuffled a little faster, now that they could see better. The four of them climbed a sculpted spiral track in the rock made smooth by old water. They emerged from the shadow into brilliant sun. The top of the butte formed a gentle bowl with an elevated rim protecting them from being seen. The central low point of the bowl showed the blackened history of ten thousand fires. Tornadoes of fine dust stirred into the air and died again where the rim of the bowl blocked the breeze. It was quiet and they were relieved to be out of the sand blast of the beach. A solitary eucalyptus stood as a sentinel and spied the countryside for them.

Dobber and Kelly laid back on the warm rock with their jackets over their faces and Simon made a quiet 'unk' to get Davy's attention. He motioned to come. They exited the cave and made for Bondi lake. At the edge of the lake he spoke to Davy.

"Ky-bah-gul-berrie." Fire, boy. They gathered firewood. They picked up what they could carry and on the walk back, Simon gave Davy two quick looks and spoke to him in a calm voice. " Blank, listen carefully. Roll your firewood away from you and drop it. Do it on three. One, two, three." Davy dropped the wood and twenty small spiders scurried into the sand.

" Those are Funnel web spiders. Fangs larger than a brown snake's 'n they can pierce a toenail. Their venom can kill anything."

Davy exploded. " Poisonous spiders, poisonous plants, poisonous snakes, poisonous fish in the shallows. Is every damn thing here poisonous!" Davy blushed at his "damn" and Simon chuckled his answer.

" Well, I guess the answer is .. mostly." Simon chuckled again.

Dopo if I die here,...Wait a minute.

"Simon. You spoke English. You speak English. " Dopo he speaks English. Dopo heard it too.

Simon shrugged as he kicked the loose kindling away from the spiders. "Yes, I do."

"But you never do it. Why don't you speak English?"

"I don't like it. Too many words that don't mean anything and hide tricks. Perhaps. Almost. My language is clear. That is what I speak."

On the way back, they heard two combative wombats huffing at each other in the brush. They sounded like small steam locomotives. Within earshot of the cave Davy and Simon stopped speaking. The angle of the sun told Davy it was about two bells. It was five o'clock and he was getting hungry. Davy took the firewood up and Simon sprinted back to where they had heard the wombats. Davy dropped his bundle of wood at the fire pit and it woke Dobber and Kelly who were sleeping at opposite sides of the butte. He left and returned with the balance of the wood and Simon followed up close behind him with his tucker bag bulging with wombat. Simon sorted out the damp kindling and discarded it. He had Kelly and Dobber strip the bark from the remaining wood and clean any ash from the pit while he dressed the wombat. The fire was hot and totally smokeless and they savored the roast. They had finished their meal in sunlight and not even the keenest eye could have seen their smokeless fire atop the Pindiri-weerona, the high ground resting place.

Davy saw Dobber catching the angle of the reddening sun to illuminate the surface of what appeared to be a coin. He sat down and looked over his shoulder. It was a copper penny with a verse engraved on it.

"Dobber. What is that you have on that thong? You have defaced a coin of the realm I do believe."

"Ah Davy. This is me love token. I had it made to send home to my girl in Cork. It was to go next week. We lads can do this one time a year." He poked at the inscription. "That there on the top is her name. That on the bottom is mine. I rhymed it and my mate scribed it. Now it's for naught but I can look at it anyway. Read it to me, will you?" He handed it to Davy who turned it to the setting sun. The calligraphy was perfect and beautiful. It was the work of a skilled convict forger.

Davy read it aloud. "For Hannah Davis /my love/ is strong/ tho long apart/ it knows/ not time / just knows/ my heart/ Dubhghall.

"Your given name is Dubghall? How did you get called Dobber?"

He fingered his earring. " Well it's a name what warders can say easy. If you don't answer quick like, it's a rap with a cudgel. I didn't know it was me that marine was orderin' when he called me by name. He couldn't say me name natural to me ear see, so I got the rap. Split my pate. 'My name is Dobber', I shouts. Dobber was a name they could say. So now it's Dobber. Me real name is Dubhghall. Dubhghall Coghlan." He said it like a fond and distant memory of home.

The men rolled their jackets up under their heads but the stone was still too hot for sleeping. Simon sat cross-legged near Davy and listened for sounds in the night. Davy laid on his back and cast his mind into the night sky. The dust of a trillion intentions waited for choices. He moved his eyes from star to star, attempting to make shapes from them as astronomers did. The clarity with which he saw the constellations was beyond his imagination. The Australian skyscape was new and foreign to him. He pointed to the southern cross. Simon put his hand on his shoulder and said in his soft positive way, " Birubi", as if speaking of an old friend. Birubi had guided Simon his whole life. He pointed directly overhead to the constellation Scorpius and red Antares. It was redder than Mars and it shone more brightly. Simon called it 'Puruprika'. The night deepened and darkened and the stars moved closer over the warm bowl. The day had had enough of the men and they slept deeply.

Dawn was still an hour away when Simon and Kelly were wakened by the bawl of a heifer. A stray calf was in the far distance and calling. Kelly walked quickly to the edge of Pindiri-weerona to place the direction of the sound better. Dobber and Davy felt the agitation around them more than they heard the sounds. They woke and sat up and Kelly came to them, excited.

"Lad? Dobber? Time ta do a little duffing. Come with? Good tucker to come boy. Neet on the hoof." He angled his head in the direction from which they had heard the heifer. His coyote eyes blazed in and out of the starlight as he turned his head. Davy was petrified.

Dobber spoke firmly meaning Kelly to hear him. "Our Kelly is up to shonky business. Aint you Kelly boy." Dobber knew Simon was close by and could demolish Kelly in short order and he was brave because of it.

"Listen to me Davy lad. If Kelly there decides to shoot through, let 'im. Don' you be goin' with 'im. For what e's thinkin', when 'e's caught 'e swings. If he brings the duff back here, we swings too. All in." Kelly snorted derisively and snatched up his jacket. He dropped out of sight into the downslope of the tunnel and cursed as he slipped in the dark. His heavy tread continued to abate and he disappeared alone in the direction of the bawling. A cadre of dingoes began whining their pitch falling plaints to summon the rest of their gang for the hunt.

The heifer stood tethered to a pole in the center of a dried-up water hole about eight feet deep. Its sides were mounded and the single trail into it was a furrow made over time by animals coming to drink. Smits had sequestered a Bidjigal runner and five Marines dressed in bush garb around it. If Kelly was within miles of the young duff he would have him. He knew Kelly would take the bait and duffing was a hanging offence. As far as the other escapees, runaways were always caught; if not now, next week or next month, but he also understood. One hour or one day of free choice was priceless and logic played no part in it.

Kelly kept low so as not to startle the young duff. He took off his yellow jacket and tied it around his waist. He did not want to spook the heifer and have to chase it. He stumbled across a furrow leading in the direction of the bawling. It was certainly a game trail and that made sense. The runner and the five Marines heard him coming. They watched Kelly enter the dried-out bowl and noiselessly they moved to take him. One marine crept and cut off the entrance and the others crawled to the top of the surrounding burm. The marine at the entrance edged toward Kelly on balanced feet with his bayonet ready for the thrust. Another of the Marines slid down and took his place on the game trail blocking Kelly's escape. Kelly saw the tether on the calf and clenched his fists and dropped into a fighting posture. He then heard the clicks

267

of five muskets cocking around him and Kelly knew that was the end of the game. He sat down with his arms across his knees and hung his head and stared at the cracks in the mud between his feet.

Corporal Billups spoke in an even tone without a quaver.

"Kelly. Lie down on your stomach and put your hands in your pockets. If you take them out, all five of us will cheerfully shoot you. Make no mistake about that. Now. Where are your friends?"

Kelly's bestial eyes burned with fury. Every man jack feared him one on one. He put his hands in his pockets and rolled over onto his belly. He tried to spit at them but he was too dry and on inhalation he breathed the dust.

"Cowards! Ptui. Need five do you? Ptui. Sure, not one of you could take old Kelly. Where are me friends? Hunh! Not friends. Just donkeys running around behind Simon. Pindiri-weerona. They are at Pindiri-weerona. Tell them you have come courtesy of Sean Kelly."

Billups turned to the Bidjigal runner. "Burnum, do you know Pindiri-weerona?" The runner nodded.

"Good. Get to Sergeant Smits with that now. Be quick." Burnum sprinted away trailing the dust behind him with his speed.

Smits received the news with little surprise. He knew Simon could not go far and he would be in terrain difficult to navigate in order to discourage tracking. That very fact made his escape from there while carrying the baggage of Dobber and Blank a slow one. He also knew if they were to escape to the outback, Simon first had to run the tidal flats. There was nowhere else to move with speed. Smits called his six-man squad and behind him they marched in double time toward Bondi Beach with two Alsatian tracking dogs in hand.

Davy could outrun Dobber on the wet sand but he kept level with him. Simon led and he trotted at a reasonable pace to stay together. The tide was out and the tidal flats were half a mile wide. Dawn broke behind a running cloud bank and it made the sunless jog within the verge of the puddled water cooler. The lapping margin washed away every footprint. The gulls played loops in the updrafts trailing fast off the small bluff running parallel to the shore. These gulls were smaller and faster than the ones at home and they traveled at a height many times of what Davy had seen. They spun with joy at the blow holes in the sand that revealed a million bivalve hiding places. They were Simon's watchdogs. These quick gulls had not learned to tolerate the intrusion of man and they reacted to the sight of him. They burst into flight along his path and Simon watched for that and listened for their call of alarm. So far there was nothing. Simon's hearing was keen and more acute than that of either Dobber or Davy despite Davy's youth. They were downwind of the settlement and once and once only, he thought he had heard dogs on the air. He did not hear them again and he was unsure of what he had heard or whether his anticipation of hearing it had made it so. He knew Smits would take up the hunt for Kelly with vigor and dispatch but not likely so quickly as this.

Simon planned to find Chukker before the day was out. With Chukker as the fourth man, the four of them could stay safe and independent indefinitely. Without him, Simon could not be awake and vigilant forever. Finding Chukker meant eight hours of running directly away from the coast and into the heat of the interior. He could manage that with ease but he was not sure about Davy or Dobber. He had to keep them on a route they were capable of running. That route brought them closer to Smits but there was not another choice. They just had to beat Smits to the punch. They would need much pituri.

Smits had six armed men and two slathering Alsatians to recover the escapees. It would be their choice as to whether they came back vertical or horizontal and it mattered little to him which choice they made. He and his team had made good time on the quick march and they believed they had the advantage now. Macquarie Rift and Belong Rift were two sandy ravines leading up from the beach level to the sun hardened clay which opened the way into the outback. Simon and the rest had to take one of these paths. They ran parallel about two hundred yards apart with no view from one into the other. Macquarie was wider and less confining so Smits and four Marines were stationed there. He put two Marines with the tracking dogs in Belong. It was narrow and steeper and it was the unlikely choice. In any case if Smits heard the dogs he could be there in a minute.

The overcast had left and the sun had come out with punishing intensity. Simon pushed Davy and Dobber past staggering. They had done their best but Simon was unsure whether they had been fast enough. He prodded them to about a quarter of a mile short of where the clefts broke open onto the beach. The wind switched back as the new tide flowed when he noticed a sudden white burst above the Macquarie cleft. The gulls had been spooked and he heard their alarm call. Someone was there. He changed his angle and cut through a series of windblown dunes toward Belong Cleft. The dunes were about eight feet high and their shadows gave them a little cover. At that instant he heard the dogs. "Down" he hissed. The dogs would not place them unless the wind switched again.

"Quiet Davy. Quiet Dobber." Dobber imagined Simon was speaking English. Davy slid low. Here he was, hiding again. It had been his own choice to be here. No matter what intention he participated in, it seemed he put himself into trouble and of all things he had lost his only escape in the pipe. Without the pipe, if Malveena showed up or Mildred needed him, he was helpless.

"Now."

Simon jumped up and they cut back sharply toward the first and highest dune and suddenly a shadow appeared from nowhere and streamed down from the top.

The shadow was Malveena Drago. She had materialized at the top of the dune ten feet in front of Simon with a flash and a dazzle of sand and she posed there in stupefied immobility. Malveena had no idea of time or circumstance. She relaxed in the safety of being nowhere. She was suspended in a vague formless flux which waited patiently for definition. Consciousness surrounded her with confidence and tranquility and it made herself important compulsions seem petty and pointless. It washed away the anger. A brightening clarity began to hum a tune of purpose just for Malveena and it harmonized her along and honored her intention to participate in the trail of one David Pilcher.

Simon eyed the pale apparition who had appeared out of the blue before him and he changed the grip on his spear. Malveena saw a boy labeled Blank who looked like Davy and she felt no need to act. Beside Davy she saw the most attractive man she had seen in her life who was labeled Dobber and he seemed just right. Her one shoeless foot burned in the sand as she came out of her torpor with her eyes locked on Dobber. Dobber had never seen any madonna so beautiful as Malveena. He climbed the height.

" Oy! Sheila. Off the pages of Lady's Monthly Museum, you is. Like a bleedin' princess of the night you is."

Dobber bent low, stepped forward with his left foot, extended his left arm graciously and swept his hat low across the sand. Dobber knew what he liked. He took two quick steps to Malveena, took her left hand in his and gave it a hearty kiss. Malveena stood there stupefied and she blushed a brilliant pink. Dobber was impressed with himself. The baying of tracking dogs interrupted his ardor.

From the top of the Macquairie Cleft, Smits heard the dogs too. He cocked his musket and charged with his men across the bluff and started down Belong Rift. Malveena saw the distant plume of smoke over Dobber's shoulder before the crack of the musket shot reached them. The hot ball singed a nice part through Malveena's hair. The convicts looked back two hundred yards along the beach and saw two Marines coming out of Belong Cleft, with two tracking dogs straining on the leash. Simon whooped and pointed to Macquairie Rift with his spear and they fled for their lives. Simon dashed and the others followed. They slid and scrambled and fell down the shadowed slope of the sand dune leaving Malveena's profile silhouetted against the sun behind them. Dobber stopped and looked back upwind to the top of the mound and protected his eyes with his hand. Malveena stood in statuesque pallidity with the sand streaming off of her shoulders and Dobber saw heaven.

Davy screamed at him. " Dobber! Come! Run!"

Malveena stood dumbfounded on the beach in a freshening wind and she put her hand up to protect her eyes against the blowing sand. She was fully awake now and in her clear untrammeled mind she was being approached by gun toting Royal Marines who struggled to restrain two frothing Alsatians. They released the dogs. The Alsatians were slowed by the deepness of the sand but the leading dog was on her before she could think. It bounded toward her in full bristle with its head down and teeth bared and pulled up abruptly in a stiff legged stop. It whined lowly and rolled over on its back in complete submission at Malveena's feet. The second dog arrived and stopped beside its mate and lay low and prone and put its head on its paws. It looked up at Malveena with doleful eyes and gave up the hunt. Malveena didn't think about the dogs. She turned in a circle to see where Dobber had gone. The wind had obliterated his trail. Oh yes. Davy had been with him too.

The wind switched about and blasted Marine Sergeant Smits with sand as he burst onto the beach from the Belong cleft and hectored the six marines to

Malveena. They saw but could not believe the submissive dogs lying at her feet. The men stood motionless at the end of Malveena's shadow and let the sand take the weight of their muskets. From the height of the dune Malveena arched her back and brought her glistening copper pipe to her eye and drained the Australian sun. She vanished in a spiral of flashing sand and took her shadow with her. The two dogs howled at the loss until the reversing wind broke the spell. Their ears pricked up and their nostrils flared and they stood with bristling hair. They had picked up the strong scent from down the beach where Simon had planted pieces of clothing. They howled a recognition and Smits shouted "Go!" Off they went, hot on the trail of Dobber, Simon and Davy who at that moment were downwind at the top of Macquairie Cleft. Simon gave them a chew of pituri and they looked at each other and laughed. They strode with pituri tinged vigor into the beckoning outback. The wind angled across the plain in front of them and eight hours away they hoped to find Chukker. The dogs scoured the beach for two hours and found the trail to Pindiri-weerona wherein alas, it proved to be deserted.

Chukker sat with his back close to the wall of the high rock cove he had chosen for the night. It still held some of the warmth of the day. He wore long pants and he was barefooted. He had a long narrow amulet hanging on a thong around his neck and red stripes painted on his cheekbones. His spear stood against the back wall beside his woomera and his leather army shoes. Chukker had built a small fire and he was cutting off the bark from his kindling. He used a narrow stiletto like knife which showed off its pearl handle in the firelight. Next to him was a small pile of clothing, neatly folded. He stopped in mid whittle and listened to the night. He slid the billy closer to the heat, just inside the rim of the fire. He reached into his tucker bag and threw a handful of leaves into the water. He went back to stripping the bark.

Simon hummed a tuneless song in time with nothing in particular. It had been a long eventful day and he was as tired as Davy and Dobber were. They had done well and they had given it everything despite the weight and abrasion of their Canary garb. They trudged behind Simon, staying within the sweep of his tapping staff. Many snakes were taking heat from the rocks. They arrived at the base of a columned cliff face that looked like organ pipes looming two hundred feet above them. Simon led them behind a fallen slab and there sat

Chukker. He did not look up and he pushed the billy onto the fire.

"Yubbah," said Simon. Brother. "Yubbah, " said Chukker. "Be-bah-ra." I heard you singing. "Ye-wi?" Simon shook his head. He was not cold. Simon poked his spear tip into the pile of clothing and tossed it to Davy. He and Dobber changed quickly and the old moleskin clothing was perfect on them. Chukker took charge of the canary uniforms. He would bury them later.

The aroma from the tea filled the small cove. It was made from strawberry gum, rose and blackberry. Davy liked the aroma of the tea. " It smells like eucalyptus."

Simon nodded. Dobber threw his hot tea back as if he were in a hurry. He stood and said, " Well mates, I'm off." He stretched his shoulders and turned to go. Davy could not believe it.

" What? You can't mean it!"

" Well lad, I does mean it. I'm goin' back. I been thinkin' on it the last twenty odd mile. I'm not one to be on the run. I know the drill. Smits 'll reckon Kelly made me do it. Maybe a touch o' the lash and maybe some time in the hole, but soon enough me times up. That's best. Goodbye."

Simon held out three pituri to him and with a smile Dobber stuffed them into his pocket and left the firelight behind. Davy said a quiet goodbye to where Dobber Dubhghall Coghlan had been standing. Dobber had not said goodbye because he couldn't bear it. Simon and Chukker continued with their tea. Dobber could leave if he wished to. Davy felt very alone and he looked to the faces of the two men he was relying upon. His eyes flew wide open and he jumped to his feet and bent over forward and pointed an accusatory finger at Chukker's chest.

" You! That! Where!"

Chukker looked blandly at Davy.

" That, that, your amulet. That is my pipe!"

Chukker was unimpressed. The tone in Davy's voice was harsh. Chukker thought the boy should do a walkabout. Simon put his hand on Davy's shoulder and spoke in English.

" Let me."

Simon spoke to Chukker. "Wi-wi yubbah jun-gun jay-moo cal-ug-ul che-pa-buddie googa-burra." Sorry brother, the bad grasshopper has run a long way

273

today, a very long way.

Chukker responded without emotion. He and Simon spoke briefly and Simon turned to Davy.

"He says he knows it is yours. He found it when they combed the beach near where you had been plucked from the blackberries. He has been saving it for you. What you do next is key. You go to him and go down on one knee. Extend your hand with palm up and he will place the sheath there. Do not thank him. His giving is his thanks."

Davy did as he was told and the pipe came home with a little buzz. He tied it around his waist with the thong and it hung perfectly. He fell into a deep sleep with his back curled to the rock and his hand on the pipe to be awakened at dawn by the tickle of sand scorpions. He jumped up brushing them away in a panic amid chuckles from the two friends.

"Harmless Davy. Just looking for salt and heat."

Davy stood and stretched and looked at the sun. Simon knew what was on his mind and fished in his tucker bag for his pituri. He handed Davy a few chunks and Davy opened his sheath and dropped them into his pipe.

"Simon, Chukker, I am going on a walkabout."

Chukker said, "Ah-yum-but." You need it. Simon nodded. If Blank wanted to go on a walkabout he could do that.

Davy brought the pipe into the sun with the strongest intention he could muster. He left Australia in a counterclockwise conduit of the widest light. The light crescendoed its brightness and when he thought it must stop it brightened more. It was warm and fine and he landed back home on the pier in the pouring rain. Davy tilted his face to the sky and let the rain wash over him.

Davy arrived home just before supper and took off his wet shoes and put them on the shoe mat. He took off his favorite shirt and pants and put them in the laundry for the last time. He removed the pituri from his pipe and put it on the dresser beside the rest of his treasures. He began to sing just as his mother walked by the door of his room. "... she's a fine gal to look at but the catch is she's a mite too fond o' ships, she lives upon an iceberg to the noren and her mate he's Davy Jones, and she combs the weeds upon her fore'ead with poor drownded sailors' bones."

"What's that Davy?"

"Oh, hi Mom. A song a friend taught me. Yes, a very good friend."

Harry jumped up the front steps two at a time. He bent to the porch and picked up the evening paper and stuck it under his arm. He had more of a spring in his step than usual. He was bringing home something he thought was good news and he wanted to share it. He sat down on the first step at the foot of the stairs and unlaced his boots. He slipped on his Birkenstocks and shifted in them and it felt so good. It had taken him years to get a pair. He didn't like quiche and Chardonnay was strictly for women but boy, after a long day, those sandals sure felt good.

He said to Janet whom he could hear in the kitchen and to Davy who was coming down the stairs, "Want to hear something interesting?" Harry unfolded the evening paper and whacked it on his knee as he sat at the table. Janet and Davy joined him. The vegetables were not finished steaming.

"I was speaking with Carson today. You know, Carson on the loading dock? He told me a very interesting rumor he had heard. Something about buyers from Asia. Foster Industries is sold all right, but it's going to carry on much of its same work, just under a new name. What do you think of that"

Davy knew better. Davy let his Australian rip when he heard that. "Pig's arse!"

Harry heard what Davy said but it made no sense. It didn't register as something in Davy's vocabulary. Janet was not so magnanimous. She leaned in to Davy like a hatchet. "What did you just say young man? "

"What?" Davy needed time to think to cover this one. "When?"

"Never mind that stuff. What did you just say?"

Davy tried. "Big source. I hear Mr. Carson is a big source for rumors. So, I don't believe the new company stuff is the truth. I think it is made up. Big source."

Janet had to admire the adroitness of her little boy. This was not something to make an issue about. She stood up and walked around Davy and touched his shoulder to end it all. She lifted the lid and looked at the beans and they needed more steaming.

As he escaped to wash up, Davy thought that might not be the only thing steaming. He spoke over his shoulder to Dopo. "Wow Dopo. Mom was real ropeable." Dopo thought that was Australian for angry and he nodded profusely. As Davy lathered his hands with soap he finalized some things to himself. He could not do the things he needed to do all by himself. Even Mildred and he together could not. He needed to get with Foster and get him back there. He had to tell his parents and get them involved. Among them he was sure they could fix things. And Tilt. He could help convince. First thing was Foster. He put his hand on the pipe sheath considering how he might best access the intention to meet with Foster and the pipe seemed to suck a little energy from him as if something was disturbing it.

As Malveena Drago escaped nowhere, her surrounding energy warmed and brightened. She participated in the full consciousness of the light and her intention delivered her safely to the front seat of her car. Slowly she emerged from her suspended state of reality. She gripped the wheel for tactile reassurance of what her eyes told her and Malveena stayed seated there and fell asleep in her happy place.

Malveena awoke to a spitting rain. In a contemplative mood she exited the Foster Industries parking lot, leaving her skid protection turned on so her wheels did not spin. She drove placidly along the usual route to her apartment and ignored the chatter of the wipers across the partially dry windshield. Those blue eyes. I landed on a white sand beach to have my hair parted by a red-hot musket ball and my hand kissed by that blue eyed Dobber. I think perhaps the boy was there too. Without thought she accepted the next color of light the traffic programming offered her. That she could do. She could manage not to think about traffic lights. The traffic lights could not bear witness against her. David Pilcher and the little girl could. She stopped off at the Entourage wine store and selected a nice Pouilly Fuissé for sipping in the bath. It would certainly dilute the experience of coming within a tooth width of being devoured by a one-ton Australian crocodile. As far as Pilcher goes, I have no interest in where he is right now. Somehow, I stumbled onto his trail but I have no idea how. And it landed me in trouble. Foster's notes said to empty one's mind of the concept of the individual and focus just on the track residing permanently in the consciousness. Hard to do, to erase the concept of an individual. Dobber. I know nothing about him to empty from my mind. Maybe I should practice on him. Malveena needed to perfect the nature of her thoughts. She would master the phenomenon of the trail.

Two bony feral dogs darted in front of her car, tousling and snapping at each other and the world. She swerved to give them a clear birth and as they cowered away, from nowhere it grabbed her again.

Which wolf will win? The one you feed.

Chapter 19: Napoleon

David Pilcher was late. He two at a timed the front steps and raced through the deserted entrance foyer of Foster Elementary School. The smell of linseed oil owned the building. He glanced at Foster's portrait and he believed the blue eyes were watering from it. Old Tilt had received a fresh batch of dust bane and he had tossed around a few experimental hummocks to test it. He had not yet squashed any of them with his foot. The opening bell was ringing and the corridors were empty of students except for Davy. He had never traveled the halls alone and the reverberating echoes from his rattling book bag and running feet bounced through the school. He had never been late for school and the thought of it grabbed him in the pit of his stomach. This was his brilliant plan to start the day but he hadn't expected it to feel like this. The whole thing felt wrong. Davy swung one handed around the door jamb to gain speed and shot into the classroom at the exact moment the bell cut out and his rubber soles chirped him to a loud stop. Tilt was impressed.

" Ah! Mr. Pilcher. Very nice entrance. Late, but very nice in its way. Do you suppose you can get to your desk without chirping again?"

Davy nodded and he tried not to flush but it was too late. Porky Gregious dropped his jaw and blinked at Davy all the way to his desk. He snorfled. Davy certainly knew how to make an entrance.

Mildred looked to say hello, but Davy would not allow his eye to be caught. He had arrived late to avoid their usual pre-bell palaver and he was not going to blow it now. He demonstrated a sudden and consuming interest in Tilt's putrid geraniums along the sill to his left and he was fascinated with the state of the window panes. He had not worked out how to tell Mildred about Australia. After an hour his neck was stiff from looking left and he gave in.

He whispered. "Mildred."

Mildred turned glacially to him and pushed her glasses frames down on her nose. She did not have a look on her face.

"Yes?"

"Later."

She said nothing but he could hear what she said. It was certainly a humph of the first order.

The day passed quickly with Tilt teaching European History in his enthusiastic bony finger-stabbing way and with Porky, the new star of the class, expounding on his growing encyclopedic knowledge of everything.

Mildred did not hurry her walk home nor did she dawdle and Davy caught her up.

"Mildred, I have been thinking." She withheld eight caustic comebacks to that and remained silent as they walked. They scuffed in the fallen leaves together and Mildred tugged sideways on her pants to make the creases parallel again.

Davy spoke to her from the heart. " Mildred, we must find Mr. Foster. We need his help. Help to get Malveena and Bully off our necks, help to stop the plant closure and help to stay out of trouble using the pipe. But first, help to find your father." She looked at Davy and saw his sincerity.

"Those are my thoughts exactly Davy, but as far as getting Foster to help us, I don't know. You can beat a dead horse but you can't lead it to water."

Davy blinked as he digested that and he came up empty. "Mildred, that is not a metaphor. It is at least two mixed metaphors. Maybe more. What you just said may be true but there is no lesson to be had from it, is there?"

"It doesn't matter, it is old."

Davy couldn't argue with that.

"What I meant Davy, is I am not sure I can do it. Do you remember what he said to us at Woodstock? That we could find him if we came with good intention? I am angry when I think of him running off and leaving us on our own. And refusing to come back to help. I want to kick him. That is not usually defined as good intention."

Davy understood her conflict. "Well, think of it like this. He has chosen to be somewhere else, perhaps in another time, doing who knows what. We need to join him in that, remembering it is for a good reason we seek him. It is our job to convince him there are better things he could do. Things that are important and things that may help many people. To convince him of that is certainly a good intention. Maybe if you think of it like that. Could you?"

Mildred walked on for several minutes without answering and began slow nods of contemplation. She thought of how she loved her father and how she wanted to help him come back. She thought of the damage Malveena and Bully would do to the town if they succeeded in their business. She thought of how hard things were for her mother. Her animus for Charles Foster was petty. She would not let it interfere with doing the right thing.

" Yes. I can think of it like that. Count on me."

They turned to each other and shook hands on it and they were embarrassed. They had never done that.

The weather reports were not good. Only with sun could they participate in the consciousness of the light and connect with Foster. The weather forecast predicted overcast with dense cloud cover and rain squalls for five days. Davy was skeptical on the face of it. The weather bureau couldn't tell what the weather had been yesterday let alone tomorrow, but the fact the seagulls had been cascading inland for three days corroborated the report. The two friends walked on, matching stride for stride and the wind danced with the leaves, in augury of the coming storms. Neither of them wanted to spoil the mood. Mildred broke the silence.

"What should I wear?"

Davy shrugged his shoulders. It was impossible to know where they would land. Foster dictated that.

"Well Mildred, just make sure to wear your glasses frames. Wouldn't want to miss seeing anything." They laughed at that but the basic question remained unanswered. Where on earth was Charles Abernathy Foster.

Charles Foster stood with his hands on his hips, looking at himself in the mirror and he chuckled at the mess he saw. He had let his hair grow long and he had cut it short around the bald spot at the back of his head so the short hair bristled. His copper pipe was secure in a sleeve sewn into the waistband on the left side of his gray unhemmed trousers. He patted it for a second time just to be sure he had it. Inside his pants on the right side were ten small pockets, each holding one coin stamped with a hammer and tongs insignia. His pants were too short and they exposed his bare ankles above a pair of scuffed brown shoes. The shoes were tied with leather thong laces too short to use all the holes, half of which were missing their eyelets. He was without socks. He had a three-day growth of beard and he looked appropriately grizzled. His blue peasant shirt was a loose pullover and it was slightly too big for him. He shrugged his shoulders a couple of times to have it sit a little better but it stayed askew. He unhooked a black felt hat from the mirror frame and positioned it just so on his head. Foster admired his reflection and he was satisfied. He was perfectly unkempt. He was now a peasant extraordinaire, one of the Italian contadini. He was ready. The sun warmed his front veranda and bounced through the glass to fill his kitchen with brilliance. He slid the heavy patio door open and walked outside and stood still with his face up to the tanning rays. He slipped his pipe up from under his shirt, positioned it to his eye, fixed his head to the sun and gave himself up to the trail.

His intention was strong and practiced and the consciousness of the light was ready for him. It understood his understanding. Foster had cleared his mind of opinion. He was uncritical, he was unemotional and he thought not of the man. He thought of his times, his places and the mark on history the man had made. He characterized such things not as good, or as bad, but as extant. The unique and timeless residue of the man's passage through the envelope of time was open and available to him. Charles Foster had prepared himself to travel without a value judgment along the indelible map of the man's transit.

A maelstrom of light began coalescing into a brilliant dynamic acceptance and there was an energy in it Charles had not felt in any of his many previous sojourns. He landed immediately and abruptly, facing the sea on a bustling wharf. It was a brilliant cool morning just after dawn on Sunday, February 26, 1815.

He saw but did not care that a beautiful fifty-meter-long square-rigged brigantine sat thirty feet in front of him. It was red hulled with the black and yellow colors of a British ship. He saw the blind sockets of ten sixteen-pound cannons watching him and he counted them. He saw the bustle of the teamsters as they loaded with speed and he thought it fine but he did not care about it. An endless train of straining men trundled biscuit, rice, vegetables, cheese, brandy and wine through his vision and it seemed a fitting thing but he saw no need for it. The ship was called the Inconstant. Its load weight and its six-inch hemp hawsers kept it motionless in the small chop splashing the pier. He felt the freshening wind titillate his shirt but it was not his business. He heard the pealing of bells from a church promising him clarification but it was a different clarification he wanted and it hit him like a typhoon. A vicious blast

281

of miasmic wind from the south east startled him into reality. At the impact, a hundred gulls complained up away from him. They screeched at him and at the ship and at the tumult disturbing their early feeding. The creeping sun was burgeoning the updrafts and en masse they gained altitude to the place for new complaints.

Charles Foster released himself into reality. The brigantine loading in front of him was indeed the Inconstant. He knew the ship. He was exactly where he wanted to be in time and place. The Inconstant was preparing for imminent departure and deck hands were testing the running lines. The sheets strained at the clews and the square sails pulled at the yard, showing new tautness here and there. The sheet tensions and tackle placements were correct. The handpicked crew left nothing to chance. Sentries in the uniforms of Spain and Royalist France patrolled past him in boredom not caring what they saw. He smiled to himself and filled his lungs gratefully with the healing air of the sea. He had followed the trail with great satisfaction.

He reckoned it was just after dawn. The penitent were traipsing up the hill in a slow fearful stream, driven along to early mass by the peal of the bells. From the highest point on the island, mother church, the Church of Mercy, Chiesa Della Misericordia, was gathering her children to salvation. It was a cold day and Foster was under-dressed in his single shirt. The quay was wet and dirty and weary of the night. Its dank morning shadow looked for relief but only isolated spires at the highest elevations showed the sun. Charles Foster's goal was Villa di San Martino and it was inland about two miles and set at a high point not far from the church. He was unsure of the best route to the villa and he cast about for a starting place. The tantalizing smell of fresh baked bread came to him from the right. A vendor was setting up his stall about fifty yards west, where a steep cobbled ramp ran down from the street and intersected with the flat of the quay. Foster fished out a single hammer and tongs decorated coin of the island and traded it for a hot bun. He cradled the hard-crusted bread in his hands to warm them. He needed directions.

"Mi scusi, dove posso trovare Villa di San Martino?"

The vendor pointed a gnarled arthritic fore-finger up the ramp and made two stabs with it to indicate continuing on and made two flips of his thumb to the left. He said nothing and wiped his running nose with the back of his hand.

He proceeded to arrange his wares as the sailors drifted over to him from the Inconstant.

Chewing on the bun, Foster set out with his longest stride and headed uphill, splashing through the rivulets of condensation gathering from the heights above. The cobbles were slippery but he pushed himself and he made good time despite the wet. He saw the sun make pale bands across the way ahead as it probed the cross streets and he welcomed the warmth. He was confident in finding Villa di San Martino, but gaining entrance could be another story. He hoped his approach would prove to be the right one. He continued his climb in unenthusiastic shallow sunlight and he was not warmer as the wet sea-wind swept up through the tunnels made by the time weathered houses. The gradient began to lose its pitch and after one-hour Foster stepped up off the cobbles and over the brow of the shallow incline onto flat terrain at the gates of Villa di San Martino. A spiked eight-foot-high iron fence surrounded the property. The fence sections were connected by fluted steel columns topped with gilded eagles with spread their wings and their heads postured in profile to the right. Two wide iron gates were latched with an enormous hasp that barred entrance to the grounds. Through the grill of the fence he saw a wide circular drive leading through to a porte-cochère. The facade above it that fronted the gate was supported by four massive twenty-foot stone pillars and embellished with a series of alternating gilded eagles and capital "N"s. The two-story villa nestled into a backdrop of rough trunked old chestnut trees and Nubian dragon trees that crept two hundred feet up a green horseshoe of ancient hills. On either side of the front gate stood one sentry. On the left in quasi full-dress uniform stood a mustachioed Frenchman with sleep still in his eyes. He attempted to be resplendent but he was tired. He stood under an ill-fitting too large helmet adorned with a white cockade and a red plume. His collar and cuffs were red and trimmed with white piping which was frayed and dirty. His white vest was missing two buttons and the turn-backs on his jacket were soiled. He leaned on his musket rather than brandished it and Foster noticed he had no flint in the lock. He had a look which hoped Foster would not make him do anything. The Spaniard at the opposite end of the gate was at rigid attention with the arrival of someone to impress. His yellow jacket and pants were spotless and his black knee length boots were polished to a mirror finish. They matched the black epaulettes on his shoulders. An elaborate Toledo sword hung on his left hip in a gleaming black scabbard. In his right hand he held a staff with a stiff pennant displaying the coat of arms of the Spanish royal house of Bourbon-Anjou. He raised an eyebrow as imperiously as he could manage until he saw what Foster held out to him.

Foster had extended his right arm slowly between the two soldiers to expose the back and fingers of his right hand and he assumed his most regal mien.

"Caballeros, aquí está mi tarjeta. Messieurs, voici ma carte. Gentlemen, here is my card."

The sentries snapped to attention and the Spaniard held his eyes in obeisance until he could release the gate and pass Foster through. They had seen this calling card before. It carried the greatest weight with the occupant of the Villa. This big rough-edged man was dressed like a paysan, a campesino, a peasant, but he had the key to the Villa di San Martino. The Spaniard lingered a few feet inside the gate and watched Foster walk away toward the villa. He stayed as close as he dared, hoping to eavesdrop and make himself important in the telling of what he might hear. Outside, the French soldier leaned sleepily against the gate attempting to not fall down and injure himself with his bayonet.

From fifty feet inside the gate Foster saw a man standing on the small veranda, facing east with his eyes closed and his hands clasped behind his back. Only his face and shoulders were in the sun and they were extraordinarily illuminated. His posture was tranquil and his breathing was slow but they belied the whirlwind in his mind. Therein a symphony of events was arranging itself to be played that day. As Foster approached him he saw il n'a pas brandi ses médailles. He was not showing off his medals. This was a man who had been promoted to brigadier general at the age of twenty-four. He appeared to be downplaying himself or wishing to be nondescript. He was dressed plainly in the manner of a merchant but upon closer inspection, the fabrics of his clothing were expensive and they were woven with innumerable small bee designs. Foster was not surprised. To no one in particular he spoke aloud and the man heard him clearly.

"Ah! The bees. Let us reincarnate the Merovingian dynasty. "

The gentleman started at the intrusion and spun to Charles Foster with wide eyes and a look of panic. He was aghast at seeing a potential assassin who was now within ten feet of him. He pointed his wavering finger at Foster and opened his mouth to scream for his bodyguards but he stopped himself abruptly. Charles Foster had extended his right hand to identify himself. He took off his hat with his left hand, leaving the back of his right extended, bowed low, swept his hat across in front of him and spoke calmly.

" I sir, am Charles Abernathy Foster, at your service."

At the sound of Foster's controlled voice, the man recovered himself. He looked again at Foster's extended hand. The crispness of the raised pattern on the gold signet ring had been lessened by Foster's fingering, but there was no mistaking the compass and square. It was the ring of a Master Mason. It was an identical ring to his own. Foster's companion put two fingers and thumb to his right temple and held it there for a few seconds before he allowed his arm to fall.

" I believe you are a travelling man. How old is your mother?"

Foster knew what was encoded in the question immediately. He mirrored the hand gesture at his temple and answered his question with alacrity.

" I believe you are a travelling man also. It happens my mother is alive and well in Annapolis, but surprisingly she is only one year old. And your mother? How old is she?"

The gentleman smiled. "Merci de demander. Thank you for asking. She has aged well, in fact she is in perfect harmony, Parfait Harmonie for lo these 80 years."

They had affirmed to each other their Masonic bona fides. The question " How old is your mother?" asked the number of the lodge into which each was inducted. Foster's home lodge at Annapolis was the first lodge in his country and it was lodge number one. The other man's Masonic lodge on the island of Malta dated from the seventeen thirties. It had no lodge number but was called simply "Parfait Harmonie."

"Well brother Foster, you have introduced yourself and I am honored to do the same. I stand before you as your Imperial and Royal Majesty, King of Italy, Sovereign of the Island of Elba, Emperor of the French, Napoleone di Buonaparte. Napoléon, at your service. Je suis à votre service, monsieur."

He tipped into a small bow and addressed Foster as one would address a peer. " I believe you and I are on the level."

Foster nodded in affirmation. " Yes, I believe we are."

285

Emperor and common man were equal in the eyes of the lodge.

The yellow clad Spanish sentry had heard every word and he doubted his hearing. He had risked much by lurking too close and he was disappointed and confused. *Nunca escuché una conversación tan estúpida. I never heard such a stupid conversation. Two big shots can only inquire after the health of their mothers? My mother lives in Annapolis and surprisingly she is one? What nonsense! They're talking gibberish. This is baloney in any language.* He could not repeat this stuff.

What impossible nonsense. And these sorts of people lead armies and become Kings. Pah.

He slouched back through the gate and closed it behind him. He poked his French compadre with his flag staff and woke him up.

Foster respected the necessity for Napoléon to iterate and reiterate his titular honors. The Corsican needed relentless reinforcement of the legitimacy of his imperial throne now being called into question in France. The Merovingian bees woven into Napoléon's clothing were one part of the statement of validity. The Merovingian bloodline of Europe was an ancient one. Many centuries earlier they had chosen designs of stylized bees to represent their family pedigree. Napoléon's bees were circumstantial evidence he continued their lineage. They came from his progenitors and through them he asserted his claim to kingship. Because of them, he claimed a much older lineage than of the Bourbons, for it was the Bourbons who were attempting to establish their king in France in Napoléon's absence. To be from an older bloodline than theirs was imperative for Napoléon to succeed should he return. In Foster he recognized one who understood the vital importance of symbolism in validating his claim to a Napoléonic prepotency.

They sat beside each other on the low railing and warmed their backs in the rising sun. The bells at Chiesa Della Misericordia stopped and they were replaced with the sweet sounds of red-tailed swallows swooping through the garden. Foster smacked a mosquito on the back of his neck which told him what they were after. He looked at Napoléon. " The church bells have stopped. Am I keeping you from attending mass?"

" No, that docility is not for me, yet I admit I do need it around me. I need it because religion is the only thing keeping the poor from murdering the wealthy." He said it as a statement of fact, not as a philosophical musing.

"Brother Foster, I sense you appreciate my strategisms. This island, Elba, is upwind of France." He nodded eastward toward the bay below them where an intermittent sun teased the whitecaps. "Down there, above the harbor, is my Villa dei Mulini. From its veranda I watch the Piombino Channel. I see the blue haze of Italy riding the wind northward. That wind can carry away more than sea mist." He added quickly, "N'est ce pas?" as if in afterthought. Foster feigned to receive it as such but he had seen the frantic loading of the Inconstant.

"Les Rosbifs have decided to move me. They want me remote from Europe. There is no question of that, just a question as to when and to where. They, the English and their man here, Campbell, have been of two minds of course. Here, I am convenient to assassinate and spare them the worry of me, yet also, from here I am close enough to France to return and do them great mischief. That is the dilemma for both of us."

Foster was unsure. Napoléon appeared to be safe. The island teemed with French and Spanish soldiers, still proud in their worn uniforms. "You seem to be well guarded by your old army corps. Protected."

"It may appear so but I have been here some months. Nine months. Months without my family and months in stagnation. Months where sunny routine has set in and security has become a forgotten purpose for the soldier. I understand it. Being near the great man is enough for them. "

Foster nodded. "I see your old soldiers love you."

" Ah. Mes vrais bougres. My old campaigners. That is true. They see me not as a monster but as a victim. Le Petit Caporal is their liberator. One who is guided by a divine hand to lead them to a new world." He lifted his eyes despite himself.

" I see too their love alone cannot protect me here. That is a task set for the English Coronel Campbell and his Royal Marines although he himself is away for three days to the mainland. So, let us not interrupt him while he is making a mistake. Yet in his absence Campbell deploys his men strategically. Should an assassin move against me, their response is calculated to be late. I am only secure with my back to the wall. I am forbidden a weapon. A dilemma is it not? Then there is you."

The Emperor stood and faced the seated Foster. He was abrupt and he spoke with brevity. " I know men and you are not the ordinary man. Who are you and why are you here?"

Charles had been expecting this question but he had not rehearsed an answer. He would tell Napoléon the full truth and let him deal with it. Le Petit Caporal was an extraordinary man with an extraordinary mind which held an understanding of esoteric concepts beyond his time.

" Majesty, I will be brief. I have observed you have things of great import to do today. I will not make you late."

Napoléon showed nothing on his face even though Foster spoke as if he knew Napoléon's itinerary rather than speculated on it.

" Your imperial majesty, you can believe fully what I'm about to tell you. I have come from another place and from another path of history to meet with you in good humor and to have honest discourse with you. I can be here because an ambient consciousness exists, a living light which offers to us, to each of us, a choice to participate or not participate in anything we can intend. My honest intention was to be here with you and so you see, here I am and here you are."

Napoléon listened tranquilly without an iota of surprise or doubt at what he had just heard. " Walk with me."

Napoléon led, one yard ahead and to the right of Foster and clasped his hands behind his back as he walked. He spoke over his shoulder.

"You are from another path of history you say. History. Simply a fable men agree upon. I am content to create my own fable. It will fall to those who follow me to make it a history." He fell back beside Foster and walked with a hand on Foster's shoulder. "Come in with me. I wish to show you my Egyptian room."

They walked inside together and the temperature dropped. It was not yet 60 degrees outside and the interior was cooler than that. The two-foot-thick stone walls and the stone flooring kept the villa cool or cold year-round. The gloss of the dyna marble floors bounced the light around and the passage was not dark, even though the morning sun had not elevated to penetrate the window openings. As they walked through the library and approached the staircase to the second floor, Foster heard the bounce of a stone ricocheting off the marble floor and a pebble the size of a marble cracked into his ankle bone. A lad of six slid past the corner and upon seeing the two men, he dashed forward and jumped into Napoléon's arms.

Napoléon laughed. "Ah, Luce dei miei occhi! Light of my eyes. Alexandre, you must not use our guests for target practice." With a hug he smothered the boy into his waistcoat.

Charles picked up the pebble and dropped it into his pocket. He rubbed his ankle and saw the corridor on the left had a hopscotch design inlaid in ceramic in the floor, where the boy had been playing and tossing his marker. A second marker sat on the last square.

"Please excuse him Charles. He is a boy."

The emperor gestured to the hopscotch design.

"Do you know what that is? That is La Peregrina. The pilgrim girl. The story is its design was inspired by the writing of the Inferno by Dante Alighieri. You see it has nine squares? They are said to represent the nine stages the pilgrim traveler must experience in order to reach heaven from purgatory. It should be so simple, no?" Foster nodded he was familiar with the pattern and continued rubbing the red welt on his ankle bone.

Quick shuffling footsteps from the left precursed a young lady who clutched up her skirts from her last turn at the game. She hurried in with an embarrassed look to retrieve her son and Napoléon touched her shoulder with tenderness. She was Maria Walewska, Napoléon's mistress. With moist eyes she pried her son away from his father. She knew the ship *Inconstant* was girded for flight to France and she knew she and their son were remaining behind.

"Vi prego di scusarmi, please excuse me brother Foster. I shall not be long. I must speak with miei cari. My dear ones. "

Foster smiled. "Naturalmente. Non abbiate fretta."

Napoléon cuddled them around the corner and mellifluous speech carried to Foster, too soft to understand.

Foster stood alone in Napoléon's library, which was small and filled to the ceiling with maps and arcane writings. Charles Foster had confessed to Napoléon he was from another time and history and the amazing idea had been received without an apparent reaction. Was the consciousness of the light something of which the man had prior knowledge? If so, how would that be manifested in his megalomania? Foster knew what lay ahead for Napoléon under the hand of the Duke of Wellington at Waterloo. But suppose Napoléon participated in the intention of the light and returned again to the battle with renewed tactics. Suppose his ego drove him to repeat it again and again until he got it right. It was an interesting possibility. He could win the battle and proceed from there into a triumphant new and parallel history more to his liking.

Foster read the titles of the books in front of him. The first one he saw heightened his suspicion of what the emperor might know. It was Thomas Young's Experiments and Calculations Relative to Physical Optics, published in 1804. Those were the first experiments proving the consciousness of light. Beside it stood the same Thomas Young's Decipherment of Egyptian Hieroglyphs. Young was the Egyptologist who translated the Rosetta Stone. Napoléon had abruptly broken off conflict on the continent in 1798 and from there spent several years in Egypt. Was Young's research on light and his special understanding of arcane hieroglyphs the impetus for that?

There was a work by Copernicus, De Revolutionibus Orbium Celestium which dealt with the celestial orbits. De Scienta Stellarum - De Numeris Stellarum et motibus was there, written by the eighth century Arab Al Battani who was considered to be the greatest theoretical mathematician of all. From Hermes Trismegistus there was a copy of Corpus Hermeticum which was more ancient than the flood. As above, so below.

Volume after volume was devoted to the literature of light and mysticism. Opticks: or, A Treatise of the Reflexions, Refractions, Inflexions and Colors of Light by Isaac Newton, published in English in 1704. Napoléon's library was armed with much but his lack of reading English foiled him.

The emperor returned quietly from his family embrace and over Foster's shoulder he watched him read his book titles. He spoke without a trace of guile. "Interesting, aren't they. Foster, if you can distill a palatable spirit from their traces of reason and insanity, history and occult, science and myth, then I commend you. I cannot do it. Let us go up."

Napoléon's voice was emotional. Foster sensed he was sharing a final gathering of memories of Elba rather than taking a tour. They walked through the dining room, the Sala del nodo d'amore, the lovers knot room. It was dedicated to the marriage between Napoléon and his wife Maria Luisa d'Asburgo-Lorena. On the ceiling, a fresco of two gilded doves in flight carried a lovers' knot among pink clouds to symbolize the love between them. Maria Luisa had chosen not to come to Elba. They entered Sala egizia. The Egyptian Room. Entering the room, a trompe l'oeil revealed a beautiful rendering of the Egyptian countryside as seen from the interior of a villa, whose columns and expansive courtyards led out to a verdant countryside running to the horizon. Brilliant green papyrus grew from an octagonal tank sunken in the center of the room. Above it, hieroglyphs and zodiacal signs ran around the perimeter of a huge circular plaster molding of the heavens. Foster saw why Napoléon wished to refresh himself of the splendor of his Egyptian room.

They walked together down to the dormant gardens huddling in the February cold. Stepping into the sun they both realized they had been too cold inside. The great Emperor paused and spoke with each guard and domestic as he passed them. Foster understood spoken Italian well. He had studied it assiduously for several years and he had prepared equally for this day with oral French studies. When Napoléon spoke French to his staff, Foster was astounded at his ungrammatical structure and his harsh inflections. Yet such inadequacies had served him extraordinarily well. He came from a noble and influential Italian family but his environment was Corsican. Its fractured patois was a mongrel of Italian, French and native Corsican. The Corsu was a harsh vowelled and indecipherable idiomatic language of mystery. In mainland France, the paysans spoke competing dialects of Breton, Berrichon, Franc-comtois, Bourguignon, Languedocien, Nissard, Flamand and a dozen other regional lingua franca. In addition, they spoke them ungrammatically as 95% of the nation was illiterate. Napoléon had not a trace of the cultured and diffident presentation of the nobility. His speech was coarse and non-patrician and surely it came from one who had suffered as they had suffered. Yet he had risen and so would they. He was Gallic yet exotic and he was certainly one of them. He promised them everything. He was their champion and he was loved unreservedly by his cannon fodder.

The wind had lost its gusts from the south east and it had diminished to a steady gentleness. It was much less active than when Foster had arrived on the wharf that morning. It usually increased at this time of day and season but not this day. Napoléon sniffed it immediately and his posture became slightly more rigid and his breathing went more to his shoulders. Sunset was at 5:53 and it was early afternoon, yet there was a feeling of closing in.

Davy and Mildred finally got their break in the weather after an interminable three days. The sky was high and the midweek pier was mostly deserted. Isolated cirrus clouds showed the direction of the moving front and they promised good weather for the next few days. One single jet plane scribed a white line across the height of the dome and with one slow stroke it gradually converted a Constable into a Dali. Mildred had ditched her balaclava and, in the sun,, her hair was red and coppered stronger than Davy remembered it. She wore her spectacle frames to help her concentrate. Davy had a long peaked black cap and a light beige jacket that used to be his father's. A touch of pipe tobacco haunted it from when his dad smoked. There was no banter between them nor any gallows humor. They held hands and combined a unified thought with the strongest focus of good intention they could muster. Davy sighted the pipe into the Dali sun and they were gone from the pier. They spun to their rendezvous with Foster inside an eccentric tilted whirlwind of surreal melting corkscrew colors which blossomed into copper fire.

They were planted in a spin at an angle close to tipping, locked in the grip of a resinous sheath. They saw the backs of two gentlemen standing in front of them, with the shorter of them somehow dominant while red tailed swooping swallows made loops for fun. Davy's hat was askew like his body angle and he held the pose. Mildred was tipped away from Davy and she felt her spectacles working slowly through the glutinous restraint and admiringly she visualized their slow slide off the end of her nose. There was no penalty for that and it was interesting to feel it. The right earpiece slipped away and with no responsibility to act she heard the frames land with a clink on the limestone veranda floor. The clink made by the falling frames mimicked exactly the cocking of the hammer of a flintlock pistol. With the speed of a mongoose Napoléon grabbed Foster and spun him around to face the assassin. He clutched Foster's arms from behind him to maintain the shield and screamed "Guard!" Napoléon then saw only two bewildered and glutinously immobile youngsters and he relaxed his grip on Foster's sleeves. He waved off the Spanish sentry who was on the run from the front gate. No wet footprints led to where Davy and Mildred stood in the center of the veranda. They were ten feet from Foster and the great Napoléon.

Foster was taller and broader and held a more erect posture than Napoléon but of the two it was not Foster who carried the greater energy. There was an aura about Napoléon which commanded attention. Davy was almost of a height with Napoléon but felt quite a child in his presence. He saw what made a leader of men.

Foster's eyebrows were frozen in the up position. Davy came out of suspension first, followed quickly by Mildred who stepped hard to recover from her tipped posture. She picked up her glasses frames as Napoléon spied the knife sheath on Davy's belt. Foster jumped in quickly. "Davy. Open the sheath. Show the pipe."

Davy flipped open the flap and the copper glimmered in the sun. Napoléon strode forward to see it. He stepped between the two youngsters and Mildred blurted, " I though you would be shorter." Foster grimaced.

Napoléon laughed at the youth of it. " I am not."

He turned to his brother Master Mason. "So, Foster. These two are friends of yours?" Foster nodded. Napoléon stood smiling between Davy and Mildred with a hand on each of their shoulders.

"Foster, I should have agents such as these." He looked at them. "You two have dropped from nowhere into the most private of conversations and stand within a dagger's reach of one which the world would throttle if it could." He did not wait for an answer as he looked to the distance and the diminishing light.

"Enough. It is time."

He shook Foster's hand. "À la prochain brother Foster, bon chance."

"Au revoir brother Napoléon, bon voyage." The different goodbyes did not escape either of them. They both knew they would not meet again.

Napoléon swung on his heel and with his shoulders back and an erect head, he walked in martial perfection toward the front gate where carriages had been gathering for the last twenty minutes. Davy and Mildred and Charles Foster watched his every step, mesmerized by the energy surrounding him like a Kirlian aura. The Emperor of the French stepped into a glistening black carriage blazoned with his coat of arms. A large gilded eagle centered a heraldic shield, perched above a small capital 'N'. Around them wrapped the Imperial Mantle, brocaded with countless Merovingian bees. He stuck his head out of the window and waved back and shouted. "Goodbye children!" Mildred and Davy felt elevated. The common touch never failed.

They walked with Foster to the warmed stone veranda steps and sat on the first step down with Foster between them. He was pleased to see them and his smile told them so. "Wait." He got up and went inside. He returned in a few seconds tossing a pebble up in his hand as he walked. He fumbled in his pocket and retrieved the stone that hit him in the ankle. "Here Mildred, a souvenir. Here Davy." Mildred stretched across to Davy with the pebble from La Peregrina and he dropped both of them into his pipe sheath and buttoned the flap.

Foster sat between them again. " I told you you could find me if you came with good intention and you have. What is happening? Have you encountered Malveena again?"

Mildred sat on his right with her head down. She was thinking of how she would phrase her appeal to Foster to return with them and she shook her head no. She had not encountered Malveena or Bully. On Foster's left, the question thrust Davy back to Botany Bay and he answered. "Yes, yes I have. I have seen Malveena. In Botany Bay. " He could not see Mildred's confused look from where he sat. He leaned to her around Foster and fibbed, "Surfing, you know?" Mildred knew Botany Bay was not where he surfed.

He recounted the entire escapade. Mildred listened in awe and admiration and when Davy came to the part about the red-hot musket ball burning a neat wide part across Malveena's scalp, she exploded with laughter. "Boy, oh boy, I would have loved to have seen that. I hope the hair never grows back!"

Foster chuckled at it too but he was worried. " Davy, was Malveena with you? I mean, was she a netherworld spectral Malveena like Woodstock or a Malveena in the flesh?"

"In the flesh." As he said it, he realized Malveena had not come with good intentions yet she had been there where he had been.

Foster began. "Davy, I am not sure how Ms. Drago did that. Someone with bad intent but with strong discipline, might, just might be able to do it, but it is exceedingly difficult if not impossible. One must empty one's mind. Even a Zen master who says to his student " You are approaching tranquility" has judged his student's state as lesser than being tranquil, deficient in ultimate tranquility.

294

The Master's mind is not empty, it is judgmental. Even the Zen master cannot truly empty his mind. So, you see how difficult it is. Then again there is Malveena. Malveena can have a completely empty and non-judgmental mind when she has a goal. I have known her for twenty years. She attaches no attributes to anything she does. With her there is no good or bad, only what is effective when she is in action. She might move that strange sociopathic mind to the right place, not even knowing how she did it. Malveena is a special case and therefore very dangerous."

Mildred asked Foster the same thing Davy was thinking. "Have you done it? Traveled a trail with an empty mind?"

"Yes. It took me thirty years of learning to do so and if I may say it, I have a reasonably good mind and a determined spirit. Also, I am not mean minded. Those are ideal starting points yet it took me decades to master it." Neither of them took his statement as braggadocios.

" As you know, all intentions exist for all time and you simply participate in that intention prepared by the consciousness of the light. All options are offered to you to participate or not participate as you intend. It is your choice. Yes.?" They nodded.

"Fine. Each of us is unique." Davy thought Mildred was particularly unique.

"What we leave behind is a record of our passage, a map of the specific intentions we have chosen to participate in, our trail. Every intention we embraced is recorded forever as our trail. The consciousness of the light had that trail ready for us as one of many to intend and we chose that one. It is still ready and forever available to choose in the consciousness of the light, but let us say, it is not you who chooses to use it but another. Your.."

Mildred interjected. "That is very er.. interesting Mr. Foster but Davy and I c.."

"Just a second Mildred. Your trail exists, yes, but this time it is not you who is using it. The trail, your trail, your record of passage, leads along the way you have passed but now it takes someone else, not you. To ride your trail has become their choice of intention. They have ridden your trail." Foster looked back and forth for affirmation.

Mildred and Davy thought they understood what they heard, but this was difficult stuff and their minds were on their purposes for being there. Davy wondered too whether a trail was how Dopo showed up and if he would understand this. Dopo understood it.

Mildred was becoming impatient. She was here to solve problems and resolve her father's disappearance and the ins and outs of the trail were for another time. And as for Malveena, enough of Malveena.

"There are two things though, which protect you or .."

"Stop! Mr. Foster!" Mildred's red hair was curling.

"We are not here for a visit, nor for a lesson on all the tricks and turns of riding the trail. Thank you anyway. There are things and people that need stopping and saving and rescuing. We are here for that purpose. Please."

"I see. Well I have a purpose too. I am off to spend some time with Nikola Tesla. His years in New York were interesting and he.."

"Tesla? New York? What of them! You plan to spin away into the void without hearing us? That is not fair!"

Foster did not appreciate being lectured by a child. "Not fair? Really Mildred. Don't be childish." He had not intended to be hurtful and he regretted how he had phrased his response. Mildred was not the age to be told she was childish. She was altogether composed as she paused thoughtfully. She spoke to Foster both dispassionately and disdainfully.

"Mr. Foster. What you are doing here is not real. My missing father is real. Napoléon has been dead for 200 years and you are with him for entertainment. The closing of your Foster Industries is not entertainment. It will destroy the lives of two thousand families. That is not entertainment. For Davy and me, someone is attempting to kill us. Not in another time frame but in our real world. You have the power to intervene. You can right these wrongs. You look at us as children, but Mr. Foster, it is not we who are behaving childishly."

Charles blinked and looked over at Davy whose jaw was set firmly in agreement with Mildred. Foster removed his hat and set it on the step. He leaned back against the step and closed his eyes allowing his hands to hang loosely in his lap and shook his head in disbelief at himself. *She is absolutely correct. What I have been doing is selfish and puerile. I will return and help them where I can. It should be quite interesting to give my regards to Bully and Malveena.*

"Mildred, you are amazing and you are on the mark on what you said. Why don't you just kick me!"

"I would love to Mr. Foster, but you are sitting down."

A tumult of sorts wafted to them on the wind. It was not threatening but it was activity. Something was happening on the route leading down toward the pier.

Napoléon's entourage moved ponderously toward the Inconstant, past the Villa dei Mulini and between Forte Falcone and Forte Stella, whose lights shone high on the bluffs facing mainland Italy. As the imperial train progressed lower, fully in the shadow of the mountain, doors opened and cast their hearth lights onto the cobbled street. One by one, two by two, the populous emptied their homes and gathered into a solemn farewell cortege which grew behind their man. Le Petit Caporal had been on Elba for 300 days. He had been their life and on that morning of February 26, 1815, he had announced he was leaving. He exited his carriage and he walked, understanding the impact of such theatre. He entered via Saint Giovanni and crossed Granguardia Square where the throng spread out to witness his boarding. The crowd murmured in an uneasy kind of reverence as he boarded the felucca Caroline, to be taken to the Inconstant which sat 1000 yards out in the bay. At 8 bells he would signal his departure for France with a single cannon shot. With four ships flying the flag of Elba and a rag tag group of 1500 old soldiers he intended to conquer the world.

Charles Foster and Mildred Craft and Davy Pilcher had come to a quick agreement on a meeting to strategize their overall campaign. They called it Operation Seagull. They agreed upon who must attend and Davy and Mildred agreed upon on a full sharing of their information. The Pilcher war room was open for business and it was going to be something big.

Twenty minutes of useful sunlight remained. With pebbles rattling in Davy's pipe, they scurried to the western exposure of the Villa di San Martino and found it in deep shadow inside the horseshoe of low hills. There was no access to the sun. About one hundred feet above them a single cleft in the limestone exposed a few trees standing in reddening sunshine on a small plateau jutting from the sheer rock face.

Foster reacted first. "Come on you two! We can make it" and he charged into the bushes and began clambering up the hill. He broke the trail for the youngsters. Scrambling onto the small plateau, they saw it narrowed to a point

297

about eight feet across and only a one-yard wide strip at the farthest end of the prominence showed sun. They approached it fearfully and they heard a few pebbles break free and bounce down the rock face from their weight so close to the edge. Davy was in shadow up to his neck and turning west to sight his pipe into the sun, the heels of his shoes were six inches from the precipice. Mildred edged forward and took Davy's hand.

"Goodbye," came from Foster and he was gone before Davy could answer. They sighted into the 5:20 PM setting sun and with pleasant prospects warming their passage, and as the undermined lip of the plateau fell away from beneath their feet, Davy and Mildred spiraled from Elba and in a joyful light they arrived home.

Chapter 20: The Mystery Shaver

Davy tugged open the gold colored drawstrings on his purple Crown Royal bag and dumped out his marble collection onto his bed. The Crown Royal whisky had been a present from Grampa Pilcher to his dad to celebrate Davy's birth. Davy was long past his marble playing days but he wanted to keep them. He grabbed a woolen sock orphan from his dresser drawer and filled it with the marbles and tied a knot in the top and put it back in the drawer. Standing there, he thought his mother dusted the dresser top more often than she used to. He admired his string of hard--won treasures and he warmed in the memories they evoked. One by one from the left he selected an item and placed it in the Seagram's bag. He had not given Mildred her diamond from Socrates nor her pebble from Elba. He would do that at the meeting. He knew exactly how he wanted to handle the presentation and he had it staged to perfection in his mind. Foster was fully onside. He had agreed to the day and the exact time to arrive to achieve maximum effect. Tilt had been apprised that Foster was coming but otherwise he knew very little except to be precise on his own arrival time. Tilt had agreed enthusiastically to participate, for two reasons. First and most important to him, he wanted to help. But second, and he would not deny it, was the lure of the pipe. Delphi had rekindled the old Tilt; the Martial man. This was the strong and decisive man Davy had seen and he was the man to spearhead the coming initiative. He could be relied upon.

Throughout all the travails with Drago and Gregious neither Mildred nor Davy had confided in their parents or any other adult except for Foster. Charles Foster had no kids and he listened. Most of the time parents did not. Even when their youngsters were no longer small, one on one discussions seldom left the realm of 'there there little fellow'. There was no room for such dismissiveness in this situation. This operation was going to entail dynamic action by a group of peers. Davy had seen the strength of group-think in the terror of Paris. He had felt the soaring heights of the combined cerebration at the Delphic symposium and he was part of the collective will on the HMS Victory. He did not understand the group phenomenon fully. Special energy seemed to come not from within the individual, but from ambient storage out there in the ether and when people in agreement called upon it, it engorged them. He did not know how it happened, but he knew it was a real thing. He had learned also, on their own, individuals feared too much and dared too little. But a team which carried the moral imperative, it feared not at all and dared anything. He was gathering that team and he was about to imbue them with their moral imperative.

Davy had engaged in some subterfuge with both Helen Craft and his father. His mother's birthday was three weeks away and that was the cover. He told Harry and Mrs. Craft he was having a surprise birthday party for her. On that basis he knew they would follow his instructions and be on time. What Davy could not know was Janet and Helen had plans of their own.

Janet and Helen had become good friends. They had coffee at one of their houses twice a week and occasionally Mildred tagged along with Helen and soon Harry was friendly with Mildred and with Helen also. Helen and Janet made the two mile walk between their houses a fitness thing. They were among the few families in town not owning a car and they agreed it was the best thing to happen to them. They were fitter and slimmer and they looked healthy and they felt good and they became co-conspirators.

The day of the meeting arrived and things were under control. Davy had fixed the time for his mother's surprise quasi-birthday party at six bells. Mildred told him to cut the nautical stuff and he reluctantly told Helen Craft and his dad it began at seven. Tilt and Foster each had his own precise arrival time. His father had cut short his cleaning job at Singh's Hilltop Garage to arrive home for a wash and brush-up at about 6:30. Janet was canning peaches and pears. She was in the laundry room finishing the last few canning jars and bopping with her earphones.

Davy's Crown Royal bag sat in the center of the kitchen table. He sat there alone and watched the sweeping second hand click its way around the clock face. He did not have prepared notes. He practiced out loud some of the things he was going to say and they seemed fine. He had moved twice from where he was sitting to get the best spot for a chairman. Opposite the clock was the best place. The big clock clicked 5:30 and the doorbell rang. *Ninety minutes early. No. Girl Scout cookies. Paper Boy. Porky.* Davy strode to the door, aggravated by the intrusion. He opened the door fast with a good scowl and it was Mildred and

Mrs. Craft.

Davy looked back and forth between them. "What the blazes are you doing here?"

Mildred answered. "What do you mean what are we doing here? You asked us to come here. What's wrong with you!" That was the kind of cutting edged question which endeared Mildred to Davy.

"But it is too early!"

Helen Craft was unmoved. She handed Davy a tube nicely wrapped in birthday gift paper. She lowered her voice. "Here, this is for Janet. Just stick it in the closet. We need to go to the kitchen and talk about something before the party." With Mildred by her side, she walked in past Davy as if this were her meeting. Mildred was as nonplussed as Davy. Helen commandeered Davy's chair opposite the clock. Davy knew the spot would be powerful.

Janet was in the laundry room waiting for the last Bernardin top to make the popping sound on the canned pears to indicate they were sealed. She heard Helen's familiar voice and she was pleased but she had not expected her.

Janet walked into the kitchen and sat beside Helen. "Hi Helen. Hi Mildred. Nice to see you. What's up?" The top popped.

Helen moved up to the table and leaned on her elbows and interlaced her fingers. She was agitated and she seemed nervous. "Janet, I can't wait any longer. We have to get this done and as far as I'm concerned this is the time."

Janet looked at her friend. "You mean you want to talk about the uh, you know what?"

"Yes. This is the time."

Davy felt weak. He was sure when somebody got around to doing this it was going to be his father. The birds and the bees thing was fine with him but he and Mildred together, with their mothers? He looked at his mother's face and he could see she was very serious. Mercifully, this was not what he had thought. Davy and Mildred sat beside each other at the round table, closer than they would do normally. This little meeting seemed to have a formality about it that made their parents uncomfortable. Janet and Helen paired off on the other side.

"Mom, what is this about?"

Janet really didn't know where to start. "Davy, Helen asked me a favor and I have said yes, I would ask you. She wants to find her husband. John. Almost two years have passed and she is mad with the not knowing and with the worry. Her anguish has not lessened with time, it has intensified. She is baffled by the means to get to him." Janet stopped and Helen took over.

"You know, the pipe. Finding my husband somehow with the use of the pipe. I believe John is alive and I have to operate on that belief. She, we, Janet and I have been conjecturing about the possibilities, the thing is, you know, we really don't know all about the problems and intricacies of the thing and you do, so, there it is."

Mildred and Davy had discussed those same things between them and Davy intended to deal with them tonight. They all knew the others had used the pipe. It had gone unsaid until now. Davy decided to test their experience. If it was terrifying or threatening for them, he doubted they could manage the upcoming project. Casually, Davy inquired.

" Speaking of the pipe, was it a good concert? I read a bit about the Philadelphia one on the Internet and they say it was the best concert Journey ever did." Helen answered for the both of them without a twinge of guilt. " Yes Davy, it was amazing. Wonderful in fact." Janet and Helen's faces were beautiful with the memory of it. Davy smiled. He understood their experience and he had no doubt about them as team members.

His mother resumed, using her parent voice. " David and Mildred. Helen and I are going to go find John Craft. The pipe may be the way. We don't know what the problems with it are, and you do. You don't need to be involved, but..." Mildred sat forward in a flash and whipped off her glasses frames and stopped Mrs. Pilcher with the palm of her hand.

" Mrs. Pilcher! Mom! How on earth can you say we don't need to be involved! We are involved. So don't try that." She had her arms crossed in finality on her chest. This was about her father. Davy agreed with Mildred. If the situation was what he and Mildred had anticipated, that Mr. Craft was hostage or in a dangerous situation, they needed more help. They had seen Mr. Tilt in action and he was the man to help them.

Davy checked the clock. The meeting time was approaching.

" Mom, Mrs. Craft, can you leave this alone for forty-five minutes? Just wait until then? There are people coming who can help us with this."

The two ladies looked at each other, not wanting to stop the dialogue now that they had broached the subject. They were interrupted by the front door as it opened and it hip bumped closed behind Harry Pilcher who shouted hello. He fussed to hide the surprise birthday present he had wrapped so lovingly in his lopsided disarrayed way and he stuffed it into the hall closet and came whistling into the kitchen. He had been helping out at the garage for a couple of hours.

Harry carried a cardboard tray with six Styrofoam cups of hot coffee and put it down beside the sink.

" Hello again this place. Mind if I join you? Two black, two cream, two cream and sugar. All I could carry. They're marked. " He pulled out one black coffee for himself and handed a cream and sugar to Janet and looked over at Helen. Helen shook her head. Harry slid a chair up to the table and sat down. The group looked furtive and they clammed up. Apparently, he was interrupting something. He looked around, puzzled. The coffee aroma drifted through the house.

Davy diffused the awkwardness. "Hi Dad. We've been trying to work something out here about Mr. Craft. So far no luck." He looked around to imply agreement. "There are more people coming later who may have some ideas. I would like to wait for them." He did not mention the pipe.

Harry was fine with waiting. "Sure. Let's wait for the rest. Gives me time for my shower and a change of clothes. Don't start the confab without me." *More people coming. Good. The party is getting bigger. Good for Davy. Janet will enjoy it. I hope she likes my birthday gift.* He stood up and he whistled his way out of the room and up to the shower, missing the two creaky stair treads.

Davy needed his power chair. " Mrs. Craft, may we please trade places? I would like to sit there for when the others come in. Is that alright with you?"

"Thank you. I can do without looking at such a clock. Get it from a stadium?" She wiggled into the chair beside Mildred and Davy sat where he could watch the time. It was 16 minutes to six bells.

The four of them sat in silence, each with concerns of his own, but as Davy sat there, some of the burden of carrying this whole mess began to lift. He should have known better than to keep it as his own problem for all this time. Simultaneously both Davy and Helen reached for the purple Crown Royal bag in the center of the table to fiddle with the gold braid and they each claimed a side. " What's in here Davy?" She patted the bag gently and accidentally she touched Davy's hand. It was cold.

Davy smiled. " All will be revealed in the fullness of time Mrs. Craft, which in this case is about 16 minutes. In fact, knowing our next guest, it will not be about 16 minutes, it will be exactly 16 minutes. Everything we and he will need to know is in this bag." He tapped it. They all began to watch the clock.

The shower stopped running and a few minutes later Harry made his appearance looking fresh and happy to be home and happy to be with his friends. He plopped down and sighed and looked around with an open face.

" So, Davy. Who are we waiting for? Do I know him, them, her, it?"

" Yes, Dad you do. You should be able to usher him in, in seven, six, five, four, three, two, one, zero seconds." The doorbell rang once. They all looked at Harry.

" Oh. I guess that means me." Harry walked with a bounce to the front door and pulled it open with pleasant anticipation of the next guest. There was a sudden vacuum in the sound. In the kitchen, all they heard from Harry was " Holy!"

Tilt's uniformed perfection loomed in the doorway and Harry dropped his jaw. A sharp click of polished heels stabbed the quiet.

"Sir. Lieutenant Colonel Fred Hill of the Royal Marines, Third Commando Brigade, at your service.

He stood ramrod straight at 6 feet 8 inches and he scared Harry into rigidity. Tilt saluted so crisply his arm vibrated. From top to bottom, from his thick soled parade boots to his olive drab beret he was the perfect man. His toe caps shone like two black stars of India. Creases ran down his pants like knife edges. He was dressed simply and he displayed none of his medals. Two immaculate green fibre straps secured a small rucksack. On each shoulder he wore a drab green patch lettered with subtle green embroidering which read 'Royal Marines Commando.' Below that, a square patch in drab olive showed a single black dagger whose unsheathed blade pointed up. All Harry could manage was a "homina homina," as an attempt to invite him in.

Davy heard what was going on and shouted out to Tilt. " Mr. Tilt. Welcome. C'mon in. That's my dad."

Tilt followed Harry into the kitchen. He removed his beret and placed it on the counter. Its black dagger patch pointed down. He swung off the rucksack and placed it carefully on the counter, making a small thud. Mildred looked at Tilt and thought he appeared even more martial than when he wore his military chlamys in Greece. He looked wonderful. The whole assemblage felt as if they had gained enormous strength no matter what their enterprise was to be. Lieutenant Colonel Hill stepped back against the sink into an at-ease position and chose to stay standing.

Davy worked his chair up tight to the table and pulled the Crown Royal bag over. He loosened the drawstrings and one by one he placed his artifacts in a row on the table in front of him. Janet had a momentary flush that she might not have put them all back. Left to right he placed them in order of his experience and named them as he placed them in line. "Nelson's button. A guillotine earring. A Hendrix guitar pick. A diamond and a ruby. A piece of pituri. Two stones from Elba." Davy planned to use them as an introduction to the phenomenon of the intention of the light. He knew these things were not yet a call to action but he could feel the unity coming.

He began the history with Nelson's button. He told of Spider and Bert. He picked up the guillotine earring and told of his head on the block and the seagulls promising the sun and of Mildred's leap to save him. He strummed the plastic guitar pick across the edge of the table and told of Woodstock and Hendrix and Creedence Clearwater Revival. He did not speak of Malveena or Foster being there. Even Tilt did not know about Malveena and Bully. That was going to come later. Davy was surrounded by pale and immobile, bloodless face masks. They were overcome by his and Mildred's shared perils. A subtle steeliness was subsuming Tilt.

Harry Pilcher was in a daze. Everyone around him was nodding as if all of this spiel by Davy about pipes and light and intention was common knowledge but Harry didn't buy any of it. These were boyish dreams from boyish books taken from his library. Yet there sat the baubles. Lieutenant Colonel Hill saw incredulity taking over Harry's face. He put his hand on Harry's shoulder and leaned in. " I assure you Mr. Pilcher what your son says is precisely so. I have been there and I have done what he says can be done. I have experienced it with him and with Mildred. You may believe what he says." Harry looked over at his wife. Her eyes looked back and affirmed the truth of it.

Helen Craft beamed at Mildred. *My girl.*

Davy gave over to Mildred and she continued the presentation with Aristotle and the Oracle in Greece and sweet poisonous gases and how Tilt had saved them from drowning in a subterranean tunnel. She neglected to mention the Kalambaki red wine. Davy picked up the diamond and the ruby and a rock from Elba off the table while Mildred spoke about Napoleon not being short and their timely escape from a crumbling ledge. She attempted a certain offhandedness but it didn't come off. She was too excited and relieved in the telling.

"Mildred, these are yours." He gave her the diamond and the stone from La Peregrina hopscotch. She passed them to her mother. "Here Mom, look after these."   "Thank you for the two rocks honey. I like the smaller one better. Diamonds are this girl's best friend." She mock modeled it on her finger. Davy and Mildred were silent.

Davy gave the ruby to his dad. "Here Dad, this is for you and Mom. Shouldn't lose it. Savvy?" At this point Harry did not savvy anything and he stared at his own open palm holding a quintessential ruby. Janet quietly took it from his hand for safekeeping. She knew from the museum it could pay off their mortgage.

Davy raced through his Botany Bay surfing fiasco and the poisonous fishes and the poisonous plants and the poisonous snakes and the crocodiles and Simon and Chukker and Dobber and the murderous Kelly and the leg breaking treadmill.

Helen Craft swung to Mildred. "Mildred Craft! Please tell me you were not on that horrid treadmill thing!"

Mildred's voice became haughty. "No Mom. I was not at Botany Bay at all. Davy went alone you see. He was there without me. I was not invited. We did not go there together. Not enough room on the pipe. Apparently, some things are better done on your own. Boys will be boys and all that." She felt better. Davy wished he had some geraniums to study.

Helen was relieved. "Well thank goodness. Your pants are hard enough to iron as it is." Davy wondered whether non-sequiturs were genetic.

He moved on to the final stages of his presentation. He must not mess this up. He had to do it in a way the adults would neither hijack the planning nor dismiss the reality of the dangers they faced because he and Mildred were just kids.

"And then there was Malveena, getting her hair parted by a red-hot musket ball on the beach at Botany Bay. In a manner of speaking, she had come to visit me."

They took his bait. Even Tilt keened. Harry spoke what they were all thinking. "Did you say Malveena? You mean 'the' Malveena, Ms. Drago? The same Vice President of Strategic Planning as at the plant? No! And why would she have the remotest interest in visiting you at Botany Bay anyway!" Davy wanted to hug his dad. It was the perfect question.

"Dad, let me tell it." He reached over and grabbed a cup of hot coffee and held onto it with the lid on. His hands were really clammy now. Davy began the dialogue he had rehearsed in terms designed not to worry his parents. It didn't work. He stuck to the script for about two minutes then the real story exploded. He had to let it fly. He and Mildred handed off between them and between them they covered it all.

They began with their deduction it made no sense to close a successful operation like Foster Industries. Helen sighed morosely and Harry's jaw tightened. From there Davy led the group to the intention of the pipe taking them to the storage room that listened into Bully's office. Harry's jaw dropped for the second time. These two kids had ridden a beam of light into a high security building without leaving a trace.

Colonel Hill watched the faces and the breathing. He studied their demeanors and their composure and their muscle tension. They might become his squad.

Davy told of the eavesdrop on the fateful meeting between Bully and Malveena. How they learned of the sale of Foster Industries to the Macau Casino Syndicate and the executive offices were to be demolished and the library gone for parking. Helen gasped at the library and Harry Pilcher began to breath faster. Mildred was getting worked up by just reliving it. Tilt continued his assessments. Then came Bully and the share deal and Malveena's forged power of attorney. A collective gasp sucked the air out of the kitchen. Davy and Tilt saw the shared emotion. It was promising.

Mildred told of her importune sneeze for the ages in the storeroom and her headlong foot-sliding panic as Malveena and Bully chased them with threats of throttling them and setting off the alarms and the hiding in the lockers. Janet was on her feet. *That pale creep threatening my boy? We'll see about that!* The veins on Harry's neck and forehead were engorged slightly but his breathing began to slow and his clenched hands began to relax. Tilt saw the change and he needed this kind of man. He saw a controlled anger; an anger Colonel Hill could mold to the task ahead. Tilt picked a cup of coffee and removed the lid. He sipped the scalding liquid without noticing it was hot while the relentless ticking clock heightened the tension. Janet began to bite around the edge of her Styrofoam cup making teeth marks. She turned the cup and crunched another indentation. She began doing it in time to the clock. 60 beats a minute. It became a squeaking, nerve wracking heartbeat.

Helen whispered. "Janet."

"What?"

"The cup," and shook her head.

"Oh."

Davy told of Malveena stalking them in her Porsche and of her bare footed sprint after them past Mullett's funeral cortege. Mildred could not contain it. " And when Malveena jumped down into the grave we were hiding in and fell in the muck on her butt, I couldn't believe it!" Mildred was in full flight.

"It was amazing. Her hands came within an inch of Davy's throat, huh Davy? And throats, I am sure she tried for mine at Woodstock. Like a wraith she was. Traipsing like a ghost and it felt as though her throttle grip shivered right through me."

Davy was nodding. The adults were enraged and looking for action. Even Tilt's eyebrows were elevated. Davy and Mildred had made no mention of Foster. Davy watched the clock. Twenty-one minutes to two bells.

Davy finished up. "So, you can guess what I meant by her 'coming to visit me' in Botany Bay."

Harry Pilcher had been looking from Janet to Tilt to Mildred to Helen to Davy and back to see what their faces read. Mr. Hill had been nodding solemnly throughout as he digested all the implications of Davy's chronology. Harry could not believe the fantastic viciousness and injustice of it all. Tilt watched the anger welling in him. Tilt had seen this kind of surge in his men and he needed to stop it now.

" Harry. I know what you're thinking. You cannot take this into your own hands."

Janet Pilcher and Helen Craft jumped up as one furious package. Helen Craft spoke in a voice which Mildred did not know she possessed.

" I cannot have those animals in my hands but I can have them in jail."

She stood erectly to her full five feet two and walked to the dect phone on the counter and began to dial. In an instant Mr. Tilt was once again Lieutenant Colonel Freddy Hill of the Royal Marines Third Commando Brigade. He flashed to the counter in one lightning gangle and gently and inexorably he cradled the phone.

"Sorry Mrs. Craft, but that is not the way."

He swept the group with his eyes. "You are all thinking about the police. Let's say it is possible to get a temporary restraining order against Malveena. What does that do for the workers who will be laid off. Nothing. There's also the matter that the evidence obtained by Davy and Mildred was obtained in an illegal act. Illegal entry. Such evidence would not be allowed even if Mildred had retained her notepad with her concurrent recording of the events."

Davy and Mildred had never thought of that. They looked down at their shoes and Mildred polished a lens opening. Davy glanced up at the clock. Seven minutes until two bells.

" Even if their testimony were admissible, remember what some of it is. Testimony from minors that includes time travel, meeting an admiral now dead for over two centuries, and conversations with Aristotle. How long do you think it would take a judge to toss that out?"

Lieutenant Colonel Tilt felt the power of the shared anger and outrage and the collective fury and frustration at the injustice of it all and suddenly, around him he had his team.

"We are all angry. That is a start and now I'm going to tell you what to do with your anger. These are our priorities. First. Retrieve John Craft. Our priority is not to go after Malveena and Bully. They can wait."

Tilt looked at his watch. He knew the timing. "Second. Get Charles Foster back here. Without him, we cannot unravel the documents done in his name with the forged power of attorney."

Harry and Janet looked at Lieutenant Colonel Tilt, confused. They saw Davy nodding in agreement, but Foster had gone up in smoke four years ago and he was presumed dead.

The red sweep second hand jerked forward with a click and the clock showed two bells. It was 9:00 PM. The doorbell rang and rang again and rang again and rang again. Short-short-short-long. Davy knew what that was and Colonel Hill loved it and flew to the door. It was Morse code for "V". "V" for victory.

The Colonel shook hands in the foyer without speaking and ushered the new arrival ahead of him through the door to the kitchen so he could announce himself.

"Hello. I am Charles Abernathy Foster. Some of you know me. I have been away for four years and now I am back. Between us we will make things right. I bring with me all of my resources. I ask you to bring with you all of your energy. Hello David, hello Mildred. Ah. Harry isn't it." He reached across the table and shook Harry's hand and nodded to Helen and then nodded to Janet. He impressed them. Harry was catatonic.

Foster smiled a beautiful smile at Davy and Mildred. "So. Are you two ready to do this? This Operation Seagull?" Mildred put on her glasses frames and answered for the two of them. "Yes. After all, a bird in the bush waits for no man."

The ticking of the big clock was the only sound.

Mrs. Craft marveled at such sagacity. Who could argue with that. Harry was so undone by the deluge of impossibilities over the last two hours that he started marveling too. Somehow Mildred made sense.

Foster looked to the Colonel. "Colonel Hill, how do you propose we proceed?"

Tilt thought 'Operation Seagull' was the perfect name. "First. Information. Mildred, Mrs. Craft, tell us about John's disappearance. Tell everything you know and every detail of where you think he might be. Tell me everything you think of. No minor detail or thought or recollection about it is inconsequential."

Mildred had memorized and pored over maps, hour after hour, for a year. "My dad flew to Lima Peru. He stayed in a hotel in Miraflores, a part of the city which was safer for foreigners. Dad said there were always armed patrols there for protection. The next day in the morning, he flew to Cuzco. The Cuzco airport is at about 12,000 feet and he called us to say he had arrived and was fine except he had had a little altitude sickness. They had given him some cold coca tea, then he was fine."

She checked with her Mom's look whether how she was describing it was good. It was.

"He and another engineer took a switch-back train north from Cuzco and then took a Land Rover by road along the Urubamba river. The main town is Quillabamba. He called from there. He told us he was going with a survey team into Echarate region. That was the last we heard. We found out later three men went out on the survey, including my Dad. All three are still missing."

"Thank you, Mildred. Mrs. Craft?"

"Mildred knows the map. I don't. I helped him pack. He took his own compass and yellow rain gear. That was all. Everything else was at the survey site on the Urubamba river, near where they were building the dam. Oh. He commented on the snakes. He had to have high boots against them. Also. Some roads were out from landslides and he might have to go above four thousand meters to go around them but he had his tea."

"Ransom demand?"

"No. Not that I know about."

Tilt showed no change externally. The lack of a ransom demand was a bad sign. He knew the high jungle and he knew the history of the Echarate area and that worried him. It was the root of revolutionary activity in Peru. The region had spawned two longstanding terrorist groups. The Shining Path and the Tupac Amaru, the Shining Serpent. One of them likely had John Craft and they were not babies to play with. Mildred picked up on Tilt's concern but withheld it from Helen.

"Leave this with me for two weeks. The rest of you, do nothing and I mean nothing. Say nothing and be good." He looked pointedly at Davy and Mildred. He looked longer at Harry. "Nothing."

He slapped his thigh and began pacing as he consolidated his approach. He needed to spit.

"I will contact all of you with instructions. The day following my call, given

311

good sun, we will go. Gregious and Drago can wait. Mr. Craft cannot. Our only priority is to recover John Craft. At that time, I will have the plan completed for his extrication. We have a fine team."

Janet and Helen were in agreement with that. A fine team. Mildred believed a balaclava would come in handy. They were curious about the coca tea.

Harry was on his feet with his arms folded. "This is ridiculous. John Craft is lost and that is tragic, but a fine team? An old geezer, no disrespect Mr. Foster, two wo.. three women who have never walked a rough trail, one past commando, a boy and me? A gaggle like us stomping through the jungle. Snakes and landslides, rapid filled rivers roaring through impassable canyons and none of us knowing a coca leaf from a petunia. Altitudes of 4,000 meters? That's 13,000 feet of thin air just waiting to choke us, not to mention freezing."

Harry's every word increased the tension and tore at the feeling of camaraderie they had felt. Charles Foster sat imperturbed and was fully relaxed. He allowed Harry to continue uninterrupted.

"The Colonel will go alone unless he needs someone, then that means me. The women are not going. Janet, I forbid it. Forget it. No way are you doing that, and that's final!"

Davy saw the stony look on his mother's face and he thought perhaps Harry might have used a slightly different approach.

Foster stood up and the strength of his presence settled things down a little.

"Listen to me. There is one way and one way only to find John Craft and that is with the trail. That is the premise of our whole operation. I do not know John Craft. Therefore, my visualizations of him and of his trail are unreliable. Colonel Hill does not know John Craft. Harry, you do not know John Craft nor have you experience in the use of the intention of the pipe. Only two here can validate his trail. Mildred and Helen, his family. They must go to Peru. They alone can take you or the Colonel along his trail and arrive anywhere near to where he is held. The next concern is the need for a quick response at arrival. The time to escape suspension and enter reality must be very short in order to recognize any immediate danger. This geezer as you put it, has traveled the most and comes out of suspension instantly. Davy is just as fast. Mildred is not far behind and both Helen and Janet have some experience. Anyone of them will be alert and ready to save Harry Pilcher's bacon."

Colonel Hill faced the group and stepped up to stand close beside Harry like a comrade in arms.

"Harry, all of you, be assured I know how to do this with you. Allow me to do it. I have operated in the high jungle. I understand how to overcome such altitude. If you will do what I ask and follow my instructions and follow my leads, there will not be just one commando. There will be seven of us. Seven of the best." He shoved Harry with a slow good-natured shove, enough to make him tip from his stance and things were good. The doorbell rang and Harry escaped and answered it. It was the birthday cake Tilt had ordered.

"Davy, come get this." Harry handed off the cake and retrieved his gift and Helen's tube from the hall closet and brought them into the kitchen. Davy followed with the cake. Tilt opened his pack and pulled out two bottles of red Kalambaki.

"May I?" He opened the kitchen cupboard where he thought he might find glasses and he was correct. Foster came over and picked up a bottle.

"Kalambaki. Greek. This should be nice. I have never had it but it has a good reputation."

Mildred joined in. "It is a really good wine Mr. Foster, why......" She stopped and made eyeballs right and left.

Janet was thrilled and surprised with her party. Tilt poured a glass of Kalambaki for everyone including an appropriate one ounce for Davy and Mildred, the children. They sang and toasted happy birthday and Mildred made a fake face as if she didn't like the wine but it wasn't fooling Helen.

Helen brought her birthday wrapped tube to Janet. "Hope you like it. Authentic." It was a poster from the Philadelphia concert, signed by Journey.

Harry brought over his package and Janet opened it without tearing the paper. She always saved the paper from Harry. The gift had an electric cord and plug and an open funnel like plastic top. She had no idea what it was. "Er. I give up. What does it do?"

"Great isn't it?"

Helen and Mildred looked at each other. They had dropped the monstrosity off at the thrift shop two days earlier. This was going to be good.

"I got it at the thrift shop." Harry fished a small bag of demonstration popping corn from his pocket.

"It is a hot air popcorn popper. No oil. You just drop the popcorn onto the heating grid, sort of like a hair dryer, plug it in and when it pops on the hot grid, the air stream blows the popcorn out and into the bowl."

Everyone was curious except for Mildred and Helen. They had seen this act before. Harry filled the heater grid with the corn kernels and plugged in the popper. The air current wound up to full throttle and like a sub-machine gun it blasted the unpopped corn out like so many bullets and everyone was a casualty except for Mildred and Helen who had taken cover. Laughter consumed the house and the wine flowed and the team was solid.

They made one last toast. "Here's to Operation Seagull! Cheers!"

Tilt began first thing the next morning. He had demanded of Harry Pilcher that Harry not take things into his own hands. He said nothing about not doing it himself.

The morning broke cool and clear. Mr. Tilt stuffed some small bills into the pocket of his brown jacket and pulled on his camel colored leather gloves. He walked down to the small thrift shop and entered, semi-singing a ditty from Pirates of Penzance. Steven was the regular clerk and he and the colonel played a little game, one week about. One week Steven would semi-sing and Tilt would guess. This week was Tilt's turn to semi-sing and Steven to guess the name and origin of the song.

Tilt semi-sang the first line. "I da da dee dee model of a dee dee major da da da." Steven was mum.

"Hah. Don't have it yet hmm? Good. Steven you are an unmusical clot. Anything interesting come in this week?"

"Not really Colonel Hill. Two Rafael Sabatinis came in, ordinary ones. Scaramouche and Bellarion the Fortunate, but water damaged. That's about it. The usual stuff otherwise."

"Your Sabatinis. Kid bound?" Tilt flexed his camel gloved hands a few times for Steven's benefit.

"Nope. Usual cardboard. Still, somebody will be happy to find them. Can't go wrong for two bucks." Steven knew Tilt's blasted song but he couldn't peg it down yet. He knew the Colonel would sing the next stanza slightly more out of tune just to make it tougher.

Tilt hummed a little hum to Steven and then he saw the shade. It was the ugliest specimen ever foisted on humanity and it was absolutely perfect. The lamp shade was an enormous eight paneled thing done in deep purple fabric with orange fringing. The finial to attach it to the harp was a Rubensesque brass nude with glass amethyst eyes, one of which had gone missing to leave an open socket. He carried the lamp shade along with him as he wandered and picked up something he had seen last week and carried it all to the counter and began to sing another line.

"I know the kings da dee dee, and I dee dee dee historical." He looked down at his purchases. "Ring these beauties up will you Steven. Still can't place it eh? Steven Steven." Tilt drummed his gloved fingers on the counter while Steve wrapped the shade in tissue and stuffed the rest in a cloth bag.

Blast. Steve knew the song but it wouldn't come to him. "Eight dollars Colonel Hill." Hill fished out the cash and paid.

"Nice gloves," said Steve.

" Thanks Steven. See you next week. Get those ears checked." They laughed. Steve wondered what Fred would do with that hideous lamp shade and he knew the song as Tilt disappeared through the door.

"Penzance you rotter. Penzance. I am the very model of the modern major general..." Tilt couldn't hear him. The door was closed. Steven had absolutely no recollection of the three reams of loose yellowed paper the Colonel carried off in his cloth bag. They would not be traced back to Lieutenant Colonel Hill. Tilt cut across the corner of the park and picked up the remnants of half a dozen walnuts the squirrels were done with and dropped them into his cloth bag.

Still wearing his camel gloves, Tilt dumped the old paper and the walnuts onto the kitchen table with a clatter. He moved the lampshade out of the way. That and the song and his yellow gloves would be all Steve would remember. He removed his gloves and put the kettle on to boil and got out two teabags. He put one bag in the tea pot and the other he broke open into a cup and sat it on the table. The Colonel went to the sink drawer for a pair of rubber gloves and snapped them on and flexed his bony hands in preparation for the dexterous work lying ahead. He stacked the three reams of paper in one neat stack. It made just the weight and shape he wanted. He went to his front closet and removed the browned shelf paper he had placed there thirty years ago. He wiped the shelf clean of any dust margin and on the kitchen table he assiduously scrubbed any prints from the shelf paper.

The untraceable walnut and black tea ink took him less than an hour to concoct. Common gum arabic made it the perfect viscosity to retain its shape. He had done something similar many times. He set up his magnifier and examined the paper and it was fingerprint free and pristine.

The lettering and artwork was tedious and it took him eight hours. The franking stamp had taken the most time. His eyes were exhausted from the magnifying lens but the work was very good. A forgery expert would spot it right away, but the man on the street would never. He wrapped the yellowed reams of paper in the thick brown shelf paper and secured the flaps with the gum arabic. The package was postmarked perfectly. His ink work franked it as official federal correspondence. It was from the Office of the Attorney General. It was addressed to Mr. Melvin Gregious, Vice President of Operations, Foster Industries. It screamed 'Attention' 'Urgent' 'High Priority' 'Immediate Response' in large upper case bold print.

From the shadows across the street Tilt watched the security hut at the entrance gate to Foster industries. It was 9:00 PM and he had been watching the guard pour coffee from his thermos and drink it against the cold for two hours. The officer finally left for the men's room. Tilt raced to the circle of light on the ground outside the empty kiosk window and sat the package down. He disappeared into hiding and watched again.

The guard returned from the washroom in short order and he spotted the brown paper package immediately. *One minute away from my post and the blasted courier brings a package. Man. What timing. It never fails.* He retrieved it and its labeling alarmed him. It was from the Office of the Attorney General and it was heavy and plastered with labels. High Priority. Immediate Response. *What the devil does immediate mean. Right now? One hour from now is sort of immediate. Tomorrow morning is not immediate. I am calling Mr. Gregious.*

Mr. Tilt watched the guard punch the speed dial on his cell phone and put it to his ear and Tilt smiled. He saw how agitated the man was and knew whom he was calling. Tilt padded away quietly to take up his position. Gregious should be in striking distance within the hour.

Bully splay footed to the phone and Lucretia turned down the television to eavesdrop. She could hear a voice on the other end but not what the voice said. Bully made a show of his irritation at the late phone call.

"Johnson, I get packages all the time. It is after 10:00 PM. I'm not coming back there for a package. Put it in my office. No, it's not locked." He paused and listened.

"I don't care how many stamps there are on it." He listened again.

" Attorney General. Fine." Another pause.

" Urgent. Heavy documents. Immediate Response. Sure, sure. Put it in my office on my desk and I will look at it in the morning."

Bully put the phone down and walked back to his recliner. He had played the big shot on the phone with Johnson but the package bothered him. Business was one thing but this was official clout. He had to go see it.

Tilt knew men like Gregious and what they responded to. He put on the last touch of his camouflage. His clothing was optically absorbent and he was next to invisible. He did not have anything exposed which could reflect light. In his left sleeve pocket, he had a folded straight razor. In a sheath on his right he had his Fairbairn–Sykes fighting knife. In a small khaki pack belted around his waist he had a can of aerosol. He carried six fiber handcuff ties. Lieutenant Colonel Hill scaled the seven-foot fence at Foster Industries at the dead spot in the camera sweep. He hugged the perimeter fence where he blended into the background. He knew by habit Bully would park in the shadow cast by the transformer on the last light standard. Colonel Hill laid down in the depression at the base of the fence and disappeared and waited.

Gregious drove to the office and stopped at the entrance gate.

"Johnson. Where's the package!"

"In your office, Mr. Gregious. On your desk as instructed, sir."

"Hunh."

Bully pulled his car through and Johnson sighed with relief. Mr. Gregious had not asked him for a delivery signature. Bully drove toward his parking spot at the farthest end of the lot in the shadow of the transformer as he always did. No dents in the Mercedes yet. Colonel Fred Hill was prone on his back with his arms crossed and totally relaxed. His mind was clear and he processed an engine sound coming toward him that said 'Mercedes'.

Bully swung his legs off of his broken front seat and closed the door with a

317

thunk. Tilt was on Gregious at the thunk and taped his mouth before he could make a sound. He whipped Bully's hands behind his back, spun him twice and rammed him hard into deep shadow with his back against the fence. Tilt kicked his feet apart hard and in a flash, he had him handcuffed to the fence. Bully's eyes were frozen to the impossible towering monster that was manhandling him. Bully struggled to breathe and tried not to throw up and he couldn't make a sound except for the bull snorts from his nostrils. Tilt slung an additional cuff around Gregious' forehead and plastic-tied his head to the fence and Bully was immobilized. The only thing Bully could do was to flap his elbows and he began doing it. Flapping had helped on the ledge in Peru and maybe it would help now.

Tilt stepped in and whispered quietly in Bully's ear. " Sir is creating a draught. Please desist from that flapping." Bully desisted.

"Sir is not going to make a sound is he. I am going to remove the tape from Sir's mouth and he is going to be noiseless. Isn't he. Nod if you think that might be a good idea." Bully nodded at high frequency.

" You may stop nodding now. Do understand it though, if you do make a sound it is possible it may be your last sound. Nod if you understand that also." Bully nodded again, faster this time.

" Good. We are agreed. Let me show you a few things I have for you."

Tilt and Bully were in the shadow and Bully could see nothing.

" Here is the first thing for Sir."

Bully could hear the snap of a flap as Lieutenant Colonel Hill extracted the straight razor from his left sleeve pouch. He extended his left hand so that only the disembodied razor extended into the light from the margin of the shadow. With one finger he flicked it open to expose the perfect blade in the light and reflected the light from the blade to bounce at Bully's feet. Bully tried to be quiet but he made a tiny cat noise. The old commando began to strop the steel on his pant leg. Bully was trying to pass out but he couldn't. Tilt reached into his canvas pack and pulled out the aerosol. He walked to Bully and lifted his chin up with the back side of the straight razor. He sprayed the aerosol on Bully's neck. It was shaving cream. He wiped a little off as he spun the razor in the light and began to shave Bully's neck slowly, very, very, slowly with the straight razor. He flashed the blade into the light to display its edge as he threw the soap from it.

" Sir, I have not done this in many years. I hope I have retained my skills. It would be a shame for both of us though likely more of a shame for you, should I go astray on my journey over your neck."

He sprayed a little more shaving cream on the side of Gregious' neck and began to scrape with the cutting edge of the razor. He took his time. He did it very, very, slowly and showed his teeth. Bully hung limply with a little meow running through him.

" Sir, if Sir continues to make that mewing sound I shall shave Sir's tongue. Understood?"

Commando Tilt had no intention of doing so but he thought it added a nice touch to the proceedings. Bully resumed nodding.

"Sir needs to think a few things over doesn't he. Perhaps in the area of some youngsters to whom he is not well disposed. I do believe he understands they should be left unmolested. Are you listening Sir? I'm sure you are. I am also sure Sir knows exactly of whom I speak. In case there is any doubt in Sir's mind, I speak of Mildred Craft and David Pilcher. They will be left alone. You will leave them alone. You will tell anyone who is not leaving them alone about our little foamy tête-à-tête this evening. I assure you, and I assure them, this is not a unique experience in which only Sir may participate. Does Sir understand my meaning?"

Bully nodded emphatically. He imagined Malveena handcuffed to a chain link fence with a face full of shaving soap and he entertained not telling her and he nodded again.

Tilt folded up the straight razor and stashed it in his sleeve. He pulled out his fighting knife and cut the air with it a few times, working it in and out of the margin of the light, making a slashing whistle sound. He lunged forward to touch bellies with Bully and with whistling sweeps he slashed off the plastic ties. Lieutenant Colonel Hill ducked into the shadow without a word and in a quick vault he was over the fence and gone. Bully stayed put for ten minutes or so and resumed breathing.

Bully sat in his car and blubbered. He was incapable of mustering a tear. He was dehydrated from the sweating. He had forgotten all about the package which waited for him in his office. All he wanted to do was to go home.

319

He zombied through his front door with his arms hanging like a dead man's and they were not remotely connected to his stride. Lucretia sat listening to Tosca at the behest of Porky. Among his many pursuits since he became king of the library, Porky had taken to opera. Lucretia could not believe this was her kid. She turned the volume down with the remote in the middle of the tenor aria `E lucevan le stelle` and Porky frowned. She ignored the little brat and turned to see what Bully was up to. He had a look about him she had never seen. He was pale and his usual florid perspiring sheen was gone.

"Bully! You look different. You look, you look, clean."

"Lucretia. He was, he was nine feet tall and all covered in black. And he had knives and razors and handcuffs and he got me. He got me Lucretia. He got me. He handcuffed me to the fence and came at me swinging his knives and razors. He.... He...."

Bully started to weep, remembering his fear.

"He kept saying Sir. Sir. One after another. Sir. And then he, and then he, ... shaved me." He dropped his head in humiliation.

Porky came close and looked him over. "Hmm. Looks like he did a good job."

Chapter 21: Krakatoa

Bully Gregious laid on his back on his bed, staring at the ceiling in the dark. He no longer felt the chafed spots or pressure marks on his forehead and wrists from the plastic ties. His terror and agitation from the fence were gone. A stultifying and impassive torpor had now replaced them. He had exhausted the capacity of his nerve endings to respond. He had used up his chemistry. It was 3:00 am and Lucretia was deeply asleep beside him. Bully swung his feet over the side of his bed and took off his pajama top and threw it. He walked like an automaton into the kitchen and put on the water for some instant coffee. His pajama bottoms bothered him and he let them drop and he stepped out of them, leaving them in a pile on the kitchen floor. He returned to the bedroom and dressed thoughtlessly in random clothing while the kettle boiled. He put on a hat. He walked into the kitchen and stared at the coffee cups hanging on their hooks. The steam kettle began a low clicking groan, working up to a whistle. He walked past the kettle and without wanting his coat, Bully exited the front door and disappeared into the night.

The temperature was dropping and the hint of a moon gradually dissolved and disappeared into the deepening mist. The seagulls were quiet and they were not interested in Bully. On other nights they would have skwarked small warnings but not tonight. They tucked their bodies in and saved their energy. Gregious lived about three miles from his office. He had never walked there and he had no idea of the distance but the office was where he had to be. There was a package there for him. He saw wet things glistening along the way but his deadened brain refused to absorb them. He moved with no thought about the direction he was taking and let the hill push him down his route and point him along the wet river road to Foster Industries.

He arrived at the front security post at 5:40 am. With his nose touching the kiosk glass, he stood and peered, waiting to be let in. Bully said nothing and he was unreactive to the salutation of the astonished guard. He made his way through the gate and up the drive to the main entrance. He signed in at the front podium and stood waiting for an elevator. He studied the light on the floor indicator. It did not change. Immobile, he watched it for several minutes then wandered off to the stairwell. He found himself on the second floor and walked into his office and sat down. The package from the Office of the Attorney General was there on his desk. He slid up to it and unfolded the flaps carefully, one by horrible one, expecting each fold would reveal something worse than the last. The glue released easily and he folded out the wrapping to expose a pile of yellowed paper. He riffled through it. Every page was blank except for the cover letter.

Bully was without his reading glasses but the lettering was large and clear and stenciled blue. He leaned his face close over the page and he could see it well.

Sir.

It was considerate of you to join me at the fence. It was a pleasure shaving Sir. Please allow me to assure Sir, although admonitions are sometimes idle, mine are not. Do feel free to share Sir's experience. A la prochain.

Signed: Your Close Friend.

Bully reacted only to the degree of sitting back to detach himself from having read it. He stared out the door of his office and did nothing. Dawn was breaking and the lenses in his ceiling intensified the dominant content of the light and made the blue ink into the color of the sky. His hat shielded his eyes and the water ran into his shoes from his mist saturated clothing.

Malveena had new wheels and she arrived at the offices early. She had found the car at an estate sale. She was there to acquire an eighteenth century writing desk purported to have been owned by Immanuel Kant but the plywood gave it away. Her car however was the real thing. She floated through security and parked not in her accustomed designated spot but at the end of the row against the fence. There was no light standard above it from which gulls could do their anointings. The Malveenic beauty was a cream colored 2003 Bentley Arnage with walnut woodgrain interior. It was a living room on wheels and no matter how hard she tried, it would not fishtail.

Malveena hummed her way to the second floor and walked past Bully's open door and came back and stared at him sitting there. The clouds crossing the lenses above him painted and unpainted him like a clown who was uncertain of his makeup. She hadn't seen his car in the lot and he was usually late, but there he was. He had an odd look about him. She did not say hello.

322

"Bully, something is different about you."

Bully began nodding and did not stop.

"Well. You agree. It is becoming to you, whatever it is, your difference. You look, ... cleaner somehow. Yes. Cleaner. You should try it more often."

Bully continued with his nod, going faster now. His eyes stayed fixed on her while his head moved. He had papers in front of him and he was early to work. Both of those things were unusual.

"Bully man, stop that nodding. Bully, what is up with you?"

Malveena walked to his desk to see what he was messing up that she could derail or need to intervene in later. The Attorney General stamps surprised her but she couldn't read the script upside down without her reading glasses. She slid around behind him and read aloud some lines from the note.

"*It was a pleasure shaving Sir. Do feel free to share Sir's experience.*"

"A la prochain? Hm. Oh yes. Until the next time."

She looked down at the back of Bully's head. Was this some bizarre love letter? No. Not to Gregious.

Bully looked up over his shoulder at Malveena with tear filled eyes. So, it was even worse than he thought. He had not known 'a la prochain' meant until the next time. He began nodding again.

"Bully, what happened?"

He told Malveena everything that had happened to him the previous evening in excruciating detail. The Stygian wraith had now grown to eleven feet tall in Bully's mind and the endless razoring had scraped within microns of his major arteries. Malveena listened without comment while attempting to decipher the whys and wherefores of the event. She could understand his fear and panic from the threatening and the tying to the fence and that, but the warning off from molesting the Pilcher kid and his sidekick, that was a different ballgame. Was she next on some hit list and if she was, when and where would the shaver strike and what was in store for Malveena. And who could the individual be who possessed such special skills yet was willing to act as the agent for two hapless youngsters. Malveena was worried, but she was inspired at the same time. Perhaps two could play at that game. This was a new dawn and a new day and Malveena was riled up. She told Bully to stop nodding and go home and had the front desk get him a cab.

Davy ran light heartedly up the front school steps. A week has passed without hearing from Mr. Tilt but Davy had full confidence things were moving forward. Porky Gregious cut him off at the main door and pulled him aside. Porky had a smile a foot wide. He had been up since the crackling of his dad's boiled dry kettle had awakened Lucretia.

"Morning Porky."

"Hi Davy. Call me Lenny."

"Sure Porky. Morning Lenny."

Lenny was jumping with his news and he pulled Davy to the side. He leaned in conspiratorially. He thought this was how you did it. He was so excited he whispered louder than he would have spoken.

" Davy, you won't believe this. This is great. You won't believe it."

Davy knew he might not believe it but he wanted to hear it.

" About 10:00 last night some ten-foot monster dressed in black came out of the shadows and swinging knives in both hands he grabbed my dad and handcuffed him to the fence at his office. Great isn't it? Imagine. Handcuffed to the fence. Couldn't move. And then you know what the guy in the shadows did? He took out an old-style throat cutting razor sharp razor and began.... well, I guess if it was a razor it had to be razor sharp, but anyway, he shaved him with it. Soap and all. Up and down his neck. Hah! Took hours to do it. Scared my dad out of his wits. It was beautiful. Never saw him so worked up."

Very quietly under his breath and to himself Davy said, " Tilt."

Porky kept his head down. He had heard Davy say Tilt. *Holy! Could be, you know. Could be Tilt. Wow! I know how to find out.*

Porky pulled on Davy and said "Let's go in," and led the way. He seemed to be on a mission of some kind.

Lenny entered the classroom all smiles and with a little head tip to Mr. Tilt as he walked, he began to sing.

"Largo al factotum della citta. Largo! La la la la la la la LA! Presto a bottega che l'alba e gia. Presto! La la la la la la la LA!" It was the opening phrase of the baritone aria from 'The Barber of Seville'. The inference was not lost on Tilt.

"Mr. Gregious, please step outside the door with me and bring Mr. Pilcher with you." He spit on the floor and missed with the dustbane. He walked sedately out of the classroom with Davy and Porky right behind and closed the

324

door.

"Leonard, what was baritoning all about? Let me answer for you. It was about nothing. What you think you know is unknowable to you. Do you appreciate what I am saying?"

Tilt's grey eyes steeled and he was more impressive because of his complete composure. He was not angry. His coolness confirmed to Porky he was the man but this was not a fight worth fighting.

"Yes Mr. Hill."

"This is the end of it isn't it Leonard." It was not a question and the three of them knew it.

"You two go back to your seats."

Tilt followed them back into the room with a very quiet 'unwise' into Davy's ear and picked up another scoop of dust bane and this time he hit the mark.

Malveena walked wordlessly to her desk and sat in the dark. The brilliance from the Fresnel lenses in Bully's office had hurt her eyes and a headache threatened. She admired the effect the good old-fashioned threat filled with flashing steel had had on Bully. The cleverness of the psychology of the towering ninja had her concerned, but she thanked him for putting her on the right track. She would threaten those kids out of their socks. *How do I isolate them and get them on their own. No. One of them alone is easier and maybe better. That should be Davy. He is the main one. How to get him one on one. If it is riding the trail, I need to know more. No more crocodiles for Malveena. And Dobber. He has a trail too.*

She cleared her head in the subdued light and contemplated how to get at Davy. She was fearful of using the pipe and light to track him down until she had more knowledge. She tugged the chain and turned on her Steuben glass Roycroft lamp. The soft light from the amber glass dome settled her down. She lifted Foster's laboratory notes from her desk drawer and sat them in front of her and stared, hoping somehow, she could penetrate the garble within. She had perused them many times but maybe one more time would be the charm. She opened Foster's commentary and began reading it again.

'3048 some action remeasured correct open minded better than urgent 3556 less than focused 4064 luxless slow back suspension interminable more ...'

Fine. She had the measurements of the pipes figured out. Word by word she began to read every line, attempting to do it with fresh eyes. Malveena's eidetic memory took over and she remembered every word coming and she could not see it as if it were new, yet she persisted, word by word, line by line.

'I have just completed my forty-eighth sojourn into a realm which is the greatest gift the universe can bestow. I have been privileged to participate in a stream of sublime consciousness. It is a stream from which we are all invited to partake. It is a stream which has existed for all time, which exists for today and exists for all time to come, should that be our choice. My choice. Your choice.'

Great Charles. My choice, your choice but how do I take the choice and not wind up in quicksand.

'They will fail in their endeavour because to succeed requires graciousness. Let their frozen disciplines corrode them. They are not equipped to enjoy the golden consciousness offered to them for their taking. Their meanness disqualifies them. '

Malveena understood too well her problems in tracking Pilcher were a product of her rancour. *How to be mindless yet focused. How to be gracious yet determined. What was the trick. How to make Davy's trail a thing apart from him to be traveled without fury. How Charles, how!* She kicked off her shoes and rubbed her stocking feet on the carpet to make some heat.

Malveena stayed at it for seven hours until her concentration was gone. She stood and stretched and arched her back to relieve her stiffness from sitting. Her neck was killing her. What she needed was a nice glass of white Puligny-Montrachet. She preferred its elegant mineral character to the fruitiness of some other Côte de Beaune Chardonnays. She reached out a bottle from her bar fridge and picked a 250 ml Erlenmeyer flask and walked with them to Foster's laboratory. It had been four years since he made himself scarce but there might still be something. There might be something she had missed. The hallway floor was cold on her feet and it energized her. She punched in the code to the door and left it open. She walked in and stood in front of the deep mahogany book case. Malveena had read the divers book titles many times but never with the intention of studying their contents for clues to the workings of the mind of Charles Foster. One book was particularly scuffed and the pages were swollen with use. *Energy Grid: Harmonic 695: The Pulse of the Universe by Cathie.* With one foot on the lowest ladder step she pulled it down. She walked with it

326

to the lab stool and sat and opened it. The list of contents confounded her. 'Mathematical values of interest.' 'The unified equations.' 'Pythagoras and the grid.' *Not in this lifetime.* She flipped the book onto the bench and poured herself a full Erlenmeyer of wine as a vent to her frustrations. She spoke to Charles Foster as if he were present.

"Charles, Charles, Charles! What is here that thrilled you. What turned your crank. I am listening Charles. Tell Malveena. Where is the secret Charles. Spill it. Give it up. You know you want to. What would have given you the clue to riding the trail and the amazing mystery of the light? What was your secret Charles? Give me a sign."

Malveena walked the floor sipping her wine and inspected the library and what books were fingered and used. She gained nothing. There was something here but what. The laboratory was cold on overcast days and Malveena was shivering in the late afternoon haze. She looked about for a lab coat but saw none. Foster's abandoned Tom Ford tuxedo jacket would do. She pulled it on. It was very big for her and she swung the sleeve ends back and forth and extended her chin and made tipsy gorilla noises and chuckled. The jacket was very warm and it felt almost as if someone had been wearing it and had just taken it off. Her imagination was getting the better of her. She ran her eyes along the row of copper pipes from the left and stopped at the right and froze. There had always been two spaces for two missing pipes. Today, there was one space only. One of the missing pipes was back in the rack.

The flood of possibilities rushed heat through her body. Foster. It was he at the fence with Bully. *Bully should be at home.* She called him on her cell phone.

"Leonard. Hello Leonard. Give me your father please. This is... Yes. Yes. I will wait."

Bully came on the phone and Malveena spoke without saying hello when she heard his first breath.

"Bully, describe the man at the fence. Now think. None of the ten feet tall and flaming devil eyes stuff. Think carefully. Describe him."

He began and Leonard listened, knowing he was one step ahead of Malveena and his dad.

"No Bully, not things like awful and rough and horrible. The color of eyes if you can. That first. Yes, I know it was dark."

She listened to his description.

"I see. Maybe light eyes." *Foster*.

"Fine Bully. Calm down. Burly? Broad shouldered? Husky, Thin? Frail, how tall? Think." She listened.

"Are you sure Bully? Skinny and well over six feet? Very long hands and fingers? Are you sure?"

Bully was positive in his description now that he had calmed down.

"Thanks Bully."

So the mystery man is not Foster. Foster is big chested and broad shouldered and ham handed. Well, so what. If Foster is back he is back. He can't prove anything. One way or another the only real problem is Pilcher.

Davy Pilcher read the final paragraph and closed his father's old book contentedly. He uncrossed his legs and rolled down onto his back with his knees bent. He closed his eyes and set Treasure Island down on the mat beside him in Harry's study. Davy wandered down to the sea virtually every day yet he thirsted for a new way to experience it. He had tasted the brine on Nelson's ship as it hammered forward into battle and that would stay with him, but Crusoe's desert island was different. It held a special enticement and he could not resist it. It was a place to be alone. A place to explore. No crowds, no noise except for the palaver of the gulls. He wanted the cutting wind and the tumbling click of pebbles as the surf retreated and to feel the earth-shaking thud of the big breakers in his bones. Maybe he could take Lenny with him. He began to practice his technique. He was now devoting one hour a day to perfecting his use of imagery and developing a sense of his own trail. He was becoming his trail and the trail was him. His island was the only thing on his mind. Day by day he refined his intention to be sure he would arrive on his island in the perfect how and when and where. He walked about inside an ambient consciousness dedicated to intention. He felt his island surrounding him and beckoning him and he was ready. His intention to the magic island was completed and incredibly strong and his perfect trail shone like a beacon in the consciousness of the light. He would have no guillotines or poisonous sea snakes. Davy's island was in the age of sail and deserted and possessed of wide sweeping beaches. His island would have no pink flip-flops washed up on the shore. He would conjure a real desert island, not an island with ladies carrying

Mai Tais and rotund gents bobbing in the sea like so many sunburned corks. It was settled in his mind.

Malveena Drago rolled up the cuffs on Foster's tuxedo jacket and refreshed her wine. The Chardonnay had warmed a bit but it was still nice. Maybe she should call Amber Glass for some suggestions on how to clear her mind of self-destructive thoughts. She had read the books Amber had suggested she read to help manage her anger. She tore out the pages she didn't agree with. They were all the same. Be one with the traffic lights, be one with this, be one with that. Be one with this idiot, be one with that moron. Maybe her stupid tennis pro had had the right idea after all. She had taken lessons some years ago. They had ended abruptly when she attacked the instructor with her racket but that was not the point. When she was fighting the ball and overthinking, he always said, "Be the ball, be its path, be its destination. Visualize. Visualize. Stop analyzing. Get your head out of the way."

Well he should have got his head out of the way too. But still, maybe that is it. Be Davy. Be the boy. Be one with the light. Visualize him in his trail as if he were you, as if you were him. If I were him I would not want to throttle him. I think this is it. If I were him. Yes. That is, it. Be the boy. Be Davy. Follow the Davy trail. Malveena was excited and she threw back the last of the Montrachet. The sun had gone for the day but the weather forecast was good for the morrow and she had overnight to work on her imagery. *Imagine the trail. Imagine what Davy is seeing, be one with the boy. Hah. Any fool could do this.*

Malveena arrived at Foster Industries at dawn with the transmogrification to Davy entrenched in her psyche. She could be him better than he could be him. The gulls from the parking lot escaped in a beautiful climbing spiral column as her Bentley Arnage entered their warm zone on the tarmac. They climbed in a tight trail, looking for help from the obstruction current coming off the banks of the Borstal and one by one, they blossomed into radiant white as they reached the first shafts of the morning sun. Malveena did not notice.

The sun was still too low for any outdoor action with the pipe so she headed for the laboratory. The light was intense and powerful there even at dawn. She had doubled up on her Carpathian makeup for this special occasion and she felt positively spectral. Her lank hair hung in perfect blackness, now minus one offending grey strand and all was well with Malveena. She caught herself

329

humming 'It's a Wonderful World ' and shuddered at its common pleasantness. The sun beckoned to her and up went her pipe to the center of the Fresnel lenses.

The pipe was at Malveena's eye and she had it all figured out and under control. *Be one with Davy, be one with the trail of the boy. Connect to his passage without a thought of why you care. The trail..the track.. the path.* The light hit her hard in a wide golden spin of singing approval and the strength of it startled and pleased her. Finally, she understood the deal and she could not repress her gut response. *Away I go and now, I have you you little brat.* She gasped at her mistake in the millisecond the thought hit her and she tried to unring it but it was too late. A tornado of scarred and buffeting copperness cut through the music and grabbed Malveena roughly and she was gone and she knew she hadn't been able to pull it off. The consciousness was cold and brittle and she felt an influence not her own, controlling her experience. It was as if the trail begrudged her presence there. It seemed in a hurry to enable her and be done with it. She had usurped and misused Davy's shining beacon trail with falseness and hypocrisy and the consciousness of the light was about to reward her malice accordingly. She was swept from the sullen laboratory at Foster Enterprises into the storm driven world of sailing ships and onto a dark and foreboding pacific island and into the cataclysmic year of 1883. Malveena was about to experience the cataclysm personally.

Malveena sank ankle deep into a dusty grey beach on the west side of the island at the center of a sweeping arcuate bay. The wind was swirling into her face out of the west and the particulate was sticking to her makeup. She was deep in the power of the intention and she did not wonder at the monochromatic sea or sky presenting themselves to her. She did not care she needed to cough yet she did so anyway. The strangely troughed and troubled sea was unremarkable to her and the fact it blended into nothing against a plain morbid grey sky was acceptable. A dark flume of something buffeted her and tipped her off balance and she came to reality. Her feet felt hot and looking down, they were covered with a soft graphite like dust that smeared when she brushed back her hair. There was no sunlight and nothing but grey in all directions. Burrowed into the beach to her right were the bleached ribs of a derelict un-masted sailing vessel and in its lee away from the wind was a half-buried rowboat. For protection she turned around out of the wind to face east and there before her was the maker of the pall.

The volcano had risen some two hundred feet over the last three months and its ash had covered the island and eliminated the sun with the scope of its billowing particulate. The seabirds had fled at the first trembles. A caldera had formed and at its lip a slim red line of molten rock had started its route directly toward Malveena and the sea. Nothing told of the time of day and the sulfurous stench seemed to burn her skin where her eyes watered. The ash from the volcano accelerated twenty thousand feet into the air and the world was grey and the air was poisonous. Nothing was green and everything was covered with ash. *So this is Davy's trail with my own personal Malveena twist. How could I be so stupid. No. No. No. No!*

The great and merciless volcano known as Krakatoa glowered down at Malveena Drago. It was about to explode and release the energy of ten thousand atomic bombs and there she was, staring it in the face. The world had never seen what it was about to unleash. Its trees were bent to the east from centuries of a constant and heavy west wind, but on that day while Malveena screamed to the heavens, the wind switched 180 degrees to come from true east. It began to grow and the volcanic ash eddied and swirled and choked her. Malveena turned a slow full circle to analyze her surroundings. The ash was worsening and small tremors made her unsteady on her feet. She ran to the rowboat and mustered all her strength and worked free a small piece of sailcloth protruding from the sand. She slung it around her shoulders and muffled her face with it to protect her breathing. She saw the small boat was not entirely buried but just nestled into the dune and as she began to dig with her shoe, she spotted an oar. A heavy groan shuddered through the mountainside and jostled her and shuddered more sand into the row boat. The east wind increased. Malveena was not in a panic. She worked. She had to get away from the volcano or die. She held the oar closer to the paddle end and it served as a poor shovel but it was better than her shoe. She had the boat free in an hour and began to lever it toward the water with the oar. She looked for the second oar and could not find it. She did not spend time to hunt. A second piece of canvas was in the boat. She had expected an easy push of the boat into the water but the tide was ebbing and the beach was widening as the east wind velocity increased. She flung her shoes into the

331

boat and levered again and again and again with the heavy oar and finally some buoyancy helped her and she was afloat in the east wind, heading she knew not where, hoping to escape the cataclysm to come.

Mr. Tilt scratched away at the board with his chalk and made crazy flat-topped mountains with his dust bane while Davy sat at his desk and practiced thinking about nothing. Suddenly Davy shivered and shivered again at a worried darkness perfusing him. He felt cold and the backs of his hands were clammy. Some distant place and time was pulling on him. A discomfort was in him about something gone wrong on his trail and he could not place it. Immediately Treasure Island washed over him with a will of its own and it filled him with pirates and booty and plunder and the slash of the cutlass. His mind's eye scanned the horizon and swept the seascape for billowing sails lest the pirates be in sight. He wished he was barefoot, sinking his feet into the Caribbean sand and swaggering with his pipe. He felt for his leather sheath at his side but his pipe was hanging on the hook at home in his closet. There was a strong energy moving around him but somehow it was unhealthy.

The wind continued to increase at Malveena's back and she moved steadily westward. She had begun her escape from the island with frantic strokes with the single oar but it exhausted her and her best efforts were a puny addition to the gale behind her. Fleeing the volcano, she was just one more piece of driven flotsam so she rested. She had no water and no food and no idea where she was, or where she was going. The acidity of the ash had reddened her hands and nose where she was uncovered. Her mascara spidered into hideous black webs along the creases around her eyes. The wind blew the foam off the wave tops and caked her clothing with salt. Brine stalactites began hanging from the edges of her sailcloth shroud.

The relentless easterly drove Malveena on through the weak daylight and through dark moonless hours into an iron dawn and on and through a sunless midday. The relentless air pressure had driven Malveena 200 miles north west. She had no idea she had entered the ancient route of the Chinese pirates, a route unchanged and unchallenged since the days of the pirate kings of the thirteenth century. The pirates still ravaged the same sea lanes from Singapore to the mouth of the Yangtze river in China, three thousand miles to the north east. Opaquely and for the first time Malveena saw a mark on her westerly horizon.

As she sped toward it in her spinning boat it became a head and shoulders peaked island. Its distance seemed close over the sunless foreshortened sea, but it took four hours for Malveena to approach to the point where she could see it was a tilted flat faced projection about nine hundred feet high and two or three miles wide, with no beach and a rock face that dropped straight to the sea. The Chinese pirates called it Enggano.

Krakatoa blew. The 180-decibel sound blast of the first explosion hit Malveena like a hammer and deafened her and knocked her down onto to the slime covered floor of the leaking rowboat. Semi-conscious and deaf, she felt the fifteen-foot tsunami lift her up from behind and propel her straight toward the jagged rockfalls on the left shoulder of Enggano. The growing surge grabbed Malveena's little boat and carried it above the rockfall and dropped it out of the wind into the dead water zone on the lee side, as the burgeoning torrent raced past the island and continued growing. The protected side of the island was quiet and alcoved and formed a large and perfect deep water harbor. Her boat was sucked back hard toward the low energy area at the lee shore and she felt a thud and bump, even though she was half a mile from the shoreline and she did not understand.

Lying on her back, there was a roar in her ears as she came to herself and saw the grey toxic vapor running west across the sky above her. Dimly, some sounds began to filter through. She listened to speech she did not understand and Malveena felt a hostile presence. She pulled herself up at a gunnel and looked around. She was in a wide sloshing bay, surrounded by the largest pirate fleet in the world.

Two days ago, at the impossible switch in wind to a strong easterly, the pirates had fled to the sanctuary of Enggano. They had battened their hatches and reefed their sails and they waited. Not one man among them had seen this wind in his lifetime. Today their fleet was well dispersed around the bay and protected within the arms of Enggano, waiting for they knew not what, except they hoped to ride it out.

The largest ship was a nine masted junk carrying the pirate king and his personal entourage. 伟大的国王 was emblazoned in brilliant gilding on its stern. Wěidà de guówáng. 'The Great King' it proclaimed. It was 410 feet from bow to rudder and had a beam of 170 feet. Its golden silk dragon pennant tailed away from its stern and reached its fraying end high aloft and twisted and switched about in the confusing wind. On the top deck at midships it had a 200-foot-long lacquered red and gold pagoda with green shuttered doorways. Its furled sails were green and gold and decorated with attacking dragons of the sea. Thirty-foot-long snake tongued silk pennants flew from every ship and on this strange day each of them stretched with a different wind. There were troop transports and water tankers, each with a two-month supply of water. Closest to the shoreline and deepest into the bay were the horse ships which measured 280 feet long. 120-foot-long eight oared patrol boats were anchored in shallower water, with their silver shafted oars at rest. The fleet was comprised of thirty-two ships, each one of them adorned with lacquered all-seeing sightless eyes to guide them in the night. The outlaw armada carried 36,000 men. Not one of these men had seen anything like Malveena. She was feeling truculent and she was back on her feet, captain of her little ship with her hands on her hips and defiant against her circumstances.

Most of Malveena's hearing had recovered and she heard the men murmur as she bobbed fifteen feet away from the 300-foot-long junk she had bumped with her rowboat. She stood erectly with her shroud like sailcloth draped over her head and shoulders. Malveena was fringed with longer stalactites now and she looked like an ancient sea creature disgorged from some maritime hell. She was salt encrusted and her black hair hung like evil seaweed. Her nose and hands had been burned a bloody pink from the acidity of Krakatoa's sulfurous ash and in that strange light they appeared to be on fire. Her double dose of mascara had pooled into her eye sockets and black lined spiderish wrinkles had guided black rivulets to make their way down her cheekbones and they had crusted there. The funereal pallidity of her natural transparent skin tones completed her presentation. Malveena could not contain her fury and she put her head back and stretched her hands open and extended her bony arms to the heavens and screamed her loudest unholy shriek at the stupidity and danger of where she had placed herself. The bantering, finger pointing crew at the rail drew back. *First the devil wind from the east and now this thing has come to devour us, surely it is a daughter of hell.*

The officer of the watch pointed and called over his gunnery officer. "Kàn zhège! Yīgè hǎi nǚwū." *'Look at this. A sea witch.'*

He was petrified. "Ko ko ko! Gèng xiàng shì nǚwū de mǔqīn." *'Oh oh oh! More like the mother of the witches.'* He called to their deck captain.

"Duìzhǎng! Kàn zhège. Nǚwū de mǔqīn!" *'Captain look at this. The mother of the sea witches!'*

The deck captain saw a deckhand uncoil a loose rope and throw it to Malveena's rowboat. She jerked it out of his hands and kept it.

"Bùyào pèng tā, nǐ zhège shǎguā. Rēng wǎng." *'Don't touch her you fool, throw a net over her.'*

The sailor loosened the belay on the boom and began to hook up the net to drop over Malveena when the greatest paroxysm of Krakatoa struck. Its 310 decibels was the loudest noise ever heard by mankind. It shattered every human eardrum within fifty miles of the volcano.

Malveena and the pirates were resting in the arms of the crescent harbor on the lee side of Enggano island. Krakatoa was 200 miles to the east and the pressure wave generated by its colossal explosion blasted toward them at 675 miles per hour. It struck the easterly rock face on the other side of the island from the ships and they did not know what they were hearing. Much of the sound was deflected over them but the air was sucked out of the harbor by the supersonic velocity of the shock wave. It passed over them and around them and it took their oxygen with it. Across the fleet, half of the 36,000 men fell unconscious. Malveena and the rest gasped for air in desperation and they hung on and hoped not to die. Then came the tsunami. They heard it before they saw it.

Enggano Island was a crescent shape. Its concave bay and its extended arms opened roughly west with its high flat face standing firm to the east. Its southern tip was slightly more westerly so as the tsunami grew from the east it passed its northerly arm first. A low whistle began at the first contact and the water level rose and raced past on the north. The new height appeared as a slight shadow on the horizon. Then the south tip was involved. At fifty feet, the water was above mast height of the smaller vessels but because of its velocity, rather than filling the bay, the weight of it passing by began to evacuate the harbor and take its water away to the west. From their central position the stunned crews watched as two mountainous streams roared by on their right and left. The water height at both ends of the island was over 100 feet now and the roaring torrents began to draw more of the water out of the bay. The ships found themselves with slack anchors in shallower water and the tsunami continued to gain speed. It was now one hundred and fifty feet higher than sea level and more than two hundred feet above them in the evacuated bay and roaring on west. The bay was almost empty. Looking to the west, two miles away, a massive wall of sea had built to a height of three hundred feet and hung there. Four hundred million tons of roiling death stood poised to release itself from the momentum of the tsunami and cascade back against the ships and destroy the bay and everything in its path. The captains of the fleet ordered anchors in. Perhaps they could ride above the impact. Perhaps not. There was nothing to do but hold on. The largest vessels were abandoned as doomed despite their buoyancy because of their inertia in reacting to the impact. The smaller vessels had a better chance to ride the crest.

Malveena Drago eyed the poised mountain of water. It had begun to fall on itself at its highest point and the cascade was beginning. She began tying a bowline in her rope to lash herself to her boat. She tickled her copper pipe and looked for the non-existent sun and laughed at her luck. Krakatoa had been here for ten million years and she had decided to drop in on the one day it was blowing up. *Karma in spades.* She secured herself with her rope through the oarlocks and settled to the bottom of the boat with her sail shroud wrapped tightly around her. She stayed low and hoped to avoid the flying debris. She thought about Dobber. She guessed he was about one hundred years old this year. She laid back, closed her eyes and waited.

The roar began. The bottom fell out of the huge wall of water first and it led the onslaught back to the bay. The pirates had been in frenzied activity to transfer as many men as possible to the smaller fighting ships. They carried no lifeboats. Sailors who have no escape will continue to fight. The first million tons of black water struck the Great King junk square amidships at the level of the main deck and it shuddered with the impact and tipped hard away, top heavy with its pagoda. Water higher up was unrestrained by impact and bristling with debris and torn trees it roared ahead and battered and submersed the Great King. Off ripped the pagoda and it tumbled crazily as the vanguard at the front of the torrent. Ahead it raced and pushed 300 feet up the mountain, breaking apart at impact into two large sections. One piece jammed into the crook of the neck and shoulders rocks. The other shivered to kindling and left polished painted debris all down the mountainside as the water fell back to the bay. Again, the weight of receding water pushed the broken-down fleet ahead of it and battered it with ton after ton of flailing logs. No vessel remained intact.

Malveena had not seen any of the carnage. With great speed her boat rode the full height of the wave and with tremendous velocity it rammed her among the collection of trees impaled in the mountain face. Her boat was the smallest and lightest and she was the highest up the incline of the mountain at about 350 feet. She had stopped moving and she was alive. Malveena released her clenched hands from the rope across the oarlocks and collected herself. She looked to the sky and two beady eyes looked down out of a hairy face. She sat up in a panic to recognize it as a macaque. A huge grey and black monkey had its arms around a tree torn out hundreds of miles from there. Its fur was singed and it was lost yet it had survived both flood and volcano. Its home was now under 100 feet of ash. Fifty feet below her, Malveena saw the roof of the remnant of the pagoda. That would provide cover. Perhaps also there was something there she could use. The rest of the survivors were hundreds of feet below her at beach level. The surviving pirate crews were spread in exhausted pods along the five miles of sand making up the bay, each looking for his mates or his ship or something to recognize.

The eruptions continued and the ash climbed up fifty miles to join the jet stream and flowed away to darken the world. Within hours, 7200 miles away, tidal gauges in the English Channel showed surges caused by the concussive air waves from the eruption. For five days those waves continued to circle the globe. The largest explosion was so violent it was heard 2000 miles away in Perth, Western Australia. Continuing 100-foot tsunamis spread in all directions and heavy swells struck South Africa's coast, 5000 miles to the west. Fire brigades around the world raced to the glow of terrible fires only to find the glow was the evening sun refracting Krakatoa's particulate. Volcanic purples embellished the twilight after a day of lavender sun and the moon shone with green and blue light. The temperature across the earth dropped two degrees and these things continued worldwide for five years.

The wind switched three days later and came strong from the west, blowing

337

back toward Krakatoa. A pale lavender sun emerged and warmed the west facing slab of Enggano for the first time. The flat rock reflecting it was about 200 feet from the summit, about 400 feet above the pagoda. There was a rift in the rock plate and the screaming sea witch of the China sea began to climb. Her shoes had come unglued from the sea water so she had fashioned sailcloth boots and tied them on her feet with her shoelaces. The sailors gave her a wide berth and thanked Mazu, their eternal sea goddess for protecting them against her black eyed evil twin. Malveena had not devoured any of them.

Malveena scaled the elevation in two hours and the sun persisted. The lavender hue across the face of the sun was intense and she had no idea whether it would derange her intention to return home but she was determined to risk it. She sighted with her pipe and arrived in her office none the worse for the strange pastel lights of Enggano, but something had changed. This particular transit in the consciousness of the light had infused Malveena with a feeling of retreat. It joined to reinforce her mood of total despondency. She had failed again and she had no solution to the difficulty with David Pilcher. She could report to the police he and Mildred had burgled her offices and thereby diffuse and discredit their knowledge, yet the video tapes would not show them doing that, only leaving. Also, how would children of that age even know what a power of attorney was if not by overhearing. She was stumped. She went to her refrigerator to retrieve a bottle of cold *Pouilly-Fuissé* for a change in texture when she remembered that she had left her empty Montrachet bottle and the unwashed Erlenmeyer flask in Foster's laboratory. She slopped down the corridor to the laboratory and punched in the code. It did not open. She was exhausted and had missed a key. She entered the code again and again it did not release the bolts.

"One Attempt Remains."

Someone had changed the combination.

Chapter 22: The Sacred Valley of The Incas

Colonel Hill unfolded the soiled dog-eared paper which Helen Craft had given him outlining the cessation of John Craft's salary. It was split at the crease line from its innumerable openings and closings and from the reading and rereading of it by Helen. It was on the letterhead of Hectares P.L.C., the engineering company which provided John Craft and his survey team to the United Nations for their hydroelectric project in Peru. They were a well established internationally recognized engineering company with a good reputation. The third world was where they operated and they knew what they were doing.

Tilt had to be certain he was not interfering with an operation which might be underway by Hectares or their insurers to recover John Craft just as he was planning to do. Two clandestine teams operating in the same area was a dangerous business for both of them. More importantly, it presented a great risk to the safety of the captives.

Tilt began his background work with calls to all of Hectares executive offices worldwide. In every case he received the same well prepared identically worded denial of the existence of an individual named John Craft. The company knew nothing. They had no employee by the name of John Craft.

Whatever was happening, they were playing it close to the vest. A quick online search showed Hectares' standard independent contractor agreement stipulated ransom insurance as a condition of employment, and that was promising. What was not so promising was such insurers maintained scrupulous anonymity. It was imperative no-one could know who was a party to transacting a ransom payment. Such exchanges were sensitive and dangerous and external interference could injure negotiations and put negotiators and captives at risk. He had to determine which shrouded company among the hundreds of such companies was the insurer. If that insurer had received a request for ransom, had they already paid a ransom, were they in negotiations, or had they been too slow and too late. That was a tough one and Tilt was getting outside of his background. He called an old friend.

" Hello, Terrence. Freddy Hill here. Royal Marines, Third Commando

Brigade." He hoped Terrence would remember their old confirmation phrases.

"How are things in the carnival?"

"Ah. Well, well. Famous Freddy Hill. Old Freddy by now isn't it. How are things in the carnival you ask? Same as usual darling. Hurry, hurry, hurry, step right up and be quiet about it. You know the drill. Someone is invited onto the ride, another is pushed off and another jumps off to get it over with. Things going up, things going down, spinning in circles, going back and forth and winding up exactly where they started, just a little darker. But I don't think your call is a social one is it? You never did social. What is satiating your danger pangs these days?"

Tilt heard a heterodyne working at low volume in the background, sliding through its frequencies, masking their conversation against intrusion. Colonel Tilt told the old spymaster about John Craft and the problematic lack of a ransom demand and his concern there may be an extraction team already in place in the region. Terrence made a little unk. Tilt laid out the entire scenario while Terrence muttered a continuous back chatter to demonstrate the extreme difficulty of doing what he was about to be asked to do. Colonel Tilt did not bring the use of the pipe into the conversation.

"So that is the rub of the thing Terrence. I'm sure it is child's play for you, but perhaps a little entertainment for a rainy afternoon, yes?"

"Famous, you must know I am quasi almost nearly retired. The carnival no longer lets me go to the well, they just give me a glass of water when it suits them. Even when I was barkering the carnival full time, every day and every night, what you are asking of me would have been difficult, let alone now. I have surreptitiously infiltrated munitions plants, I have hacked the archives of states, I have without their permission audited drug lords, I have even plumbed a certain secret sauce. But an insurance company? Harder than the Kremlin. Worse than the Vatican but much the same, for if one does get through the firewall, they are a confusion even to themselves, ensconced in an ambiguous jargon. Totally impenetrable. Next to impossible. And to make it even more interesting, Famous Freddy can't even tell me which company among thousands of companies is the insurance company in question."

Tilt listened in silence to Terrence complaining, appreciating the demonstration of temperament from his virtuoso. Listening was a small price and Tilt was happy to pay it.

" I take it then Terrence, it is too difficult for you. Old Terrence by now isn't it."

There was a short silence and a small chuckle.

" Your tactics have become exceedingly obvious in your dotage darling. However, I appreciate the goad. I am told rain is predicted for the morrow so the carnival may not be busy. I shall work on your little problem but do not badger me. One badger and you are on your own." He put down the receiver.

Colonel Hill had been glib and understated with Terrence as was expected between them, yet he was very worried, but not about the mission. Operation Seagull was simple enough. Foster's ingenious method of inserting a team by using the consciousness of the light was a masterstroke of stealth. There were no engines to be heard, no rivers to be swum and no jungle paths to be slashed open with machetes. To extricate John Craft from captivity in Peru was more routine than most operations Tilt had managed, even given the inexperience of his little army. The red flag for the colonel was there had been no acknowledgement of a ransom demand. It made no sense for a terrorist group like Tupac Amaru or even a lone wolf thug to confine and guard a trio of professionals for over a year without a ransom demand. He knew the nature of the beasts. Such cowards denied their malignity with the rationale of having some enlightened moral imperative. They were communists or they were nationalists or they were freedom fighters or they were religious zealots. Take your pick. It still came down to the same things. Money and power. Period. In John Craft's case Tilt suspected an unplanned haphazard encounter had occurred along the jungle trail. Neither party had expected it, not the engineering team nor the terrorist group if that is what happened, and that could lead to a quick confrontation and a violent end. That was the worry.

Freddy Hill listened to his Westminster chimes and the clock struck 2:00 am. He was studying online satellite imagery of the Echerate region where Mildred's father was seen last. He had found nineteen flat areas suitable for a compound but only three had useful tree cover for a secure encampment. He concentrated on those. He was planning to make the raid into Peru in starlight and in that light, he needed to be able to guide his team down from altitude largely by memory. He would use his infrared goggles but they too had limitations. His

341

tea was cold and his focus was waning even though he had installed a blue blocking program on his monitor and used maximum brightness to increase the flicker rate. His eye fatigue was reduced tremendously but he was tired after ten hours of work.

The telephone call startled him even though he was expecting it. Tilt turned on his heterodyne harmonics and punched the speaker button and waited for the tinny voice.

"Hello. Famous Freddy. Famous Terrence here. How are things on the carousel?"

"Ah. Famous Terrence. How are things on the carousel you ask? Well, I can tell you better how the horses run after we speak. I presume this is not a social call."

"Perfectly correct darling. The flight manifests I sourced show John Craft did embark and deplane as Mrs. Craft has described and the hotel records in Quillabamba agree."

Tilt relaxed a little. Memories under stress are seldom accurate but Helen Craft had been right on.

" I have paid a gentle visit to the electronic records left lying about so carelessly by Hectares engineering, to look for repetitive same dollar amount payments. Insurance premiums you know. They have nine payees with repeating amounts. Four are to rental property lease payments. Four are ongoing cash inducements to smooth the engineering road in Lagos, Quebec City and two in Lima. Generals and parliamentarians need to eat too. The ninth was to a company called Spic Ltd., which is domiciled on the island of Malta and advertised as a telecommunications company, but it is not. Its registration in the European Union is as a limited license insurance carrier. As they say in America, Bingo."

"Terrence, I thought you said this was impossible, impenetrable, Vaticanesque and difficult."

"It is. All of those. That is why it took me eleven hours darling. For mere mortals it would have been weeks if at all, but I am not done telling. Don't interrupt. Really Freddy. So. How to tell if a demand for ransom was made. Nothing in the document files one way or another, but there is a giveaway all the same. There was a sudden change in their book value of reserves allocated for impending obligations, within three weeks of the Craft disappearance. That allocation has been carried over to this year but reduced by two thirds. So, these are my conclusions."

As instructed by the old spy, Tilt did not interject.

"Freddy, John Craft and his team were insured. The protocol of the insurance company is not to notify the family of a ransom demand. False hope is worse than no hope at all. So the demand was made and the captors have upped the ante and negotiations continue. The captives are still alive. Rather, the captive, singular, is still alive, given the two thirds reduction in potential ransom obligation. That would be the leader, John Craft. I am sure the others have been released. If not, the Tupac Amaru or the Shining Path or whoever would have boasted of their end as a lesson to tremble the world. By the way, Spic does not engage in, or hire or farm out extraction teams. They negotiate. But what I know from past experience is you have scant time remaining to intervene. The kidnappers will cut their losses and move on very soon. You know what that means. Oh yes. I think I have not wished you Merry Christmas. Merry Christmas darling." The empty speaker continued heterodyning up and down the scale and Tilt turned it off.

Juan Ignacio Hidalgo huddled behind the stocky trunk of the ancient polylepsis tree and turned up his collar against the freshening wind. He cupped his hands around his bent cigarette and put his last match to it. The end paper flared at first draw and illuminated the brilliant red striations of the rough tree bark. With relief he took a long drag and filled his lungs with the smoke from the mixture of tobacco and coca leaf. He needed the help of the coca. The prisoner he was forced to guard was at an altitude of 14,000 feet. The thin air sucked the fight out of the man and made him easier to manage. The high altitude starved Hidalgo of oxygen also but the coca kept him breathing well. Bits of tobacco and coca leaf stuck to his lips and his tongue and he spat them out. He never could roll the paper tightly enough. The hot match head stuck to his skin and burned his finger and he cursed. The wind curled around the six-foot trunk and spun the hot cigarette ash onto his jacket and he rubbed and smudged at the tiny burn holes. His day was just beginning and he was already aggravated and cold. He had ten hours ahead of him before his relief came, if it came and he sighed and his breath frosted in the cold of the dawn. His boots leaked and his feet were wet. He had taken the boots away from the Craft man as he was ordered to do but they were too small for him. He had to cut them to make them fit better and now they leaked and they still didn't fit. In the dying night he looked to the east and to the timeless Castor and Pollux twins of Gemini. He knew soon they would spin away and leave him alone. Juan Ignacio asked himself how it had come to this. He was an educated man. He was a Hidalgo. He was possessed of a name which was traced to the 12th century and he was a proud descendant of the great liberator, Simón José Antonio de la Santísima Trinidad Bolívar y Palacios. The great Bolivar. And now, this proud descendant stood shivering in leaking boots, in thrall to a bloodthirsty thug named Alejandro Charca and guarded a freezing goat pen.

"Do not worry, Juan my friend, buen amigo. We will be rich men. You and I together. The foreign mining pirates will pay us. Oh yes, they will pay. Now, more than ever. Do not doubt it. I know how to drive the deal, I am negotiating. Hard. For you Juan. It will soon be concluded, my friend, Juanito. Hold fast. Be strong. Soon I will give you what you deserve."

He hated the implied diminishment in 'Jaunito'. Little Juan. It was the same spiel last week and last month. He would get what he deserved. What he deserved was to regain his birthright. He should have listened to his wife. His beautiful, wonderful, French Canadian wife. They had met during his second year at McGill University. *Ah Camille.*

Juan. Dearest. Do not go back to Peru. You see the news of the turmoil. Please love, stay here. Let us be here in Montreal. Yes, your father has gone, God rest his soul, but to return to the family lands is not safe. Bring your mother here. Let us have the family life here in Quebec. It will be beautiful. This is Canada. We will be safe, we will work and we will be happy. Dearest do not go home, it is not a home for you any longer. It is not a home for us. Do not risk it.

Camille had stayed in Montreal and she had been right. Juan Ignacio had been lured home to Peru by the military junta in the middle of his third year at McGill. His family name had become anathema in his absence. He was the intended example, the sacrificial lamb to be used by the new regime as a warning against the evils of inherited wealth. They took his land and they took his father's assets and they intended to take his life in a very public way. He fled to the jungle and here he was, at the mercy of a kidnapping monster bent on self extermination. Juan Ignacio Hidalgo had become an unwitting exile and an unwilling participant. His prospects had been distilled to his execution by a madman on the one hand or his execution by a thieving military on the other. And he was impoverished. His wealth had been redistributed as promised to the people by the generals, but not to the Indians who still hauled 150-pound sacks of coffee beans on their backs or to the five million hovel dwellers surrounding Lima, who starved and raged and killed each other with the approval of an army that brutalized all opposition. Yet he was of Peru, where power came and power went but the old families always emerged. He was of the old families and he must find a way to emerge.

He swung his rifle to his other side. The carry strap abraded his shoulders and they never seemed to heal fully. The 1891 Mauser carbine weighed 9 pounds and hours of it pulling down on him wore him out. *The bloody thing would not dent a tin can if I did fire it and the blasted hammer self cocks. The only thing likely to get shot with this bolt-action antique is me.*

The bleating of the goats announced a brilliant sub-zero day on the 21,000-foot Salkantay mountain. The sun was golden on the permanent snow cap at the pinnacle, seven thousand feet above the camp. Hidalgo stood motionless, trapped in the shadow of the Condor Massif facing him from the west side of the valley. There were many higher mountains in the Vilcabamba range but this southwest face was the coldest and at 14,000 feet, Juan Ignacio was never warm. The sweep of the wind ran uninterrupted for twenty miles and reached velocities undreamed of from the quiet valley below. He crushed the end of his cigarette and put the remnant in his left shirt pocket. Juan Ignacio did not want to be selected as a target because of a burning coal on his cigarette.

The stultifying mindlessness of his patrol exhausted him. His days were the same ad nauseum. He looked for mountain cat footprints. The cats were on full prowl at 14,000 feet and their rust-colored gray and black coat made them nearly invisible at dawn. He patrolled past the wire enclosures of the goat pen and tested the padlock on the gate. He was mortified at his role in this stupid dangerous mess so he avoided speaking with the prisoner and talked to the goats. There were some kids in the mix and their silly enthusiasms helped to break the monotony. He pitied the captive but at least he could sleep with the animals and keep warm. He reached for his cigarette and he realized he was out of matches. He counted the goats. They came to the fencing and the kids hopped a greeting to him as he walked by. He counted the prisoner.

The mist billowing from the tumult of the rapids two miles below began to thin and a few thousand feet above, the *hut hut hut hreek* of the eternal condors proclaimed the ascendancy of the sun. Light bathed the massif on the other side of the valley and Juan made an internal hello to the enormous condor petroglyph chiselled deep into the cliff face across the canyon.

Commando Hill was ready. He had called then visited each of his team personally two days earlier with instructions and an outline of the plan. He asked Foster to bring his pipe and to cut an extra one. If they were separated or if Davy lost his pipe they had spares. Regarding dress, warm, dark, dull and unreflective, quiet and comfortable. Faces. Dull green gray black. Hair, covered. His commando team understood and agreed.

Mildred was worried. Despite the fact she had the most invested in this expedition she had doubts about herself.

" Davy, I think this is gonna be a problem for me to do."

"Really? Why Mildred? This chance is what you and your mother have been waiting for. This is what you want. To rescue your father is what all of us want." Mildred nodded and spoke with a concern Davy had not heard in her.

" Yes, it is what I have prayed for. I can't tell you how much I want it. The problem is I also want to get at the people who did this. I want them to suffer the way my father has suffered. I can't get away from wanting revenge on them. I want *piranhas* in their bath water. I don't know if I can block them out and think just of my Dad, knowing they are there and need to be dealt with. My intentions for them are not good."

Davy understood fully. If they traveled with anything but good intention it would be to a parallel opaque and useless netherworld. It would be of no use to them and of no use to Mildred's father.

" Mildred, we will have to try another way. You must think only of that trail your father has left. Think nothing of why we travel it, but only that it is a record which remains in the consciousness of the light and it represents your father's passage. Also. The trail you make to find him has to be the strongest trail of all. The rest of our team can only participate in the pathway to wherever your dad is by following you. We do not know him. We know you and your mother. If you go astray, we all go astray."

He saw he had made a mistake in his emphasis on her crucial role.

"But I know you can do it, so just relax about it. Maybe you need to look at it just as an adventure, as fun. What do you think?"

That was it. Mildred relaxed. "Thank you, Davy. That is exactly what I need to do. If you can't have fun what can you have." Davy could not argue with that. He had full confidence in Mildred and in operation Seagull.

They met at the Craft residence an hour before sundown. Helen's house had a clear western exposure to the setting sun.

Tilt began the briefing. "Well, we are a fine, fine looking team. Commandos extraordinaire if I do say so myself. Listen up now and focus like you have never focused. What I am about to say will decide the success or abandonment of our mission." The group keened to Tilt. Abandonment had never been raised.

"We intend to arrive where John Craft and his survey team are being held. Intend is the key word. First. Mildred and Helen, you must intend and visualize three things. One, John Craft. Two, flat ground. Three, red barked six-foot-wide polylepsis trees, in that order. Second, the rest of us will also think of three things. One, Helen and Mildred together. Two, flat ground. Three, red barked six-foot-wide polylepsis trees." They had no idea what a polylepsis tree was but six feet wide and red barked was good enough. They did not question the colonel's instructions.

" Wide red-barked trees are easy to conjure. Flat ground however is ordinary and becomes difficult as a result. Work on it now. A sixty degree 20,000-foot-long ice-covered slope is not a useful place to land. Having said that, one unknown remains." They had not expected an unknown.

"If you wish to leave the team because of this unknown, I understand and I applaud the courage of your decision. We will be landing at altitude in or near the sacred valley of the Incas. It is a place unique on our planet. Sacred energy blasts out from the ground as a palpable physical power. I am unsure of the effect this cosmic stream may have on the activity of the light. Light is bent by energy. Light travels at different speeds under different influences. Given that, I do not know if we will stay together in a trail even with a unified intention. In the sacred valley there are no rules. The energy does what it wants. It is possible it may reject anything coming into it or it may embrace and welcome a like

347

consciousness. I do not know if the valley can or will override our collective will and destroy our participation with the light. I do not know. If this is too much, just shake hands and leave here and wish the rest of us well. We love you and respect you."

No one looked around to see what the others were doing. There was no question of leaving. "Good. Thank you. Charles, do you have your two pipes?" Charles nodded in the affirmative.

"Give one to Janet." She placed it in her right zippered pocket as Tilt had instructed her to have available.

"I have four belts with stuff sacks attached. Harry, Helen, Mildred and myself will wear them." He passed them over. "They contain a 35 metre 8.1 mm rope. It weighs three pounds. Do not remove it until and when I ask you to do so. I will instruct you at the time. I see each of you has the knife I issued you. Good. Keep it clipped to your belt. Likewise, do not open it unless I request it. Here."

He passed around a large thermos. "Fill your canteens with this tea and drink some immediately when we arrive. It is coca. Tie off your canteen so it does not rattle. There is more tea in my pack along with a flare gun and wire cutters." He also carried a taser but he did not reveal it. Tilt reviewed the group. Harry was good. He even had a black hockey mouth guard to cover his teeth. Mildred had her balaclava and had not shined her walking boots.

"Helen, I see you have added a little tasteful glitter to the camouflage around your eyes. May I?" Tilt wiped off the sparkles and smeared around some of his musty concoction. It was impossible to tell whether Mrs. Craft had blushed.

"One final note. We must assume there are three captives. If fewer, so much the better. Pipe one is Davy. Davy, you and Mildred and I will use that pipe. Pipe two is Janet. Janet, you and Helen will use that pipe. On return, you will bring one of the hostages. Pipe three is Charles. Charles, you will embark with Harry. You two will bring John Craft and another hostage when we return. We will hold hands both coming and going. We will stay holding hands until each person is free of the effects of the travel. Remember. Flat ground. Now. Let's go outside. I see the sun is ready for us. Good luck and hold tight."

Bully Gregious measured it for the third time to be sure. He was leaving nothing to chance. *Good work Melvin, same measurement again. 152.4.* He spun the pipe cutter with care and off dropped the final cut. He ran the emery cloth around the end and blew away the dust and smiled at his good work. *That looks good.* He flipped it end to end and began polishing. In five minutes he was done. He had his own pipe and it was time to make amends.

Bully's episode with the razor wielding monster ninja had clarified his thinking. Malveena had messed him up and pressured him to collaborate in wrongdoing and he was finished with it. He recognized the lie he had told himself for what it was. He had deluded himself. He was not a victim. He had cooperated with Malveena willingly out of laziness and passivity and an inability to withstand the energy of her marauding sociopathy.

Bully was unsure of the use of his shiny new toy. He had shared such a pipe just once with Malveena and it had dropped them onto a slithering sub-zero ledge above a yawning chasm. He had even lost his belt. He had asked her then what she had been thinking and that was the key. So, what should he think. Who did he need to talk to make things right. *The Pilchers. Janet and Harry. The Crafts, Mildred and her mother. These people are ordinary people. Housewives, children and families. They are probably not doing things which would put me on a ledge. I will think of them. Also Foster if he is still kicking. We cheated him with the power of attorney. Maybe I can still fix it. Even Gargantua the shaver guy. He was doing the right thing for those kids.* He shivered at the memory. He shivered again and put his hand to his neck and felt for a carotid pulse. It was accelerating at the thought.

Bully was not a planner but now he was trying. What should he wear. Some of the group might be outside. It might be at night. *Need to be seen.* It could be raining. *Need to be dry.* It could be cold or foggy. *Need to be warm.* He knew what he needed and he remembered Lucretia thought it was ugly and wouldn't let him wear it. He bellowed to the missus.

"Lucretia, where is my yellow rain slicker?"

"Where do you think it is. It is with the rest of the yellow rain slickers."

" But there is only mine. I am the only one with a yellow slicker."

"Exactly. That's where it is."

Porky heard the exchange and got up to get his dad's rain gear. It was hanging at the back of the front hall closet. Bully took it from Porky and smoothed out the plastic wrinkles on the way to the bedroom full length mirror. He put in on for the first time and modelled it. It was beautiful. The off gassing of the volatile organic compounds was olfactory heaven and they filled the room. Lenny fled the scene and opened the vinyl sash on his bedroom window to let in some air.

Bully admired himself. He was billowing, canary yellow and shiny. *Good. Could see me from a mile.* Something hurt his back. He inched a fat hand up between his shoulder blades and ripped out a three-inch cardboard tag. It said 'Do not remove this tag' and Bully felt jaunty by disobeying the order and tossed the label on the floor. He looked good and felt good and there was no point in waiting. He tested to see his pipe fit into his inside map pocket. The sun was reddening as he walked to the balcony and sighted to the west. *Good people, wherever you are, here comes Bully.* He felt an ecstasy of embryonic approval unlike anything he remembered in life as the last of the sun transported him. He smiled. There was no belittlement, no derision and nothing false in the light to trick him. He did not want it to end.

The goats were sleeping and quiet in the alcove away from the wind. The magnified Andean constellations were brilliant and enormous and a waxing gibbous moon shone a white light to give Hidalgo a shadow to keep him company. The ground was freezing again and the clay slush from the aquifers stayed indented under his feet. He decided to foot print a big 'McGill' into the frosted mire. He was on the 'G' when he heard the wheeze of Alejandro's breathing floating up the rock face at the edge of the plateau. He was early but not surprisingly. Alejandro did not like schedules that made him predictable. One could never be too careful. As he gained the flat his gait was a little more energized than usual. He was puffing as always because of the belly he carried but less so today.

"Juan Hidalgo. Any problems?"

"No. A few cat calls but distant. Nothing else."

"Good. I have news. The best news. You have three days more to guard the swine in the pen. Goats too." He laughed a yellow grin and put too friendly a hand on Juan Ignacio's shoulder.

"Juanito, I have done it. The big bosses have agreed. Three days. We have done it. The money will be in the bank. Hah. Money for me and for you. Kings. We shall be the new Inca. Oh oh oh such kings." He was perspiring from the excitement of his confidence, but Juan Ignacio sensed something was sideways. Alejandro's presentation was malignant.

" Three days more and we are rid of the scum and we will both get our just deserts. You and I will get what we deserve."

The malice in the tone of Alejandro's voice removed all doubt. In the mind of Alejandro Charca, what Hidalgo deserved was a Mauser bullet and eternal rest in the valley of the Incas. It was precisely what Hidalgo had feared. He would leave the mountain that night.

"Good." was all he said. He walked past Alejandro and started down the difficult path at the western rim. He stopped with his head at the level of the plateau and looked back at the unfinished 'McGill'. He would not stop his slow descent until three miles below when he arrived at trails leading eventually to the hovels of Lima, 600 kilometres northwest. From there, he knew not what, but Juan Ignacio Hidalgo would not die at the hands of a maniac.

A sleepless John Craft had listened to the murmur of the guards' conversation but the wind had blown apart the words. He saw Charca beginning to doze at the base of the huge polylepsis. This was not the guard to aggravate or confront. Craft fingered the scar from the first time he had tested Alejandro's alertness. The rifle butt had come straight and hard to his face against the wire mesh barrier and split his chin.

Craft was awake with the cold. He found it impossible to sleep despite the warmth of the animals. The moonlight was enough for him to make his next written entry. Hidalgo had given him paper and pencil as a small gesture of empathy from one species of prisoner to another. John wrote poetry, made observations of the day, drew birds and sometimes doodled. Most importantly, every day without fail he wrote five lines to his wife and daughter. He did not miss. Every day was a new visit with them on paper. He kept the pages dry under his shirt against his heart and they kept him warm. He had lost his compatriots from the survey team but John still had one reliable friend. His friend lived across the valley a couple of thousand feet below and they saw each other every day. He stretched thirty feet with open arms and the sun traced his bevelled feathers and the mighty condor of the Andes preened himself in the rock.

The Tilt commando team arrived quietly on the plateau at the goat camp,

351

facing east toward the pens. The forces of the energy in the sacred valley had broken their hand holds and the group was spread out like so many dreary statues. They were immobile and quiet and John Craft did not see the shadows appear on the small mesa as he nodded in the cold and dreamed over his writing. Sitting asleep with his back against the red polylepsis was Alejandro. Davy and Charles Foster began to escape agglutination first but they were not yet lucid. The quality of things was slightly different under the competition of the energy within the valley. Helen Craft saw some goats and observed them and saw a skeletal man pondering a paper and how nice and she had no need to react. Janet did a slow circle sway waiting for the music to stop. Tilt was nowhere to be seen. Mildred took a little balance step. She gazed through the holes of a heavy wire mesh enclosure just like a zoo and there were goats and could be a zoo and she knew about zoos and the goats began bleating and they did that. She watched a man who sat writing and rubbed his ear while thinking and he could do that. Her dad did that and she was at peace waiting for clarity. Harry began to creep into awareness and through his black mouth guard he breathed a quiet slushy 'hoo' as he saw the power of normalcy cycloning toward him. Somewhere deep in Alejandro Charca's dreams the goats were making odd sounds. Little hoo owl sounds maybe. Odd for goats to make owl sounds. He awoke without a reaction and stood noiselessly. He was invisible in the shadow of the ancient polylepsis and he was at the backs of the commando team standing just fifty feet away in front of him. Silently he slid the safety off his Ouzi machine gun while he crept to a central position on the plateau. From there, one sweep of the small gun was all he needed. Fully focused on the intruders, Charca neither heard nor saw what happened behind him.

Bully Gregious' bulk landed him heavily at the frozen brim of the precipice. He teetered on the brink with his heels hanging over the 14,000 feet drop with a look of bemused wonderment on his face. All that kept him from falling three miles down the mountain was the west wind at his back. His instinctive gyroscope warned him to tip forward but it seemed to be an unimportant thing in the starlight. The windswept shadows of gnarled polylepsis branches grasped to pull Bully away. Six postured frozen forms spread themselves across Bully's field of vision. He saw the dull statues of the people he had been thinking about begin to thaw and move and it was interesting but it needed no action. He observed a man moving stealthily in front of him. Without interest he heard the man with the machine gun order the dull statues to turn around and put up their hands and they did and Bully thought it good and he would too but didn't have to couldn't make him. He smiled childishly to the easterly stars and the brilliant little dog Procyon beckoned him and surrounded him and hit him between the eyes with a million candlepower and he was wide awake. He was off balance backwards above the canyon and he flapped his shining yellow arms to balance forward. *Again with the ledge.* He wiggled forward on his toes and gained a few inches. The astonished commando team stood with their hands up and beheld the amazing Bully. They said not a word and looked past Charca to the furrowed fountain of clay sludge that was shot skyward by Bully as he blazed through the muck and belly butted the kidnapper from behind and knocked him to his knees.

The Ouzi flew into the darkness as Mildred raced to the impact and ripped off her balaclava and thrust it down over Alejandro's head and flattened him the rest of the way onto his stomach. Bully splashed in a circle around the hapless Charca with his fists cycling like John L. Sullivan on a poster. Foster arrived at the same time and began winding his rope around and around Charca's hands behind his back while Davy quickly wrapped his belt around his feet and cinched it tight and dragged the thug backwards in the mush, filling up the red balaclava with slop through the eye holes. Bully ceased his Marquis of Queensbury and sat on Alejandro Charca and pinned him helplessly in six inches of ooze. They heard the sharp clicks of cutting metal and looked for the noise. Tilt had seen the whole thing from inside the goat pen where the light had dumped him. He was feverishly cutting the cage wire to join the fray but to no avail. The fight was over as he pushed through to the action with a tribe of forty liberated goats behind him. A kid hopped to Mildred and began to chew on her shoelace. She batted at it and it responded with a perfectly placed butt in the crook of Mildred's knees and knocked her flat into the muck. She stood up with cold sludge running out of her sleeves and looked at the crease in her pants and the remains of her shoes. *Why do I bother. Muck and more muck.* Janet Pilcher had missed the whole event. She was swaying happily in her glutinous suspension, contented with the music in her misty miasma and totally disinterested in reality. It took ten minutes for her to make clarity.

Helen Craft had neither seen nor heard the last of the fight. She was standing flush against the front of the cage at the goat pen and she was quiet. Mirrored against her on the other side of the wire mesh was John. They had not spoken. They held fingers through the holes to touch and they didn't move and with quiet tears they breathed the pure safe air of the Andes. Charles watched their touching reunion. Over Helen's shoulder, John Craft's eyes were sentimental but they revealed more than that. From deep within him, his latent refusal to capitulate to his captors burned hot. He was a man to remember.

The Commandos of Operation Seagull decided not to risk the dangers of lugging Alejandro Charca down from the plateau in bad light. The goats were underfoot and one little butt meant a quick trip to the bottom of the canyon. Dawn was just six hours away. The valley below promised nothing but a dangerous trek and it came into sun much later in the day. They were better off to stay at high altitude where the light for the trip home would arrive earlier. Tilt was disappointed in not having the opportunity to use his taser. He remembered Tom Swift stories from his childhood. Tom Swift and his Electric Rifle. Now called t.a.s.e.r.

Bully Gregious could not take his eyes off Tilt. He was the fence guy for sure and he could tell Colonel Hill was itching to shave some spots he had missed. Bully saw him scratch his neck. That was a signal. He was threatening a shave. Tilt smiled at Bully in acknowledgement of Bully's quick action and soldierly initiative. Bully was sure the smile was ironic.

The Pilchers sat close together and reflected individually on the happenings and the strange world at their disposal through the light. Davy reckoned either the shadows were playing tricks on his eyes or Dopo was hopping in the mush and stomping to finish the 'Gill'.

Foster was proud of the youngsters and to have been part of the escapade. It had not been a smart thing to do but it had been successful and that was enough. He sat down beside Bully.

"Bully, do you have anything you want to tell me?"

Bully nodded. Mr. Foster had not called him 'Melvin' and that bode well.

"Yes Charles, I do. I have much to tell you."

They walked together and sat down beside each other with their backs against rough red bark. Bully was proud and shiny in his yellow slicker and

Charles was stolid with his face painted dull in his camouflage gear. Bully began and he poured out his story and spared no details. He told of the connivance to manipulate the shares with Malveena's forged power of attorney, of the chasing and harassment of Davy and Mildred and the negotiations and the agreement of purchase and sale with the Macau syndicate and the lay offs at the plants. Charles nodded along in a manner of affirmative listening and drew every possible detail from Bully. Bully told of the recent shaving episode with the twelve-foot ninja and Foster struggled to suppress a guffaw. A certain Colonel had been busy. He wished he had been there to witness it.

"Bully, thank you. And thank you for your action tonight. It was heroic and generous and I will not forget it. I will also not forget what you and Malveena have done."

Bully waited for the 'Melvin'.

"Melvin, you must now promise me. You will keep this event and our conversation from Malveena. This is a demand. Understand?" Bully understood very well.

" You and I and Malveena are going to have a cordial little meeting. We will meet in our executive offices and this is how it will go. At ten o'clock tomorrow morning you will call Malveena to your office. After she is seated, get up and close the door with authority and sit down. Say nothing and tell her to wait. I will knock a few minutes later. You will go to the door and open it and stand there looking out for thirty full seconds. Then say simply. 'Hello. Please come in.' Nothing more. I shall do the rest. Melvin, do not spoil my surprise."

Foster gave Bully's shoulder a little shake and a warm smile. They were pals thought Bully, just like the old days.

The shadows of the four-thousand-year-old polylepsis were trapped inside the spans of themselves in the overhead noon-time sun. Harry had retrieved Alejandro Charca's Ouzi machine gun from the mud and with it he herded him toward the footholds leading down from the plateau. For show, Harry loudly clicked off the safety. Mildred grasped Charca's shirt collar and jerked her sopping balaclava off his head. Charca staggered with stiff limbs and stumbled. He slid and fell and tumbled down the rock footholds and away from Harry's grim threat, scraping and cutting and concussing himself as he scrambled to save his life. Harry put the safety back on and placed the gun back in the muck.

The sun was not hot but it showed a brilliance which in all the world was reserved for the sacred valley of the Incas. The plateau began to steam in the warming and its rising vapour weaved Bully Gregious, Colonel Freddy Hill, Janet and Harry Pilcher, Helen and John Craft, Charles Abernathy Foster and Mildred and Davy into its spell. The little band of friends sighted to the sky. A kaleidoscopic glow built and hummed and warmed through their pipes and they held hands. Suddenly a tumult began from below. It rose and grew nearer and louder and it continued to grow in sound and in speed and in force and in fury and with one firm hand, it swept them into in an all-consuming updraft of light and carried them above the peaks and through the stars and made them know what it was to be Inca and to be Condor. Secure in the grip of the eternal consciousness of the light, they descended and they arrived. They were safe and they were together and they were at home.

The graven bird watching from his cliff face across the valley had seen much in his thousands of years but he had seen nothing more interesting than this.

Chapter 23: Foster Renews Acquaintances

The wine was warm and the bath water was cold and she had been dozing. Malveena peeled a small strip of skin off the knuckle of her big toe from where she had abraded it pulling it out of the bathtub faucet. She had fallen asleep in the warm water and a jasmine scented candle had burned through its rim and run down into the tub. She stared thoughtlessly at the rafts of wax floating around her. It had been a week since her return from the fiasco at Krakatoa. On two occasions since then she had attempted to enter the old password to the laboratory. There was no question the combination had changed. Malveena could certainly work out the new one if required but it was not pertinent. Whoever had changed the password had done it not to increase security but to forebode something to come, yet nothing else threatening or apparently related to it had occurred. She pulled the plug out of the tub and as she stood, bits of wax ran to her and stuck on her legs. She poured the balance of her wine into the swirl of the drain.

Malveena towelled off and walked into her bedroom and pulled on her silk charmeuse kimono. The message light on her telephone was blinking. She punched the playback button and listened to Bully's message while she tied her belt.

" Malveena. Gregious. I need to speak with you first thing in the morning. Be in my office, ten o'clock. Something urgent has come up."

Malveena replayed the message. It was Bully all right, but the usual uncertainty and trepidation in his tone was absent. His assertiveness bothered her. Her digital clock flipped to midnight as she punched the speed dial to get him back on the line.

Bully picked up the phone on the second ring. He had been expecting the call and his voice was firm. " Hello Malveena. Thank you for returning my call. Don't talk, just listen. Be in my office at ten, as my message to you indicated. I expect you to be on time. Good night."

Bully hung up the phone before Malveena uttered a word. She had to swallow her invective. She hammered redial but it went to his voicemail. She smashed down her receiver. She was furious, but more than that she was confused. It unsettled her that Bully was so sure of himself. That was strange enough on its own but his request for a meeting with her was more puzzling. He disliked meetings in general and specifically he abhorred meetings of any kind with Malveena. What he was doing was unnatural.

She sat at her dressing table and looked in the mirror. She was a wreck. She set her alarm and slipped into bed and rolled over on her right side and pulled her enormous stuffed bear up against her stomach. She laid there expecting another night of fitful and disturbed sleep and she was not disappointed.

Bully and Porky Gregious sat having breakfast on their back patio. Lucretia was still in bed and Porky had toasted four frozen blueberry waffles for him and his Dad. They each had two and Bully was just putting his finishing touches with the syrup. It was going to be a fine day and it was better than fine in Bully's mind. For the first time in 20 years he had one up on Malveena. She was going to get it in the neck and he could hardly wait. If he knew how to use the upload and the download and the whatever load he would upload the embarrassing bits of their upcoming meeting with Foster to the Internet. He should ask Porky how to do it. The music from Porky's bedroom percolated through the screen door and wafted out across the patio. Bully did not listen to music but this was something different.

" Leonard, is that your music? What music is that?"

" On my computer. Great isn't it Dad? That is Borodin." Bully frowned. It did not sound boring to him. Porky continued.

" Alexander Borodin. He is amazing. Russian. Dead too. That is one of his string quartets, I think number two. Yes, I am sure, number two. Do you like it?"

" Lenny, that is amazing. You are amazing. You are a neat kid."

Porky did not bat an eye and he got up and walked to his bedroom. This was the first time in his life he had heard a word of approval. He fiddled in his bureau drawer and pulled out a flash drive and downloaded the string quartet for his father.

" Here Dad. I put the music on here. Just push it into your office computer in the slot which fits this end. The music will come up onscreen and ask you if you want to play it. Just click once on it."

Bully took the stick without a comment and looked at the clock. He needed to shower and get cleaned up. "Thanks Lenny."

Malveena arrived early at the office and clicked her car door locks closed with the remote control. She began to walk away from her beautiful Bentley when a seagull landed on the hood. The gull stepped around with soft shoes a couple of times then spread its feet and settled its beautiful white front into the warmth. It ignored her shoosh. She was sure it had raised an eyebrow at her. She strode through the front door and took the stairs to the second floor. She walked quickly past Bully's open door and started to insert her key into her office door when it registered as to what she had heard. She left her keys dangling in the lock and walked back. He had a smile like a Cheshire cat and he was listening to something which sounded like Brahms.

" Bully. You're listening to music."

" Yes Malveena, I am." He was proud to have found where to put the memory stick. The music was beautiful and it was familiar to Malveena but she could not recall who had composed it. It was not Brahms.

" Bully, what is that you're listening to?"

" Strings Malveena."

" Thank you Bully. I know that it is strings. Who composed it?"

" Alexandra Borden. Russian, you know. String quartet. His second, actually." Bully was pleased with his new knowledge and he wanted to impress Malveena when he realized, there she sat and he had not done what Foster had said to do.

" Sit Malveena."

He got up and closed the door to his office with authority. That was what Foster said to do. He sat behind his desk and beamed at Malveena in an unnatural way.

" There is something wrong with you, you know Bully. You realize you asked me to sit, do you? I was already sitting. What's going on?"

The setup was so delicious, Bully was squirming in anticipation. The squirming aggravated Malveena even more.

" Gregious, what is so special about today? You never close your door. Even so, you just closed it."

Bully began nodding as he looked at his digital clock, then he looked at it again. It had just flipped to 10 am. He had 5 minutes to wait. Malveena sighed at the silliness. She had not slept well and she was not in the mood for games. There was business to do. She closed her eyes and rubbed her temples with the tips of her elegant fingers. Apparently a third party was coming. Fine. She decided to sit and wait and to say nothing and let Bully stew. Bully saw the fatigue and dishevelment and spoke to her.

"Malveena, you look like you slept with rats."

"Thank you for your concern Bully. While we are waiting, pull your box of transaction files over here. We need to prepare the share certificates for the transfer of ownership to the Macau syndicate. It's not ..."

The knock on the door was harsh and Bully jumped even though he was waiting for it. He moved quickly to get it.

"That must be Fo.. I wonder who that cou.. I'll get it." Malveena did not bother to turn to look to the door behind her.

Bully pulled open the door and smiled at his old pal. Foster pointed Bully to his desk. Bully walked ahead and sat obediently. Charles Foster entered and stood in front of Malveena beside his old leather topped desk, comfortable in the brilliance of the overhead Fresnel lenses. Foster rubbed a slow circle in the leather of the desk top. He had on a light camel jacket with an open necked white shirt and blue slacks and burgundy loafers. He was not carrying a briefcase.

There were only two chairs. "Bully, go to my lab and get my lab stool. The combination is '4444'."

Bully got up and a surge of embarrassment flooded through him at the memory of the last time he used the one-time code DORK. He was sure the rescue team was still laughing at him.

" I suppose that 4444 stands for something else like DORK. You gave me my one-use password as DORK. Your friend. DORK Charles, DORK!" Bully was still hurt.

Charles was puzzled then understood. "Bully, no. It was not that. Nothing like that at all. It was an acronym for Foster Original Research Laboratory. F.O.R.L. The numbers are the same. Not DORK. Sorry Bully, that you thought that. Grab my stool from the lab."

Foster walked past Malveena and stood at the window and looked toward the river with his hands clasped behind his back. The gulls were circling in turn, each of them looking for the highest vantage point. Foster had placed bristled protectors on every lamp post and the adults had given up the attempt. The mixed feathered youngsters were convinced this time it would be better but eventually they looked for something else to sit on. He had missed this view and he enjoyed it while he waited for Bully to return.

Bully rushed away, embarrassed again but not so much. He was back in two minutes with the lab stool and not a word had passed between Foster and Malveena. She sat calmly and waited for Foster to bring it on. Foster sat comfortably on the high lab stool with his feet on the lower rung.

"Well, well. Malveena. Good morning."

"Good morning to you too Charles. You are not dead."

"Ah Malveena. Your mastery of the obvious has not diminished. That is a good thing because there are some obvious things to deal with. I understand you and Melvin have been busy little beavers since I have been away on my little sabbatical. Deals here, deals there, shares here, shares there, that sort of thing? That is what the little birds tell me. Are they correct?"

Bully moved a little more to the front of his chair. He had not expected any 'Melvins' and there had been one in the first thirty seconds. Malveena said nothing and did not acknowledge Charles had spoken. She knew exactly to which 'two little birds' he referred and they were not seagulls. Bully nodded commensurately.

"I was also amazed in my absence you two were able to transact agreements which contravened the company by-laws unless and accept for waiver by my personal signature. That is a marvel of contemporary business."

Bully began to perspire. Charles had said "you two", which meant him as well, not just Malveena.

" Tell me Malveena. How did you get around that little inconvenience?"

Malveena was implacable. She did not answer Foster. She answered no questions to which she knew an adversary already had the answer.

Bully was determined to help. " Power of attorney. Malveena has your power of attorney."

" Yes, thank you Bully. The little birds did happen to mention that fortunate happenstance as well. It is an amazing thing really. Poof, presto chango, when required to be there, there it is. A power of attorney."

Bully was watching every nuance of Malveena's posture. He watched her facial muscles and her breathing. There was not a twitch of an eyebrow nor a shift in her seat. If she was getting it in the neck one would never know it. Malveena went on the offensive.

Charles Charles Charles. Sadly, things do change as one ages, and those changes are not always good. Unhappily, your mind is not what it once was. In fact, Charles, you are past it. It is tragic, and believe me, I am entirely sympathetic to your plight. You once had a fine mind, but now, well, it pains me to say, you are senile. You gave me your power of attorney, in fact you forced me to accept it and now you don't remember doing it. Sad to see. You have given me the authority to act in your stead and now you wish to rescind it. Apparently, you also forget you designed it so should you become ill, mentally incapable, the way that you are now, the power of attorney is irrevocable. Irrevocable Charles. Sad."

"I see. Irrevocable. That is a big word. I need help with it. If I search hard within my dimming capacity I see vaguely that it might mean that I can't take it back. Bully, fish out a copy of it from one of your boxes there."

Bully slid over the cardboard box he hoped it would be in and began to look. Bully filed documents in careful chronologic order by tossing the next one on the last one in the box. The power of attorney was down 14 spots and he found it quickly and handed it to Foster. Foster looked at it carefully.

"I have to say this is a beautiful piece of work. Congratulations on a job well done. So, let us not examine it and let us assume for just a moment that it is valid. Suppose that it is. The question is what have you done with it. If I were a gambling man, I would bet you have done something interesting. Melvin, slide your box over here." Bully did not notice, but the reference to gambling was not lost on Malveena.

Charles Foster was looking for the Macau International Gaming Syndicate deal. He trusted the accuracy of the report from Mildred and Davy. The impact and shock of what they had heard from the storage room made the memory of it indelible for them. Those kids knew what they had heard. Foster begin to riffle through the box and came upon a document of preliminary terms and conditions. He finally came to the agreement. It was a purchase and sale agreement between Foster Industries and Macau International Gaming.

362

" This is it. This is certainly something interesting. You two. Don't talk. This will take me a few minutes."

Foster read the document quickly. He was very familiar with the form and content of such agreements and as he read Malveena began to fidget. She was losing her resolve. After 20 minutes he sighed and put his head back and closed his eyes. Foster slammed the forty-page agreement down on the surface of Bully's desk and shot the sheets of terms and conditions 10 feet over Bully's desk and fluttered them down the wall.

" Gregious, do you know what you have done? Do you have any idea what you have done! After all my work. Years of it. " He shook his head.

Bully had no idea what Foster was talking about. He thought they were buddies but once again he was getting the Melvin treatment.

" But I, but we, I thought...."

" Never mind. Let me tell you what you have done. You have really done it this time. Let me tell you. Bully, you have outdone yourself and in fact, which I never thought I would hear myself saying, you have outdone me."

Bully was pleased to hear that, but he was sure there was another shoe about to drop. Malveena was astounded and silenced.

" This agreement, this pile of terms and conditions and caveats is the most, the most, beautiful thing I've ever seen. You have, you have .... made the best blasted deal under the sun."

Foster slapped his thigh in glee. Bully had had his eyes closed and his face contorted waiting for the hammer blow. He didn't think what Foster had just said was one of those. Bully and Malveena looked at each other in stupefaction.

" What?"

" I had been working with the Macau boys for two years when I left. We have a separate ancillary agreement already done to take affect when this agreement or an agreement like it is executed. I walked out on the discussions knowing they would be back, but I never dreamed when they came back they would be willing to give up this much. Beautiful job you two." Foster laughed a big gut laugh.

"Now Malveena. Bully. About this power of attorney thing."

Malveena jumped in with petulance.

"Well Mr. Charles Foster, too bad about that. My word against yours, and the signature, your perfect blue inked Charles Foster signature will tell the tale. I have the original paper. Good paper makes good friends. You are too late and I have your power of attorney. Signed, sealed and delivered. What do you say to that, you big Abernathy you!" She was triumphant.

It did not have the effect Malveena expected. Bully wanted to hide and he began a soft mewing. Charles Foster was composed and sure of himself. He smiled the smile that both Malveena and Bully knew meant that he had it all under control.

"Malveena, I could not agree with you more. About good paper making good friends. That is so. However, bad paper just makes a mess and your power of attorney is bad paper."

"Prove it!"

"I will be brief and please do pay attention. You have made a lovely attempt. The signature is perfect and it is indistinguishable from mine. The form of the power of attorney is immaculately correct and the blue ink is perfectly correct in its color. Your attention to detail was one of the things which gave me confidence in bringing you along and teaching you all that you need to know about the business. Notice that I said 'all that you need to know'."

Bully mewed his rejoinder to Malveena. "I told you it wouldn't work."

"Shut up you idiot."

"Well Bully, if that is so, you were correct. Malveena, I am first and foremost an inventor and here in my pocket is one of my inventions." He pulled out his leaky old fountain pen.

"Charles, we have seen that thing a thousand times."

"Yes, but you have never wondered why it is special, have you. To your eternal chagrin you will now find that out. My pen", he wiggled it between his fingers, " is not remarkable, but what is in it is unique. Since day one, without a single exception, every corporate document signed by me has been signed with this pen and therefore with my one of a kind ink. Its chemistry is unique. It leaves its own signature. It has trace components that no other ink has and in fact, every three months the composition is changed slightly. So not only is the ink unique to me, it has a built-in time stamp to tell exactly when a document was signed. Your pretty paper has nothing of the sort. Your lovely artwork, my dear, does not have Foster ink and it is a forgery. Sans aucun doute. Game, set and match."

Bully was not sure he understood but by the look of Malveena they had lost. The room was quiet and somehow Foster seemed unbothered by the whole exercise.

" Listen. You might not go to jail. There is a way."
Malveena almost brightened and Bully resumed mewing.

"This is how it stands. My patents pending and those coming for approval need a different production configuration than the current plant along the Borstal can offer. The plant has to come down and yet there is barely enough room even after rebuilding. That, by the way, also means shutdown until operations resume. I don't want that."

The entire scenario finally coalesced in Bully's brain as an idea.

"Wait a minute. Let me get this straight. You already started negotiations with Macau before I met them?"

"Right."

" In addition, you have made a wholly separate but related deal with them already."

"Yes."

"You wanted and want to sell the plant and library, just as Malveena and I had planned to do?"

"Yes. Exactly. I did and do. But like my martinis, with a twist." He chuckled at himself.

"Here is the background. The plant land along the river is small and if expansion is in the cards, it cannot be done on that site. The library. It was fine in its day but it is the wrong building for this generation. More land is needed. I have 70 acres where I live. The separate deal with the syndicate, signed and lying in wait, waiting for a reasonable share deal like yours, is as follows. Construction of a modern environmentally perfect, high tech plant will be done on my homesite. A new library will be there. It will also house an attached training, research and apprenticing facility. The plant itself will require an additional 500 workers above what we employ now. The deal I made with the Macau syndicate is a simple one. They are buying our, my, shares in exchange for the Borstal site and library building and a 25% interest in one of my pending patents on artificial intelligence. They don't want robots beating their games."

Malveena and Bully were overcome. They had sneaked and colluded and slogged through crocodile swamps and hung from muck sliding ledges attempting to do precisely what Foster had been doing all along. Bully had not been able to expunge the sentence containing the words 'might' and 'jail' from his mind.

" Charles. Jail. You said 'jail' and with a 'might' attached. Jail?"

" What you planned, you and Malveena together, is called I believe, fraudulent conveyance. That can mean jailtime, yes. Let me finish about the deal with Macau."

"The Macau boys will endow an annual scholarship for local students for intellectual property ideas. Their construction team will build the complete new plant and library first and make it ready for occupancy and production. In the meantime, the status quo continues for the workers. The day we open the new plant, Macau commences with tearing down the old one and we get our money and they get our voting shares relating to that plant alone. Our full current work force plus 500 new hires will start in my new facility. Oh. There will also be a small garage where I can tinker with my Auburn."

Malveena interrupted. "Charles, it went to the police pound and then out at auction. It is gone. We did not know it was yours."

"Thanks Malveena, but I knew what would happen. A subsidiary of mine in the middle east bid on it for me by phone and got it back. Amazing antiquities near Beirut Lebanon. Ancient cut slabs of rock bigger than my house. Now, about jail."

Bully Reddened and Malveena went whiter.

"As I see it, this is your choice. In fact, not a choice. This is what you will do. Malveena, how many workers have been laid off at the Borstal plant site?"

She did not respond, wondering where the trick was in the question.

"Come on Malveena, you know exactly. How many."

"404. Exactly."

"Thank you. You and Bully will give to me your shares in numbers which when sold to the syndicate will provide sufficient funds to cover the lost wages of those 404 workers. I will direct those funds to the appropriate employees so they are indemnified fully. I estimate you each will have about 10% of your shares remaining. You will be alright. That is it. Oh. The fact I am back is no longer confidential. Also, I will announce publicly, in a spirit of generosity and good will, you two have decided to divest enough shares to assist all our faithful and much appreciated employees. Agreed?" There was no disagreement.

The news of Foster's safe return spread with Twitter speed and around the world a collective sigh of relief emanated from the subsidiaries of Foster Industries. Charles Abernathy Foster's firm hand was back on the tiller.

The world press prowled Charles Foster's 70 acres. The drinks table was set at the north end of the front steps and apparently news was happening there at the table, as the press corps seldom left it. Foster made them wait for him and they were happier to see him as time went by. After two hours they positively adored him and they were loud about it. Foster and Roger Tam of Macau International Gaming ambled leisurely to the center of the front steps. Tam had forgotten to wear Bully's watch and apparently his wife had forced another Patek Philippe on him. Behind Tam on his left was his cadre of Armani automatons with lovely frozen smiles. Corporate had instructed it.

Behind Foster on his right stood Malveena Drago. She was haughty and alluringly cadaverous in her deep purple pinstriped 1930's gentleman's business suit. Her matching mascara and touches of purple hair coloring were perfect compliments. Porky and Lucretia stood to her left beside Bully, who was nervously obsessed with tucking in his straining shirt. Porky smirked and tucked at his own belly while Lucretia dead-faced at the loss of Bully's shares. Summer on Mallorca had become a weekend at Disneyland.

Roger Tam and Charles Foster signed off on the amended contract in full view of the mob. The moguls shook hands and smiled for the cameras and the deal was done.

Davy and his mother and father poked along the wide beach and breathed in the smell of the sea. Dopo kept them company, unseen and quiet. Harry had broken off a silvered branch from a shore bound log and punched fake blow-holes into the sand with it as they walked. Janet exhaled in relief and contentment. They did not talk and they did not need to. The heat and the sun and the light onshore breezes were rejuvenating and wonderful for the three of them. The tide was out and they had wandered randomly about five hundred feet offshore, close to where thirty or so small sailboats were moored at the marina. The mainsheets played an endless symphony on the aluminum masts.

The boardwalk and railroad tie dock extended about 600 feet out and stopped in a wide deck at the marina entrance. The passage dug for the fleet at the marina was deep and filled with water at low tide and the boats came and went into the bay beyond the breakwall. The channel was fifteen feet deep there and the crab fisherman, mostly kids, were trying their luck. They all had their licenses and knew to toss back the little ones. The crabs had to be six inches long or they were rejects.

Janet said it first. "I'm hungry."

Harry was thinking the same thing. "Good. Me too. Let's go get a hamburger and some yam fries."

That was their usual choice and nothing else was said as they walked off the beach to the promenade. They washed off their feet in the foot shower and put their shoes back on. Davy rubbed his side in muscle memory but he had not brought his pipe because he knew it would speak to him of where and to when he could go and he wanted today to be like before with his mom and dad. The gulls peppered the dock surface and broke open their clams as always. They made wider and wider circles by the thousands to stake out their territory and to stay connected to the scope of the updrafts. They were joyous in their work and they could feel the ease of the day.

Chapter 24: Low Alcohol Beer

The mundanity of the classroom was a tremendous relief for Freddy Hill and Mildred and Davy. None of them had any thoughts of the pipe. Davy let the soft routine of the school day unfold around him. It was turbid and slow paced and plodding and it was terrific. Mr. Hill turned every topic over to Porky for his elucidation and he allowed loquacious Lenny to expound in full flow. Mildred smiled and polished her lens openings. She was much contented with her Dad coming back to make them a family again and her life was full.

Davy reached into his Dad's discarded brown accordion folio and fished out a handful of envelopes and spread them out. They were sticky on Mr. Tilt's desk. He was looking for the one intended for Tilt. He found it and slid it across.

"Mr. Hill, this is your invitation. I don't know if you have a girlfriend or whatever but my Mum says if you do please bring her along. Or any friend. You know. Or on your own. Can you wear your uniform? The one with the commando dagger on the sleeve? That would be really good."

The envelope was hand lettered in black India ink, in an ornate gothic script and it was addressed to " Lieutenant Colonel Freddy 'Tilt' Hill Esq." Tilt liked the artistry of the salutation. He knew how difficult it was to do good ink work. And the flap. Little glue spots showed they had brushed on their own glue like the old days. He opened the letter on the spot. It was an invitation to a barbecue at the Pilcher home. Tilt had perused the guest names as Davy spread them on his desk looking for the right envelope. The one notable omission was Malveena Drago but he might have missed it.

"My Dad wanted to thank everyone and have a relaxed time to celebrate what we all did. It says 'rain or shine', so let's hope we are lucky with the weather."

"That is wonderful of your parents. I accept. Thank you, David. Thank your parents. Do they require a written response?"

Davy frowned. He did not know about that time-honored protocol of R.S.V.P. and Tilt recognized such was no longer de rigueur. He would do so anyway. He thought it might be impolite to ask about the guest list but he was curious all the same, regarding Malveena.

"David, who else is invited?"

Davy read the names from the remaining papers. "Um, Mildred, Mr. and Mrs. Craft, Charles Foster, Bully Gregious, Lucretia and Porky, er.., Lenny Gregious, and me and my Mum and Dad of course. And you."

"Oh." Tilt seemed disappointed and then he brightened.

"I can bring anyone I want? Or two maybe?"

"Well yes, but I .... wait. Mr. Tilt, you are looking tricky. What are you doing?" Davy had seen that kind of look on Tilt only when he was becoming the colonel.

"Well, I am pleased you ask, because I need your help." He drummed his fingers on his desk.

" Mr. Tilt, I am afraid of your answer. What or whom do you intend to bring?"

" Not a 'what', but as to the 'whom' Davy, it is actually three. No, four. They are friends of ours. Socrates, Plato and Aristotle and to complete the package, the fellow we saw disappearing up the hill, Proclus. Maybe we can give him some help. I suspect your other guests might not enjoy the Pythia quite so much. Unless of course, you have a gaseous cleft in your back yard where she could moan and do some oracling?"

Davy was speechless. He was sure they had no cleft to speak of in the back yard. He pursed his lips. Aristotle. Proclus. What an astounding idea. He unintentionally let his right hand feel for his pipe sheath. His personal phantasmic list was growing to much more than the four Tilt was considering. Bert and Spider. **Dobber and Chukker and Simon at least.** He could see Chukker loading up his woomera and going after the neighbor's cat and stuffing it in his tucker bag. Davy's pipe world began overloading his mind and filling his backyard. He stopped and smiled to himself. *I think I will ask Simon to pass around the Pituri.*

Tilt saw the glint in Davy's eye. "I see. Tell me, now who is looking tricky?"

Davy's head spun at the possibilities. He needed to tell Mildred and the whole pipe crew, one by one, they could play the same game. He thought it would make a nice surprise for his Dad.

"Um. I think Mr. Tilt, that we have to be really careful on who we bring first and in what order each one arrives. Napoléon, fine. He knows Foster and they can buddy up. But my Australian friends Simon and Chukker for example, they have to come last where I can look after them. I can't be going off to collect someone and leave them to their own devices."

"Yes Davy, this is going to be interesting. Your dad might need more beer."

At six bells the school bell rang to close the last class of the day. Davy and Mildred walked out together and they were calm and contented together on the outside and itching on the inside. Tranquility was dull and each of them knew how the other was feeling. Davy explained Tilt's thoughts for the guest list at the barbecue and Mildred laughed out loud at the thought of the conglomeration they could put together.

"That Tilt! You might know!" Mildred thought of the characters she had encountered. The tie-dyed girl in the muck at Woodstock might be fun. The orange bellied times reporter, Randolph Arbuthnot Scrivener from Paris popped into her head and she smiled. She then felt a little tremor inside. She was not eager to fight that bloodthirsty little red hatted Jacques again.

Harry had not done many big barbecues like this one and he was a bit nervous about it. He seldom drank beer but it was a staple of barbecues so it was a must. He wanted something special. He knew American beer was lower in alcohol so he would get some of that. He relied upon the clerk and he was pleasantly surprised they had a nice American craft beer on sale. He had never heard of Sly Fox Instigator Eisdoppelbock but that was not surprising, he rarely bought or drank beer. The Eisdoppelbock had a nice label. A rust colored stylized fox head looked rakishly to its left. He should get something exotic in addition as a second choice. Many of his guests and friends had traveled and he admired their sophistication. Immediately he spied what he wanted. Boquebiere Apico. He looked closer to be sure it was beer because it was in tall slender 375mL half Bordeaux bottles he thought usually held wine.

"Is this beer?"

The clerk nodded yes. "This is the Beer Store."

"Oh. Yes. What about the alcohol content. Is it stronger than the Sly Fox?"

" Well, it is a Quebec beer, some Quebec beers have higher alcohol, so let me look, no, it is the same. Both the same."

That was good. On a hot day people drank fast and Harry did not want anyone to feel unwell. He got two cases of each.

He practiced offering. *"Hello Lucretia, may I get you a Sly Fox?"* or perhaps, *"Welcome Colonel Commando sir, how about a nice cold Boquebiere."* The Boquebiere had a real cork too, and that was classy. Harry decided he would uncork every one of them himself. The cork popping would add a festive flavor to things. He could say 'et voilà ' with every one he opened. *There you go.*

The day of the barbecue was hot and sunny. Harry was perspiring already at 10.00 am as he lugged the bags of ice from his car trunk. He carried in ten bags of ice and put them in the bathtub and covered them with an old horse blanket. That would keep them cold forever. He had scrounged two large galvanized tubs for the beer and for the red cream sodas he got for the kids. White wine cooled in the ice tubs too along with club soda and spring water and he was all set. The ladies could make spritzers if they wanted. At 1:00 pm he dragged out the tubs and placed them in the shade under the edge of the backyard trampoline. Each tub held a different one of the special beers. One was American and one was Québécois and different, yet they were identical in one interesting way. Both labels read, *Alcohol content: 15 %.*

Lucretia was seldom invited out and she was giddy with the invitation, even to a barbecue. Bully looked forward to the day also. It was a special occasion and he decided to do something equally special for himself. He rented a tuxedo. Charles Foster had looked so good in his Gucci Tom Ford in Bully's office, he wanted the same.

Malveena walked past the open office door and stopped in her tracks. She was sure it was Bully in there and equally sure it was a tuxedo but the incongruity of it jarred her. She walked in without leave and watched Bully strain at doing up the cummerbund which he had upside down.

"Crumbs Bully, crumbs."

"What?"

"Crumbs. You have the thing on upside down. The pleats go up. Catch the crumbs."

"Oh. Thanks. How do you like it? Nice huh?"

Malveena could not bring herself to tell him he looked good.

" Gregious, what on earth are you doing? A tuxedo?"

"What's wrong with that. If it's good enough for Mr. Amati it is good enough for me."

"Bully. Amati was an Italian violin maker. I think you mean Armani."

"Right. Fine, if he wants to make violins, that is his problem. I still think I look great in this Henry Ford. "

Malveena feared to continue but her curiosity got her.

"Bully, where are you going?"

"Not just me, everyone is going. Big barbecue you know. Me, Foster, Davy and little Red Hat, why, everyone."

Bully was slow about certain things and he had not grasped the obvious corollary that Malveena had not been invited. She said nothing and unlocked her office and sat behind her desk in the dark. She hated barbecues and hated everyone whom would be there more or less and would not attend had she been invited yet it bugged her she was not invited. *A few attempts to throttle their kids and people get testy. Apparently, they consider it unfriendly.* Malveena was going to the barbecue.

At home in front of the mirror, Bully held his chest up and modeled his tux and the effect was astounding. Bully was big and round and beautiful and Lucretia hated it. Porky ignored the tension between them. It was business as usual in the Gregious household. Porky could see another hour of this fussing before his mom was ready for her grand entrance at the Pilcher's. Same old stuff. They were still an hour from leaving.

"Mom, Dad, I am going to walk on over to Davy's place. Maybe I can help set up or something."

Lucretia was not really listening and she gave back an unhearing 'fine fine' and Porky was out the door. He could use the walk and maybe he could help cook stuff up on the grill. He would be early somewhere for once. The day was predicted to be the hottest of the year to date and as he walked, the air was filling with the density of the vapors climbing away from the heating ground. He arrived in good time just as Helen Craft and Mildred arrived. Mildred held the front door open as Helen twisted through, with a huge covered bowl filled with potato salad. She said hello to whomever was there as she came in. Janet answered from a distance and came toward the door. Harry poked his head around the kitchen door jamb. "Hi. Where's the man?"

Helen made an exasperated frown. "Hi Harry. Sorry. John got called in for a second job interview. Some kind of bridge or rail trestle project in New Guinea. He will be here when he is finished his meeting." Her speech was terse. The thought of another jungle expedition was too much.

Porky filtered through the house, away from the adult tensions and went out the back door into the yard. He walked to the trampoline and climbed up onto it and jumped a couple of times, hoping no-one was watching. It was fun but he was lousy at it so he gave up and swung down off the edge onto the grass. He spied the cream soda and grabbed one out of the ice. He ambled over to the glade made by the spread of the beauty bush in the corner of the yard. A flock of bush tits flushed up and twittered happily away to the next bush as if Porky had just done them a favor. Davy dragged over the last of the eight chairs for spot and sat with him.

They heard and more than that, they felt the burble of an old style external exhaust system from the street. It took over the air and agitated the water in the tubs into ripples that trickled over and ran down the galvanized sides. Foster gunned the engine of his Auburn a few more times to announce his arrival and to get reacquainted with the habits of his baby. Tilt swung open the passenger door and closed it with a perfect thunk. Together they entered by the side gate and looked around for Harry. They spotted him at the implement shed on the other side of the trampoline and walked to say hello. He had just finished the last lawn trimming before the party and was brushing the cuttings off his pant legs.

"Hi boys, you are just in time. How about a cold beer." He looked for their partners.

"Came on your own?"

Foster answered for the two of them. He was about to leave for a pipe trip to pick up his guest, as was Tilt.

"Thanks for the offer of the beer Harry, but I am on the way to get my guest in a few minutes. I will certainly have a beer when I get back. You Freddy?"

" 'Fraid not right now. I am doing the same thing. I will be back in short order and I shall do extravagant justice to the hops at that time. I won't be long." He spied Porky and Davy in the glade under the beauty bush.

"I see Leonard and David. Excuse me. I will go say hello."

Foster turned on his heel and headed through the gate and put the top down on the Auburn. With the top down, the air in the open car would be trapped and hot until he made some speed but Foster wanted the car ready to roll when the time came. He planned to amaze and astound and petrify his guest with a down shifting clutch popping 100 miles per hour spin through the countryside. He would not let him get behind the wheel.

Mildred headed across the lawn to say hello to Davy and Porky and Tilt followed along to share his plans. They all smiled and the common impulse was instantaneous. The ex-Delphics greeted each other.

"Tilt, Mercutio."

" Mercutio, Davidus."

" Davidus, Tilt."

Porky didn't get it but he could see the camaraderie and the feeling was good with him. Tilt spoke quietly to him.

"Leonard, I have a favor to ask. It will not take much of your time at the barbecue but I am bringing a guest a little later whom I would like you to entertain. I will have to leave him alone with you for just a few minutes. He will be wearing a himation, that is a, a..."

Porky interrupted. "Greek, is he? I know about those. Sure. Maybe he can teach me some Greek. You know, the himation is actually the...

"Thank you, Leonard. I will see you in a while."

The friends all smiled at Porky's open willingness and Tilt walked to the gate to find a private spot in the driveway. Davy followed. He knew what was needed. Mildred was close behind. Porky stayed in the shade and shook the cream soda to make it shoot.

Davy flipped open his leather sheath. "Here. You are going to need this."

Tilt took Davy's pipe and the receptiveness of the grip surprised him. Mildred looked around to be sure everyone else was occupied as she approached the big commando. She finger wiggled Tilt down to her height and cupped her hand and whispered in his ear. He nodded twice and smiled and winked. He was off to recruit Proclus. He would corral the other three great minds later. It was important for Proclus to arrive first.

Freddy Hill had been unsure of how to recreate the circumstance to be with Proclus. He had seen the man from some 75 yards distant and watched him

375

carefully but he had not heard his speech, nor was he aware of Proclus in history or his philosophical positions. Tilt had visited the C. A. Foster Memorial Library and he was amazed and pleased by what he read of Proclus the man. Proclus had ultimately succeeded Plato and expanded upon his tenets. Commando Freddy Hill planned to connect with Proclus by envisioning the passing of the intellectual torch between him and Plato. He would likewise weave in what he recalled of the physiognomy of Proclus. That should be manageable. It was.

Proclus turned away and up a cleft to his right and out of sight of the symposium he had fled. He had worn a heavy himation as a cloak in the style of the day and he was drenched with sweat. He re-attached the peronai at his shoulders to free the garment a little and continued west up the incline toward the setting sun. The sun was in his eyes and his head was down to guard his step when a shadow materialized and shot down the path to him. Something from nowhere towered close and directly above him. It was the man from the symposium. *How can this be. I saw him not one minute ago wearing his chlamys, in discourse with Aristotle, a hundred yards below us.*

Tilt was close to seven feet tall in his gleaming combat boots and Proclus' uphill line of sight made him seem taller. The dagger patches on his beret and shoulders were subsumed by his deep olive tone commando kit. His Fairbairn– Sykes fighting knife was on his hip and his carry pack on his back. Protected within Tilt's shadow, looking over Tilt's shoulder Proclus could see the constellation Orion, the constellation of the Giant Hunter, setting with the sun. Proclus looked at what must be Orion's dagger on Tilt's hip and his game bag was on his back. He saw the man before him, the one who a minute ago was 100 yards below him on the plateau in the olive grove. Surely this was he who had sat in symposium with the god children, the god himself, who now appeared before him out of the ether. This was the god from the constellation. The Hunter Giant. The Orion.

Tilt saw his wonderment and extended his hand to Proclus and spoke evenly. " I wonder, have you seen Elysium? Would it please you to do so, to come with me, fair Proclus? For a time, at least?"

Carried by the setting sun against the backdrop of the constellation Orion, Tilt and Proclus traveled together hand in hand. Golden peace carried them and

Proclus saw the Borstal stream of Okeanos, and felt the good life free from toil. He gave himself up to the spinning presence of the honored gods as he traveled the shore of the timeless ocean into a land forbidden of melancholy and filled with ease.

Charles Foster was looking forward very much to renewing acquaintances. He sighted his dull patina-green copper pipe from the driveway at the Pilcher home and the high sky responded to his intention with vigor. A thousand gulls flew in a subtly diminishing circle a mile up and their closing vortex helped him collimate his intention. He was sublimely consumed by his concentration on the surf and the man and the island and the era and he flashed into a hard-blown sandblast on a cold rocky prominence. He recognized nothing. He had not seen the westerly exposure of the island of Elba but he doubted it was like this. This flora was sparse and bent and the view was more punitive than alluring. The sun was setting on his back. He faced east out of the wind but where the devil was he. His view led down an extreme slope of impenetrable bush to a precipitous continuation into the sea. There was no beach to be seen in the miles of coastline his eye followed from his vantage point. Foster turned into the sun behind him and a man was stripping olives from branches he fed with one hand into a machine whose crank he turned with the other. Foster's shadow cast was behind him and the other man did not see him until he spoke.

"Excuse me."

"Foster!"

Bonaparte wore a Phrygian cap and had his sleeves rolled up. His hands and forearms were covered with sap and juice. At the sound of their voices two redcoats tore up the path and Napoléon waved them away. He could see the regret at his condition etched on Foster's face.

"Do not be sad my friend. This too will pass. You have a need of me?"

Foster thought the phrase a strange construction. The great ones always assumed they would be sought out for action.

"No. I have come to give you a respite from this monotony. A party. Pleasant people, good weather and good drink. Nothing more and nothing grand. If this simple interlude suits you, come. If it does not, then goodbye and good luck. I am sorry for your state."

Napoléon grinned and shook Foster by his shoulders, man to man.

"Your interlude is welcome and it suits me admirably. You may guess this island of St. Helena is not the center of polite society. It is a soulless stone set in a grey sea, thousands of miles from civility. Wait here a few minutes. I will clean up and put on my imperial best. After all, you say it is a party, un événement social." Charles looked at the sun.

"You must be ready to leave within half an hour or we cannot go. We depend on the sun."

The Emperor of the French returned in twenty minutes. Foster placed his right hand on Napoléon's shoulder and sighted into the remains of the low reddening sun. With a martial flash it spiraled them away from the ridged rock called St. Helena, inside a loose and widely sweeping counterclockwise corkscrew. It tightened and brightened and funneled them away from the island it rejected and took the light with it and left the rock behind in the dark. As it made the equator it flashed to heat and gathered massive dextrorotatory energy into a new spin to the right. The Imperial Legion of Honor lavallière hung importantly on Napoléon's neck and the light made silly reflections off it. Consciousness and Foster's intention carried them in a projectile of glistening brightness. Together and free, they obliterated vast oceanic expanse and the breakers in Borstal bay became victorious cannons to their ears as they swooped low along the beach ahead of the climb to the barbecue.

Davy and Mildred huddled in the Pilcher driveway. "Mildred, who do you want to have here? Or, do you want anyone I guess is more like it. Don't feel you have to do it."

She pushed her Balaclava back off her forehead. "Thanks for that Davy. I am fine with it and I have two people in mind. I think I can collect them if I intend correctly. But I saw you give your pipe to Tilt."

"Yes. I did. I will go later. My friends will need some chaperoning. If you want to wait, you can use it after Tilt returns, otherwise we can see if my Mom will let you use hers. No guarantees." Davy sensed Mildred was keen to get on with it.

Janet was in the kitchen squeezing deviled egg mixture from a tube into the waiting egg halves. Davy reached for a filled one and ducked a swat and laughed but he didn't get the egg.

"Leave those alone. Go outside."

378

Her copper pipe was drying in the dish rack and was newly washed and polished for the big day. She did not like fingerprints on it.

Davy looked at the pipe and at his Mom. Janet looked at Davy and at the pipe and back to Davy, who was waiting. He said nothing and Janet stopped her squeezing of the icing bag and morphed into her 'out with it' look.

Davy lost the contest. "Not for me, Mom. For Mildred. Tilt has mine."

Janet shook her head and pointed with the icing bag toward the door.

"Fine. Take the pipe. Get out of here. Go trampolining or something."

Mildred had never been able to get the tie-dyed girl lying in the rain and mired in the muck at Woodstock out of her mind. There were half a million stoners to wade through if she was going to connect with her now. And the rain. If it is the wrong day, rain. She would see how her first traipse into the human scavenger hunt went and then consider the girl. The man she was after presented operational problems of his own. He was Randolph Arbuthnot Scrivener, correspondent for the Times of London who was working smack in the middle of the terror of the French revolution. *Make one wrong move around the guillotine and you could kiss your head goodbye which is a trick in itself.* She could not risk the marauding death squads of the Jacquerie.

Scrivener had mentioned the Royal Mail packet boat and his frequent comings and goings. She would intend a rendezvous with him there, on the packet boat. She remembered his face and voice and mannerisms perfectly and Mildred formed that part of the intention easily. His new location on the boat was the trick but she would suffer no more rampaging mobs.

Mildred came to reality very quickly in a cold and queasy sun. Right and left and round and down in every nose diving, trough sliding possibility of a gyroscope, the boat persisted with its nauseating stomach-turning pitches. In total relaxation there in front of her, in a slat wooden deck chair, sat her target. Scrivener had lashed his deck chair between two twelve-inch tackle blocks and he basked in the smell of the sea under a struggling sun. The insane chop of the channel told him he was homing. He had a dormant black square ended cheroot clamped between his teeth and he was wet from the sea spray. He loved the sea and eschewed the cabin whenever he could. He sat with a rug on his knees and a bag from which he was tossing bits of breakfast to the herring gulls. He watched the spinning wave tops while the gulls swooped over him in their short, side slipping arcs and shrieked orders for food. Scrivener always kept back tidbits from breakfast to feed them and he was just tossing the last bits. He spied Mildred and she stepped forward quickly to receive his outstretched hand for something to hold on to on the swinging deck.

He patted her hand. "You are the young lady of the Paris doorway, aren't you? Yes, you are, I am sure of it." He was pleased with himself to have remembered and he smiled broadly and Mildred returned the pleasant smile.

"My dear, I did not see you embark but you have made a wise choice. Wise choice. You are right to leave France. The terror is too much. It will subside in time but you do not want it to take you with it."

He was exactly as Mildred recalled. Today his colors were even brighter. The orange brocade waistcoat of the Paris time was now replaced by one done in a brilliant violet, contrasted against a yellow silk lined suit jacket, done with black brocade. He was a bit more rotund than at their last meeting and Mr. Scrivener seemed more satisfied to the same degree.

On this trip to France, Scrivener had acquired a plumbago pencil for the first time and he was thrilled with it. It was a new invention from one of Napoléon's scientists and he was aching to make notes with it. The graphite pencil required no ink, did not leak and needed only simple sharpening to expose the next bit of writing surface. For the sharpening purpose he had added a small Italian stiletto to his outfit. Its purple cloth sheath matched his waistcoat and it had an acuminated point for good stabbing if need be.

Mildred had her man and she wasted no time. "Mr. Arbuthnot,.."

"Scrivener my dear, Arbuthnot Scrivener at your service."

"Sorry sir. Mr. Scrivener how would you like a story for the Times. A story, a story so fantastic your London Times readers will hardly believe it. You will experience it yourself and even then, you may not believe it either. That is why I am here to see you. You are invited to a party that is out of this world. Shall we go?"

"Why bless my soul, indeed we shall. I shall sharpen my new plumbago when we get there. Let them break open the ale, let the frolic begin, Scrivener is coming."

Mildred held his hand firmly and sighted her lens-less copper telescope by putting one end through her lens-less spectacles opening and swinging it to the sun. The joviality of the happy Arbuthnot stoked the energy of the pipe to party fever and it poised in a gull competing vortex high above the Pilcher yard. There was a singing glee in the smiling consciousness as Mildred spun home with her happy companion.

Harry was testing the heat of the barbecue and Porky volunteered to sample the first hot dog off the rack. It was perfect. He walked with it and his second cream soda back to the glade and sat at the head of the arc of eight chairs. Davy was second to assess the hot dogs and he came and sat on Porky's right hand. They heard a crackle and a sort of exhalation and saw Tilt standing there with a tall man in a himation who appeared to be fresh from Tussaud's. He was a man in wax looking at the glade. *The Greek,* concluded Porky.

Proclus began to leave the pleasantness of his uncritical agglutination and saw that thing which only Elysium could offer him. A symposium, waiting for Proclus.

Tilt recognized that Proclus was lucid and they moved forward. They approached the glade but did not enter. Porky lounged and brandished his hot dog. Proclus recognized Davy from the Delphic grove. *The god child and another with him.* Tilt made the introductions.

"Gentlemen, may I present philosopher Proclus. Proclus, may I present Davidus and Lork...Plenar... Porcrates." Porky said nothing because he was confused and Proclus admired the aplomb of one so young. *His name is Athenian. And regal. Porcrates.*

Proclus looked hungry and Davy played the host and handed him his untouched hot dog. "Proclus, welcome to our barbecue. You would have a cold drink, I believe. Please sit. There, beside Lenn... Porcrates."

Davy went to get another hot dog and a drink for him and Proclus. Tilt was at the ice tubs inserting ten unscathed bottles of red Kalambaki from his knapsack. He shrugged, "Mildred."

Davy knew the Kalambaki was what Proclus would like. He had been denied it at Delphi. Tilt surrendered the pipe to Davy. Davy dropped it in his sheath and had Tilt open the wine for him.

"Thank you, Mr. Tilt. I will be back shortly with two guests."

"See you when you return. We can trade off again." They exchanged nods. Tilt opened himself a Sly Fox as Davy carried the Kalambaki to Proclus.

381

Porcrates was holding forth as loquacious Lenny and Proclus was enthralled. He received the Kalambaki with thanks. Tilt sat on the other side of Porcrates and his head spun a little with his first draught of the ice cold fifteen percent beer.

Davy walked out his side gate onto the front lawn and eyed the sky. Mrs. Williams spotted him scoping with his telescope out of her front window. She had bought him a fine pair of brown corduroy pants to replace the too short jeans which the poor boy was wearing. The cords were right there on her table. She glanced back out the window and he was gone.

Davy arrived back on H.M.S. Victory at the right time. It was eight bells on the midday watch and the crew was changing. He was looking for Spider and Bert. The smell of powder was up strong from the main gun deck and the wind was changing. Hard aport rang out and the Victory dug in on the starboard heading and the rigging whistled as the sails snapped full. *Ah. Now she has the weather gage. She has the tactical advantage.* Davy was back in battle mode. Spider saw Davy first. He shrieked with pleasure.

"Davy! Davy lad." Bert heard Spider's call and he threw back his head and keaked. Davy had never heard such a cackle. They surrounded him with hugs and rib breaking slaps on the back. The sea was heavy and Davy began two stepping to keep his balance. Bert laughed at the lubber and Davy agreed with a chuckle. "Listen you two. You just finished your watch? How much time do you have?"

Bert answered. "A hour, old cock. We has a hour for ourselfs."

"I am throwing a party. A big celebration with my friends and parents. Good food and good drink and safe on land. I am here to invite you. So? What do you say? You won't be caught back late."

The three mates spat on their hands and sealed the agreement. Bert and Spider had no idea how Davy was going to do it and they did not care. They were willing. The three ran to the fo'c'sle deck and Davy sighted his copper pipe to the sun. He could not stay on target as the Victory pounded down the troughs with the push from the wind at the stern. Davy counted the time to the heights of the troughs. It was eight seconds. He would sight on the up-roll like the gunners did.

They entered the next deep trough and Davy began to count. *One, two..*

"Now! Hold hands and cinch your grip and don't let go no matter what.

Quick Spider! Take mine! Bert! Grab Spider!" Spider crushed Davy's hand as instructed and Bert did the same for Spider. *Six, seven, eight* and precisely on the height of the up-roll, at four, post meridiem, strong maritime sun filled the lumen of the pipe and hammered its approval of the seamen. They exceeded the clouds in their flight and imagined a place called home from somewhere above the day. The three friends landed near the implement shed twenty feet from the trampoline. Spider and Bert had a death grip on each other and the circulation in Davy's hand was mostly gone when he pried free from Spider. Janet was looking out from the kitchen sink window as she unwrapped some bacon for the hamburgers and saw Davy and his chums. *What nice boys. So well behaved. They are not rough, they are hardly moving.*

Bert came out of it before Spider and his only words were, "Well I be pitchkettled!"

He began to stagger immediately. His crew had been on the sea for ten weeks and they could walk the deck but not the ground. He made his way under the trampoline into the shade and half rolled and sat down. He was not conspicuous there and it suited him. Spider left the agglutination stupidly and when he recognized Bert he toddled to safety out of sight and collapsed against a perspiring galvanized tub. The men from the Victory owned their private spot close to the beer. They passed the libations to the folks as they came through one by one. Harry kept alert to pop the corks. Davy stuffed them with hot dogs and potato salad. Otherwise, they helped themselves to the tubs. Two beautiful eight-year gulls had smelled the cooking and had landed near Bert. He toasted one with his second Sly Fox and it bobbed twice in response with a little gurp noise.

Chapter 25: The Menagerie Grows

Tilt received the pipe from Davy. He began to focus on his next sojourn, but before he could contemplate the next move, something changed. It was not sudden but an energy seemed to be building and it silenced the talk. It was not electric, it was more than that. It was momentous. There was a tremendous crack and the smell of voltage and disruption. There before them stood Charles Abernathy Foster holding hands with the Emperor of the French, Napoléon Bonaparte.

Charles Foster was into reality and aware of the surroundings at the Pilcher household in seconds. He stayed in his position and looked in an inspecting way at Napoléon who appeared haughty even when he was trapped and immobile in a suspended state. It was Foster's first opportunity to see le petit caporal deprived of his magnetic emanations. The Corsican was built of intention and the light had felt it.

Before Napoléon could become clear headed and be aware of his surroundings, Mildred arrived from afar with a broad smile and a slight bounce, holding hands with Randolph Arbuthnot Scrivener. He was resplendent and beaming and it seemed to him they had gone from the pitch of one ship to the heave of another but that was fine and he need not concern himself with it. The horizon rose and fell before him and the ship rail seemed fence-like but ship designs were not his problem anyway. He felt for his notepad by reflex and it was there and it could be there or not be there without consequence. Mildred was out of suspension in the trail in an instant. They had landed in the middle of the trampoline and Scriveners weight had put them into a nice bounce. She stopped and rolled off and let him simmer down on his own.

Janet Pilcher went over the ingredients again. The vanilla ice was in the freezer. She had the vanilla pods to split, the peaches and the raspberries. Lemon juice! She flung open the refrigerator door and it was in the door rack. She tapped the box of confectioner's sugar on the counter. *All set. Let's do it!*

Through the kitchen window she saw Mildred return and Janet was at her side in a flash. She ignored the yellow and violet man going up and down on the trampoline. She held out her hand and Mildred plopped the pipe in it. Mrs.

Pilcher had deviltry in her eyes.

"Mrs. Pilcher, is my Mom in on this, this whatever you are up to?"

She lifted an eyebrow and tilted her head which said yes and she rushed inside with the pipe and grabbed Helen.

"Helen, where will he be?"

"Either at the Ritz or on the Imperator with Kaiser Wilhelm or maybe with Jenny Melba but if we just go for him with a positive attitude we are fine either way, aren't we?"

Janet agreed. They had the positive attitude of two white wine spritzers each and they were fine.

They sneaked outside and stood beside Foster's Auburn. The deserted front drive suited them perfectly. Helen put her hand on Janet's shoulder and Janet put her head back to fill the pipe with the sun and Mrs. Williams saw her. That family certainly loves astronomy. She reached for the cords to run over and give them to Janet for Davy but when she looked back out the window, Helen and Janet were gone.

Lieutenant Colonel Fred Hill of the Royal Marines, Third Commando Brigade, saw someone resembling Napoléon materialize about the same time as a violet and yellow brocaded florid faced man arrived to bounce on the trampoline, but Tilt was unphased. He left on his mission to Greece.

The south wind swept up hot from the Pleistos Valley below and flowed through the olive grove and up the tilt of the plateau toward the reflective faces of the Phaedriades. Artimes the scribe sat upwind of Socrates, Plato and Aristotle. He was worried he had not heard their windblown dialogue well enough for perfect transcription and in addition to that, the wine had not been good. The Athiri had been acceptable but the two reds presented by Dartis the steward had disappointed. The thinkers were in foul moods. They stood together looking toward the bay of Corinth in the distance, freshening their faces in the sea wind. The day was particularly hot and each of the other philosophers had been particularly stupid.

Artimes was pleased to have a break from the writing. He closed his eyes and massaged them with his fingertips. He moved his neck and stretched out his cramped left writing hand. A fluster of yellow breasted great tits burst up around the narrow canyon and startled him with their alarm calls. Ten feet from

Artimes stood Commando Tilt in his olive drab war attire. Tilt looked past Artimes toward the backs of the philosophers and spied one of Dartis' amphora with dribbles of red wine drying on it. Artimes saw the look and waggled his finger and pinched his nose. Tilt got the message. The wine had been poor.

Tilt approached the seating at the symposium. Socrates turned and with a pleased look he gestured for Tilt to sit. As Socrates approached, Tilt asked, "How are you?"

Socrates was confused. He was often asked, whether he was, that is, did he exist, or why he was, that is, the meaning of life, but never at any time, how, he was. He had never turned his mind to how he was. They sat beside each other and Plato and Aristotle joined them. Tilt knew the answer before he asked his question. " I see you have left your wine unfinished. Kalambaki? " He knew it was not. Plato shook his head.

"No. What we had was not good. I am embarrassed by what we have to offer."

"Then I have a suggestion. Would you like to come with me to a symposium? You know Davidus I believe, as well as Mercutio. There are others and in addition," he laughed at the coincidence, "we have red Kalambaki. I do not know if you will be invited to sit, but, there is the wine." He laughed again. They laughed too. Of course, they would be invited to sit.

They did as they were instructed by the eminent Tilt and walked to the edge of the precipice and squinted at the shimmer from the gulf of Corinth and held hands while Tilt attached himself at the end. He mumbled something they could not quite hear to imply some mysticism in his actions. He postured into the waiting light and together they were taken.

Tilt relaxed in the bath of warming intention when something chilled. There was a dappled dimness fluttering around and it settled on his face. He resisted the degradation with all his energy, yet the dapples faded to grey and one by one they melded with a surrounding swarming blackness and Tilt was within it and helpless. His grip on the transit in consciousness was gone. The combined energy of the other three had hijacked his intent and now they were on a trail of their own. Their collective strength of will did not change Tilt's destination, but it reshaped a pathway which knew their desires. Plato, Aristotle and Socrates disagreed on much, but not on the mysteries of the underworld. Of those they had a common need and they would satisfy it now. Even so, Tilt struggled to break their wills.

The blackness paled into a troubled rivuletting vapor as worry and woe pulled them on. They floated above the river Acheron which they would one day cross when newly dead. The land of Erebus awaited them on the other side. They spun to lie on their backs with hanging arms and began to fall and fall and a voice spoke 'soon' to them all and they sped in a hard arc over the boatman Charon who would ferry them across that river and he raised his wet head and whispered 'soon'. The river roared on and became a molten torrent as it coiled around the earth and plunged deep into the abyss of Tartarus, a place of torment and anguish.

Three large minds gripped Tilt with their dark and morbid intention and they began to follow the glowing molten torrent into oblivion. He battled against them with all his strength when suddenly he was torn by a strange conflicting surge. Another energy was at work. It was a vile and villainous energy which demanded them all for itself.

The grasping hands of Thanatos, the messenger of Hades steered them away from the abyss. It was he, and he alone who would form their choice for death. It would not be left to them he triumphed, but it was too late. They were too far west and his dank ether of permanence no longer held sway. A suggestion of grey insinuated itself into the void and gradually it spun into a growing amber. The heroic quality of the four travelers had preceded them into the netherworld. The incorruptible hand of fair-haired Rhadamanthus spread over them as they westered over the Isles of the Blessed and into strong new light. They were at the western edge of the earth and above the Elysian plain where life is easiest for mankind. There, Rhadamanthus ruled in strength and they believed the voice saying welcome and they passed over soft parkland and heard hope filled music and Tilt felt his control return. They landed as one, facing the glade where Porcrates and Proclus held counsel with each other. Tilt allowed the weary trio their recovery in their own time and headed straight for the beer. He bent low to greet Spider and Bert and looked into the ice water in the tubs. "One of each, please."

Janet and Helen landed softly and quietly on a deep luxurious carpet. Above them, a huge illuminated glass dome centered a large rectangular room lit by 16

387

sconce lights. Twelve arches were closed by curtained round topped glass doors to wall the room and they stretched to an eighteen-foot ceiling. There was a sixteen-foot-wide fireplace at one end of the room and the periphery of the floor was surrounded by groupings of upholstered and leather chairs and small round tables. They had no idea where they were. They were alone in the room. A strange motion queasiness came over both of them that they could not figure. A deafening blast and another and another from all around them answered their questions. They were on the Imperator, the largest cruise ship in the world and the pride of the German fleet. It was 1913. A single red jacketed steward sped past them with no intention of stopping. Helen waylaid him.

" Chef? "

The man did not stop and pointed a wagging finger back in the direction from which he had come. He increased his pace with no apparent desire to be called back to where he had been. The ladies walked toward the shouting. There they saw the great man, the Chef of all chefs, chef to royalty, chef to the famous and a chef for the ages, George Auguste Escoffier. He was instructing his staff in no uncertain terms and although he was surprised to see Janet and Helen he liked an audience to his greatness.

"Yes? What is it? Be quick about it." He played with an end of his immense pure white moustache was as wide as his face.

Janet hesitated and Helen took over.

"Ah. Chef." She made a small bow with her eyes closed. "We are emissaries. Our patron the Emperor, who, for both your and our sakes shall go unnamed, desires your company and your service."

She gestured to Janet.

"He is the guest of this lady, in her home."

It was on such emperors he had built his reputation but solely in grand settings such as the great ship Imperator. He stated flatly, "I have never worked in a private home."

"Yes of course. It is difficult. I understand why you have never. I am sure the Emperor will understand it too. It is not your fault. He was misinformed. He was told that you could do anything that grande cuisine demanded. He, I, we, did not expect it to be untrue. I apologize for asking. Janet shall we go?"

"Really! You woman! Of course I can do anything! I am George Auguste

Escoffier! Chef!" He put his head back and crossed his arms and began to breath very fast through his nose with his lips pursed.

"Yes. Your reputation is good but, well, I understand. You fear exposure in a small kitchen setting. The emperor was hoping for your Peach Melba, but fine, we shall look elsewhere for the right man.

"My reputation is good? Good, you said? My reputation is good? The right man you say! Madame, you have found the right man and you do not see it. I am not only the right man for this, I am more than that. I am the perfect man." With his declaration some of the purple left his face.

"Oh. Good. Then you will come. Janet held out her hand and began to walk away very slowly so he had to reach to take it. He did.

Napoléon stood alone on the lawn as Foster walked to Harry to have him uncork his cold Boquebiere. He looked back to check on his comrade in the center of the yard. Napoléon heard the pop of the cork clearly. He had released himself from the control of the suspension faster than anyone had. He did not reveal he was lucid. He moved his eyes to survey his surroundings but maintained his posture.

In front of him he saw the bouncing Scrivener lose the last of his bounce and blink into the day. Scrivener's face was red and happy. His loose straight cut bright yellow coat was brocaded with black curlicues. Purple cloth covered buttons led up each of his lapels. His wide purple cuffs had two buttons and on his left side he carried his notepad inside a large flap covered bulging pocket. His red hair was windblown and tangled from the packet boat and he loosened his stylish yellow fringed cravat. Arbuthnot Scrivener's waistcoat was blinding violet and made of silk and it strained over his belly. The curlicue coat terminated at his knees above bright violet spatter-dashes covering his legs down to his soft black leather shoes which he closed with yellow buckles. He could not see a way down from the trampoline.

Napoléon strode forward and offered a hand. He wished to assess the potential of the trampoline for reconnoitering by bouncing high enough to see the lay of the land. He was already calculating escape directions where the lack of shadow would betray him.

Scrivener was pleased to have his assistance and he thundered to earth off the rim of the trampoline. He was removing his notepad before he landed on his feet. He knew who the man was.

"I say. Randolph, Arbuthnot, Scrivener, correspondent for the Times of London, at your service. May we have a chat?"

He and Napoléon walked to the beading cold tubs beneath the trampoline where Bert dispensed a frosty Sly Fox Instigator Eisdoppelbock to Scrivener and handed Napoléon a paper cup full of chilled red Kalambaki wine.

Mildred was pleased with her recruitment of Scrivener and he was enjoying himself at the barbecue. He was interviewing everything that moved and scribbling furiously with his new plumbago pencil. He was dressed in layers against the weather of the packet boat and the day was becoming very hot. The graphite from sharpening his pencil had blackened his hands and he had smeared it along his temples where he wiped the perspiration. He was now well into his second Sly fox, which for easy access he carried in his notebook pouch.

Mildred returned her focus to the girl at Woodstock and sighted Davy's pipe above her. The rising air was at high velocity from the heat of the land and it added force to the obstruction currents coming from the escarpment to the south. Mildred could see a galaxy of gulls, just specks of pristine white at thousands of feet above her. They spun into a columnar formation and made a perfect target for her eye. They collaborated.

She arrived at Woodstock in the sun as she intended. She was close to the spot where she and Davy had seen the girl in the muck but she was not there. Mildred wanted to kick herself. There were now one million people at the festival and what had she been thinking. It was an impossible idea.

" I know you! I remember that woolly red stocking thing on your head. I saw you and you friend doing the jangle walk behind Jimi Hendrix." It was the muck girl. She put her hand on her mouth and laughed behind it.

"Uh, yes. That was pretty weak."

They laughed together and Mildred asked. "Want to go on a trip?"

" Well I have just come back from one, so, absolutely. By the way my name is Tie. Last name, Dye. Tie Dye." She was serious and Mildred nodded. Tie removed what used to be a flower from her hair and stuck the stem through the wool of Mildred's balaclava as an adornment. She smiled and closed her eyes and moved her shoulders around to the music playing in her head. Mildred took her hand firmly and Tie began to dance. They bopped away into the sun and arched along impossible rainbows and came down into Davy's menagerie. Mildred returned the pipe to Davy and came back to watch over her friend as she came to herself.

"So Tie, how was the trip for you?"

"Whoo. Full chromadelic. Right up there." Mildred could never have said it better.

Tie Dye spied Napoléon immediately upon leaving her viscous suspension which she had experienced as very little different from her usual lucidity. Also, it did not strike her she was approaching someone who had been dead for some centuries. He was standing in the sun near the implement shed looking at the wine he wanted, in a paper cup. Foster had stepped away to get himself a Boquebiere and he hand gestured to Harry that he needed uncorking.

Tie Dye drifted over and said hello. "Hi. I am Tie. Aquarius." She giggled. "You don't have to tell me your name. You are famous. You are Napoléon. French guy, right?" She looked him up and down and wondered what his Imperial Legion of Honor would look like on her neck. She hit him with her hip.

"You are not short. I read that you were short five foot whatever. You are not. Why are you not short?"

Napoléon looked for help. He could not see Foster and he had wine in a paper cup. " I am not short because you are accustomed to English feet. English feet are smaller. The true foot of measurement is the French foot which is bigger. French feet are longer."

Tie checked his boots carefully. His feet did not look long and still he was not short. She looked up to his face. He could not tolerate it.

"Excuse me, my dear. I have to ...walk."

Miss Dye headed for the invitation made by the clinking under the trampoline and crawled in and sat between the tubs out of the sun. Bert made her a spritzer.

Napoléon headed for the kitchen back door, in need of a washroom and a place to hang his jacket and lavallière. He entered the kitchen to see Janet and Helen looking guilty and pleased. They had gotten every pot and pan in the house out and spread them on the counters. Studiously, they were examining a man in a chef's attire standing at the counter of the kitchen island. He was facing the window to the yard and swaying blearily and holding on. Napoléon hung his jacket and medal on the coat hook at the door. He was wet from perspiration. He approached Janet, looking down at his wine. He lifted his head and asked, "Crystal, madame?"

"No, that is not me. I don't know a Crystal; my name is Janet."

Over Janet's shoulder a now wide awake and truculent Chef bellowed at the sweating kitchen help. " Drink that down and get over here. Vite." He pointed.

" Bring that pot and find the lid!" Napoléon threw back the wine and dropped the cup and looked-for escape but Chef was on him like lightning and threw him at the pot. "Vite!" The emperor obeyed in shock and his apprenticeship in Janet's kitchen began with Escoffier Peach Melba.

Harry had just finished his first low alcohol Sly Fox and the 15% was beginning to pay dividends. It seemed Helen and Janet had some kitchen help and he couldn't see Davy at this moment. He began to hum an old tune.

The sun had moved some in the hour and on the protected side of the implement shed away from the house it beat and bounced off the white anodized aluminum surface. Davy was on his way to retrieve his friends from Botany Bay. He wanted no part of the brutal Kelly or the hardnosed Smits. He had to be careful and he chose the scrub territory near Chukker's campsite where the four were last together.

He intended for and landed at Dobber first. Dobber was on his way back from Chukker's deep rock cove to captivity in the Hyde Park barracks. Davy intercepted him.

"Blank! You froze me bones. I didn't hear you." Dobber fingered his gold earring and felt for the leather thong on his neck as he always did when he was nervous. He thought Davy had followed him.

"Dobber, I need you to stop here. Right here, for just a few minutes. Please." Dobber agreed for Blank. He needed the rest anyway.

Davy intended to find Chukker and Simon together somewhere on the trail. He ran back over the last rise and out of Dobber's sight. Blank sighted with his dulled copper pipe and landed right in front of his two wandering friends. They were two miles west of Dobber and they did not bat an eye that with a small zap Blank had appeared from nothing right in front of them. If Blank wanted to do that he could do that. They had been west and they had filled their tucker bags with the Pituri chew they made. They said nothing and waited for Blank to speak.

" Come."

They ran behind him, slowing their usual pace to match his, happy to see young Blank safe and well after his walkabout. They came upon Dobber in short order, sleeping soundly against a ghost gum tree fifty yards or so from where Davy had left him. He heard their steps and sat up with a smile at the three of them.

Blank filled them in. " I am inviting you to enjoy good company, good drink and good food. What do you say?"

Simon asked. "Where are we going Blank?"

" My house. We will have beer and eat some hot dogs."

Dobber liked the beer idea but the look on Chukkers face was horrible. His English was not nearly as good as Simon's and he hoped he had misunderstood what Blank had said. Simon blurted with scarcely contained anger.

" Blank! Do not ask this of us. No. It is not to be done. Our kinship system sometimes even gives kin names to our dogs. They are our cousins, our brothers Blank. Blank, no. What, where, what kind of place is it. We do not care to walk it. We will help you here. Stay with us."

Davy realized then they had taken him literally to mean to eat dogs on the hoof. He should have known better. Simon and Chukker's society had few words and they spoke directly without secondary phrases like 'hot dogs' to describe a wiener and a bun. They had no fanciful terminology. After fifteen minutes of slow and careful backtracking and explanation of the party at his house they relaxed. Perhaps Blank did not come from a land of devils after all. Davy asked both Chukker and Simon to bring their stash of Pituri. They could share it with many at the barbecue. The two Bidjigal men were pleased at that. It was the thing to do, to share. Dobber was assured the beer was cold and plentiful. They linked to Davy's hand and trusted the light.

John Craft had finished his meeting and he sat on Janet's back steps having a beer with Helen. Escoffier had been instructing incessantly in the kitchen behind them but now he was silent. Janet was demonstrating to Chef and Napoléon how to make deviled eggs.

Davy and his friends arrived from Australia with a clockwise spin just inside the side gate, connected with firmly locked hand grips. Dobber and Chukker and Simon stood frozen in the deepest and most rigid agglutination. Davy made his way toward the ice tubs and finagled a cup of beer from Bert. It was cold and they touched cups together like they did on the Victory. Harry came over and unloaded a bag of ice into the water.

"Hi Davy."

"Hi Dad."

"How's the beer?"

"Good Dad, thanks."

"Good. No more." Harry walked back to the barbecue, singing a little more loudly.

Socrates, Plato and Aristotle settled into their clarified environment looking directly at Porcrates and Proclus. This was surely the symposium Tilt had promised. But there was Proclus. Seated. They realized then it was Porcrates dominating the proceedings. Yes. Another of the god children. He has asked Proclus to sit.

They waited. It was improper to request to sit. They waited.

Lucretia had completed the finishing touches on her trowel work. With the air conditioner blasting in the car, Bully was still hot in his tuxedo but he was determined to wear it. There was just one car in Pilcher's driveway when they arrived. It was Foster's Auburn. As they came to a stop on the grass boulevard, Lucretia saw what could have been the back end of Malveena's Bentley disappear left, around the corner at the end of the block. She said nothing to Bully and waited for him to come around and open the door for her.

Bully and Lucretia entered by the side gate. Lucretia steamed ahead with her best red carpet walk past three statues in her way and smiled the star smile but no-one important saw it except for Scrivener. She stopped and stood in an aggravated stance waiting to be acknowledged. Scrivener looked past her and spied the man in evening dress walking behind her and he made for him to get the scoop. Porky saw his parents also. He spoke to Proclus while Socrates, Plato and Aristotle listened from where they stood outside the glade.

"Proclus, my Mom is so mean to my Dad. Mean. All the time."

"Well, that might not be all bad." Porky did not understand that.

"You see Porcrates, there is very little difference between meanness and love.

394

They are both generated independent of the receiver and they are both done for the purposes of the doer. Love carries a satisfaction in what it represents, or in what need it satisfies in the holder of it to manifest a judgement the receiver deserves it. Meanness is no different. It also belongs only to the holder of it, it is the same judgement that the receiver deserves it and the same doer can change the wind in two seconds and dish out one or the other to the same person. They are the same. Neither one of them exists. And the use of the one non-existent thing is sometimes for nothing more than to demonstrate the other non-existent thing."

The big three had heard every syllable clearly and they now saw Proclus differently. They had not known he was capable of something like that which they had just heard. He deserved to sit with the god child.

The senior philosophers were hungry and thirsting for Kalambaki red but given what they had inflicted on Proclus over the years, to ask to sit was anathema. Porky had his third cream soda on the table in front of him and Proclus was on his third low alcohol 15% Sly fox and feeling philosophical. They each had a hot dog in hand. Porky looked up at the three anxious men and over at Proclus. All Proclus could think to say to Aristotle, Plato and Socrates was, "I see you."

Plato addressed Socrates. "That is a marvelous thing to say. It really is the essence of simplicity yet deep. To see. To comprehend, to gather all together and assess it quickly, to have made an instantaneous judgment and come to an encompassing conclusion. Perhaps I have misjudged Proclus. And I am hungry." Porcrates saw the uncertainty on the faces of the three stately men.

" Please gentleman, please come and sit with us. Would you like a hot dog?" Porky held up his half hot dog and wiggled it in the air.

The three elders entered the symposium and sat with humility. Porcrates addressed them together. "I will get you what you need." He waggled the hot dog. "One of these and some Kalambaki red. I think you prefer it. Proclus my friend. Another Sly Fox?"

"Thank you no, Porcrates. Please bring me a Boquebiere Apico."

The three older men looked at each other and Plato spoke for the three of them. "We will have the same."

Malveena Drago made her eighth left turn and pulled over to the curb.

Foster's and Bully's cars were at the house. That was the barbecue for sure. She had been around the Pilcher block twice but had not had the courage to crash the party in the face of their fury. She wanted to be there. Perhaps she should use another way. Like Woodstock. She could see them. They could not really see her. She could hear them, and they could hear her only dimly if at all. But today she had dressed to kill and she looked terrific. Once more the thrift shop had made Malveena wonderful. Should she waste that?

The air conditioning was too cold in the Bentley Arnage and she had made a mistake with her boots. They were too hot. She turned off the engine and ran the windows down and let the breeze blow through. Malveena opened the door and swung her feet out and worked the boots off her swelling feet and tore a nail. She sucked her finger. The blasted things had grips to snug them on, but getting them off was a different animal. She put her head back and closed her eyes. Here she was alone, sitting outside the happy party just around the corner. Somehow, she always managed to trick herself out of the good things. She manoeuvred the headrest and tipped the seat back and slept. Dreams came fast and strange and howling. No matter how they morphed from one fantasy into the next one the theme was wolves. Always at each other, always trying for dominance, always nudging Malveena with their bristled shoulders. Competing. Pushing. Slathering. The one you feed. The one you feed. The one you feed.

Davy stood at the gate protecting his vulnerable friends. They had not yet left their heavy suspension nor become aware of their surroundings. Dimly they saw odd men dressed strangely in a glade and they could do that if they wanted to. Someone dressed like a red-capped parrot was jumping up and down on a stretched skin and so why not. They saw the staff sitting out of the way under the skin and serving the others, so that was their place and fine but what they did not see was the impact into reality coming like a tsunami. A blast of spinning heat seared into them like the back of a frying pan and they gasped and tottered back with the impact. Chukker and Simon dropped to a fighting crouch and flashed their woomeras into throwing position. Davy jumped in between them with a purposeful laugh and pushed down their arms.

"Come with me my friends. We will get a beer." He waved at Harry and put up four fingers. Harry nodded as he sang full voice. Four hot dogs coming up.

Foster was happy and relaxed and enjoying himself immensely. He had tried both low alcohol beers and a nice paper cup of the Kalambaki and now he sipped a white wine spritzer to cool off. He did not see Napoléon anywhere in the yard. He looked in the implement shed and it was empty. He had Harry uncork a cold Boquebiere Apico to take to Napoléon and he found him in the house. He was humming in the kitchen wearing an apron and covered in red splatters. He was on his third attempt at making the raspberry sauce for the Peach Melba spécialité and Escoffier was at his shoulder. The sous chef would do it until it was satisfactory.

Foster walked passed them to the freezer behind them. Harry had mentioned he had forgotten to bring out the beer mugs. Foster extracted two frozen and frosted mugs and filled them with the Boquebiere and gave one to Escoffier and the other to Napoléon. He lifted his spritzer to them. "Cheers".

"Thank you, Foster." Napoléon looked to Escoffier for permission to have it and Chef nodded. Of course. It helped the creativity. They each took deep rejuvenating draughts and Napoléon went back to his sauce. Charles returned with two more bottles of the same and put them in the fridge and it was not long until he could hear both men singing through the screen door. If he was not mistaken, Janet was putting in some harmony on the thirds above.

Dobber played nervously with the gold earring in his right ear as he and Simon and Chukker scouted around the periphery of the yard and arrived at Harry. The Sly Fox beat anything they had ever tasted and it helped them coast. They had finished their third hotdog each and were just getting warmed up. They marveled at the propane making the flame on the cooker. Harry was wearing his usual apron which said, "I look better naked."

Simon translated for Chukker. To them that was self-evident. Of course everyone looked better naked. Simon began discarding his pants but refrained at seeing Dobber's disapproving head.

Mrs. William's cat was named Frank and it was a sociable copy of herself. It had heard the ruckus and smelled the food and dropped down off the fence into the yard and began to investigate. Chukker quietly untied the flap on his tucker bag. People petted Frank in turn and he was determined not to miss anyone. The cat rubbed against Chukker's leg and he bent down as if to pet and in half a second he had it in the bag and closed the flap on it. It squawled blue murder and Chukker pretended not to hear it. Davy dashed across from the conversation he was having with Foster and released the cat. Chukker didn't react. He looked at two squirrels running on the fence top and tested the weight of his Woomera.

Escoffier gave Napoléon an eight-minute break and he was reluctant to take it. He did not want Escoffier to spoil his sauce. Out of habit he hung his Imperial Legion of Honor lavallière on his neck and entered the back yard to the pop of a cork. He walked to Harry and refilled his mug from Foster's beer. They walked together to Davy.

Charles and Davy stood beside each other, leaning against the rim of the trampoline benefiting from the shadow cast by the implement shed. They did not talk, the way friends had no need to do. Both had spent some time in the shade of the beauty bush grove and for the time being they traded off to give the others a spot. Their friends deserved turns to listen and interact with the great personages. Davy had become quiet despite the fine company and the beautiful day. With his father's permission he had a paper cup of beer in his hand but he hadn't touched it and it was warm. Harry had just uncorked Foster's third Boquebiere and he was happy and he and Napoléon hummed a little concertina ditty they knew from Elba. Davy's party had been a great success and the mingling of people who proved in the end to be just people was amazing. Yet he was melancholic. Charles had seen it coming on.

"Davy, something is burning. You are thinking. That is a dangerous thing. " Davy laughed but Charles Foster was correct.

"Yes, I am thinking. I am thinking it was very easy for Bully to cut himself a pipe. Around the world there are billions of Bullies. Look at the chaos and confusion here today with just twenty or thirty comings and goings. I was just imagining the mess of a thousand or a million, let alone billions, doing the same thing."

Charles did not answer for a few seconds. He did not want to make his response too rough.

"The billions are already doing it. The thing is they don't really need a pipe for the real chaos." He let that comment sit while he considered the rest of his response. He would not have broached his observations to the boy unless Davy had asked.

"Davy, I have now enjoyed the pipe over fifty times. I have used it in many

398

eras over a span of thousands of years and on every continent. As I see more, I understand less. Of all the eras and times I have experienced, this one, right today, is the most damaged. There is a terrible number of people in such bad shape around the world and so much more of what we do makes so little sense. We are overcome with mean-mindedness."

Davy's intuition had told him exactly what Foster was saying and he hung on his every word. Napoléon nodded. The same could be said of his France.

"There is a sense of desperation and fury and hate which seems almost to be contagious. Humanity inhabits a common envelope of existence and consciousness that is interdependent. Within it we share a continuum of a common ethic and when that ethic is perverted anywhere, it degrades us all. The meanness is affecting the consciousness. We are infected with vicious, contagious aberrations that arrive out of the blue and we have them and we do them and we don't want them but they have us. We are all meaner. Jimi Hendrix had it right. When the power of love overcomes the love of power the world will know peace."

From under the trampoline, came. "Right on man!" Miss Tie Dye had spoken. Whatever she said was good with Spider. He was smitten. His girl sat in a lotus pose looking pleased with her contribution, having just downed her fourth spritzer as mixed by Bert. Spider leaned closer. "Oy, miss. Does ye come here often then?"

Tilt stretched his long arms in the cloister of the beauty bush and stood to get out the kinks. He had been sitting there for an hour and he was stiff with residual tension from the deadly flight over the Acheron. As he walked into the sun he signaled to Spider and from his post under the trampoline the boy acknowledged the uniformed man. Spider dashed into action with a cold one for Tilt. Helen and Mildred waved at Tilt from the steps and Chukker had his eye on him too. He was too much like the fearsome Thardid Jimbo from home. If Blank wanted a cannibalistic giant here, fine, but Chukker kept Tilt in view.

Harry found the flash drive of songs he had put together and pushed it into the player and ramped it up a little. He waited for Janet's 'turn it down' but she was too busy singing in the kitchen. The joint began to jump. Simon and Chukker heard strains of dreamtime and began to stoop and bounce and stoop and bounce with the beginning of a stomp and a quiet plaint began to grow from their throats. At the first hard beat, Bert and Spider pulled Tie Dye out into the sun. They had the sailors' horn pipe flying in two seconds and their feet were flipping and they sang in the tempo of the music. *And when we're hauled into Liverpool docks them bloomers all come 'round in flocks....* Tie closed her eyes and moved in a random sway and somewhere in her head she was with it. Helen was off the porch steps and dancing with John with brand new accidental incidental steps as the spritzers tempo kicked in.

Scrivener walked right past Lucretia and pulled Bully into the yard in front of her. Scrivener had seen him from across the yard and he was amazed at Bully's beautiful suit. Bully had seen him from across the yard and he was amazed at Scrivener's beautiful suit. They were of a size. Scrivener handed Bully the cold beer from under his pocket flap and they walked toward the back door, talking, while Scrivener plumbagoed his pad.

Scattered around the Pilcher's back yard was the most astounding aggregation of characters Lucretia had ever seen and it lured her forward. The invitation had not said the barbecue was a costume party. Had she known, she would have worn her devastating Cleopatra outfit and brandished her rubber asp.

Chapter 26: A Starburst of Gulls

In the corner of the yard easiest to defend, someone who looked like Napoléon in his full medaled glory was bantering with Charles Foster. The beauty bush glade showed promise with toga type handsome men sitting beside her Porky and two sailors did what could have been a hornpipe right in front of her. In the center of the yard a hippy girl was dancing with her eyes closed to the tune Harry was blasting from the player. From the kitchen came singing in French and it sounded like Mrs. Pilcher was doing a descant against it.

Lucretia was without a libation and Bert left off dancing long enough to remedy that with a white wine spritzer. She accepted it as her right. Simon and Chukker were doing a foot stomping caribberie frog dance to the rimshots from the blaster and Dobber made his best copy of it right behind them. They wound in a rhythmic stepping line around the yard and gifted one and all. It was time for the Pituri and they handed it out and every person took it. Harry's hands were full and they set a piece beside his grill. He thanked them. Escoffier poked his head out of the back door and stood with hands on hips, looking for his underling. Simon bopped up the steps and gave him a Pituri and Chef took another one for the singing lady in his kitchen. Napoleon saw him casting his eyes about and bid adieu to the trampoline. He raced past Simon, accepting the handout. He had to get back to his Melba sauce.

Helen and John popped a chewy Pituri into their mouths and started a good chaw. Mildred had been dancing close to them and had a little chew herself but stuffed it away as Davy had suggested.

The happy Bidjigals snaked and stomped past Lucretia and put one in her hand and Simon said chew and she did because to her left, Lucretia's eyes had locked on a very tall man in commando attire. He was tilted in a gravity defying posture, engaged in jovial conversation with a gentleman who appeared to be wearing a toga. As he spoke, the man of interest thrust a long arm into space as if he were pointing at a star with his finger. In one second she knew Colonel Tilt was the guy. Lucretia was excited and she walked to him slowly, in her best brittle attempt at a sashay. She drank her drink hurriedly so as not to spill it and chewed her Pituri like a vamp. As she caught Tilt's eye, her high heel stuck in the lawn and pulled off her shoe. Tilt increased the speed of his own chewing as she approached. She dropped onto her black mesh stockinged foot and without losing a stride she kicked off her other shoe and stayed on her laser guided track to the eleven-foot Ninja.

"So, you are the one who hogtied my Bully to the fence, hmm? May I shake your hand?"

In a poisonous coquettish way, she smiled up to Colonel Tilt in his handsome commando uniform and grasped his hand. "Did you bring your razor by any chance?" Tilt began to realize he might need it.

She flaunted an alluring bony shoulder. "Never mind, you Ninja you, never mind. You do good work."

Tiltus ran in a panicked gangle to the safety of the beauty bush and sat as deeply as the space allowed while the great minds ruminated and chewed their Pituri. Lucretia proceeded to follow him at lady-like correct pace.

Davy had accepted the Pituri the same as the others but he had dropped it into his pipe sheath without chewing it. He had seen its effect in Botany Bay. It was meant to be chewed once or twice then passed on to the next chewer. A couple of chews gave you energy and interest. An hour of chews made you happy and high and with any more chewing than that, you slept for a day. Calvin Reynolds, the young marine at Botany Bay could attest to that. Davy had no idea what chewing stage anyone was at. His guests all had their own Pituri chaw and the whole assemblage was chewing as if they had never chewed before. It seemed they were at the happy stage.

Socrates and Proclus led the way to the trampoline and they were met there by Scrivener whom they did not recognize immediately. Scrivener was wearing an immaculate black Gucci Tom Ford tuxedo with the cummerbund grooved upward.

"Excuse me, Mr. Socrates, sir. I have one little point to add to my exclusive biography of you. What is your age?"

Socrates was willing. " I am not sure. What year is this."

Scrivener had no idea. "Master Pilcher, what year is this?" Davy told him.

Socrates nodded. " Then I am 2397. And three months." Scrivener scribbled the number down thinking Socrates did not look a day over 2300.

Resplendent and boisterous in his elegant violet, black and yellow brocade, Bully Gregious flashed past in a blur and rolled onto the trampoline just as Proclus was climbing up. Lucretia wandered happily looking for her shoes. She was almost positive she had worn some. Bully began to jump and attempted to sing an up up and away song but he couldn't remember one and sung an anthem from boy scouts as he bounced. Proclus began a counter bounce and he had the knack of going high and his himation fluffed up and down. Lucretia thought of kilts. Chukker jumped high off the grass with every Proclus bounce and Simon jumped high off the grass with every Bully bounce as they chanted a continuous monotone *hungayukka, hungayukka*. Bully loved his satin waistcoat and rubbed it as he jumped. Porcrates chanted "Dad! Dad! Dad!"

In the kitchen, Escoffier and Napoléon had completed a perfect raspberry purée and the poaching syrup was cooling. They clinked their cold mugs and had a drink of the Boquebiere. Chef gestured to the kitchen island.

" You know, monsieur, if you want it, I am sure you have a future at the island. "

"Merci monsieur Escoffier. I am positive you are correct. Definitely, my future will be at the island. It is called Saint Helena."

Out the kitchen window Napoléon saw the height Proclus was attaining on the trampoline and made for it. Proclus was singing too but in a tempo having nothing to do with the music from Harry's player. His beat was trampoline beat and the down beat came with every landing. Bully was managing double time with the scout songs. Napoléon clambered up and small hopped between them and picked his own node and he was soon pounding eight feet above Proclus. He turned his shoulders thirty degrees at the height of every bounce and soon he had the neighborhood trapped in his mind. He might need the information. He enjoyed his Pituri. Its juice made him feel slightly strange. Dobber stood at the edge and clapped his hands in time with whomever he watched bouncing at that moment and loved everything about the day. His pendant flipped out of his shirt top and he tucked it back in.

Mildred and Helen climbed up under John's adoring eye and held hands and bounced into an open spot. They let go of their hands and rode a rebound up toward Napoléon and came eye to eye in the same bounce as him and continued on.

They were now on opposite bounces. "You. Know. Mum. That. He. Is. Not. Short." Janet nodded. " He. Is. Not." Thanks to the Pituri, Mildred felt not one bit queasy. Davy motioned to her and she stopped her bounce and swung down. He had Porky with him. The three of them huddled and set off together to select the wood from behind the implement shed for the fire pit. Simon saw them and carried some logs and began arranging them in a pattern to burn longer and smoke less. With Davy occupied, Dobber and Chukker sneaked into the implement shed and slid the tin door closed behind them. The amber plastic window made enough light. They had seen the glint of the tools and now they had a private look.

Malveena awoke in her car after an hour's rest. She was unrefreshed and uneasy and her feet throbbed. The short sleep had decided nothing except she needed different shoes. The day was still bright and she had time.

She exited her Bentley and heard an enormous bang as a transformer somewhere exploded in the heat. She walked in bare feet into her apartment and flung her boots at Charles Foster and they rebounded off the wall. She threw her keys onto the kitchen counter at that miserable Lucretia and slammed her purse onto the chair neck of that idiot marine who parted her hair with the musket ball. She did not throw her 1934 one of a kind Lady Carol coat sweater. It went to its hanger. Her apartment was hot but the white Montrachet was in the wine cooler. She opened the cooler and the light did not come on. She double clicked the light switch. There was no power in her building. The warm wine disappointed but it calmed her all the same.

She knew what to do. She pulled on her Yuiki Shimoji track pants and tightened her Louis Vuitton sneakers. She loosened off the laces. She remembered reading where tightening your laces too much could make you feel angry. She grabbed her copper pipe. She kissed it. "Little baby, do your stuff!"

Malveena landed fully alert on the woodpile behind the shed at Davy's house, wrapped in a smoked and pulsating envelope of separation. She slid down the pile and a loose splinter poked through her track pants as she struggled for balance. She pulled at it and tore a hole as it released. The envelope thickened a little with her aggravation.

She assessed her state of awareness. Malveena saw and heard dimly what was around her, and she was less removed from contact than she had been at

404

Woodstock. She could not believe the racket. She heard chanting and stomping amid the buzz of accented speech. Sounds of high harmony drifted against a beefy baritone. A blaster blasted percussive music and she could hear the sound or squeak of a ..trampoline. Surely she was mistaken. A tuneless but perfectly timed sea chanty duet bounced to her off the back of the house.

Malveena worked her way around onto the lawn to see Lucretia acting oddly friendly with Foster. Malveena's gelatinized vision was not good but she knew these people well enough to make out most of them. In fact, she thought she could see Bully across the way in his tuxedo but he seemed to have red hair. This was going to be beautiful. They could not see her or hear her and she began to prowl. She was going to find out what they were saying about her. *Lucretia. She will be the worst.* The envelope thickened a little at the thought and Lucretia was harder to see as Malveena approached. The Pituri was talking and Lucretia was pleasant and funny in her conversation with Foster. Malveena was surprised at it. *You know, I may have the wrong idea about Lucretia. I have always goaded her. In speaking to Foster just now, she sounded nice. Not one negative word.*

The veil lightened a trifle. She walked along into the group and stood between Bert and Spider, in the middle of their hornpipe space. Not able to see her, Spider shivered involuntarily as she got closer but kept on tempo. Malveena smiled at their chanty and started a little movement to the beat. Tie Dye moved close to them doing a nice sway and Malveena copied it. She was at the party and almost dancing and the envelope thinned a bit more. She wandered to the fire pit where some people were clustered. Porky and Davy and Mildred were there looking at their handiwork and Simon was putting on the expert touches.

" Great work Simon. Thanks. That will be a great fire." Porky put up a high five hand and Simon stared at him.

Malveena was close enough to see Mildred's red balaclava and her envelope began to stifle her and thicken. *Wait. The guy Porky just called 'Simon'. Is it possible?* Her restraining veil pulsed with the thought. *He was with Dobber at Botany Bay. He and Davy and another.* She was confused. She wandered the lot and listened to every conversation. *The people are so friendly. The ones in the glade are serious but laughing at the same time. Having much fun at what they do. Harry is the perfect singing barbecue host and Janet is sampling deviled eggs with Napoléon in the kitchen?* She laughed at the absurdity of what she was seeing. Her veil was much lighter and flimsy and the sun felt good.

She walked and listened and was at the barbecue and drank in the sun. She was enjoying herself and in the sunshine every so often she made a shadow. She whirled in a circle and swung her arms to the music with her eyes closed as Dobber came out of the implement shed with his pockets full of nails. She felt the whack as she hit him but Dobber, who swatted at a little shadow, did not.

Malveena could not endure it. The closeness. Dobber. She moved to within four inches of him. He was beautiful. It was Dobber. He walked back to join Simon with Malveena walking at his side, one inch from his shoulder. He sensed the proximity but it eluded him. He sat on the lawn and shifted to avoid the nails in his back pocket and Malveena sat cross legged opposite him, watching him talk.

The kitchen door burst open and out came sous chef and head waiter Napoléon, with his tray of the famous Escoffier Peach Melba. "Et ainsi, le chef-d'oeuvre! And so, the masterpiece!" He held it high above his head with both hands.

Chef looked out the window to see the reception. He refused to mingle with his patrons but today he wanted to. He would honor them by accepting their accolades. He stepped out to great applause and before he knew it he was swept across the lawn and to the ice tubs for a bottle of Kalambaki red. Janet charged along behind him with a wineglass. She had found twelve glasses in four different styles in various cupboards. Escoffier seized her and kissed her hard on each cheek and once hard on the lips. Harry stopped singing then laughed. All around the yard, the Peach Melba was the best.

Napoléon swirled his wine. It was difficult to see the legs in the sherbet glass but it was tasty none the less. Harry turned the music down and put in a second memory stick of big band music. He moved to the fire pit and started the kindling. The sun was low after a hot day and the wine was wonderful with the dessert. Simon preferred the red cream soda and stood and moved with Artie Shaw and watched the group circle and sit around the fire. Porcrates was on the trampoline by himself. Happy with Pituri he soared high, not caring. He could see the odd star coming as he bounced.

Malveena sat very close on Dobber's right. He felt nothing and he did not move away, but there was a pleasantness there.

The evening moved on with the bands playing in the background and Tie Dye and Escoffier danced barefooted on the lawn to Moonlight Serenade. Scrivener danced alone in his tuxedo with a stiff arm extended to his partner as he chewed. Bully walked slowly in his finery, dipping and pivoting to the music of Pituri land and turning constantly to catch the firelight on his silk violet waistcoat. Lucretia watched him in admiration of his girth. Little Spider had downed a Sly Fox and he was tacking nicely. Bert was moving on the same wind. From the glade came an ongoing quiet unison chant in slow time against the music and it was beautiful. It gradually diminished to nothing. They slept in their sheltered windless symposium wrapped in their himations, covered by horse blankets.

Davy and Simon and Chukker laid on their backs looking at the stars. The Bidjigals were lost. They had never been without their guiding star Birubi. They would not find its Southern Cross here. They looked for their Antares, their 'Puruprika', so red and bright. Simon spoke in his soft voice.

"You know Blank, your pipe, your pathway to the past is Bidjigal. We have such a pathway in our Songline. It traces our ancestors to creation and sings not just there. It sings today and forever in the future. We hear its language and we learn its music and we continue and we remember. It is all in our Dreamtime. Our myths do not mean past. They are made today and have been made in the future. Blank, I like how the night is getting colder now."

John Craft placed a couple of logs on the fire at Mildred's urging. She was cold. John admired the perfect structure of the first setup but now he was having trouble remembering it. He was fading fast with Pituri and the low alcohol Eisdoppelbock. Dobber was fiddling with the thong at his neck and his hand gradually dropped as he succumbed to the laze of the fire. Malveena slid closer to him. Her meanness was subsiding and the firelight glowed on Dobber's earring. She began to sing to him knowing she would not be heard. Her voice was from the heart and it was pure and amazing. *"There's a story, the gypsies know is true, that when your love wears golden earrings, he belongs to you. An old love story..."*

The entire group heard it and every one of them looked to the sky then to Harry's player which was turned down low and now crooned Perfidia. Chukker sat up. That voice was bad gurbuny. From the fog. Malveena stopped singing and moved to touch Dobber with her hand but she couldn't get through. She smelled the hot dogs and couldn't have one, she saw the wines and she could not share them. She wanted friendship from the group but she could not have it.

Around the circle, eyes were closing and closed. Janet was curled on her side and sound asleep. Escoffier leaned against the shed with his arms crossed in a deep Pituri dream. They were all gone and hopeless until morning. Davy was alert as was his Dad who did not touch the gift from Simon. Mildred was back to herself too. She had asked Tilt to bring back the Kalambaki and she had not had any of it. The night was cold and most guests could not go home. Those that could, did not. Bully and Lucretia were out cold by the fire. If Bully rolled over he would go up in smoke or put it out. Tilt was beside Napoléon on the high ground of the porch leaning against the wall staying warm against the house. Davy and Harry and Mildred began covering the sleepers with blankets one by one. Malveena was warm and unseen beside Dobber and she spooned in. He was soundly asleep and he had no idea one millimeter away was the madonna of the dunes who ghosted through his dreams. Malveena could not contact him and just imagining the warmth did not help. It had become a cold night. Under a load of self-recrimination, she laid awake shivering and waited for the dawn and for sunlight to fill her pipe. She was getting colder. Blast the cheap blanket. The envelope dimmed a little. She was freezing and she had had it. She uncovered herself without disturbing Dobber and stepped around the sleeping people and out the gate and headed for home on foot.

Malveena lived about an hour's walk uphill from the Pilcher house. She looked at her watch. It was 3:05 in the morning. First direct sun at her twelfth-floor apartment was about 5:50. Pilcher's house was in the shadow of the bluff for about half an hour longer. Dobber and Davy would certainly be in shadow until she arrived. She had time. As soon as the sun hit her balcony she would come to real time with her pipe, then into the Bentley and heavy foot it to the Pilchers. Davy needed sun to take Dobber away and she would not let him.

Simon and Chukker had been up since four and ready to go. They had spent the night on the trampoline. They went to find Dobber and with him in tow they rousted Davy.

"Shh. Quiet Blank. We are going now. Come. Bring your pipe and get us home." Chukker had slipped quietly out the gate and was fifty yards down the street. He walked on the grassy boulevard for he did not like the paving under his feet to give away the sound of his tread.

Davy was barely awake. "What? But. It is the middle of the night. I need sun for the pipe. Go back and sleep."

Simon shook his head. Dobber rasped quietly. "Blank lad. Chukker did not sleep. He has felt the gurbuny voice. From the fog. It brings a mean and sickly spirit. He watched against it all night. It was here and strong around us. He felt it leave a while ago but it will be back. It has a longing for this place. There is something here it wants."

"But we need the sun."

Simon stiffened and began walking away. "Then we will walk until we find it."

They closed the gate quietly behind them and headed downhill and caught up with Chukker. Dobber's pilfered nails began working their way out the hole in his back pocket.

Malveena entered her apartment a little after four and she was happy. Everything was under control. The power was still out for several miles surrounding her building and it was strange territory without the lights. The stars were new to her again.

She placed her cell phone light on her vanity table and looked at herself in the mirror and she looked fine. Her makeup was a bit strong perhaps. She began removing it and it felt good to have it off. Dobber would not like it. He was a simple man. A convict. *I wonder what he did to become a convict.* She shrugged. It didn't matter a bit. This was no time to be coy. She would declare her love.

The sun had not yet reached the Pilcher house or the western down slopes leading to the flats and to the river. The per-dawn air was cool and promising and there was scant noise from the gulls. They were farther inland taking full advantage of the heat in the farmlands. Harry had a large pot of coffee to pour and a second one about to perk. He liked the old-style percolator. It was something to watch bubble up as the sky lightened. The aroma of the freshly brewed coffee stirred the lot of them and they awoke one by one, refreshed and with the feeling of a nice experience. They filtered onto the back porch and into the kitchen. Harry began filling the aggregation of cups. Coffee had just been introduced in Napoléon's France and it was very expensive. He was impressed. Scrivener was not. He was a tea man to the end. He had tried coffee of course.

Foster took John Craft aside and handed him a cup. Helen overheard Foster's generous job offer to John. It started in one week without a jungle in sight. Mildred looked around and realized Davy was not there. Neither were Dobber nor Chukker nor Simon. A highly tuned engine wound down at their front door and a heavy door closed. Malveena had arrived with time to spare and she strode to the house. She was nervous about seeing Dobber and nervous too about facing the crowd but not deterred. What did she care. She smiled at herself. *Love conquers all.*

Malveena did not ring the bell but entered through the side gate. People were talking and mixing as she approached the porch. Bully looked more like a parrot today than he did the night before.

"Hello Bully, hello everybody."

Bully said hello to her as did most of the guests as she stepped into the kitchen. Helen and Janet saved it for later. Porky offered. "Coffee Malveena?"

"No thank you Leonard, but, where's Davy, and the, the others?"

Scrivener answered. "Off harpooning something, like as not."

"No, all joking aside, where are they? Millicent, do you know?"

Mildred answered. "Not Millicent. Mildred. And no, I don't know. I checked on them half an hour ago and they were gone. Walking I would guess. That is what they do Malveena."

Malveena turned blue and her rage was boundless. She kicked the kitchen island with her running shoe and left a red mark. "Gone? How can they be gone? Harry Pilcher! They are your guests and they are gone and you don't know where they are? What is wrong with you? Janet Pilcher! They are with your Davy, Davy, Davy, oh wonderful Davy brat, who left and did not even say where he was going?" She kicked the island again. Tilt regretted now he had omitted the razor from his kit.

"And you, you red hatted Millicent sidekick. You and your big shin kicking boots. Why are you not there too wherever there is and nobody would know where you were. I would know if I had been invited here! But no. Who would invite Malveena. No wine or hot dogs or Boque.. Boque.. beer. Not even a peck on the cheek. Nasty old Malveena. Give me a break! Get a little rough with a couple of kids and you are a pariah." She pounded the island top.

" Foster! You boob. This hate stuff was supposed to be all done with. We had a deal and now there's a big 'let bygones be bygones party', a big 'feel good barbecue' and I am not even invited. Not even invited! Who wants your rotten little failure party any way!" She began to grind her teeth.

Scrivener could not accept more of her. "Madame, be civil or be elsewhere!" She just looked at him in his black tuxedo.

"So, scribbler. You stole Bully's tuxedo. Typical." She did not know of what he was typical but it worked. " Nothing but a scribbler."

"And my wine. I would have brought some real wine. Not that Kalambaki rot, and served it with the Peach Melba and helped..."

Janet interrupted the desperate tirade quietly. "Please Malveena. Malveena, you were invited. You were invited to the barbecue."

She blinked. "What? What did you say?" She said it in half of her fury voice but only to give herself time. She had heard exactly what Janet had said.

"You were invited. I wrote the invitation myself. And I am really sorry you don't like us Malveena." Harry ran upstairs to Davy's room.

Malveena was powerless as Harry burst back into the kitchen carrying his old brown accordion folio. "Freddy. Is this what Davy delivered your invitation in?"

Tilt affirmed it. "Yes. That is it."

Harry exhaled slowly and shook his head. "I tossed this thing away in the bin and Davy obviously retrieved it. The glue that holds it together is breaking down and it makes everything sticky so I pitched it. "

He held it upside down and shook it. Nothing. He felt inside and a divider was stuck closed. He pried it open and from it he retrieved a glue dappled, beautiful black India ink hand written invitation to Ms. Malveena Drago Esq., Vice President of Operations, Foster Industries. Malveena snatched it with wet blazing eyes and held it to her front and the rasp of her grinding teeth made their arm hairs stand on end.

Aristotle interjected. "Miss, I am pleased for you that you are now in the thrall of decorum. I also have one question of such obviousness that I fear to offend you with it, but why are you not going after them?"

Malveena dashed from the yard and through the gate and fired up the Bentley. She had no idea where Dobber was but she headed downhill. The streets in the lee of the dominating bluff were still quite dark.

All the while during the confrontation, Plato had been sitting at the kitchen table with pen and paper, writing something in India ink. The room was quiet from the drama of it all but it was time for farewells and departures. Foster came to Napoleon and shook his hand.

"Want to go for a ride before we head for Helena?" Napoléon smiled as he settled his jacket onto his shoulders. "Bien sur mon ami. Allons-y."

They walked out the front door and Napoléon gave his regal wave as he stepped into the passenger seat of Foster's Auburn and pulled the door closed. Spider and Bert were right behind and clambered into the back seat over the sides as Spider stuffed the remains of a muffin into his face. Foster laughed.

"Hah! Good. I will take you too." They soon found themselves shadow strobing past lamp posts at 100 miles per hour.

Tilt proceeded to lead his charges into the yard. Socrates, Proclus, Aristotle and Plato had deduced everyone should gather around the trampoline and all go at once. It was agreed. Tilt related his little sojourn through the underworld to Proclus and attempted to enlist his help for the return voyage. He was unsure whether Proclus could resist the big guys but he would find out soon enough. The philosophers called over Porky and one by one they shook his hand. Plato unrolled the scroll he had just made in the kitchen.

"It is with great honor we of the Delphic Symposium, confer upon you, life time membership in said symposium at the level of Philosopher, First Class. Be well." The applause was strong and Porcrates blushed and beamed as he received his scroll. The members of the Delphic Symposium who signed the document were Socrates, Plato, Aristotle. And last, Proclus.

Mildred and Tie Dye and Scrivener had become good friends. They went outside and talked as they sat on the rim of the trampoline and waited for the light.

Janet finished dotting the 'i's on the recipe for deviled eggs for Escoffier and pressed it on him. Janet and Helen each took a hand and led the old gentleman into the garden. The lawn was imprinted deeply with their footprints and their feet were wet from the dew. It was warming there and it was just a few minutes until the sun was right.

Malveena was panicked and desolate and embarrassed and angry and almost out of her mind. The road was still dim but improving and soon it would be sunny and Dobber would be gone. She had no idea whether she was heading the right way and she sped to cover as much ground as she could. It was barely dawn and few people were out. She ran her wiper. It was still cold and condensation was on the glass. There was a soft frost on the ground and she swerved toward a cat that crossed the road and left its prints behind and marked up the boulevard. She slowed and stopped. She gunned into a spin and headed back the mile to the Pilcher's. Just what she thought. Tracks. She rolled down her windows and blasted the heater and crept along keeping the tracks in sight. They sparkled and every so often they bristled.

The tracks began spacing wider. Simon had picked up the pace and they jogged. Dobber's medallion swung out and back and out and back as he ran, hitting him in the heart with every stride.

Malveena stopped her car and got out and had a close look. There were four sets of tracks. It was Dobber. The first sun passed the brow of the escarpment and its rays streamed parallel to the shape of the land. Along the frosted boulevard a trail of glistening points ran back over the hill. She looked closer without her glasses. It seemed as if they were nails.

She spotted her man, walking now, about 100 yards ahead. Davy would soon have use of his pipe. She ran two steps and stopped to refresh in her mind once again how she would declare herself. Malveena said not loudly. "Dobber."

Dobber turned, followed in turn by the other three. Davy, Simon and Chukker turned away and continued on without him. Dobber stood and waited as Malveena approached and he tapped his medallion nervously with each of her steps. He could not understand all this and he tapped his coin in time with Malveena's tread. His madonna of the Dunes walked to him and stood three feet from him and the sunlight reflected from Dobber's trinket and distracted her eye.

"What is that thing you are tapping?"

He looked down and felt the deep engraving. It shimmered in the sun and Dobber grinned up at Malveena.

"Yes. Me love token." He continued feeling it.

As ice formed in her, Malveena breathed, "Read it to me."

"I don't read Miss, but I knows the 'scription by heart. Davy, he lerned me it.

413

I made the rime myself. I hopes you likes it." He began to recite and the darkness began to look for Malveena.

'For Hannah Davis /my love/ is strong/ tho long apart/ it knows/ not time / just knows/ my heart/ Dubhghall.'

"That's me, Dubhgall. If she will have me when I get back, God willin', or out here, fresh like, we be joined."

Malveena stood without substance in a lost world, devoid of thought. Darkness fingered through the tunnel of her pipe and spiraled around her. It grew into soft and understanding hands that spread and touched and misted to a gossamer thing which pulled on her. She shrunk into the swirl of its dark invitation and breathed in its gases of promise. It howled a high and mournful beckoning that made the party goers look for it. Malveena succumbed without resistance to its dark escape and she loved nothing. She raised her pipe to the morning sun and through it she fled to elsewhere. Malveena climbed like a rocket and felt the burn into a howling torrent of regret that spread wide for her above the world. She sped to dark cold suns unseen and looked at nowhere and sped on and on and screamed her screams and did not know what she wanted.

Chukker stopped and looked back at the empty Bentley. The street was deserted except for Dobber. Chukker shook like a wet dog. The voice from the fog no longer sang. The gurbuny was gone. He spoke in Bidjigal to Simon. Simon laughed and translated.

"He says, let's go back. They may have muffins."

Foster finished Napoléon's joy ride with a brake tearing smoke filled screeching stop at the Pilcher driveway. Napoléon, Bert and Spider teetered forward with white faces and sprinted across the lawn to the warm tubs of beer. They cracked a Sly Fox and filled three paper cups and drained them. Janet and Helen and le Chef were putting in time waiting for the last arrivals and after two 7:00 am spritzers each, the three were in a contest. The one who could say 'spritzer' clearly was the winner and the prize was a spritzer. 'Zripster, rispterz' it went. No one could quite win the prize to the amusement of the others. For no reason except for the unrestrained love of it, Napoléon and Escoffier launched into the Marseilles.

Davy and Dobber and Chukker and Simon jogged through the open gate and up to the trampoline as if they had never been away. Mildred and Davy exchanged a relieved smile.

Davy came over to Mildred. He looked around at the impossible bunch having a wonderful carefree day. His pipe hummed in approval and little Dopo hummed along with it.

"Mildred this has been great. Are you happy? Happy about how things have worked out? I am."

"Yes Davy. I am too. In fact, you and I should go out and paint the town green."

"Red. You mean red."

"Definitely not red. I wouldn't like a red town. Green would be nice."

One by one the friends tightened their circle and held hands as one. The circle was complete. Smiles moved across the trampoline with love in every direction and a perfect column of pure awareness began to form and gather in brightness like a searchlight. The strength of such consciousness had never been seen. It brightened and dazzled and made the day seem dull. Together they put their heads back and moved their minds to the timeless light connecting them. Prepared, in unison they dropped a hand and melded into their group. Mildred and Tie Dye gripped tight between Scrivener and Bully. Lucretia and Porcrates stood behind Bully with a death grip on his coattails. Harry and Janet and John and Helen surrounded old Escoffier. Charles Foster had Napoléon in a firm grip. Tilt centered Socrates and Aristotle on his left, with Proclus and Plato on his right. Chukker and Simon were on a Songline deep in Dreamtime holding onto Dobber and Davy. Dopo held on for dear life. Their column into time blazed like a thousand suns and it carried them away.

High above, the gulls began to gather. They gathered from the farmlands and the sea and still on they came, in ever increasing numbers, in a vortex which whitened the sky for miles and continued to grow. Suddenly from below them, a billion candles of light shot their galactic transporting column past the gulls and into the void. A billion gulls made a billion cries and they flashed their whiteness to a billion-point starburst and they rode the winds.

End

About the Author

Other Titles by W. Lawrence Nash

The Perfect Monster
Frank McCord and the Foghorn Blues
Frank McCord and the China Blues, or, Here a China, There a China,
Everywhere a China China

On the way:
Frank McCord and the Time Crystal Blues

W. Lawrence Nash is a graduate of the University of Toronto. He is a past
member of the American Association for the Advancement of Science and
the Cognitive Neuroscience Society. He was the CEO and President of a
publicly trading gold and diamond mining company and he has expert
certificates in diamonds. He is a student of the advanced physics of
harmonics and he kayaks and sings for fun, often at the same time. He
resides in the remote reaches of British Columbia Canada and he is the father
of three wonderful grown up girls.

CPSIA information can be obtained
at www.ICGtesting.com
Printed in the USA
LVHW081243041122
732312LV00003B/435